Julia Widdows was born in London and now lives in Brighton. She is an award-winning short story writer, and has run groups using writing as a therapeutic tool. This is her first novel.

D0246125

www.rbooks.co.uk

DORSET COUNTY LIBRARY

204963218 Z

LIVING IN PERHAPS

Julia Widdows

DORSET LIBRARY SERVICES	
HJ	26-Aug-2009
AF	£6.99

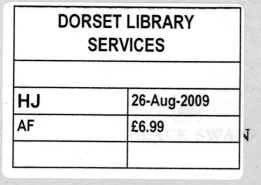

TRANSWORLD PUBLISHERS
63 Uxbridge Road, London W5 5SA
A Random House Group Company
www.rbooks.co.uk

LIVING IN PERHAPS
A BLACK SWAN BOOK: 9780552775014

First published in Great Britain
in 2009 by Doubleday
an imprint of Transworld Publishers
Black Swan edition published 2009

Copyright © Julia Widdows 2009

Julia Widdows has asserted her right under the Copyright, Designs and Patents
Act 1988 to be identified as the author of this work.

This book is a work of fiction and, except in the case of historical fact,
any resemblance to actual persons, living or dead, is purely coincidental.

A CIP catalogue record for this book
is available from the British Library.

This book is sold subject to the condition that it shall not,
by way of trade or otherwise, be lent, resold, hired out,
or otherwise circulated without the publisher's prior
consent in any form of binding or cover other than that
in which it is published and without a similar condition,
including this condition, being imposed on the
subsequent purchaser.

Addresses for Random House Group Ltd companies outside the UK
can be found at: www.randomhouse.co.uk
The Random House Group Ltd Reg. No. 954009

The Random House Group Limited supports The Forest Stewardship Council (FSC), the
leading international forest certification organisation. All our titles that are printed on
Greenpeace approved FSC certified paper carry the FSC logo. Our paper procurement
policy can be found at www.rbooks.co.uk/environment

Typeset in 11/14pt Giovanni Book by
Falcon Oast Graphic Art Ltd.
Printed in the UK by CPI Cox & Wyman, Reading, RG1 8EX.

2 4 6 8 10 9 7 5 3 1

**For my parents,
who knew the value of education**

1

Names

Cora Eileen. Such an ugly name.

I can't believe it's mine.

I couldn't believe it was me they were talking about when they read that out in court. I wanted to shout *There's been a mistake!* Maybe I did make some kind of noise. I certainly heard a ringing in my ears. But perhaps that was just the shock.

You see, I'd always thought I was Carol Ann.

Cora Eileen. My real name, my true name.

The name my mother gave me.

I'm adopted. I didn't know that until I was sixteen. I never dreamed it. Of course, I *did* dream, like any kid, that underneath this too, too ordinary exterior I was really a foreign princess; that my parents, fleeing execution at the hands of the mob, had entrusted me as a baby to this simple childless couple, and that – one day – all would be revealed and I'd come into my rightful inheritance. Castles, and white horses, and more money than could easily be spent. But I reckon that's par for the course when you're nine years old and you've already downed too many fairy tales.

I've got a younger brother, Brian. I never dreamed *he* was adopted. He was much too boring to be anything but theirs.

They never told me I'd been adopted when I was growing up. It wasn't *the done thing*, then, to let your little ones in on the family secrets. I always thought we were flesh of their flesh. My mother sprang it on me when I was much older. Saved it up as a present for my sixteenth birthday. But she never told me what my real name was. Maybe even *she* thought that would be a bit much.

It's so important, what you're called. It colours everything. 'Name, please?' some complete stranger asks, and you have to own up. School is the worst place. They call your name out, they tick it off in registers, they make you write it on all your books, and it's there, sewn into every bit of uniform, for anyone to find. And if you've got a stupid name or one that sounds like a rude word, everybody hears it, and the smirking, snickering rumour of it runs round like wildfire. Higginbottom. Sucksmith. Lipshitz. There's no escape. I don't know how the parents let it happen. Why don't they change it by deed poll, swap it for something less visible? I can see that people might feel strongly about *the family name*. But who needs to hang on to a family heirloom, a great tradition, like Raper or Boggs?

I was Carol Burton. It was all right. It could have been better, but it could have been a hell of a lot worse. At my school, it was a mid-range sort of name. It wasn't as classy as Suzannah Grey or Natasha Maynard. But it wasn't nearly as bad as Suki Wooster. S*ooo*ki W*ooo*ster. Or Mildred Clark, which made you think of a hundred-year-old charwoman.

But Carol Ann Burton – I wonder why my parents didn't get round to making it official? Why they left me on the record as Cora Eileen? I know they're the sort of people who aren't confident with paperwork, who don't like to *bother* anyone official, but even so. What did they think would happen? That I'd sail unruffled through life and never find out?

It's quite clever, really. Coraeileen, Carolann. Slurring the names together, letting them slip into something else. I guess they wanted to change it, yet they didn't want to stray too far from what I'd been used to.

I've done that. I've slurred my name, let the sounds slide together: Carol-Ann, Carolann, Carolyn. Because Carolyn is a much prettier name. Someone called Carolyn would be dainty and attractive. Her pure white kneesocks would always stay up. She'd have a pretty young mother who shared her tastes, who'd pay for her to go to ballet classes and drive her there in a pale-blue sports car. A Carolyn would have a feminine sort of bedroom, with billowing curtains and a princess-and-the-pea bed. And she'd have loads of friends, other pretty girls with shiny hair and nice manners and gracious homes.

Sometimes with new people I tried to let them think my name was Carolyn. Not Carol Ann. And now I find out it's really Cora Eileen.

Brian got to stay Brian. He didn't have an alias.

Every week at home I used to read the obituaries in the local paper, searching for someone who had died of something interesting, or spectacularly young. I began to notice that often the older ones had mysterious pseudonyms in brackets. You'd see 'Ayling, Ronald Arthur (Pip), in his eighty-third year, beloved husband of . . .' or 'Pope, Doris, née Mottram (Kitty), aged seventy-six, widow of . . .' And further in, after all the grieving relatives have had a mention and the name of the cats' home, donations in memory of to be sent to, it would say: 'Further enquiries to J & S Brewer, Fnrl Drs, High Street.' And sometimes I'd be tempted to make further enquiries, to telephone J & S Brewer, Fnrl Drs, and ask them if they knew why the late Ronald Arthur Ayling was known to his friends as Pip, or why Kitty Pope, Kitty Mottram as was, forsook the name of Doris. I have always been curious. I have an absolute thirst for knowledge. It's the only thing worth having.

My dad's first name was William – letters always came addressed to Mr W. Burton – but everyone called him Ted. I never knew why, and it wasn't the sort of family where you could casually ask. They were great at let's pretend. Let's pretend that what you see is what you get.

We weren't adopted from birth. I would have been five, and Brian four, when they got us from the children's home. I imagine it was always hard to shift brothers and sisters. Who'd want a ready-made family, when what you truly wanted was a family you'd made yourself? And I'm talking about the days when perfect white babies could be got at birth, if you were a hungry adoptive couple, with faulty tubes or faulty sperm, with a marriage certificate and your own house, preferably church-goers, within a certain age bracket. Babies were yours for the picking, like fruit off a tree. Nobody much wanted older kids, or black babies, or children with handicaps. And since they could get a flawless white baby with no bad habits, why should they?

It was 1960, the year they picked us. As adoptive parents, perhaps they were a bit too old, or a bit too poor, or perhaps they didn't have the right people to give them references. They certainly were on the old side, so maybe they wanted their instant family straight away. Or maybe we were a bargain. Buy one, get one free. They could have dug in their heels, hung on for a *tabula rasa*, a little unetched baby with a windy smile. But how long would that take? So we were what they got: one of each, slightly worn, five and four.

I don't remember any of this. All I know is what I've been told. Like being given the corners of a jigsaw puzzle and being expected to fill in the rest by yourself. Or, more likely, leave it at that: be satisfied with the corners and never mind the picture in the middle.

And now I find that I didn't even know my own name. My own name, the one I started out with. If only they had bothered to change it officially, I would never have had to hear it called out like that, so incriminatingly, in court.

Think of how it must look, on a report, a lengthy official one, pages and pages of it, full of the judgements of worthy, highly qualified people, about the background and character of its subject. And the subject's name in big black letters at the top: Cora Eileen Burton. Now, how would that look? Wouldn't you start to think, straight away, before you'd even read it: *Cora Eileen, she sounds a hard-faced sort of creature?* She sounds like the type who'd be guilty. Who dunnit.

2

A Happy Childhood

I've been talking to someone recently. In here. *Here*'s another story. I'll get round to that one, in my own good time.

She came into my room without knocking. You have to keep your door open, here, during the day. She just tapped on the door, firmly, as if to say, 'I'm here, but I'm coming in whether you like it or not,' and then she was in. She sat down straight away, without asking if I minded.

'Hello. My name's Lorna. I'd like to talk to you.'

What she meant was 'I'd like *you* to talk to *me*.'

I don't care for all this first-name-terms stuff. It's supposed to make everything feel relaxed and informal, but it just makes me more suspicious. I'd rather she said, 'My name's Dr Smith,' or whatever. They don't give you a chance to find out anything about them, not even their place in the pecking order. What are they hiding? A long and distinguished career in psychotherapy is my guess.

They think that if they get you to call them Lorna, or

Mike, or Trudy, you'll slip into thinking they're only a nurse or a trainee and you'll say something more revealing than if you thought you were talking to a psychiatrist or a social worker. And they kid themselves that they're being egalitarian and all-pals-together. That they're not patronizing us. But I'd like to know exactly who they are. I'd like to see the framed certificates, please.

So Lorna smiled and put her hands together in her lap and looked encouraging, and I just sat there. I wasn't going to make it easy for her. She was going to have to *squeeze* each little drop out of me.

We both waited.

'I thought we could have a bit of a chat.'

I shrugged.

'Why don't you tell me something about yourself? We could start with where you live. Your home.'

Well, I wasn't going to fall for that.

I'd much rather have chatted about something interesting. I'd rather have talked about *anything* other than me. What came to mind was Louisa May Alcott, and the bit where Jo March cuts off her hair. I'd found the book on the window sill in my room, tucked behind the curtain. I don't know if it had been hidden or just left there, forgotten. I didn't care – it was something to read, and I was already halfway through. So I smiled brightly at good old Lorna and I said, 'Have you ever read *Little Women*?'

I must say I enjoyed watching her reaction. Various expressions chased each other round her face, until finally one overwhelmed the others and her features settled down into a simulacrum of *patient interest*. She thought she could wait. Hear me out, then pin me down.

But I ran her ragged. All round the houses we went,

never touching home. Round the rugged rocks the ragged rascal ran. I'll say.

So – oh, Lorna, die for this! – I had a happy childhood. Happy enough. Let me start by describing our home.

Whatever they say about it now, I don't remember the children's home. As far as I'm concerned, I have always lived in the same house, the same little bungalow with rectangular gardens, back and front. Two parents, Mum and Dad, two children, Carol and Brian. Our mum and dad have names, too. They are called Edie and Ted, but we don't call them that. In fact, whenever I hear another adult – invariably an aunt or uncle – call them by their first names, I get a little squeeze of fright. Who dares to be so familiar, so intimate? And who dares to forget that, really, who they are is *Mum* and *Dad*?

There is a garage, and a car which he drives, she doesn't. There are no pets over a certain size. There are weekdays, when he works, and weekends, when he doesn't. He works at *the firm*. I don't know what it does, and I don't know what he does there. It is called Gough Electricals, but that still doesn't shed much light. She used to be a bookkeeper there, but now she doesn't go out to work. Now – in the long, elastic present I'm referring to, my childhood and life so far.

For Brian and me, the days are mapped out by school and Sunday school. We are nothing if not well behaved. We're terribly well brought up. We wear the correct school uniforms, and satchels on our backs. Neither of us is bright enough to get a place at the grammar. I go to the girls' secondary modern, he goes to the boys'. We do homework, we are Cubs and

Brownies, Scouts and Guides. We ride second-hand bikes.

Our home is set in a sea of bungalows. They're all very neat and tidy but with a somehow seedy air about them, like all those suburban streets whose inhabitants wish they were a little grander. They're pre-war, past their best – a bit like their owners. At the end of our road, right next door to us, there's an anomaly, a much older house, a spacious double villa left high and dry from an earlier age when the town hadn't crept this far. Tucked between hedges and trees, it hides away, ignoring the neighbours, trying to pretend we don't exist. Trying to pretend it's sailing alone through the fields, just like it used to. Whenever I walked home down our road, I wondered what it must have been like before the bungalows existed. A house right in the middle of nowhere, with the high road in the distance curving away across the fields; just the leaves rustling and cows tearing at the grass, no modern din of lawnmowers or transistor radios. Once or twice when I was playing outside I dared go as far as the front gate, crouching down and peeping through the bars at it: a fairytale house in bungalow-land.

But I'm not going there just yet. I'm staying away from that particular house.

The bungalows are L-shaped at the front, with a big bay window swathed in net curtains, because this was the main bedroom, and no one wants the postman or the milkman or the neighbours staring into their bedroom. The path from the front gate goes straight as an arrow to the front door, set in the corner of the L. Each front door has a rising sun or a sailing ship made out of stained glass in its window, and two more little windows either side to let some light into the hallway. The windows are always of frosted glass, to thwart prying eyes. In some of them you can see the outline of a pot plant, or a vase of flowers. If the flowers look especially healthy or brilliantly coloured, you can bet they're plastic. They're given away free with soap powder and petrol, and they look so real and last so well, and, after all, are *so convenient*.

Because these houses are small and set all on one level, they're popular with retired people, or middle-aged couples whose children have grown up and gone, or couples who never had children. But our parents had children, in the end, and they needed to expand. A few of the bungalows expanded outwards, sticking on a sun-lounge, or a utility room to house the freezer and the washing machine. Ours expanded upwards, into an attic bedroom in the roof. This is my first taste of injustice.

Although he's fifteen months younger than me, Brian gets the bedroom in the roof. Even though it could be argued that he is more likely to trip on the stairs, or need help in the night for a nightmare or a wee – and it's true that he frequently wet the bed – or simply that he might like to be nearer Mum and Dad than I (being older) would, *he* gets given the room in the roof. He is a boy. Boys always get privileges, earned or not.

I have the smallest bedroom, the one right next to the garage. It's plain as a nun's cell, despite the eye-jangling wallpaper. A narrow bed, a single wardrobe, a small chest of drawers, all white-painted wood. A bookshelf with a few Enid Blytons and my Bible and prayer book. The only softening touches are the fluffy pyjama case on the bed, and a print on the wall of a puppy and a kitten sitting amicably together in a basket. The view from my

16

window is the front path, the front gate, the hard standing for the car. Even so I used to spend a lot of time staring out of my bedroom window. I put my head under the net curtains to look out: I couldn't stand that film of nylon between my eyes and the outside world. 'You've been gawping out of this window again, haven't you?' my mother would say, tugging the curtains straight. As if looking out of a window was a crime. Well, it was fine to look out, but you mustn't be seen doing so.

My gazing wasn't strictly observational: it was the sort that cows do, looking soulfully into the middle distance while their jaws keep moving and sometimes their tails lift to let out squirts of dung. Gazing out provided a view for my imagination to rest on and blank out. Maybe that's just what cows are doing, stuck in the same old field, as they while away the dismal hours.

But I wanted to be up in the roof, under the sloping ceiling where model biplanes dangled. I wanted to be able to lie in bed and gaze out of the dormer window, over the roof tiles and the neat back gardens, to the low hills and greenness inland. There's a feeling, when you're up there, of being alone, complete, like being in a well-defended castle on a mound. As if you could pull up the ladder and shut the trapdoor and no one could come up unless you said so. But you can't. There's just an ordinary door and a steep flight of red-carpeted stairs leading down to the hall.

I don't think Brian could have cared less which room he had. He isn't an imaginative sort of boy. His talents lie firmly in the realm of the practical. He built model aeroplanes out of plastic kits and made stupid noises with his mouth as he flew them round in his hand, but I'm sure he didn't imagine anything other than 'Here is an aeroplane, flying along.'

We live near the coast, though you'd hardly know it. Eastwards, everything's so flat you can't see the sea at all. The horizon is a line of houses. Our road is right at the inland edge of the town. But the soil is full of sand, and the trees are the sort you get near the sea, stunted hawthorns and pine trees, growing in fixed, crouched positions, as if the wind never blows from any other direction.

We're near the main road out of town, and on summer weekends there's always a traffic jam, because of the day trippers. They want their glimpse of the sea, and then when they've had enough they want to go home – all at the same time. Hot and thirsty and sunburnt, with quarrelsome kids in the back. Maybe they sit there in the stalled queue and look out of their car windows and wish they lived here, near the sea. Perhaps they catch a glimpse of Dad doing the garden or us on our bikes, and they wish they were us and not them, not stuck in the traffic with another fifty miles to go yet. I'd see kids with their sticky mouths pressed up against the windows, staring out at me, and I'd know they wanted to be me. Me astride my bike, with my suntanned legs and my chewing gum, and no one telling me to *for God's sake, sit still!*

Perhaps they did.

I've always found it too easy to think of *perhaps*, to live in perhaps. The perhaps of being a Carolyn, the perhaps of people who wished they were us. It's so tempting. So much better than real life.

3

The Hedge

At least I don't have to share a room in here. I'd hate that. Because I've never had to share my bedroom. I never dreamed of going to boarding school and sleeping in a dormitory with half a dozen other girls. Where would you ever get any privacy? And what if they snored? What if they had nightmares, or smelly feet? That wouldn't do for me. I've been used to privacy, and being on my own. A certain amount of loneliness. Aloneness. I'm not sure what the difference is.

God knows what a room-mate might get up to, in here. From what I've seen so far, the others are all completely barmy. Mad as hatters. Snoring and smelly feet would be the least of it.

I know I sound quite cheerful, but I'm not. I try to look cheerful and careless, to anyone who's watching. *Nothing to worry about, that's me!* It wouldn't do to wander around with your tail between your legs, forlorn, or looking guilty. Especially looking guilty.

*   *   *

'Give some people an inch and they'll take a mile,' my mum used to say. 'Hold out the hand of friendship, and you never know what you're letting yourself in for.'

So we didn't know our neighbours. We didn't really know anyone in the road, beyond a pleasant nodding and helloing when we passed. That was what you did – you never ignored anyone, but you never became too intimate.

'I wouldn't want people always in and out of the house,' she said.

It was unlikely. My mum and dad weren't very encouraging. They had no one you might term 'friends'. My mother went to church regularly, and my father irregularly, but they kept the busy church community firmly at arm's length, turning down everything except the most formal invitations. The only people who came to our house were family, and the only people we visited were family, my dad's two sisters Gloria and Stella, his cousin Bettina, and my mum's brother Bob.

We certainly didn't know our neighbours with *the hedge*.

In the fashion of the neighbourhood, our front garden was divided from our other neighbours and the road by a chain of white links slung between foot-high posts. The back garden had a low fence of brown palings. The aim was always to be able to *see* – to see the neighbours in their gardens, the washing on the lines, the people going down the road. And to *be seen*. To be seen doing the neighbourly thing, which was keeping your own patch trim and tidy. And following the rules, cleaning the car at weekends and no bonfires before seven. There might have been frosted glass and nets at every window, but outside all had to be crystal clear.

We were at the outer edge of this oasis of good citizenship. We lived in the last bungalow in the street. Beyond us was a wilderness of thistly fields, scrubby woodland, tumbledown sheds and half-hearted fences. Old tyres, discarded machinery and scruffy ponies were corralled back there. And right along our inland boundary, shielding us from this wasteland and from the house next door, the very last house of all – *the old house* – ran the hedge. Solid as Sleeping Beauty's thicket, a wall of evergreen laurel, it stretched from the pavement at the front to the far end of our back garden, and grew untrimmed to the height of our roof. At least, it grew untrimmed on their side. On our side, Dad would snip away constantly with the shears, keeping it as tame as he could. But he wasn't brave enough or furious enough to get up on a ladder and have a go at the top.

'That hedge sucks all the life out of the garden,' he always said. He'd walk up and down the lawn, examining the grass, shaking his head and tutting, trying to make out something poorer in its colour or texture which he could blame on the hedge. It was true that bedding plants didn't flourish near the hedge's roots. The soil beneath it was dry and starved.

'It's so inconsiderate,' my mother agreed. 'It casts so much shade.'

'Only in the morning,' I pointed out, when I was old enough to notice. 'Not when you want to sit out here.'

I wanted to defend the hedge, and its owners. I was fascinated by the idea of something *different*, something secretive and wild. I just didn't have the words to say it.

And it was true: on summer afternoons our back garden was a blaze of sun. You couldn't get away from it;

there was nothing higher than a foot tall to cast any shade, apart from the shed. My dad laid out the garden on the basis of interior decoration, and maintained it as neatly as a room kept for 'best'. The lawn was a carpet, a perfect rectangle, smooth and free of weeds, with a strip of bare brown earth – the parquet – all around it. Then he ran dwarf plants round the edges, like wallpaper, alternating the colours: white alyssum, blue lobelia, red salvia, ginger French marigolds. To earn our pocket money I pulled up weeds and Brian mowed the lawn, but Dad always did the edges himself. He couldn't trust anyone else to get such straight edges as he did.

So the hedge stood for all that was threatening: the un-neighbourliness of our neighbours, their suspect desire for privacy, the proximity of behaviour that was not fit for the scrutiny of others. Well, of course, my parents didn't say this, they couldn't have put their feelings into words. But the way Mum said, 'I wish they'd do something about that hedge,' whenever she came in from hanging the washing, and the prim click-click of Dad's shears in the summer dusk, were quite enough.

We knew that there were a lot of them next door. It was a big house, full of loud careless people. You could tell that from the sudden and various noises which came from beyond the laurel barrier. My parents never tackled them about the noise, or about the vast size of the hedge. They were fearful of any kind of interference, in case people interfered back.

'You just never know with *people*,' my father said. 'You never know what they'll stoop to.'

And anyway, they got a funny kind of satisfaction from complaining, from having a permanent reason to feel disgruntled. A perfectly ordered world would have been less rewarding on that score.

I was playing on my own when I found the hole in the hedge. I couldn't believe my father had missed it.

It must have been spring, because the daffodils were out and the buds hadn't burst yet on the trees. I would have been eight, coming up for nine. I had some complicated game going on in my head and was pretending to hide down beside the shed. The space was too narrow for my dad to slide into with his shears. The long stems of the laurel splayed out, pressing up against the shed wall, leaving just a low passageway for me to creep into. I crept. There was no chance that Brian had been here before me, because he didn't like spiders. Neither did I, but some things are too good to miss just because a creepy-crawly might fall down your neck.

And there was the hole. The laurels gave way, and formed a sort of tunnel. I pushed my head and shoulders into the gap. Inside, disappointingly, the tunnel stopped. Laurel twigs criss-crossed in front of me. But I was in, and it was easier to go forward than back. I crouched down, dropped on to hands and knees, and inched forward. The ground stank of dirty old leaves and mushroomy damp. I peered through the thick stems to the light beyond. I was at the back of some kind of flower bed, filled with leafless bushes.

For the very first time I could see into next door's back garden. It wasn't as I had imagined. For a start, it was nothing like ours. It was so much bigger. Towards the house there was an abandoned bike, and a tree stump, and a swing. In the other direction, a sagging tennis net, and an old wooden summer house, its window panes cracked and its wood peeling. Their lawn wasn't lawn, in the sense that I understood the word. The patchy grass was almost knee-high. In the borders dead plants leaned against each other with their seed-heads still on them. The far end of the garden was full of trees, gnarled bare trees planted in rows. I recognized this from our *Children's Encyclopaedia*, the double-page spread that depicted a mixed farm in glorious detail: this was an orchard.

Something moved. My eyes flicked back to the summer house: there was a man. My skin prickled. I kept absolutely still, barely daring to breathe. A twig stuck into my ear, but I ignored it. At least the man was far away and had his back to me. I realized that he was completely absorbed in what he was doing, though I couldn't for the life of me work out what that was. He didn't pause or even look up. He was painting a huge board propped against the wall of the summer house, but the bit he had painted and the bit he hadn't painted looked exactly the same.

I stayed where I was for a good five minutes, burning with cramp, itching with fear. But part of me felt triumphant. The man I was spying on was *our neighbour*. The owner of the hedge.

Suddenly I wanted a garden like that. I'd never seen anything like it. Untidy, haphazard, full of secret corners. Different things could go on there – you could ride a bike on the lawn and just throw it down where you finished with it. You could play tennis, you could hide. And whatever people did do there, it didn't involve manicuring the grass and mowing stripes into it.

I never crawled through the hole again. The laurel

burst with bright new leaves to fill the gaps, and started shedding old dead ones. They scattered like dandruff along the foot of the hedge. Spiders began spinning businesslike webs. Anyway, I knew it would end in trouble. Most things did. If I tried again Mum or Dad was bound to spot me backing out of the hole. Or I'd be discovered in the act of spying by the people who lived next door. And you never knew with *people*. I could imagine the shouts: 'Hey! What do you think you're doing? Get out! Get back to where you came from!' Or worse: taking me by my collar and marching me, red-handed, or, rather, green-kneed, back to my parents. I could see the pair of them, clustering in our front doorway, their faces anxious and uncomprehending. 'What on earth were you up to? Making an exhibition of yourself! And *us*.' Explain that away.

I relied on my imagination, my usual tactic. In my mind's eye their garden expanded even further. The pock-marked lawn stretched in all directions and grew almost as green as ours, the thicket of shrubs I'd crouched in sprang into a forest, the summer house into a play-palace fit for Marie Antoinette. In my head I played – and won – endless games of tennis. I cycled like the wind up and down, up and down, never hitting a pothole, never catching my shin on the backspin of the pedal as I put my foot down to heave my bike round the corners. In my head, I never had to put my foot down to heave it round corners. I was perfectly competent, and that garden was mine. All mine.

Sad to say, those little chats with Lorna have become a daily event. I thought I'd beaten her, that first time she came into my room. I thought I'd won that round, and she wouldn't try again. Shows how much I know.

We meet in a small room off the front hall. Mid-morning or mid-afternoon, usually. Someone comes and gets me from wherever I am, Mike or Trudy or whoever is on duty. 'Time to see Lorna,' they say. Or just 'Carol?' and a hand signal, a beckoning finger and then a point towards the front hall. They don't let me go on my own, just in case I never get there. They always take me right up to the door.

There's a table which is not quite a desk, and two chairs beside it, facing each other. It's not exactly formal but it's certainly not *in*formal, either. I expect Lorna thinks it strikes just the right note. Whatever that might be.

Today she asked me what I was good at, what I liked doing, and I said, 'Nothing much.'

'Oh, I'm sure that can't be true.'

She pressed her lips together as if she was cross. There was a long silence. I examined my fingers. As far as I was concerned, we could go on like this until the end of the session. It didn't matter to me.

Then Lorna coughed in a fake sort of way, and pushed with her fingertips at the edge of a folder beside her on the table. A folder which was shut. 'I've been looking again at your records,' she said. 'You've had rather a tricky time, haven't you? Almost four years in the children's home before being placed for adoption. Some rather difficult years with your new family. And then this latest business. Still, at least you always had your brother with you.'

She didn't say anything else. After a bit she let me go.

But outside, I thought: Why can't *I* look at my records? They're *my* records. Why can't I see what everyone's been saying about me?

I should have said piano. When she asked what I was good at, that's what I should have said.

4

Piano Lessons

Lorna's had another go at asking me to describe my home. She's persistent, I'll give her that.

I said, 'It's a big white house, with a big garden. There are lawns and paths and flower beds. There's a long line of steps down from the front door to the gate. The slope is very shallow. There are a hundred and twenty steps, but only in sets of five. Five steps and then a flat bit, then another five steps.'

'Do you often count things, Cora?'

She always calls me that. It's just a name on a piece of paper, it isn't me. I've half a dozen other names I'd prefer. I'd like to say, 'Don't call me that,' but I think that's what she wants. What she's after. To get a rise out of me, to get me to say something I really mean. So I don't. I just look steadily back at her when she uses that name. I don't even blink.

'Only sheep,' I replied.

'It must be a very *big* garden,' Lorna said. 'I make that forty sets of steps.'

Either she's innumerate or she's trying to catch me out. I tend to think the former.

'Yes, it is a big garden,' I replied. 'There are yellow tulips, and white seats to sit on.' I wondered how much detail I could go into before she realized. 'My favourite seat is by a sundial,' I said.

But, actually, she has never come out into the garden here with me. When you go outside you always have to be with a member of staff, or in sight of one, at least. Lorna has never come and sat with me in front of the sundial, and looked down the path between the long beds of yellow tulips.

But every day she must climb the hundred and twenty steps, the *twenty-four* sets of five steps, to come to her place of work. And not notice them? Now, that is what I call unobservant.

That spring, when I turned nine, I started piano lessons. It was a very Carolyn sort of thing to do. I'd badgered away at them to let me. We had an old upright piano, black as ebony, standing there useless in the lounge. It had come from my mum's own mother's house, apparently, along with the noisy pendulum clock on the mantelpiece and the convex mirror above it, a circular eye that made your top half bulge weirdly when you peered up into it. All these things were *old*. Old was not desirable, or attractive. They only kept them out of sentiment, and a sense of duty. They liked things spick and span and new; things they had chosen themselves from the big stores in town; at least then you knew where they had been. The piano took up space, and always needed dusting, and nobody could play it. 'Why not?' I kept on. 'Why not, *please*?'

My mother took me the first time. We walked. The roads round our way are flat, and perfectly straight, laid out on a grid pattern. I was surprised to find that the house where I was to have piano lessons was just like other houses. I had imagined it would be enormous and grand. The sound of musical instruments would drift out from tall, open windows. There ought to be huge trees around it, and hedges and lawns, and a wide flight of stone steps up to the front door. I didn't recall imagining this beforehand; it was just that when we got to the little pebble-dashed semi I realized that that was what I'd expected. Not a concrete path, rose bushes snicked down to their knuckles, and a holder for milk bottles in the porch with a dial to tell the milkman how many to leave.

My mother rang the bell. The door was opened just a foot wide by someone who peered round it suspiciously: a youngish woman, dumpy, with rollers in her hair. Was this the musical type?

'I'll take you through to Mum,' she muttered.

We squeezed awkwardly round the door and into the narrow hallway. A big pushchair took up most of the space. I noticed a little boy at the back of the hall. He was bumping a push-along toy crossly against the skirting board.

We were shown into the front room. The piano was there, along with a dining table piled with folded ironing, a mirror engraved with flowers, a kitten calendar on the wall. So disappointingly *domestic*.

Another dumpy woman, much older, dressed in a grass-green Crimplene frock, turned round to us from the piano bench. She looked like anyone you might see walking down our road, pegging out washing, getting off a bus.

'So this is Carol. I'm Mrs Wallis.'

I gave her a tight smile. My mother hovered, somewhere between the ironing and the mirror.

Mrs Wallis pointed to the bench, and I sat down. She showed me how to find middle C, which I already knew. And so we began.

If someone was having a lesson when you arrived, you waited on a seat in the dark hallway. The busy times were after school on weekdays and on Saturday mornings. The little boy could sometimes be heard crying, or his mother shouting, or someone would run noisily up the stairs. All quite thrilling, compared to our house. Mrs Wallis, when she heard these things, would sigh between clenched teeth. She had large hands which she brought down firmly on my hands, and later, when I got on to the pedals, she would sometimes press down with her foot on my foot. It was an odd way of being guided, like being crushed. And you couldn't do anything right under her physical force, you couldn't find the right place because you were just held there, and the next time, on your own, it would be back to guesswork, as usual.

But I met Barbara at the piano teacher's. She was sitting in the hall one day when I arrived. 'I know you,' she said. 'You live next door to us.'

I was astounded. I didn't recognize her at all.

'You live next door to us in Cromer Road. You live in the bungalow. The one with the windmill.'

She was right. There was a model windmill in one of the front garden beds. I omitted to mention it when I described the garden. It wasn't quite a garden gnome; it was a windmill.

'I don't know *you*,' was all I said.

'I'm Barbara Hennessy,' she told me, as if that would jog my memory. I shook my head. Upstairs there was a crash, and a wail. In the front room a rendering of 'The Bells of St Mary's' fell apart and then carried, falteringly, on.

'She's not married, you know,' Barbara said with a glittering look, glancing at the ceiling. 'All the parents think they're being dead brave and compassionate sending their kids here for piano lessons. Helping Grandma pay the bills.'

None of this made any sense to me, but I loved the way her face assumed a wicked expression. Maybe I'd never seen a wicked smile before. I asked her if she had a lesson next but she said she was just there to pick up some music. Her lessons were usually on Saturday mornings, and this was a Tuesday. I was relieved, in a way, because if she had a lesson booked I was sure she had more right to it than I, who also had one booked then. I had never waited with anyone else on that uncomfortable seat before.

She went in to collect her music. I heard her voice, to and fro with the piano teacher's, just like two adults having a conversation. She came out, smiled at me, said, 'I'll see you around,' and then, at the front door, 'What's your name?'

I slurred it. I tried the Carolyn trick. Perhaps it would work.

Later my lessons were changed to Saturday mornings. My mother had stopped accompanying me by then; it took up too much of her time. I walked there on my own.

I went in as Barbara came out. She always smiled at me. Then one day she was still there after my lesson. Not on the seat, but in the road outside.

I came out into the sunshine and turned right on to the chipped asphalt pavement. Barbara appeared from a gateway, from between hedges: an apparition. She had on a red tartan kilt, a cream woolly jumper. Her hair was messy and loose and fell into her face. A kilt and a cream jumper and messy hair were suddenly my aspirations in life.

'Are you going home?' she asked, and we walked together. My heart was bumping with excitement in my chest, and I must have had a stupid grin on my face all the way back to Cromer Road. Because Barbara had waited, expressly for *me*.

I've just met someone, the first person I've encountered in this place who isn't a zombie. Thank God. I was getting jolly lonely. Her name is Hanny Gombrich, which is another good thing.

I like to have a friend, an accomplice.

5

Activity

They've put me down for Activity.

That's what they do here. You don't *choose* an activity, or *do* an activity. You get put down for it.

Mike came into my room and told me. 'Come on, Carol. You can't stay here all day. I've put you down for *Activity.*'

His voice is falsely jolly. I can see from the look in his eyes that he's afraid I won't go along with it, won't go along with all the enthusiastic suggestions about chats and activities and time for tea. And what if I don't? Then he'll have to use an alternative method of persuasion. I've seen a few examples of that already: not a pretty sight. So I get up off my bed and follow him. Besides, I'm curious.

I can't imagine what kind of activity it will be that scrupulously avoids the use of scissors, knives, needles and pins, thread or wire, or there again, blunt instruments. Every minute of the day in here, we have to be saved from ourselves. Or each other.

On the way to the back of the building, where Activity

takes place, we walk down a corridor beside a courtyard. I've never been down here before. In the yard two washing lines are strung with tea towels and plain, white, functional-looking aprons. They're flapping and struggling in the wind. For some reason that makes me feel happy. Maybe because they look as if at any second one of them might take off. I follow Mike slowly, keeping an eye on those energetic aprons for as long as I can.

Whatever it was my dad got up to at Gough Electricals, it required him to wear a blue boiler suit. He had two – one on, and one in the wash. When I was little I hated to see that man-shaped blue outfit swinging on the washing line, puffing up in the wind. It frightened me, made me afraid to go outside. Worse was sometimes if Dad had a holiday and my mother took the opportunity to wash the two boiler suits at once. Then they would hang side by side on the line. It was all too easy for me to imagine a whole family of brothers who worked at Gough's, a line full of boiler suits, a human-sized row of cut-out blue paper dollies dancing their way menacingly down the garden. I wasn't normally a nervous child, I was just full of fancy, and sometimes the fancies took me in the wrong direction.

Whatever he needed the boiler suit for, my mother wouldn't let him go out of the house in it. Boiler suits were not as respectable as she would have liked him to be. So he took it in a canvas bag, and set off for work in a white shirt and a brown tartan tie, brown jacket and cavalry twill trousers. Not quite a suit, not proclaiming falsely, 'Here is a man in a suit, who goes to work in an office.' But certainly not overalls. Heaven forbid *overalls*.

Then they invented drip-dry nylon shirts and she bought him some of those. She was always eager to sample the modern, to find labour-saving new inventions. He had one white, one blue and one cream nylon shirt. They billowed disgustingly on the line, like swollen corpses. The white one soon faded to cream, the cream one turned nicotine-yellow. The blue one stayed blue. He went back to his white cotton shirts that Mum had to iron. He wore the nylon shirts for gardening, sweating away inside them, because she said they were too good to throw out.

'They're still fit for something,' she said. 'They're not finished yet.'

They never would wear out. That was how she was.

It was *clay*. The Activity was clay.

I haven't touched clay since my last year at junior school. I haven't smelled that smell – wet and earthy. Gravelike.

They had already cut out our bits of clay for us; they were taking no chances. Otherwise we might strangle each other with the cheese-wire or poke our own eyes out. When we came into the room, the little cubes were already wired off and set on wooden boards in front of each place at the table. A woman called Dulcie was running the show. She stood at the front in a clay-smeared coat, and watched us shuffle in.

'Hello, everybody. Sit down.'

A long pause, while chairs scraped and we glanced resentfully at each other's bits of clay, to see if they were bigger or smaller.

'Now, you can make anything you want with your clay,

36

so long as you use your hands. I want to see those fingers really working!'

We couldn't have those sharp wooden scrapers, the wire-ended moulders, the neat metal scalpels, that I remembered from school. You could try to mould a shape using just your fingers, or, with Dulcie's hovering help, make a pot. Or just tear it up and roll it into little balls and drop it on the floor, as the woman next to me did. No one batted an eyelid. It was all Activity.

When I did clay at school we had to make a coil pot. No choice about it, a coil pot was what you made. The teacher in charge of the pottery room was very particular. She really didn't like just anyone getting into her pottery lessons, and so there were only about half a dozen children who ever progressed beyond coil pots to glazed animals, and vases, and moulded tiles. Goodness knows how much money had been spent by the generous county council on the pottery room and the kiln, but only a handful of kids benefited.

I couldn't make my coil pot work. The sausages of clay I rolled dried up so fast that they cracked and broke when I tried to force them into curves. So that was that – my one and only lesson with clay. Our class was sent back to drawing on shiny kitchen paper with blunt pencils, and to another teacher, a trainee, who drifted between the desks, saying everything we produced was 'Lovely. *Lovely!*'

Rose, the woman next to me in Activity, kept pinching off little bits of clay and rolling them between the tips of her fingers, gazing all the while into the air. She dropped the clay balls on to the floor as if she didn't know what her fingers were doing. They pinched and rolled and then just – opened themselves. And hey presto, nothing there! Rose had a huge wart on the back of her ring finger, just where a diamond in an ostentatious setting would be. She wore no real rings, of course. (That's the sort of thing they remove from us, in case we find some fantastically ingenious way of injuring ourselves: stick our heads through them and hang ourselves, I would guess.) Rose didn't say a word, but sometimes a little squeak issued from the back of her throat.

The only activity I've ever been any good at is piano. Legitimate activity, that is. It took me a long time, but eventually I was good at those scales, up and down, down and up, my fingers trilling so fast that you could barely follow the movement, like the whirring legs of a cartoon animal. I was damned good at 'The Bells of St Mary's'. I liked everyone to be able to hear me, all through the bungalow, plinking and plonking away. I liked to think of one of them coming in and saying, 'Oh, my dear, that was lovely. Now do play such-and-such for us.' I bet a Carolyn sort of mother would have said things like that. Encouraging things. Carolyn's mother would have sat down next to her on the piano stool, arranging her pleated chiffon skirts, and played a duet, elegant white fingers rippling like sea anemones over the keys. I bet she would.

Perhaps I wasn't so good. Perhaps I was dire. Maybe there was nothing about my playing to admire, except the sheer volume. I was fond of the loud pedal and had got into the habit of pressing it down, before Mrs Wallis could press it down for me.

Without even thinking about it, I found I had made a face out of my clay, a face dominated by a huge nose.

A caricature sort of face. I squashed it up again before anyone could see what it was and deduce something about me from it.

6

The Wren

'How come I haven't ever seen you at school?' I said to Barbara Hennessy, walking back from piano one day.

This had become a habit. Every Saturday she'd wait for me and we'd walk home, slowly, together. I don't know what she did for half an hour while I had my lesson, but she was always there when I came out, jumping out from behind one hedge or another. Sometimes she didn't appear for yards, and I'd worry that she had finally got bored with me. But then, with a thump and a scattering of leaves and flower heads, she'd be there in front of me.

Now she sounded very casual. 'We don't go to school that much.'

She toed a pebble carefully along the line of kerb-stones. A strategic kind of pause, only I didn't know it then.

'I've seen your school, I've seen them playing *netball* in the playground.' Her voice made netball sound disagreeable. 'Anyway, we don't go there. *We* go to the Wren.'

And that was how I discovered that St John's C of E

Primary School, run by the church and the county council, wasn't the only place you could go.

'I've never heard of a school called the Wren.'

'I'll show you it, if you like,' Barbara offered. 'It's not far.'

It was far, but then that was Barbara, as I'd come to appreciate in time, always bending the truth to her own ends. We made a detour and eventually came to a long, leafy road full of old houses. I was looking for something I recognized as a school, peering as far as the end of the road, when Barbara stopped in front of one of the houses and said: 'This is it.'

I stared at the ramshackle building. Enormous trees lined the front fence, and a big flight of steps ran up to the front door. It was like a distorted dream-version of the house I had imagined my piano lessons would take place in. Above the door was a half-moon window with 'Wren House' painted in curly script, but there was nothing – no noticeboard, no signs, no tarmac playground or netball posts – to indicate that this was a school. Except maybe the row of paper chains hanging in one of the front windows. I didn't know whether to believe her or not.

'You can come with me one day,' Barbara offered. 'They won't notice.'

They *won't notice*? It seemed to me that schools were designed to notice. They noticed whether you were there or not, whether you were late, even whether you arrived too early. They noticed if you were sitting up straight, if you weren't listening, if you were on the wrong page, if your pencil wasn't sharp enough. And they made it their business that everyone else noticed too. 'Now stop, everyone. Look at Peter. Has Peter got his left foot in the air, or his right foot? Which foot should he have in the air? That's right. Now show us, Peter. Show us you know which is your left foot.' I couldn't believe a school existed where they wouldn't notice me.

'I'll have to get the day off my school,' I said.

Barbara shrugged.

'It won't be easy,' I told her.

'Forge a letter from your mum, saying you're ill,' Barbara suggested, as if this was the most obvious thing in the world.

We were never off school. We were never allowed to give in to coughs and sniffs and tummy aches. My mother liked us out of the house from eight thirty sharp until four o'clock, unless we were actually contagious.

'My brother's good at doing grown-up handwriting,' she added. 'And *your* brother can hand it in.'

We had established, in the course of our conversations, that we both had brothers.

So that was what we did. I stole a piece of paper and an envelope from the bureau drawer, and Barbara got her older brother Tom to write the note. I tried to persuade Brian that handing a fake sick-note to my teacher was a brave and cunning act, something only a *boy*'s daring could carry through. When this didn't work I pulled rank.

'You've got to do what I say. I'm older than you.'

No dice.

'Then I'll tell Mum and Dad what you've been up to.'

This was a bluff. I knew of nothing wicked he'd done, I had no interesting inside knowledge of Brian. Not at that stage. But there must have been something he felt shifty about, even then, because he gave in.

'All right,' he grumbled. 'But it'll cost you a sherbet fountain.'

I liked that feeling. I liked it that I had bent Brian to my will.

Barbara and I arranged to meet at the roundabout near the end of our road. I set off for school at the usual time, and then hid in the bushes. It was dark inside but I didn't want anyone else on their way to school to see me. The undergrowth stank sharply of urine. I wasn't sure if it was cat or human in origin. I was afraid of getting my school clothes dirty. I was even more afraid of spiders falling down my neck. It reminded me of my adventure, climbing through the hedge the previous spring. That was Barbara's garden I had peered into. And now here I was, waiting to go on another adventure, with Barbara herself. As my aunt Stella often said, wonders will never cease!

I waited a long time, crouching in the acrid semi-dark. It occurred to me that perhaps Barbara wouldn't come, hadn't ever meant it, that I'd be stuck there all day. Perhaps she was already in school, sitting up keenly at her desk, reciting something off the board. Perhaps she had tricked me. And Brian might get an attack of nerves at the last minute and fail to hand in my note. Or my teachers would spot the forgery. And then I'd be *expelled*! The only people who ever got expelled were really wicked boys, boys who were out of everyone's control. Maybe that's how they would see me.

Then I heard voices, and saw Barbara, accompanied by two smaller children, wandering along the pavement in a careless, meandering way. I burst out of my hiding place, hysterical with relief.

'Shouldn't you be there by now?' I asked.

43

Barbara only shrugged, and said, 'Not really.'

I stared at the little boys. Barbara didn't introduce them. They both had curly hair and neither of them had bothered to comb it that morning.

'I'm Sebastian. He's Mattie,' the dark-haired, slightly taller one said, pointing at his brother. His voice was husky, which sounded odd, coming from such a small boy.

Barbara was busy looking me up and down. Self-consciously, I pulled some dead leaves out of my hair.

'Give us your woolly,' she instructed briskly.

I was in my brown-and-white-check school dress and brown botany wool cardigan, with white socks and brown lace-ups. She was wearing lime-green nylon shorts.

'Don't you have to wear school uniform?' I asked.

'No. They don't like uniforms at the Wren. They wouldn't want to see us all looking the same.'

We exchanged cardigans. Hers was made up of left-over wools crocheted into circles of different colours. Some of the colours hadn't even lasted a whole circle, and were finished off with something else. She pushed the sleeves of my school cardigan up to her elbows and buttoned it unevenly at the front. I thought I'd got much the better end of the bargain.

When we reached the Wren, Barbara marched straight up the steps and pushed the front door open. Sebastian and Mattie ran off towards the back of the house and Barbara went into the front room. There were half a dozen children round a big table, painting on leaves and pressing the leaves down on to sheets of sugar paper.

'Oh, hello there,' said the woman in charge, looking up

and smiling in a vague, short-sighted way. She didn't seem annoyed at Barbara's lateness.

We sat down at gaps round the table and joined in painting leaves. No one took a register or even glanced at me. There were two children who weren't doing anything much. One was poking a ruler in the fish tank and the other just looked out of the window for ages.

In the middle of the table was a big tray of leaves from the garden, and we chose whichever we wanted, and painted them however we wanted, and stuck them down on paper to make patterns. I thought it was like something out of infant school, but I didn't say so. Barbara got the giggles and was painting on her hand and trying to stick it in other kids' faces. The boy next to me took a dry horse-chestnut leaf and crumbled it to pieces all over my sheet of paper, just to annoy me.

After a very long time we were sent out to a sun-porch at the back of the house to wash the paint off our hands, and then we went into the garden and ran about under the trees. There was no playground, just worn-out grass covered with old beech mast. We ran hard, and shouted and screamed, but only for the sake of it. At my school, you rushed about and yelled at playtime for the sheer relief of being out of the classroom, but here you didn't feel the same need. I think I galloped around, bursting my lungs, to try and make some kind of impact on someone, but it didn't work.

After a while, the woman in charge of our classroom came to the top of the steps and asked us to come in. Barbara took no notice, so I copied her. She had to come back several times before she succeeded in rounding all of us up. We stuck our mouths under the cold tap in the

45

sun-porch. The water was warm and tasted green and metallic. Then we slouched back to our room.

The other children were already sitting on the floor in a circle. Barbara and I flopped down with them. The woman – I couldn't call her a teacher, she lacked that glint of suspicion in the eye that marks a teacher out; in fact the only suspicious thing about the glint in her eye was its innocence and joyfulness – read a story aloud. There were cushions on the floor and you could lie back on them and lounge about while you listened. Afterwards we acted out parts of the story. Everyone joined in, except one boy who sat in the bay window and picked his nose in a leisurely sort of way.

I looked at the woman in charge. Drilled my eyes into hers to see if she would look back and *notice* me. She had untidy red hair and big lips covered in peachy lipstick. Her upper lip was just like the lower one, completely unindented. She wore a black dress covered in swirly red roses, with a full skirt and a wide neckline that kept slipping, always showing one set of petticoat and bra straps or the other. Barbara said her name was Gail. Not Miss or Mrs anything. Just Gail.

Needless to say, Gail didn't notice me.

At lunchtime we went into the sun-porch, where there were two big wooden tables and assorted chairs. Barbara put her carrier bag on the table and I put my satchel on it. Barbara took out a plastic box and a thermos flask. I just sat there. 'Where's your lunch?' she said.

'What lunch? We have school dinners.'

'School dinners? This *is* school dinner.' Everyone around us was getting out paper bags and plastic boxes and greaseproof packages of food. 'Here, you'd better have some of mine if you haven't got anything.'

And that was when I found out that you could have such things as grated cheese and lemon curd and sultanas in sandwiches.

Barbara offered me some of her drink. The shiny lip of her flask was covered in slips of beige like tiny pieces of seaweed. I caught a whiff of the drink and felt sick.

'It's only *coffee*. Don't you drink coffee?'

I shook my head, and saw a look in her eyes that showed me I wasn't coming up to scratch. But afterwards she admitted that it did taste a bit of thermos. I settled for another drink from the cold-water tap.

The day was strangely long. There was no clock on the wall in the front room, and I didn't have a watch. The sun came round into the front garden, and the boy picking his nose turned and faced the other way, so that it didn't shine in his eyes. Barbara and I made some pastry, using a pair of scales and a bag of flour and some rather hairy lard. Around the room, other children were sorting coloured marbles into jars, building things with bricks, and measuring the height of the bookcase. I thought it must be counting and measuring that we were learning now, but I didn't see why it had to be disguised as something else.

Barbara and I took our grey dough out to the kitchen to put it in the oven. The kitchen was huge and old and smelly, and there was a pile of dirty teacups in the sink. A clock hung over the boiler in the defunct fireplace.

'Is that the right time?'

Barbara nodded. 'Think so.'

'It's only five to two!'

'So what?'

47

'I thought it must be nearly home time.'

Barbara found some matches in a drawer and lit the oven. It made a booming sound as the gas caught and she leaped back. We left our pastry resting straight on the oven shelf, as we couldn't find a baking tray for it. We knew that no one was counting the minutes until we came back, so we ran outside into the garden again.

Barbara led the way to the end and we slipped behind some bushes. From there we could see through the slats in the fence into another garden beyond. There was a clothes line with underwear swaying on it, enormous flesh-coloured knickers and long-line brassieres with cups the size of balloons. We fell about laughing.

I gulped for air. 'Have you ever seen the owner?'

Barbara nodded violently. 'I've seen her asleep in a deckchair, wearing a swimming costume!' And she gestured eloquently with her hands to describe the voluptuous sight. I felt weak with laughter, and it was the happiest I had been all day.

We went back and retrieved our pastry, which was brown at the edges but still grey in the middle. Gail said we could take it home. It was nearly half past two and people were picking up their jumpers and their lunch bags and drifting out.

'Bye-bye, everyone,' Gail said cheerily, waving both hands in the air. 'See you all tomorrow.'

We waited on the steps until Mattie and Sebastian came out and then set off for home.

'I'm much too early,' I said to Barbara. 'We don't usually finish for another hour.'

I thought she might invite me to her house to wait out

the interval, but she just said, 'Then you'll have to hide in the bushes again, won't you?'

When I saw Barbara the following week at piano I said bravely, 'I didn't like your school much. I thought it was boring.'

She blinked sleepily. 'That's why we don't bother to go all the time. You don't *learn* anything there. Except Izzy and Tom. And they're clever anyway, so they probably taught themselves.'

School dinners cost a shilling, and I had missed a dinner that had been paid for because of going to the Wren. My mother always sent the right money at the beginning of each week, so at the end of term they gave me the shilling to give back to her. I kept it, of course. And that was how I learned that crime *does* pay.

7

Nearest and Dearest

There's a lot I don't think about. Recent things.

I'm only eighteen and already I'm living in the past. I'm like an old lady with nothing to fill her days and nothing to look forward to, who dwells continually in some lost golden age, *before the war*, when she was young. Either I think about right now, today, breakfast, dinner and tea. (Or breakfast, lunch and supper, as they call it here. I don't know what happened to dinner. It doesn't feature, not at midday or in the evening. *Dinner* is off the menu.) Or I think about way-back-when. When I was little.

I'm only eighteen. I should be able to look to the future. If I was a Carolyn sort of girl my life would be full of things to look forward to: invitations, parties, the purchase of fashionable dresses that would fit me like a glove. Maybe an engagement ring. I bet a Carolyn sort of girl would have her wedding all planned out in her head by the time she hit puberty. She and her mother would smile at attractive small children when they were out and about, and remark to each other that Julie was a nice name for a girl and Mark a very good choice for a boy. All this long before there was any suitable man on the horizon. Because of course, for a Carolyn, there always would be, some day. No question. Simple as that.

If I think about the future I see only a door slamming shut.

Lorna has been chipping away again. Or she tries to. She keeps asking about my mother. Frankly, the woman's *obsessed* with my mother.

There are little gems, little jewels, I could hand her. But I don't.

I could say how she would dry my hair with a towel, roughly, poking my scalp with her bony fingers and almost pulling my hair out as she rubbed it between the folds of towelling. I hated hair-washing day. But she didn't mean to hurt me.

Or porridge. She could make it thin as gruel, or thick as rice pudding. Either way it had lumps in. Little blunt lumps which broke apart into dry oatmeal under your teeth. And then she'd nag us if we didn't eat it all up. Summer was better. In summer we had cornflakes instead.

But does Lorna want little gems, or does she want facts and figures? Does she like stories – where there's the risk of fiction – or does she like the safe, calculable nature of maths? And why does she want them, anyway? She's got my precious file. She's not getting anything else.

She sits down. She laces her fingers, and glances out of the window with great interest. She opens her mouth with an intake of breath, as if she's going to comment on the butterflies that flit past or the way the clouds have built up on the horizon, or, indeed, the shape of a gardener's bottom as he bends over the tulip beds.

Instead, not quite looking at me, she says, 'Tell me about your mother.' And she swings her gaze over to mine, like a crane with a demolition ball wild on the end of its chain.

Oh, no. You don't catch me that way, Lorna.

I won't fall for such tricks. I tell her instead about a Carolyn sort of mother. I don't think she'll notice the difference.

Of course, my mum is not my mother. Lorna forgets that. She forgets her question is a paradox. Who *does* she want to know about?

My mum is a tall woman, not exactly thin but spare, nothing but muscle to cushion her bones. She stands and sits very upright, as if to relax would be to let something go. She is as tall as Dad, taller if she wears heels of any kind. Her short hair is always tightly waved. She does this herself, with curlers which go in at night and come out first thing in the morning. Dad's cousin Bettina is a hairdresser, but she's never been allowed to get her dye mixes near Mum's hair, which is the same shade of brown as it must have been all her life: middling brown, like milk chocolate, stippled with a few grey hairs. She doesn't wear make-up, only powder for special occasions. I can't see what this is meant to achieve as an aid to beauty, but it makes her feel respectable.

She always dresses in the same way, whether she's visiting relations or cleaning the house. This is because she has *standards*. She wears a skirt and a blouse, and shoes and stockings. She owns a pair of slippers but only wears them for moving between bedroom and bathroom. A woman who pads around in bedroom slippers all day is, according to Mum, a slouch. (She probably means *slut*, but even the word itself is a step too far for Mum.) If it's cold, she puts a cardigan on over the blouse. In winter she wears a vest. She's a great advocate of sensible underwear. To do housework she puts a nylon overall on top of her skirt and blouse. To cook she wears a flowered apron with a bib. When she is serving the tea to guests – our relations – she ties on a perky little waist-apron with a frill round the edge. When she goes to church she wears a mackintosh, neatly buttoned up even in warm weather, and a hat.

Hats are her weakness, if she could be said to have a weakness. When we went into town we would sometimes make a detour to the hat department in the big shops, and have a look, though not try anything on. I remember her owning four hats: a brown angora beret, a black pill-box (for funerals), a green velour bucket, and a red squashy shape with a small crimson feather. Most often she wears the beret. I never once saw her in the red hat.

When she goes to church she carries a large handbag, and keeps her Bible inside it. A lot of people at church carry their Bibles in their hands. Some of them have normal little Bibles but with lots of texts and bookmarks and ribbons poking out. Some people have those big soft-covered black Bibles, with curled-out edges from constant pious use. My mother never carries her Bible in her hand, and thinks all those big flashy Bibles and ribbons are just a way of showing off. Needless to say, I longed to be given a big black Bible. Or, better still, a white one with gold lettering on the front, like a girl had in my Sunday school class.

It was my mother who insisted on the church-going. She had to keep Brian and me up to scratch.

'Well-brought-up people go to church,' she said. Well-brought-up people, she implied, did God the politeness of believing in Him.

My father went along with it, though only so far. He managed Christmas and Easter, and showed some signs of actually enjoying Harvest Festival. The rest of the family, Gloria, Stella, Bettina, Bob, were very remiss in their devotions. They were fond of a lie-in on Sunday mornings, I suspect.

My mother used to be a bookkeeper but when we were little she never had a job outside the home. She kept constantly busy with cooking and cleaning and knitting and sewing. She knitted all my jumpers, and Brian's, and she knitted thick winter socks for Dad. She sewed my dresses.

'Isn't she clever, your mum?' my aunt Gloria often said to me, holding up an unrecognizable slab of knitting, destined to become a pocket or a sleeve. Another trick of hers was to lift the skirt of the dress I was wearing, to admire the tiny hem stitches. 'Auntie!' I pushed at my skirt, trying to hide my knickers from the company. 'Please!'

'I could never do all that, Edie. I really couldn't. Such patience.'

Gloria's humility was put on to increase the compliment, but I saw my mother's look: no, *you* couldn't.

The only other child in our family was Mandy, Bettina's daughter. I envied Mandy her shop-bought dresses with their machine-finished buttonholes and narrow machine-stitched hems. Sometimes Mandy wore dresses identical to those I'd seen other girls in, flimsy checked frocks with gathered skirts and sashes, daisy prints with puffed sleeves. My dresses were never the same as anyone else's. My mother used patterns that had been around for years, and then gave them a twist of her own: lasting quality. They had big hems, with 'lots to let down'. They were never skimpy, and the buttonholes never came unravelled. But I longed for a frock that was up-to-the-minute, shoddy as only shop-bought products could be, and then tatty enough to be chucked away. Even Mandy's cardigans were made on a machine: the automated sheen of their surfaces was thrilling. I wished mine could be like hers.

One day when we were going past our local wool shop I noticed in the window a pale green cable-knit jumper very like the one Mum was currently making at home. 'Look,' I said. 'That's just like the one you're knitting.'

'It *is*,' she said. At first I thought she meant 'It's the pattern I'm using.' But when we got home, I noticed that the pale green wool had gone from her needles and been replaced by brown yarn for my next school cardigan.

'Where's the green one?' I asked. 'Who's it for?'

'At the shop,' she said. 'It's for whoever buys it.'

And that was the start of her new job, her home knitting career.

Mum liked us out of the way while she was doing this, concerned that our mucky fingers would spoil the goods. Just as she liked us off her clean kitchen floor, away from her plumped-up settee cushions and smoothed bed-spreads. Just as Dad liked us out of the flower beds with that ball, and off the nice sharp edges of his lawn. We couldn't put a foot right.

My new friend Hanny Gombrich is Jewish. That was the second thing she told me, after her name. We met in the gardens here, where we're allowed out for an hour in the morning (weather permitting), and again in the afternoon. I knew she wasn't a zombie that first time because I caught her eye. Everyone else here avoids meeting eyes. Or they're too drugged-up to be capable of noticing you. I caught her eye and she looked back at me for – it must have been – all of three seconds. It was such a relief. It was like a hand reaching out and pulling you up out of a deep, deep well.

So she said hello and told me her name, and when I raised my eyebrows (I couldn't help it, it wasn't the kind of name I'd come across before) she explained, a bit curtly, that she was Jewish. I said I hadn't ever met anyone Jewish before.

'Where have you *been* all your life!?' she cried, so I said maybe I had met some but I just didn't know it. Then she made a noise in her throat and laughed. She said it was the noise her grandmother made when she was being disparaging about *goyim* – that's the rest of us.

8

Next Door

'Come round to our house,' Barbara said one day.

These were the words I'd been waiting for, for months. She had found me slouching home from school, towing my more or less empty satchel as if it was a bag of stones.

'Only don't say you live next door.'

'Why not?'

'Because we don't like the people who live in this road. They're *suburban*.'

'Oh. OK.'

I dropped off my satchel at home and said, 'I'm playing out.' I ran off again before my mother could say, 'Playing out *where*?' Not that she usually did. It was just my guilt that made me dash away.

Barbara was sitting on the kerb, waiting for me. She jumped up, grabbed my hand, and pulled me past the laurel hedge and in at the peeling gate, which today was propped open with a brick.

The house was tall, with steeply pointed gables and symmetrical windows and a wooden veranda all the way round. The two front doors stood side by side. There was lots of fancy fretwork, just like a gingerbread house, which could have done with a lick of paint; and on closer inspection the windows – no net curtains at all – weren't very clean. We ran up the front steps, and they juddered beneath my feet like the steps of the old passenger bridge at the station. My stomach felt the way it did when a train went under the bridge while I was on it: flipping over with nerves and excitement. Barbara kicked open the left-hand door and we stepped into the darkness of the hallway.

A long staircase was straight ahead and at its foot was a doorway with a heavy blue curtain across it, trailing on the floor. She swept this aside and we were in the next-door hallway, the other half of the house, at the foot of *their* stairs. This hall was dark too, with pictures all over the walls, and a table full of sprawling plants in lead-coloured bowls. Barbara cantered down the passage towards the rear of the house, with me following close behind, grabbing at the back of her cardigan, fearful of being left alone in such a strange place.

The kitchen was full of light. There was a big window with glass shelves set across it and striped spider plants cascading down the panes. Barbara took a glass from the draining board, filled it with water, downed half of it, opened her mouth to yell 'O-ma!', and then finished off the water. She didn't offer me any. She rinsed out the glass and turned it upside down again to drain.

I heard a slapping, slippery noise behind me.

'Oma!' Barbara cried out joyfully.

Oma was composed entirely of circles. Her face was round, her wire-rimmed spectacles were round, the top of her body with its sloping shoulders and shelf of bosom was round, and her great fat stomach, covered with a sky-blue pinafore, was another circle. Her skirt was ankle-length, and her mannish cotton shirt was filled to bursting. The noise I'd heard was her trodden-down slippers. I thought she looked repulsive.

'My little Baba!'

She took Barbara's cheeks in both her hands and pressed a kiss on Barbara's nose, which was about the same height as hers.

I leaned back against the cupboards, making myself small in case she did the same to me. But she took no notice of me at all.

Oma was Barbara's grandmother. She lived with the grandfather in one half of the house, and Barbara and her parents and brothers and sisters lived in the other half. Of course Barbara didn't bother to explain this at the time, just left me to work it out as best I could.

The house had originally been two properties but when the family moved in they knocked a doorway through in the downstairs hall and another upstairs, for ease of movement. Such casual vandalism impressed me, especially since the upstairs doorway was still unfinished, a rough hole gashed in the brickwork, with no curtain across. The two families maintained separate households, with separate sets of furniture and meals, but when they felt like it they stepped through into the looking-glass world of the other house and had a chat or borrowed a pan or sat down and cuddled a child.

That first afternoon we stayed in the grandparents' half of the house. It was very quiet, and half light, half dark, like the paintings by Rembrandt I later saw in books.

Much later. It smelled of strange food, and beeswax polish, and the scent of the jars full of drooping flowers which stood in every room. Despite the cool air inside the house, the palms of my hands were sticky with sweat. I didn't know how to *be* with a friend. I was glad when I heard Oma slip-slop away upstairs. We sat down on the threadbare carpet in the front room, and Barbara told me her story.

Barbara's grandparents were called Mr and Mrs Van Hoog. They were both short and fat, and said very little. Barbara's mother was their daughter. Tillie Hennessy now, but once upon a time she'd been Mathilde Van Hoog. Now *there* was a name, though not one you'd want to take to school with you.

The Van Hoogs came from Holland. They'd both been painters long ago, and the walls of their house were filled with their paintings, and paintings done by their friends. Then they had Tillie, and Mr Van Hoog's father had said that he must stop messing about being a painter and earn his living. They were sent to England, to East Anglia, where a distant relative ran a nursery business. This was before the war. Mr Van Hoog worked at the nursery and Mrs Van Hoog looked after Tillie and painted all the plants and flowers her husband brought home for her. There were pictures of auriculas in pots, and sheaves of roses lying on a table, and stripy red-and-white tulips leaning out of a glass vase. Bouncy peonies and vivid poppies. Then the war came, and Mr and Mrs Van Hoog lost all their family back in Holland.

'Shot – or starved,' Barbara said bluntly, and we exchanged looks of horror. All the grown-ups we knew had been in the war. We were used to stories of loss and destruction murmured like gossip over our heads.

When we'd finished giving each other suitably horrified looks, she went on: Mrs Van Hoog stopped painting altogether, and they both worked in the nursery, which had been turned over to vegetables for the war effort. But Tillie grew up wanting to paint. They didn't stop her, but they didn't particularly encourage her either. They felt that painting always led to grief and frustration. She worked as a life model for an art school, to help pay her way, and that was where she met Patrick Hennessy.

'A life model,' Barbara told me, 'is someone who poses *naked*.'

This time my look of horror was genuine.

And that was it, Barbara said, although I felt the story was only halfway there. When her grandparents retired and sold the nursery, they moved here to the coast, bought a house big enough for the lot of them. Tillie'd had so many children that there was no time left for her to paint.

'How many children?'

'Six.'

'*Six?*'

Barbara nodded casually, as if this was normal.

Patrick taught at an art school, and painted pictures in his spare time.

'I'll show you,' Barbara said, uncrossing her legs and standing up. 'But not today.'

This was my cue to go.

I saw Tillie Hennessy naked before I ever saw her clothed.

The day I got to go into the Hennessys' side of the house, Barbara kicked the front door open as before and this time turned left, into their big front room. Above the mantelpiece, facing anyone who walked into the room, was a huge painting. Of Tillie, naked. Only I didn't know it was her, then.

I hadn't seen much flesh. We were a modest family. The bathroom door stayed shut, and bedroom doors when people were changing. My mother went quickly to and fro in her ankle-length dressing gown as she readied herself for the day. I never saw my parents undress to sunbathe or to swim. If we went to the seafront, it was for a stroll after all those awful trippers had gone home, and if we ever sat on the sand with a picnic between us, the only people who ever rolled up their sleeves or took off their shoes and socks were Brian and me. Cousin Bettina, sunblushed and bulging out over the straps of her summer frocks, amounted to indecent exposure, and left me feeling quite shocked.

In the painting, Tillie was pale and bony. There was something both natural and awkward about her posture. She was caught half sideways, sitting on the edge of a chair, holding on her knees a naked baby. Her breasts drooped against her ribcage like small flat saddlebags. Behind her shoulder was a table with a blue-and-white cloth and a big vase of blurry flowers. A mirror, or something, on the wall caught the light and shone it back like a flat white shield. The baby, a big baby, like those enormous versions of the infant Jesus, crouched on her knees, his back curved. She held him by the upper arms – not like you would hold a baby, I thought. Her face was turned to him and her hair hung like a curtain.

I didn't even think it was a very good picture. Let alone nice.

'It's a fake,' Barbara said, seeing the direction of my stare.

All at once a little cushion of air let down inside me: relief. I didn't know what she meant at all, but my insides told me that it was a made-up picture, not a painting done of real naked people. So that was all right.

'That's my mum, with my brother Eugene. But Eugene wouldn't sit still for a minute – not one single minute, which Tillie had told him would happen all along – so he painted *her*, for days and days, and he took a snapshot of Eugene and painted him in from that. That's why he looks like a monkey, I think.'

'*Who* painted it?' I asked. My insides had contracted again.

'My dad, of course. Honestly, painting Eugene in from a snapshot. It's as bad as those people who do portraits by post of your bloody corgi!'

And she turned on her heel and marched off down the passage to the kitchen. I followed, as I was meant to. Beyond the kitchen, sitting on the back step in the sun, was her mother. Fully clothed, thank the Lord.

I saw Hanny Gombrich today in Activity. I was glad she was there, as I hadn't seen her again in the gardens and I thought she might have been avoiding me. She made penguins out of her clay, sweet, neat little penguins, and then she lined them up according to size. None of them was more than three inches high. She said she would like to get hold of a book about penguins so that she could see what the other species look like. At the moment she can only do King Penguins. She tried another kind but it ended up looking like a skittle. Then she said, 'But books are rarer than *live* penguins in this place,' and she gave me a tired kind of look, a 'Wouldn't you just know it?' sort of look, and let her hands fall slack in her lap.

She said that she was in here because she wouldn't eat. It's true that she doesn't seem to fill her long loose dresses, and her eyes are enormous, with half-moons the colour of purple crocuses beneath them. She asked me why I was here and I said that I was an orphan, I was adopted, and I hadn't got over the shock of my mother telling me about it so suddenly.

She didn't say anything to that. Instead she went on, 'A Jewish girl starving herself. Ironic, isn't it? My grandmother can't bear it.' Then she told me that her father wasn't really Jewish, because *his* mother wasn't, and Jewishness is inherited through the mother's line.

'Maybe I'm Jewish,' I said, 'only I don't know it.'

She gave me a look, and I think I might have offended her again.

9

My Relations

What amazed me about Barbara's family was that they all seemed to really *like* each other. That made me think about my own relations.

Every Saturday afternoon, almost without fail, my dad's cousin Bettina visits us. Which means that Mandy visits us too, virtually every week. We hate Mandy, Brian and I. It is the one thing that we are united in – our hatred of Cousin Mandy.

I've always thought the name Bettina sounds bouncy, like bedsprings. Bettina is the fun of bouncing on beds, and *in* beds. She's quite a bit younger than my dad and his sisters, and she always seemed to me like *a woman of mystery*. She never mentioned her parents, and no one ever mentioned her husband, if she had one. She must have had one at some point, I always thought when I was younger, since she had Mandy.

Bettina lives across the far side of town from us, in a district that looks much like ours, with scrubby trees and sandy roads. But it's just a bit more built-up, and a bit less respectable. She has a flat above a hairdresser's in a short parade of shops. The hairdresser's is called 'Charisse' and Bettina is the second stylist. The first stylist is Maureen, who owns Charisse. I can see why she wanted to call it that. I know what she was after. Sort of French, sort of Hollywood, sort of glamorous. Sort of an uphill slog, too, maintaining that image, since everyone else calls it 'Maureen's'.

Maureen used to work in a fashionable hairdressing salon in London, and that's why she calls herself and Bettina, who do all the cutting and curling, *stylists*. It costs slightly more to be attended by the first stylist than the second stylist. The only other person employed there is the shampoo girl, a woman of about ninety whose name is Ida Carr. She sweeps up all the fallen hair and writes names down in the appointment book with a very blunt pencil, which she keeps licking to make it write at all.

Occasionally my mother goes for a perm at Charisse. I go with her, waiting for her on one of the plastic chairs, smelling the smells and watching everything that goes on. For an ordinary shampoo-and-set Bettina will oblige in our kitchen, but a perm she considers more technical. Home perms, Bettina says, look like something the cat's dragged in. Even in qualified hands. Better to come to the *salon*.

This is why we've always hated Mandy. She's six months younger than Brian and two years younger than me, but she makes us feel foolish, and not because she's clever. In some ways she's stunningly stupid. But she's one of those effortlessly knowing, worldly girls who can mimic adult gestures and tones of voice perfectly whenever she wants to. Mandy spends the hours after school (late night Thursdays) and Saturday mornings in the salon, flicking through tired magazines, sorting pins and curlers into their different trays, and rearranging the artificial flower display. Customers are always giving her sweets. They bring sweets in specially for her. At Christmas they come bearing little packages wrapped and labelled for Mandy. 'Put this under your Christmas tree, darlin', they say. At Easter she gets more chocolate eggs than anyone I've ever come across. And on her birthday – 'Mandy's coming up to seven soon,' Bettina would shamelessly advertise; 'Ooh, when's your birthday?' the customers would ask, and Mandy would lisp 'Next Fwiday' – she has hair-slides and colouring sets and tiny baby dolls in baskets, anything small enough to be wrapped and slid into a handbag and then produced like a magic trick when the customer is under the dryer.

'Just a little treat for Mandy,' they say. 'Bless her.'

What is it they know, or suspect, about Mandy? Brian and I discuss this in low resentful whispers. We hope it is a life-threatening disease that they nod and murmur about as they tie plastic rainhats over their fresh shampoo-and-sets. Otherwise, what is fair about the loathsome Mandy, not even pretty, receiving so many undeserved tributes?

And she's such a fraud. Our sense of injustice glows hot every time we see this sly know-all give way to a wide-eyed lisping baby as soon as any adult comes into earshot. Don't they notice? Why are they taken in? Their voices turn to honey and they croon, 'What was that, Mandy, sweetheart? Won't they let you have a turn?'

Haven't they heard the way she speaks to us out in the garden, or seconds before they walk into the room? Don't they notice our dropped jaws and scowling expressions? Or is it that they just don't care? That they know something about Mandy that makes them favour her above us at every opportunity?

She's younger, for a start, and that puts us at a huge disadvantage.

'She's younger than you, remember,' they keep saying.

Which means that any cheating on her part has to be overlooked by us – 'Mandy doesn't understand the rules yet' – any dispute over whose go it is on a bike or a skipping rope is resolved, in her favour, by an adult intervening. She gets let off any chores that have to be done, by virtue of the fact that she's supposed to be too little to be of any help. So we'll be drying the tea dishes or sweeping up the grass cuttings, and there is Mandy, pausing astride *my* bike, watching us with a glazed, soppy expression, mouth hanging slightly open, as if she doesn't really know what's going on. And then she'll ride off, fast and purposeful, standing up on the pedals. Her jaw is set, and she's whistling 'Colonel Bogey' as professionally as any station porter. And the grown-ups never *ever* notice this bit!

Mandy is small and scrawny, with legs like sweet pea stalks, and a little, baffled, white face covered in blotchy fawn freckles that stand out as if they're half an inch in front of her skin. Her eyes are very light grey with pinpoint pupils – she can look either stupid or very, very mean. Her hair is a wispy aureole of red strands that get sweaty easily, and stick to her forehead, which turns pink after any exertion. Are these all signs of imminent demise? We hope so. We don't mind weeping at her graveside, if it means that our bikes are our own on Saturday afternoons.

The rest of the family routine goes like this. Every two or three weeks we go to tea on Sunday with my aunts Stella and Gloria, and every two to three weeks Stella and Gloria come to tea with us. Sometimes Stella isn't there when we arrive, or leaves before we do. The assumption is that Stella, being a single woman, has a duty to see to her love life, while the rest of them, being married, have a duty to fulfil family obligations. Sometimes, though less often, Stella doesn't make it over to tea with us at all. Then Gloria says to my mother, 'Stella's not with us today,' and gives a quick flick of her eyebrows. She'll never say, straightforwardly, 'Stella's out with Gerald this afternoon,' or 'Wally has taken Stella for a drive.' It's always as if some plot or intrigue is taking place, some *I told you so* or *let's see what comes of this*.

None of the women in the family likes cooking – it isn't something you *could* like. Cooking consists of toiling for hours in a steam-filled kitchen. It means roast meat and boiled vegetables and fried eggs and bacon and burnt toast. So, for a treat, on days when the aunts are coming to tea, or we're going to them, everything is shop-bought and served cold. Tins of ham and fruit cocktail and evaporated milk are laid in. Battenberg cake in perfect squares or fruit cake laced with fat red cherries is bought from the grocer's in town. Sometimes boxes of cupcakes with orange or caramel icing. I like these best because you can carefully eat away the sponge from underneath, saving the thick layer of icing for last.

After the meal they send us children outside to play, while they drink more tea and talk. At our house it's fine, we can play French cricket in the garden – if we're careful – or ride our bikes up and down the pavement. But at

Stella and Gloria's there is only a small paved backyard. The shed and the coal bunker take up most of the space, and there's usually washing hanging from the criss-cross line. The only thing you can do is prise up bricks to find woodlice and tease them, or climb on the coal bunker and stare over into the neighbours'. Where what you see is much the same.

We aren't allowed into the street. It's steep and there's a busy road at the bottom. And besides, playing in the street in this part of town is *common*. There are no wide grass verges here, no tarmac paths perfect for bikes and hopscotch. It isn't children's territory.

In winter we have to amuse ourselves indoors. At home we can go to our own rooms, but at the aunts' we must be visible, sitting on the scratchy brown carpet and playing Ludo or Monopoly with sets which have lost most of the pieces. Or cards. They always have packs of cards, often with new unbroken seals. But we have to play with the old packs, where the corners are bent up. We play pontoon or snap or sevens, in a lacklustre sort of way. It's hard to fill the time. There is no question of whining, though, or asking to go home. It's like being in the waiting room at the dentist's – you just have to sit still and be quiet, while the time ticks slowly away.

What they really want is for us to be out of the way so that they can gossip. If we are in the room they lower their voices and spell out certain words. Any hint of the alphabet and my ears would prick up. I don't think Brian was tuning in at all, but I did, all the time. They didn't seem to think that we could spell. And even before I was sure what M-A-N did spell, I knew it was one of those things to look out for; it meant intrigue and danger and suspense. Whenever there was an M-A-N involved, you had to watch out. How true.

Then there was Bettina's. We didn't visit very often, because the flat was so small and the only place for children to play was on the wide pavement outside the shop, which again was *common*. Though we knew for a fact that Mandy played out there all the time in the fine weather, from the familiar way in which she shouted greetings to other kids outside, or shouldered the bubble gum machine in passing, with the confident air of getting something free in return.

When her mother was out of the room, she would lean from the upstairs window and shout, 'Oyah! Derek! Give us some!' to a boy riding a bike one-handed while eating a sherbet dip, or 'Oyah! Phyllis! Saw you last night. Uh-*oh*. Not sayin' 'oo with!'

We knew what *common* was, and Mandy was its living embodiment. Only the grown-ups never twigged.

But every Saturday afternoon, almost without fail, Bettina and Mandy came to visit us. Bettina, after a long morning in the salon, would fling herself down in an armchair and shuffle her broad squashed shoes off her swollen feet.

'That's another week done, thank God!'

We weren't allowed to take the Lord's name in vain, but Bettina was never rebuked for it. My mother would hurry to fetch a cup of tea and the biscuit barrel.

'Mandy, would you like a Bourbon cream?'

Mandy, with her roomful of girl-toys and hoard of sweets, never brought anything with her.

'Go and get your new puzzle,' my mother would say to me, with a little nudge, 'Mandy might like to see it.' Or

71

'Why don't you get out the bikes and let Mandy have a go?'

Nothing in the wide world takes so long as standing by and waiting while someone else has a turn. Mandy was a helpless creature, needing to be entertained. We had to be the hosts. Not that she ever showed hospitality to us when we visited. She would take us into her bedroom, a boudoir with frilly pink curtains and matching bedspread, a nature reserve of fluffy animals. Slyly she'd open the door to her bedside cupboard and show us the store of sweets inside, the Crunchies and Milky Ways and Love Hearts, arranged like a shrine. Sometimes she would even take one out, unwrap it slowly and put it into her mouth, her pinprick eyes on our faces, disingenuously, as if she was looking in a mirror and not terribly interested in her reflection. We'd swallow helplessly.

'I can't give you any,' she would say. 'Your mum doesn't let you have sweets before tea.' Or, less truthfully, 'My mum doesn't want me giving things away.'

Bettina didn't know or care, we knew that in our hearts. But we had nothing cunning in our repertoire with which to answer back. Then Mandy would itemize what was left, and rearrange them, and slowly shut the cupboard door.

Brian and I plotted. We planned how we would distract her, and then one of us would creep in and steal some of the sweets from her hoard. We had it worked out down to the last detail, but we never put our plan into action. Somehow we knew that when Mandy found out that one of her Milky Ways was missing, even one little Love Heart or Rowntree's Fruit Gum, a great convincing wail would go up and all the grown-ups would rush round her, cooing sympathetically. And *we* would get the blame. The blame for coveting one sweet out of a shopful. The blame for *being greedy*.

What was it she lacked that we had? What was it that made us so fortunate? And Mandy so deserving of their all-out sympathy? We just couldn't work it out.

I don't like to think about why I'm in here. There are quite a few things I don't like to think about. So I have to find other things to fill my mind with. There's a hell of a lot of waking hours in the day to fill when you're only thinking careful thoughts. Even the sleeping hours you can't rely on.

I read somewhere that old people can remember all kinds of things from their childhood but they can't recall what they did the day before. I can see why they might want to do that, might want to dwell on the *then* and not the *now*. I hope I'm not getting like that. I'm only eighteen. I've got to have something to look forward to, haven't I?

In place of friends, we always had just family. There weren't even very many of them. My favourites were Dad's two sisters. They have wonderfully unsuitable names. Like me, really.

If you asked me to describe two women named Gloria and Stella, this is what I'd say:

Gloria is one of those terrible names full of hubris. Like Victor. Why do parents name their children like that? How do they think they're ever going to live up to such a pompous name? *To the victor the spoils. In excelsis gloria.* They give birth to a tiny red screaming baby and say, 'I know! Let's call him Victor!' Or Gloria.

Besides, Gloria is a barmaid's name. A woman who dyes her hair an unnatural shade of red, like copper-beech leaves. A bosomy woman with thick lipstick, which she leaves in a U-shape on glasses and on the resting filter tips of cigarettes. A woman who prefers men, and hasn't really got time for women. Sic transit Gloria.

Whereas Stella, that's a prettier name. I can see why you might go for Stella. That name would fit a baby *and* a grown-up. *Our dear little Stella, our star*. Stella would be a finer-boned creature altogether, with cloudy light-brown hair and a vague expression, wide-set grey eyes. A Stella could never be forceful. Indeed some people might say she was put-upon, she shouldn't let others take advantage of her sweet nature. But Stella would smile, vaguely, prettily, and say that it didn't matter. A Stella would be a magnet for men, not consciously, not trying to attract them, but finding them at her elbow in droves, falling for her sweet helplessness, wanting to take care of her. Honourable men.

That's what I would have said.

Only *our* Gloria and Stella are the other way round. Stella has broad hips and broad cheekbones, a kind of ox-like distance between her eyes which doesn't lend to the impression of intellect. Her hair might have been cloudy once, but now it's whipped into a dry frenzy by a vivid chestnut rinse. She favours knee-length pencil skirts, and sling-back high heels, and blouses with a froth at the neck or all the way down the front. I can picture them so clearly: thin nylon blouses of shell pink or baby blue, which always show the line of her brassiere straps and the way the flesh of her back bulges above and below the fastening.

Stella has never married. The right man has never come along, or has never popped the right question. She's always got a *boyfriend*, if these huge men, determinedly peripheral characters, could be called that. It's certainly what she calls them. There's Dimitri, who I heard about but never met, and Wally, who drives a van, and who once waved to us as we walked down the high street, and Gerald, who travels in paint, and isn't in the area much, due to the nature of his job.

Once, while we were visiting, Gerald called at their house to retrieve something of his. He didn't seem like a boyfriend so much as someone who was angry, and in a hurry. He stayed in the hall, with one foot apparently nailed to the front step, and I saw his hand gesture impatiently at Stella to cut the introductions short. No one else seemed to notice this. They were busy craning their necks and saying, 'Oh, is it Gerald? Tell him to come in. Come on in, Gerald!'

I always seem to see the things other people don't see.

Gloria is older than her sister, smaller, thinner. She has doubtful, worrying, washed-out blue eyes. Her mousy hair is lit with a glamorous flash of white at her front parting. 'Oh, my awful grey hair,' she says, sweeping it back with one hand, but I thought it was the best bit of her. She never tries to dye it out.

Gloria is married to Eddy, who is in the merchant navy and away for long stretches of time. She puts up with this very well, but I know the rest of the family believe that it isn't the exigencies of a sea-borne job that keep him from home so much, but other girls in other ports that Gloria doesn't know about. Or even suspect. (Eddy is a good name for him; *Eddy* sounds shifty. Wriggling away, impossible to pin down. Not like reliable *Ted*.) I know this because, as Stella says, little pitchers have big ears. Because my parents never got the habit of telling us things, I quickly acquired the habit of listening out. Listening in. You could usually pick up something worth knowing when one of Dad's sisters was around.

Stella and Gloria, and Eddy, when he's home, live together in a little house in the hilly part of town, back behind the beach. The *old* part of town, my mother says, disparagingly. Beet Street, their road is called. Something to do with the sugar beet, my dad says; not that he knows what. The streets are short but meandering, and the houses come in various shapes and styles, though all of them are small. Stella and Gloria's house, in a terrace, is painted brick-red with white steps and white window ledges. The front door opens straight on to the pavement and above it there's a sinister indentation where there was once another window, filled in and painted over long ago. A lot of the neighbourhood houses have them, I don't know why. The house once belonged to Stella and Gloria's, and my dad's, parents. Every so often Stella picks up some object and says, 'Oh, this old thing! It's about time we got rid of this.' And Gloria always replies, 'Oh no, that's Mum's, we can't just throw it out.' So everything stays there, just the same.

The only relation we hardly ever saw was Uncle Bob. He was our mother's brother, and he didn't live in our town. He lived in Basingstoke, in a flat at the top of a three-storey block, *purpose-built*. The fact that it was purpose-built seemed to make living in a flat all right. He worked for a company that made pipes and tiles for the building trade. He worked in an office with a desk and a telephone of his own. That this was good I knew from the way my mother dropped it into the conversation. Bob, you gathered, was a step up in the world from hairdressers and flats over the shop, and a husband who went to sea, and working in a fish-and-chip shop as Stella did. It was a step up from Gough Electricals and a blue boiler suit. All this went unsaid. But it was felt. It was felt.

10

Our Fortunes

So – now I had a best friend. I hugged this notion to me. I carried it round. It made me feel warm every time I remembered it.

Not only a friend, but a fully functioning paid-up normal human being for a friend. Someone other people might want as *their* friend. Not just that desperate pairing up I'd seen in playground and classroom, of two hopeless kids with nothing in common, in order to stave off being absolutely on their own. I hadn't ever done that; I had my pride. My strategy was hopeful hanging, wistful drifting, pretending to the casual observer that I was absorbed in doing something or just temporarily on the edge of the crowd.

One of the good things about Barbara was that she didn't want to know too much about me. Only: What's your favourite colour? (Blue.) How high can you jump? (Don't know.) What grade piano are you? I'm grade three. (Oh dear – grade one.) Are you right-handed or left-handed? (Right.) Have you ever seen a ghost? My brother has. (No, but I once saw a cloud in the shape of an old man's face. Absolutely correct in every detail, even the hairy beard.) Do you know what sign of the zodiac you are? (*What?*) Can you do this? Look, I bet you can't. (No, I couldn't.)

These were the kind of questions I could answer without feeling shame. These were not questions to trip the unwary, new to the perils of friendship. These questions were not pass or fail.

Barbara said, 'Come round. Just come round. I'm always bored.' She said it in the reasonable tones of a shopkeeper saying, 'We're always open,' or a generous host who promises, 'Just drop in – we're always here.'

I knew I'd take her at her word. I couldn't resist.

So I got to know Barbara and her constitutional boredom. She was like some fickle, spoilt princess in a fairy story: she needed constant amusement. I soon discovered it wasn't to be a friendship of equals. But then, is there ever a friendship of equals? I was happy enough, ecstatic even, to be allowed in as the junior partner. Barbara was a wonderful source of information, and she made me laugh. She made us both laugh until our sides ached, until the muscles of our faces assumed a jaded rigor, until our leg bones melted. I've never laughed like that with anyone else.

'You're Gemini, that's the Twins. Look.' She showed me a picture in the back of a magazine. 'You're going to have emotional problems this week. Don't think about throwing a party. You'll be full of self-doubt, but try and look on the bright side, because financial matters are on the up and up.' She rolled over, swinging the magazine away from me. 'I'm Aquarius, the Water Carrier. *I've* got emotional problems too . . .'. She paused to give a belly laugh. 'The moon in Taurus – we don't want to know about the moon in Taurus – blah, blah, blah. Wednesday is a good day for a party. Time to make up quarrels with those nearest you. Financial matters could cause worry. Well, that's OK because you can lend me some of yours.'

I didn't know what to make of it all. We didn't have horoscopes in our house.

'Is it true?'

'No, of course not. Whoever gives a party on a *Wednesday*? They're for weekends, so that people have got time for hangovers.'

We didn't have hangovers in our house either.

Barbara chucked the magazine aside. 'What would you do if you found a thousand pounds just lying in the road?' she asked. 'No – ten thousand pounds?'

'Take it to the nearest police station,' I said, without having to think.

She screwed up her face. This was not a good answer.

'What if you didn't? What if you kept it? What would you do with ten thousand pounds? Just lying there, all over the road, piles of notes. And no one can see you picking them up.'

I had to admit it was tempting, when she put it like that. So I bought loads of sweets, and a pair of fur-topped boots, and a silver Rolls-Royce. Then she (who found herself in just the same happy circumstances, coming across a stranded load of banknotes lying in a deserted lane) also bought a car to drive alongside me, and loads of presents for her family. I hadn't thought of my family at all. The new-found wealth quite put them from my mind. I felt mean beside her. But then she bought a snow-white horse with an exceptionally long mane and tail, and I did just the same, and while we were galloping around her back garden, prancing over low jumps and shying at tree stumps and tennis nets, I forgot all about the presents for the folks back home.

When we had collapsed in the grass, puffed out, due to the high-strung nervous energy of our thoroughbred steeds, it occurred to me that now I was part and parcel of those squeals and laughter which back at home we heard issuing over the hedge. I hoped my squeals and laughter were indistinguishable from genuine Hennessy ones. Otherwise I'd be rumbled. I put the thought away, out of sight.

Instead I said, 'But if you *did* hand the money in to the police station and no one claimed it, they would give it back to you. Eventually. Or some of it, at least.'

'Would they?' Barbara screwed up her face suspiciously. '*Would* they, though?'

A worm of doubt crept inside me. Barbara seemed to know. She was so very worldly-wise. She had opinions and knowledge and used big words, and didn't hesitate to exercise them all at every opportunity.

I gazed at her. Her long dark curly hair looked as if it had never seen a comb. The clothes she wore were her sister Isolde's hand-me-downs, she told me, hardly worn, well cared for, until they hit Barbara. They didn't suit her. She stuck on any old thing, and any other old thing to go with it. Given a bit more flair, a bit of care, she could have looked bohemian. As it was, she resembled the child of neglectful parents, a mother too poor or too browbeaten to notice her skirt had part of the hem hanging down, her unpaired socks, her collar half out and half in. Today the blouse she wore had a grease stain down the front. Her skin was slightly olive, and there was a big bruise on her wrist, the colour of a plum. 'My brother shut it in the door, the stupid nutcase! He wants his brain seeing to. Have you got any brothers?'

But she knew. She already knew there was Brian. She had even seen me with him, out on his bike on the pavement.

'Have *you* got a bike?' she asked, something else she knew the answer to. 'We've only got one. It doesn't matter because we don't like cycling very much. We used to have another but I think Eugene took it down to London with him, or maybe he left it somewhere and it got stolen. My mum's got a bike, too – it used to be my grandma's – but we don't ride that one. It weighs a ton. Does your mum ride a bike?'

Tricky ground, now. I was less keen on this line of questioning. Was it suburban to ride a bike, or not to ride one? I shook my head.

'*My* favourite colour's blue, too,' Barbara said. So I was saved from answering. I could have rolled over and embraced her for the flightiness of her brain, the way her thoughts short-circuited, flashing here and there and here again, like a butterfly flitting about a high-summer border, completely spoilt for choice.

Her next question was 'What do you want to do when you're grown-up?'

We were lying under the fruit trees at the end of their garden. I stared up through the thin curtain of leaves, floury and puckered and twisted with disease, to the pure blue sky beyond. We liked to chew on grass stems, something strictly forbidden by my mother. ('There are creatures in them. You swallow them and they get inside your body and . . .' But she never followed up on this promising information.) So we lay and chewed the juiciest stems we could find and contemplated what we would do with our lives, should we survive the invasion of the grass-stem parasites.

'I was going to be a famous dancer,' Barbara said, with her air of awful self-confidence, 'but Tillie said you have to start ballet classes when you're about four to be any good. And I haven't started at all yet. It was either piano lessons or ballet and at the time I had a verruca which really hurt.'

I had never thought about the future. To me it wasn't a long and tempting gallery with intriguingly labelled doors leading off. With pictures of what might be at intervals along the walls, and every so often diamond-paned windows letting you peep outside at different views. The future was school stretching endlessly ahead, with maybe the treat of a half-term holiday in the offing, the final reward of the Christmas break miles on down the road. Right then the thought of the summer holidays coming to an end scared me. The future was new shoes to break in, a new class teacher to get used to. The thought that I would one day be a grown-up, out in the world, that I would wear shoes without socks, shoes with stockings, have a job, have a husband, was grotesque.

'I'm not going to marry,' Barbara said, writhing to get a stone out from under her backbone.

'Oh, nor am I!' I said, with relief, finding that this was an option. Of course it was an option; my aunt Stella was not married. But then Stella's whole purpose in life – leaving aside her career in the fish-and-chip line – was to

Find A Man. A perfect, or, at a pinch, less than perfect M-A-N with whom to *settle down*. Settling down was what my mother called it, as if unmarried men and women were dangerous and erratic, liable to set off chain reactions of inconstancy in others, in settled married others. People who were not married were unanchored, brittle things, casting around hopelessly for a set of rules and regulations that applied to them, and were liable to get cracked and damaged in the process. More damaged as the years slipped by. The only way to stop the rot was by getting married. The rules for married people were quite clear. My mother felt happier when the rules were clear. So settling down seemed to be the ultimate end for everyone, no matter how old they got before it happened. I couldn't really see how you *could* avoid it.

'I'll go to London and have fun,' Barbara said. 'I'll be a single girl. But I might have children, in the end.'

'I won't have children,' I said, just to see if the sky would crack.

'No, Isolde's not going to have any children,' Barbara went on, in a perfectly reasonable tone of voice. 'She says she doesn't like them.'

So all things were possible in the Hennessy world-view. In their best of all possible worlds.

When I got home, nobody said anything. My mother was busy with the Hoover, then with the treadle sewing machine. So perhaps the roaring of one and the clattering of the other – and always in the background the cheerful musical tones of the wireless – covered up all evidence of my treachery.

11

Reading Matter

Someone left a magazine in the front hall today. It was lying on a chair as I walked through. I could hardly believe my eyes. Some of the pages had come right off the staples at the back and I managed to pinch a couple and bring them up here. There's a quiz. It's that cheap kind of paper where the colour print comes off on your fingers. But you could starve for want of reading matter in this place. Anyway, I like doing quizzes.

Question six. (Unfortunately questions one to five must have been on the facing page, which I didn't manage to get hold of, along with the title of the quiz. So I don't quite know what we're supposed to be finding out here. It could be 'Are You Huggable?', or 'Would Your Best Friend Recognize the Secret You?' It could be almost anything.) So – question six: 'When buying a pet would you choose (a) A cuddly Labrador puppy? (b) An elegant Siamese cat? (c) A flamboyant South American parrot? Or (d) A goldfish?'

Well, it's obvious that you shouldn't go for the

goldfish, not even granted an adjective. Who wants to be indescribable? Maybe the whole thing is entitled 'Are You Completely Lacking a Personality? Find out now by completing our simple quiz!'

I'd definitely choose (a). Or (b). You can catch a disease from parrots. And goldfish swim happily around with great long ribbons of fish-shit trailing beneath them. Not very huggable.

See, Lorna? See what your rules and regulations reduce us to in here?

When, for days on end, for reasons I couldn't begin to imagine, Barbara failed to intercept me out in the street or on the way home from school, I took my courage in both hands and went to call on her. My passport was that phrase of hers: 'Just come round.' I hoped she truly meant it. My heart was beating hard. Her sister Isolde let me in. She showed me into the front room and sat me down. 'Barbara's busy at the moment. Would you like to wait in here?'

She was only a year older than Barbara, but seemed terribly grown-up. Her well-shaped legs moved in a carelessly elegant way. She wore slip-on shoes with tiny heels, over bare skin. Her insteps were high and pale.

I sat upright on the middle of the big settee. It had carved legs, a high back and scrolled arms. It was prickly and unyielding. Barbara had told me it was stuffed with horsehair. I imagined it stuffed with the taut flesh and hard bones of horses, too.

'Would you like a book to read while you wait?' Isolde asked me. She was the perfect dental receptionist in embryo.

I nodded.

'Behind you.'

I turned round and knelt up on the seat. Covering the wall behind me were two huge bookcases with glass fronts, and between them an alcove also filled with shelves that were stuffed with books.

'I don't know what to choose,' I said, looking back over my shoulder for guidance.

Isolde shrugged, a magnificent loose shrug. 'Take anything you like.'

But it was like trying to find a particular headstone in an endless cemetery. There were no signposts and much of the writing was hard to make out. The titles meant nothing to me: *A Tale of Two Cities, Antic Hay, Life of Marie Curie, Dr. Box's Book of Remedies, Tropic of Cancer, The Treasure Seekers, Saturday in My Garden, The Way of All Flesh*. The bindings were mostly old and dull, some with flakes of gold or ornate patterns pressed into their spines. They looked like books picked up at second-hand shops and jumble sales, books that had sat unopened for years.

I was about to reach for one called *Birds of Northern Europe*, which at least looked as if it must be about what it said, when Isolde pulled out *Alice Through the Looking Glass*. 'This is funny,' she said. 'Have you read it? *Alice in Wonderland* comes first, really, but it doesn't matter. You can borrow it if you like.' She shrugged her shoulders gracefully, and dropped the book in my lap with the careless generosity of one who has far more of everything than they will ever need. And she left me to it. I was still reading when Barbara at long last came bouncing into the room.

I treated their house like a public lending library after

that. I carried *Alice* home and read it by the summer day-light that came through my bedroom curtains in the evening. It took me ages to finish. I was a slow reader. Barbara said it didn't matter how long I borrowed it for, nobody else wanted it. But the speed of my reading improved by leaps and bounds. I found you didn't have to sound every word in your head. You could breathe in the words, whole sentences, paragraphs, suck them off the page with your eyes. And reading was fun, it was good, it was a *delight*. I liked Alice, cussed, confused Alice, and I loved the talking Tiger Lily, and the wicked greedy Walrus and Carpenter.

Next I took home not one but four books, in case what I had chosen (without Isolde's advice) turned out not to be interesting. I kept them under my bed so that I wouldn't have to explain them to Mum. I forgot that she vacuumed under there regularly. When she asked I said they came from the school library. I blushed as I said it. I worried that she might have known I was lying. But she didn't. She didn't notice my hot face or the artificial tone in my voice. It's weird how adults don't suspect the most obvious duplicities. I was only an apprentice liar at this stage, but even so she didn't notice anything. After that I didn't bother to worry about her finding them.

And anyway, it was true: those first four books *did* have library cards inside the front covers. One had a page full of old date stamps, the others had little cardboard pockets for the slips to go in. I asked Barbara about this.

'Oh, our books come from all over,' she said. 'Patrick picks them up when he's out and about. Anything that takes his fancy. Some of them are old books the libraries sell off. He says he's going to read them all one day, when he's an old, old man and has the time. And then Isolde and me used to *play* libraries,' she went on. 'Isolde had us make cards for all the books and we would check them in and out if people wanted to look at them. We sat at a table by the door of the front room, and she was going to charge fines if anyone didn't hand the books back pretty quick. It didn't work – nobody borrowed anything. And they wouldn't have paid up, anyway.'

For all the books there were in the house – propping up the front-room walls, languishing in piles on the landing, sitting on the sill in the dining-room window under the damaging rays of the sun with the tasselled tails of other people's bookmarks hanging out – they were not a bookish family. I never saw any of them but Tillie with a book in her hands, and I'm sure she was just looking at the pictures. Barbara, to my knowledge, never opened anything but a magazine, and Tom thought of all books as school textbooks and therefore beneath his consideration. Sometimes to get up the stairs I had to squeeze past Sebastian, crouching on the bottom step, scanning that week's *Beezer* with great concentration. Mattie was very partial to individual letters, finding them everywhere – W in the house gable, Ls in the banister rails – but had trouble cementing them into words. Only Isolde impressed me with her knowledge of books, as with her knowledge of everything, which she seemed to gain by osmosis, extracting information with her X-ray eyes, like an alien invader who can suck your whole history out of your brain in less than a second.

To say my tastes were catholic would be an understatement. At junior school there was one lesson a week when we could visit the school's library, a dank room next to the sickbay. Everyone fought over the *Tintin* books, which were just like comics only in book form and for some reason allowed in the library. To help the slow readers, I think; to encourage them that not all books were deadly books. Of course, I never got one. Never fought hard enough in the scuffle. I had to take out what was left, *I* got the deadly books – *Children of the New Forest*, *The Old Curiosity Shop*. They were printed on hard lavatory paper, in tiny writing, and smelled of must. I couldn't ever get beyond page one. There was nothing to interest me, and, anyway, what they really smelled of was school.

But the books I borrowed from the Hennessys felt different. In that first armful I took there was a book called *Scoop*, which was sort of funny, and another called *Tales from Shakespeare*, where at least all the tales were fairly short. There was *Emma*, which I couldn't get on with at all, despite the title which attracted me, and a picture book, a book of paintings by an artist called Van Gogh. He seemed to use very thick layers of paint, and rather eggy colours, which I didn't much like. There was a horrible navy and yellow one with a field full of wavy lines, and another of an ugly man wearing a fur-trimmed cap and a bandage. Some of the paintings were only shown in black and white, which made them even worse. But the book itself, its heavy shiny paper, the layer of tissue in front of each colour plate, and its small blocks of print surrounded by acres of luxurious white space, fascinated me.

Tillie caught me lugging this one back. 'Oh – do you like him?' she asked.

I stopped dead in my tracks. Guilt suffused me,

whatever Isolde had said about it being all right to borrow. I like to think that my mouth was not hanging open. I'd like to remember that I made some trenchant statement, but of course I didn't. I couldn't.

But Tillie was kind, and said, 'I'll find you something else about painting, if you want.' I nodded. I might have whispered, 'Yes, please,' but only because I'd been brought up to be polite to adults.

She looked out a huge book of Dutch paintings for me, which I took home and never wanted to bring back. There were flat white winter landscapes, and bowls of fruit and flowers and dead gamebirds which looked so lifelike, if a dead bird could be said to be lifelike. There were plump plain women corseted up to the eyeballs in voluminous plain dresses. I loved the light, the crystal clear images, the verisimilitude of these contentedly plain faces. No fat custard layers of paint here. No leaf-print splodges, but colour put on with a feather, stroked on so thin that daylight or candlelight could gleam through. Flesh-light. The gleam of expiring light in a gamebird's eye.

Thus began my education.

At the secondary school where I went when I was eleven we read bits of things. We read bits of *Pride and Prejudice* and I thought Elizabeth Bennet was shrill, and a snob. We read bits of *Great Expectations*: Pip seemed quite unsympathetic, a weedy, boring boy. We read a bit of Wilkie Collins's *The Woman in White* and I thought it was a ghost story. We read the whole of Scott Fitzgerald's *A Diamond as Big as the Ritz* and hadn't got a clue what it was about. We did a few scenes from *Julius Caesar*, pushing back the desks so that we could stand up and read aloud out of the abridged school version, the one with the interesting bits taken out. It was all nothing to me.

But at home I read other things. Whole, undiscriminating. Carried home by the armload from the Hennessys', read in patches of sunlight on their staircase, read lying on Barbara's lumpy bed, posting my toes through the holes in her crocheted bedspread. I learned to read while around me Barbara carried on with whatever she was doing, to read and still make believable responses to her questions, and to filter out her running commentary. Sometimes she'd deliberately flick the book shut before I had a chance to mark the page, saying, 'Come *on*. Let's *do* something!' and then I wasn't able to resist her. But quite often she let me read. There were no hours the length of those hours. Time is much quicker these days.

I read lots of books about sex, written by men, which was an eye-opener for a naive and virtuous girl of eleven. I got to know all about putting it in and then taking it out in time, about the way in which women had to be dismembered in order to be described – 'her eyes, her lips, her luscious breasts, her narrow waist' – about 'a clitoris the size of a boy's thumb'. What was a clitoris anyway? And how big was a boy's thumb? I looked at Brian, whose hands were large, and judged it to be about four inches in total. It was all information, but was it *good* information?

Without guidance, I read anything and everything for fear of missing something – and still there were huge gaps. I came back to Eliza Bennet and her distant cousins and began to laugh at them and worry for them. I thought Mr Elton seemed like a good catch for Emma until it proved otherwise. I read *The Mill on the Floss* and assumed that Maggie would come out all right because she was, after all, the heroine. I read *Madcap of the Fourth Form* and *Tristram Shandy* and *A Pony for Patricia* one after the other, without breaking stride. Without a pause for intellectual breath. This is how you read when no one tells you. I read like a great white shark, moving forward with my mouth open, eating porpoises and number plates and witch balls; I read like a giant whale with its krill-gleaning, ocean-cleaning grilles.

12

Hennessys

I haven't really described them properly yet, the Hennessys.

Ask about *them*, Lorna. Instead of harping on about *my* bloody family. You're barking up the wrong tree.

I loved them all at first, indistinguishable, just the brilliant Hennessy-ness of them. So many, and so vibrant, and so loud! To think that they were tucked away just next door. All those long bored hours I'd spent kneeling up on my bed, elbows on the window sill, gazing out over the front path and the motionless sails of the miniature windmill, daydreaming. Surely a Hennessy must have strolled by at some point? Or a Hennessy vehicle chugged its way out of their tumbledown garage? Not that I could recall. Not one that had disturbed my imaginary worlds, anyway.

And who did I come to love best? Well, darling Tillie, obviously. And then Tom. My fortune and misfortune. Ah well.

Darling Tillie. It's the phrase that keeps sort of slipping into my head. I've never in my life called anyone *darling* out loud. It's a fussy kind of word, a word that fussy, over-fond mothers use to their children in the street. Or under-fond mothers use without thinking, like they use an ashtray without looking. 'Don't, *darling.'* But it suits her, it suits Tillie. Such a darling.

Tillie was thin and fair. She wore faded jeans and a matted jumper which hung away from her sides like a bell. The sleeves were too short and showed her knobbly wrists. Or sometimes she wore an old checked shirt of Patrick's, with frayed cuffs and a tear at each elbow, and all the buttons hanging by a thread. I didn't think she looked like anyone's mother. She probably wasn't their *real* mother, I thought, at first. Not the mother of all those children. She certainly didn't look like any other mother that I knew. Barbara was three months older than me, and Isolde was a year above her. Tom was a year older again, and Eugene was so old that he didn't even live with them any more. He lived with friends of theirs in London for some reason that no one had yet told me. Tillie looked about eighteen, to my eyes. She wore no make-up and her whitish-fair hair was hardly ever combed, let alone styled. She even moved like a girl, forgetful of herself. She sat down with her knees wide apart and her bony elbows resting on them. Or she stood leaning on one hip and chewing at a hang-nail. She had no interest in her appearance. In summer she wore a garish red and white striped dress, tight in the bodice and with a full skirt, like a little girl's dress. The gathers of the skirt were always squashed into flat creases, because she never ironed anything. Another outfit she had was a lemon-yellow sleeveless blouse, pierced all over with tiny eyelet holes, which made her skin look the colour of dirty washing-up water. She wore this with a skirt of shiny green material. I couldn't understand how someone who was supposed to be a painter, and was surrounded by paintings, could have so little awareness of how they looked.

Patrick Hennessy usually wore jumble-sale clothes with spatters of paint on them. But I once saw them when they were going out somewhere grand. He had on a black suit with satiny lapels, and she wore a tight crimson dress of rough-surfaced silk. Her hair was pulled back into a couple of tortoiseshell combs and she had on dark lipstick which drained all the colour from her face. The tips of her pale lashes were brushed with mascara, so that when she looked straight at you you saw a row of black dots just above her eyes. Her feet were in high-heeled sling-backs with a latticework of black straps over her toes. She hadn't scrubbed her fingernails, and bits of hair were coming down from her combs before she'd even left the house. I thought she looked strange and unfinished, more like a little girl in dressing-up clothes than a grown woman. Patrick obviously thought she looked marvellous, and kept squeezing her up in his huge arm, or putting his hand on her crimson bottom. I really wished he wouldn't. Then they went out, Tillie tap-tapping down the wooden steps in her sling-back shoes, swaying because she wasn't used to high heels. Patrick called out to us back in the house, and Tillie waved her little black beaded bag, and then they were gone, hidden by the hedge.

Patrick was much older than her, or seemed older, seemed anyway to be the right age to be the father of so many children. Tall, with a laughing brown face and curly dark hair, he was the king of bonhomie. I was a bit afraid of him, afraid of what he would do next, whether he would ignore me or – worse still – notice me. He stepped over me, once, when I was reading a book at the top of the stairs. I was waiting for Barbara, who unselfconsciously and happily spent hours on the toilet, talking to me from time to time through the closed door. 'Nose in a book,' Patrick said, 'that's the ticket. That's what I like to see. A little scholarship. What're you reading?' I held it up, an old green paperback Philip Marlowe, price one shilling. 'The Lady in the Lake, eh?' And he took the book from my hand and tapped me smartly, painfully, on the head with it. 'That'll teach you to stick indoors reading on a fine sunny day,' he called out, laughing, as he cantered away down the stairs. I could never tell whether he was joking or not.

Barbara said that he and Tillie took turns to name the children, and all the names he'd chosen were characters in operas. Eugene was for Eugene Onegin, Isolde was from Tristan and Isolde, and she couldn't remember what Sebastian was from. Tillie had chosen Tom, Barbara and Matthew, because they were names she liked at the time. What if they had more children? I asked. They wouldn't, Barbara said firmly, because she'd had the op. I didn't know what she meant, but I looked wise. I never liked to appear ignorant in front of Barbara.

I liked all their names. They seemed to fit admirably. I didn't feel the need to make rude or witty remarks to myself about the Hennessys' names.

What Barbara wanted from me was an audience, a side-kick, a constant companion. No one in her family would do. They were all too busy with their own stuff. I wondered why she didn't turn to Isolde. I badly wanted a sister. In her position I would have made great use of a sister. But it was a point of honour for Barbara not to get on with her. They had been little girls together, had shared a room, were lumped together for presents and treats by their numerous relations and friends. Isolde's clothes were passed down to Barbara, Isolde's toys. But it was difficult for me when Barbara dragged my arm and we ran off giggling, flinging ourselves into the bushes or hiding behind the summer house; I wanted Isolde to come too. I wanted her to be allowed into our games and our secrets. But she was too old. Too grown-up, superior, disdainful of our silly behaviour. Which made me yearn after her all the more.

Sebastian and Mattie, the two youngest ones, were much the same age and size. Mattie had very fair hair just like the roof of a haystack, and ran around the house all the time in wellingtons, kicking his feet out at the sides. It was dangerous to get near him. He was always making a noise. Sebastian, who was an inch bigger, was much more calm. His brown hair grew into tiny perfect corkscrew curls that I wanted to reach out and touch whenever he came near. He had sombre round dark eyes like chocolate drops, and a kind of look – a 'pity me' look – which could always get him out of trouble. He knew he had this look and he went about using it on people when it suited him.

And then there was Tom.

Tom was the most like Tillie. Tall and thin, he had the same white-fair hair, but it grew in curls. Not like Sebastian's, which had an inch of straight hair before the curling started, but right from his scalp, springing out round his head like bunches of grapes. His face was rounder and sharper than Tillie's, rounder at the cheeks and more pointed at the chin. His eyes were very light in colour, and although he had eyebrows and eyelashes you could hardly see them. But it didn't spoil his looks. There was something about him that was compelling.

The Hennessys weren't like anyone else I knew. They had three dimensions and the rest of us, I saw now, had only two. But maybe, thinking about it, they were just so alluring because they let me into their lives without ever questioning my presence. They gave me an inch, and I took a mile.

Things happened in the Hennessy household that never happened anywhere else, not that I knew of. They were relaxed and slapdash in a way that delighted me. Tillie washed dishes with the cuffs of her jumper dipping into the water, seeming not to notice. Or the flopping unbuttoned sleeve of her shirt would catch in a stack of cereal bowls waiting to be washed, so that they fell to the floor with a resounding crash. Milk and strands of leftover shredded wheat sprayed all over the floor, and two of the bowls split neatly in half, their white china insides grinning between the layers of sunshine-yellow glaze. 'Oh bugger!' Tillie shouted. 'Bugger-bugger-bugger.' A chant unknown to me. Our cereal bowls at home were made of convenient melamine so that even if our mother knocked them carelessly to the floor they wouldn't break. Nor would she jump lightly up and down and shout so merrily if they did.

To help in the kitchen, Patrick thumped the gas water-heater to get the washing-up water going and sang the duet from *The Pearl Fishers*, both parts, alternating them. He loomed big against the cupboards, his feet enormous, spanning each floor tile. He would try to put things away, but was always asking, 'Where does this go, then?', holding up a cup by its handle as if it were a small fish he'd caught, or an egg whisk or a place mat, looking like he had no idea of its function, let alone its home.

The Hennessys all liked doors to be constantly open so that they could look – and shout – through them, but also shut, so that they could come flying through, kicking them open for preference, flinging them back on their hinges. You could hear Patrick's voice from all over the house, booming out instructions or singing bits of opera and Irish jigs; and the flip-flap of Mattie's boot-tops as he ran up and down, making crowing noises; and Isolde clicking about in her heels and sighing heavily. 'I think I must have been a changeling,' I heard her say, more than once.

All in all, it was a rich diet for a girl like me.

And then there was Tom Rose. He was a friend of Tom's, always hanging round the house as if he had no home of his own to go to. Like me, I suppose. I was always disappointed if I found him there, too. But Barbara took his presence for granted so I didn't dare complain. 'Oh, it's just Tom Rose,' she'd say.

We would sit on the floor in Tom's room, just bare floorboards stained with varnish, and he would teach us things: card tricks, and how to roll dice properly. He taught Barbara and me to play poker. Isolde wouldn't join in, but she watched from the doorway with her arms folded and her nose in the air.

'Corrupting the children again,' she said.

'We *want* to be corrupted,' Barbara told her. And giving me that glinting look, she added, 'We're not goody-goodies, all timid and feeble, must-do-what-your-mummy-says. We're not *bungalow* kids.'

When Isolde stalked off Tom called after her, 'Interfering bitch,' and glanced conspiratorially at Tom Rose, who snickered with amusement. And that was that. Nothing happened. No fire or brimstone rained down on him for being rude, or disloyal about a sister, or for using such a word. Nobody came crashing up the stairs saying, 'I heard that!' No one suggested he wash his mouth out with soap and water.

Once, even, I was in the kitchen and Patrick was having a sort of mock fight with Tom (I thought it was a mock fight), and had grabbed him by both arms from behind. Tom, who was nearly as tall, struck backwards with both elbows into his father's ribs, with all his might. Patrick yelled and let him go, laughing and crying out, 'You bloody little sod!' I froze. My ears turned crimson, and I could feel a prickling sensation all over my face. Could other people hear that sound as if a huge pane of glass had smashed, the tinkling of the slivers of glass as they fell to the ground? Tom was hovering in the doorway, cackling at his father's discomfort. Patrick rubbed his ribs through his grubby jumper, and said, 'Little sod,' again, in wonder.

No one ever uttered a swear word in our house. We knew there were words one could not say, or even hear, without being defiled. But we didn't know what they were. So, how come, from out of that startling sentence, spoken by a father to his son, could I unerringly pick out

101

the words I knew to be wrong? *Bloody* little *sod*. And no one baulked, no one froze – except me – no one else *did* hear the glass crashing to the ground. Tillie went on with her washing-up, glancing over her shoulder, untroubled, and Tom hopped up and down in the doorway, and then, laughing, sprinted off down the hall like a dog that really wants to be chased.

They even arranged their house differently. I just assumed that the biggest bedroom was reserved for the parents, the couple, the heads of the household. At Gloria and Stella's the bigger bedroom automatically belonged to Gloria and Eddy, even though the high marital bed was so seldom busy. Stella was banished to the back room, being single. And Bettina, who spoilt Mandy in every way possible, still claimed the bigger bedroom for her own. It went without saying. Until I knew the Hennessys.

It was Tom who occupied the big upstairs front room. The curtainless windows let in all the sun. He had louring posters on the wall, Che, and amorphous bubbling shapes, and Dalí's soft clocks. He lay on his bed and threw darts at Che's handsome warrior features. The room smelled of socks, and old cardboard, and something sweet and sour. Tillie and Patrick were relegated to a smaller room at the back of the house, where all the furniture was pressed up against the walls to make way for their bed. Barbara had a room downstairs which she referred to as the study. '*I* sleep in the study.' It looked like an ordinary bedroom to me, though desperately untidy. This was another shock – that you could have a bedroom downstairs in a house that was not a bungalow. And Isolde had stepped through the blue curtain into next door and taken up residence in one of her grandparents' spare rooms, gradually moving all her possessions through after her.

Right at the top of the house Patrick had opened the attics, painted them white and made them into a studio. A long breeze blew through all day, and here he painted, or in the garden if the weather allowed it. It was Patrick I'd seen through the hedge that day, preparing one of his big canvases. I often caught sight of him down by the summer house, hammering and stretching and sizing. It was what he did, while the children ran round him, slamming tennis balls and jumping on molehills, playing poker, swearing, kicking open doors. And while Tillie washed up and washed clothes and squeezed dough and sat on the back step with one of her home-made cigarettes (the type of cigarettes I thought only men were allowed to smoke) and looked at books and taught us things.

Now that she knew my name, Tillie sang out, 'Carolyn-nie, Caro-lina,' when she met me in the hallway or the kitchen. She always seemed cheerful, energetic, girlish. There was one day I remember particularly, when she seemed so full of light, and everything amused her.

Barbara and I were perched on the kitchen table, eating apples, and Tillie was drying knives and forks with a frayed tea towel. 'Where do you live, Carolyn?' she asked.

'Oh, not that far . . .' I said. I glanced at Barbara. I knew she would kill me if I got any closer than that to my address. Heaven forfend that *Barbara* should be the one to introduce something suburban into the Hennessy household.

'You're at the Wren as well, then?'

'No. I know Barbara from piano lessons,' I replied, glad to tell a truth.

'Would you like some ice?'

Tillie must have seen the perplexed look on my face, and went into peals of laughter.

'Look, I've made some ice cubes. What do you think?'

She opened the fridge door. She had laid out the ice cubes on three plates, blue and green. The cubes were made from frozen orange squash, lemon squash and lime cordial. I thought her taste in colour exquisite then. We sat on the veranda in the shade, sucking ice cubes till our cheeks hurt.

It was that same afternoon that Tillie asked about my reading matter and pulled out the huge book on Dutch masters especially for me. She hefted it on her knee and said, 'I think, Carolina, that you'll like this.'

And nobody before that day had ever consulted my tastes, or entertained a single thought about what it was I liked.

13

Shopping: One

I miss being able to go out here. I've heard that in time you're let out on little journeys, though always accompanied by a member of staff. If you're deemed fit to go, that is. I don't know who decides. Or what *fit* looks like. As far as I can see there aren't any prime candidates in this place – except maybe Hanny and me.

I miss stupid simple things like going shopping, and being able to just wander about. I lie on my bed here and think about all the shops I've known and what was in them, and I imagine the kind of shops I'd like to visit and what I'd buy there if I could. If I suddenly found ten thousand pounds lying in the road. And if I could suddenly get out of this bloody place.

When Brian and I were little the shops at the end of our road seemed the ultimate in adventure and indulgence. There was a sweet shop on the corner, the wool shop, the greengrocer's, and another one which every so often went out of business and opened up again as something quite different. Our favourite, Brian's and mine, was the sweet shop. We homed in on the comics, the counter full of sherbet fountains and penny chews, the rack of cheap plastic toys hanging by the door. As the streams of trippers flowing past increased, the shop-keeper grew canny and expanded his stock into ever new and fascinating lines until it spilled out on to the pavement. Bottles of fizzy pop for thirsty travellers, crossword puzzle books for the beach or the homeward traffic jam, postcards, sunglasses, buckets and spades, inflatable lilos, plastic boats and plastic cars to keep the kids quiet. Then ballpoint pens to write the postcards with, straw bags to carry the drink bottles and the toys in, rubber beach shoes, sunhats with cheeky messages, ashtrays with plaster seagulls perched on the rim. I'm sure most of his trade was homeward bound. This was the last port of call to buy that hat, that postcard, that blow-up sea monster they'd looked at and longed for down on the prom, and then thought better of. Last chance to spend their money.

The wool shop was Mum's favourite. We never passed without peering into the window, where the display was protected from bright sunlight by a layer of cellophane the exact same colour as Lucozade. Inside the shop it was shadowed and dim, as if the contents were precious, easily disturbed. The balls of wool were stored in little cells on the back wall of the shop with all the intricate precision of a beehive. My mother understood the mysteries of two-ply and four-ply. There were long conversations about buying eight ounces now and having the rest 'put by'. Mrs Drew, behind the counter, would store the other balls of wool in a crumpled clear cellophane bag, marking it with a pencil, to be claimed when needed, or not, as the case might be. She was consulted over the glass counter about patterns and quantities and needle sizes. Under the glass, which I was commanded not to lean on, were rows and rows of cotton reels, in all the colours of the rainbow and far more. Below these were glass-fronted drawers of hair ribbon, lace, elastic and bias binding. Everything came in a choice of colours. The sweet shop didn't offer rubber rings or beach hats in every shade imaginable, just bright yellow plastic and white cotton. But it was the prerequisite of the wool shop to imagine that human beings liked to make a choice, a slow and deliberate, tantalizing choice. Now should it be lilac, or should it be mint? There again, the lemon was nice.

Brian didn't care for the wool shop. He couldn't see the point of all that deliberation. He couldn't care less if his jumper was grey or green, so long as it wasn't pink. It was a female place, a quiet, careful, female place. Even more so in that, as I later discovered, under the counter in discreetly thick white paper bags, Mrs Drew kept the bulky supplies of sanitary towels her customers whispered requests for. Kotex, and Dr White's. Twelve luxury towels, the packet said, making them sound like an indulgent treat, like a Badedas bath. When I was sent I always bought Kotex. Dr White's, with that medical aroma, was a scary name. Sickness, emergency, catastrophe was Dr White's arena of action. Not swathing oneself in luxury towels.

Then there was the café. This was not on any of our usual routes, being up the main road, beyond the roundabout, on its way out of town. Also, we were forbidden to go near it. It was a place for trippers, that hated category of humankind. Trippers were common. And the road was busy, with no pavements. We were likely to get sucked into the traffic and tumbled to bits, like the unidentifiable, torn but still furry things we sometimes spotted in the middle of the tarmac. 'Don't ever let me catch you going near the café,' my mother warned. No, we won't ever let you *catch* us, we replied.

The café was a bungalow, too, of sorts: a low ramshackle building with a wooden frame and an overhanging wooden canopy at the front. It had a forecourt of muddy pink gravel for cars to pull into in search of thick white cups of strong tea, and egg and bacon breakfasts, and soup of the day (tinned). There were peeling posters along the front, for long-gone circuses and firework displays and somebody or other's big band sound which just showed the mouth of a saxophone and lower legs of a musician in the kind of trousers nobody wore any more.

The fact that the café was prohibited made it more appealing to us. Mandy was always pining to go along there when she came to visit us on Saturdays. Whether we would give in or not felt like a matter of power, until she learned to threaten, 'If we don't go, I'll tell that you did anyway.' So we usually went, creeping along the roadside on the strip of dirty grass between the traffic and the bushes, hoping no one who knew us was driving past. We didn't ever go inside. We just hung around and peered in through the grimy windows, and read the menu, which was fixed to a post out front. Sausage and egg. Egg and chips. Sausage, egg and chips. And beans. You could have beans with any combination. Mandy used to stand nearest to the door, her nose raised to catch the seductive scent of frying pans. Then we'd tear another strip off an old poster and scurry home, out of harm's way.

In town there were the big shops. Behind the seafront was a huge main street, with slabs of buildings: department stores, offices, banks. Sometimes I would go in with Mum on Saturday mornings on the bus, if there was something important to be bought, like new shoes or a winter coat. It was the one activity where Mum didn't find my proximity a nuisance. I don't remember Brian coming with us, though he must have, sometimes. Even he must have needed shoes, and school uniform, from time to time. I don't remember us being driven in by Dad. Shopping, my mother implied, was a female duty. 'Oh, I daren't trust your father,' she'd say. 'Goodness knows what he'd come back with!' Men were impatient, awkward shoppers: it made them choose badly, neither wisely nor well. And they couldn't see the point of the shops we preferred, where leisurely choice and comfort were doled out in equal measure. Because shopping was also, just possibly, a female *pleasure*.

I thought the department stores were heavenly. A world with looser purse-strings was on display here, an arena of endless *things*. Everything was arranged to engage the senses. You walked from place to place on patterned carpet, taking in the sights, the scents. There were chairs at the end of the counters, not for the sales staff but for weary customers, and on the top floor, after a smooth upward ride in the lift, there was a tinkling restaurant. A department store was like Mandy's bedside cupboard full of sweets, repeated over and over on a grand scale, and catering to every taste.

The salesladies, dressed in black with white collars,

had fierce plucked and painted eyebrows and fiercer hairdos. My mother never tangled with them, if she could help it. She liked to find what we were looking for herself. It was purgatory if the right size was not there, under our hands. She hated to ask, and if one of the gorgons bore down on us with a 'Can I help you, modom?' she would always put the item hastily down, muttering, 'No thanks, we're just looking,' and hurry off to another department. Like shoplifters almost caught in the act.

But I loved it. I would have liked to test the gorgon's mettle, and mine. I would have said, if she'd let me, 'Yes, do you have this in blue? In a size ten? Do you have anything similar, only *cheaper*?' But that would have paralysed my mother with embarrassment. These ladies were not to be troubled. They were formidable, like headmistresses. They mustn't know what you were up to. What were the limits of your purse, or the size of your bust. As far as Mum was concerned, it was better not to be noticed at all.

14

Mixing

Lorna doesn't ask about my brother Brian. Not at the moment. I don't know why she's so circumspect. Perhaps she's saving him up for a special occasion.

When he was younger, Brian was small but thickset, built like a tortoise or an armoured tank. He had short dark hair, run through with a wet comb until you could see its tracks across his head, like plough marks on a field. He wore National Health glasses with brown wire rims and his eyes were hazel. He wasn't a *thinking* boy; he was good with his hands.

There were only a handful of other children who lived in the bungalows, and we often played with them, although they weren't what you'd call friends. I think we might even have hated each other. But it was a case of expediency. Children herded together because adults expected them to, and what else was there to do? 'I'm playing out,' we used to call, following up quickly with a slam of the front door, so that the words 'Don't slam that door!' always pursued us up the path. Playing out was the main pursuit for children of primary school age, an all-encompassing term, slippery and useful.

There were two sisters, younger than us, who were often out on the pavement, chalking squares for hop-scotch or jogging up and down to the slow slap-slap of a skipping rope. I'd get Brian to tie them into harnesses of string, and then we'd gallop them down the pavement, imagining they were our chariot horses. Sometimes the string was under their arms, but sometimes we made them hold it in their mouths and pulled it tight. And there was a very small boy who rode a tricycle with a huge bin on the back. I'd keep him distracted and Brian would sneak up and put great heavy bricks in the bin, or rattling sticks and stones, for the pure pleasure of watching him pedal away, stop, frown, go round to the back and look inside. If it was bricks, he would take them out and care-fully stack them in the gutter, so that he wouldn't bump into them; but if it was sticks or stones he would often have a look and leave them in there, then pedal off again, noisily. Leaving us in a helpless heap of laughter. He always fell for our tricks.

We were forbidden to go into the fields or along the main road: much too dangerous. We had to keep to the pavements outside the bungalows. Neither Brian nor I asked anyone back to our house – we knew without enquiring that our mother wouldn't have liked it. Nor did we get asked into anyone else's. It wasn't the done thing. Or maybe they just didn't like us.

At school there were groups of girls that I hovered on the edge of, girls I would seem to get friendly with one day, but come the next day I would be back at square one again, ignored, left out, not knowing how I had got there. I used to look at pairs of 'best friends' walking arm in arm around the playground, or sitting side by side on the steps, and not know what it was that cemented them together. Then Barbara came, loose and friendly, seeking me out. She didn't seem to mind at first when, out of shyness, I rebuffed her. She didn't seem to care whether or not I wanted to be her friend, but she kept on offering. So that was how it was done, I thought. You opened up like a flower, taking the sun, taking the rain, the wind, whatever comes. I looked at the pairs of girls with a new eye, cool and detached now, because I had a friend, too.

I noticed that Brian had made a sort of friend as well, a boy of his own age called Pete whose family had moved into the road behind the shops. He and Pete didn't talk much. They rode fast up and down on their bikes, or dodged behind bushes and made machine-gun noises. They knew what they were doing, and they didn't need to chat about it.

I don't know why we found this friendship thing so hard to do, Brian and me. Why we hung back, and couldn't make ourselves likeable, and didn't understand the rules. Maybe it was a hangover from our years in the children's home, or getting adjusted to our new family. All that time I just can't remember. Must have had some effect on us. Well, that's one of my theories. It's almost something I might welcome a professional opinion on, from Lorna or some eagle-eyed colleague of hers. Almost, but not quite. Not worth going out on a limb for. I mean, it's just a theory.

Brian must have seen I'd started to go next door, but he didn't comment on it, and he didn't tell on me. It was an unspoken knowledge between us, something to do with my parents' hatred of the hedge, with the frightening glamour of the shrieks and laughter that came from beyond it, with my deep desire not to be suburban and the deeply ingrained suburban nature that was in both of us.

Or maybe I'm making all that up. Maybe he was completely unaware. Which would account for his formidable discretion.

Barbara never came to call on me. As far as I know she never set foot on our garden path. Maybe she didn't want to taint herself. She'd drift past the front gate, and if I spotted her as I was gazing out of my bedroom window I would hurry outside. 'I'm just playing,' I'd call to my mother. 'Playing out.' Once, stooping to put empty, rinsed milk bottles on the doorstep, Mum glanced up and asked, 'Who's that?'

'What – that girl?' I sounded terribly innocent. 'Think she lives up near the shops.' Brian's friend Pete lived *up near the shops*. It was a useful address, nicely unspecific, by which anyone exotic could be safely located and explained. My mother took no more notice, went inside and shut the door. The windows of our kitchen and our lounge looked out on to the back garden. If they hadn't, she might have noticed more.

I'm glad I've got a friend in here. I'm glad I met Hanny. You wouldn't want any of the others for your boon companion. I went into the lounge this morning and there was a blonde woman standing in the middle of the carpet, just wringing and wringing her hands, scrubbing them with invisible soap and water. So I backed out into the hall, and there stood Rose, with a bread roll she must have stolen from the breakfast table, tearing it into tiny little pieces without looking at what she was doing, and scattering them all over the hall floor and down the corridor. A trail of bread balls: Hare and Hounds, but nobody wants to catch up with Rose.

God, it's just like being back in the school playground, except that *everyone*'s friendless now. Apart from me and Hanny.

The Hennessys, like kings and queens, didn't mix with common folk. Or that was the impression they gave. They lived aloof, certainly the adults did. Just as much as my parents, only in a different way. Their home was their castle and they carried on as if they'd been there for generations, ever since the house was built, pretending that they couldn't even see the incursion of neat little red-brick, red-roofed bungalows, creeping up to their very doorstep. And like kings and queens they only consorted with other royalty, ambassadors from foreign courts, a flock of outlandish friends who alighted at intervals, arriving from nowhere and departing at the drop of a hat.

'Whose car is that outside?' Stella enquired, one Sunday afternoon when she was round to tea. 'That great big shiny Humber?'

My mother flashed her a 'don't ask' look, but my father, undoing the bottom two buttons of his knitted waistcoat and settling back in his chair with a sigh, said, 'Oh, you know, *next door*,' and tossed his chin and flung up his eyebrows in one speaking gesture. I liked the way he could do that. It made me think I knew what he had looked like as a boy, a schoolboy sitting unimpressed at the back of the class.

'Next door?' repeated Stella, lightly. She knew all about the hedge outrage. Not above a bit of stirring was good old Stella. 'No – I was just thinking – I like the look of that car.'

'Blocking the road up with some visitors or other,' grumbled my father. 'Causing inconvenience to other people. Ought to build a proper driveway. They've got enough room.'

'More tea, anyone?' asked my mother, already filling Stella's cup.

'And I liked his waistcoat,' added Stella, teasingly, plying the jug of evaporated milk over her mandarin orange slices.

'Whose?' Dad asked sharply.

'Chap getting out of the car when we arrived. Red, it was. Silk, I should think. Bit of a swagger, a red silk waistcoat.' And she glanced at my father's grey-marl cable knit, handmade by my mum.

'Give it a rest, Stella,' said Gloria, who had finished eating and was sitting with her arms folded. 'Honestly, man-mad,' she added, as if that was all it had been about.

One Saturday afternoon, in the summer after I met Barbara, Mandy was at our house. As on every Saturday afternoon. It was hot and overcast, and I suppose we were all irritable. 'Why don't you go out?' my mother suggested. 'Mandy might like to go to the sweet shop. You've had your pocket money.' Her voice was wheedling and kind. Oh, thanks a bunch. Mandy has a temple to confectionery in her bedroom, Mum. Mandy is a nutritionist's nightmare. Mandy *is* dental caries.

Of course, we said nothing and sidled out, followed by

Mandy, who gave us a sly, opaque look, and wiggled her fingertips at the adults in her version of a goodbye wave.

Outside the sweet shop, the mica glittered in the pavement. We stopped to read the dirty postcards on display, hoping to prolong the moments while we were still in possession of our pocket money. Mandy rammed the bubble gum machine, casting a look up through her lashes towards the open shop door. 'This ain't much good,' she said. We went inside. We chose the cheapest things – penny chews, red liquorice bootlaces, translucent purple lollipops, gob-stoppers that left your tongue ripped and raw – all so that we could control the sharing out, handing over as little as possible to Mandy. She stood back, empty-handed, in her pocketless pink shift-dress, waiting to be given.

Back on the pavement, the sky was pewter and there was a roaring noise in the clouds, maybe an aeroplane with engine trouble, maybe thunder. Mandy gave the bubble gum machine a final vicious smack on its top and a single egg-yolk-yellow gumball dropped out. We walked home, not speaking.

Down our road came a four-legged hunchback on a bicycle. A low screaming sound issued out of it. It was Mattie, on the back of their old silver-painted bike, with Tom pedalling and steering. They shot past us, Mattie's arms stretched out wide. They must have veered round the roundabout, which was thankfully quiet at mid-afternoon, and came back, following a serpentine path, swinging from side to side on the sandy tarmac of our road. Swerving a violent ninety degrees, they disappeared through the gateway and were enveloped by the hedge.

'Who's that?' Mandy asked. Brian looked vague, as

blank and invisible as Mandy herself when the chores were being given out. 'You must know them, they went in right next door to you.' She turned back to me, accusing. I shrugged.

The hunchback appeared again, tearing out through the hedge, clearing the pavement airborne, and landing with a yell. This time its back half was starfish-shaped, legs sticking out at an angle, arms held up in the air. I recognized Barbara's brown sandals, her tanned and scratched legs. Tom, hunched over the handlebars, pedalled madly. They screamed in unison, a pair of unmatched threadlike piercing squeals, as they passed us. Brian clapped his hands over his ears. They seemed to be doing it *for* us, or *at* us, this reckless display. They're claiming me, I thought. Or maybe they're just teasing me. It was impossible to tell.

Mandy turned, walked backwards for a couple of paces, following them with her narrowed eyes, still licking at her lollipop, the insides of her lips stained blue. Before she turned around again she gave me one quick flicking glance, just the way a snake's tongue darts out and in; and I knew that whatever Brian failed to see or failed to remark on, Mandy had spotted in a second.

After that, it was as if the rest of the Hennessys suddenly became visible. Their magic cloak had been lifted. I quite often saw one or another of them going up and down our road. The Van Hoogs' insect-like car crawling along, with Mr Van Hoog, who could hardly see over the steering wheel, peering anxiously ahead, his hands on the wheel like two mouse paws. Or Patrick's van pulling away, evil-smelling smoke belching from the exhaust. He drove a van because it was better suited than a car to transporting the large canvases and other pieces of equipment he used. The art school he taught at was in another, bigger town, inland. He turned off at the round-about and roared up the open road with his rude black smoke pouring out behind, like Mr Toad, keen to get away. Once I even spotted Tillie riding her upright ladies' bicycle with the basket on the front, pedalling stolidly along on her way back from the shops.

I never hailed them in the street. I was shy of presuming too much. And the Hennessys, being Hennessys, didn't appear to see me.

Although that's what it's like, being suburban. You think about whether you are going to greet people. Will greeting them get you in deeper, deeper than you are prepared to go? Will ignoring them, and maybe pretending to have something in your eye, let you off the hook, or will it cause offence? You're always weighing up and balancing these tiny social commitments. You fear to get sucked in.

With the Hennessys, though, I was prepared to go as deep as I could. Deeper than I could see, or breathe.

15

Observation Skills

'You're a good observer,' Lorna said to me this morning. 'You're observant, and you've got a good mind.'

Oh, thank you, Lorna. Thank you! How kind of you to let me know.

Well, Lorna, here's what I observe.

You are plain, and short. I hate short people. You sit with your little legs tucked neatly beneath your skirt, calves together, as I imagine you've done since schooldays. You wear ginger lace-up Hush Puppies, in a broad fitting. They still crease up over the widest part of your foot. I would say you have corns. Working upwards from the feet: your tights are cream, always the same shade. Do you buy them in bulk? Never take a chance on Chocolate, or Bermuda Beige? You wear, every time I see you, either a black skirt or one in light and dark brown tartan against some intermediate shade that I'm not even interested in finding a name for. You smooth down your skirt when you sit, and again when you stand. You wear a beige twinset, or a yellow jumper with lacy panels down the front which reveal layers of underwear. If you're going to go for teasing lacy panels, what's the point of a petticoat and a huge bra and maybe even something else underneath? The bra is one of those ones that come up to the armpits, and the tops of the cups almost up to the shoulders. I know, it's the sort Bettina had to resort to, to hold everything *in* and *up*. Sometimes I can see a gold locket round your neck; sometimes it must be tucked inside. You wear no rings, not even a fleshy diamond like Rose in Activity. Your complexion is pale and puffy. You favour just a dab of green eyeshadow, and lip-coloured lipstick. Your hair is coarse, with so many grey hairs in it that it's turning from black to pinstriped. You have a pony's fringe and two heavy wings of hair to your chin. It makes you look terrible. Yet you take such great care of your hair. It's always immaculately cut and immaculately combed, this great thick Cleopatra's wig of a hairstyle. Whatever for? It doesn't suit you at all. And I do know what I'm talking about. Don't forget, I am related to a second stylist.

Only I never told you that, did I?

Oh, and you always smell of some faint, sweet, cloying scent. Some man, years ago, must have said, 'Oh, Lorna, what a lovely perfume,' and you believed him. You didn't think he was just passing the time, or flattering you to get you to do something he couldn't be bothered to do himself, in the domestic or the bureaucratic field. You always wear that scent. *My* scent, you probably think, as you dab the stopper behind your ears and on your wrists, and you glance to see how low the bottle's getting.

See, aren't I a careful observer? Mind like a razor, too.

*   *   *

The gardens here are very neat. Big bland lawns, long straight flower beds, filled with all the same thing – butter-coloured tulips or sky-blue forget-me-nots – as if someone had taken a single colour and poured it out into a paint tray. Along the front of the building, which is white, lies a bandage of blood-red tulips.

Maybe it's to help the gardeners concentrate their minds. They don't look all there, to me.

The Hennessys' garden was a total mess. Mr Van Hoog, freed from straight nursery rows once he was retired, liked to throw the plants in all together, letting them fight it out. The front garden was heady with lavender and sprawling roses whose long stems were bent back down to the earth in thorny hoops. There were leaves mottled and splashed as though paint had been thrown at them, and flowers shaped like snapdragons, although I could see that they weren't just simple antirrhinums. Tom told me their names once and I thought I would remember them because it was him that told me. But I was bewitched by the shape of his mouth as he pronounced the unfamiliar words, and barely registered the names of the flowers.

In the back garden, the children ruled the space. There was lawn to the side and the back of the house, an overgrown shrubbery (which was what I had crawled through when I breached the hedge), the old tennis court, and finally the orchard and vegetable patch. Mr Van Hoog wasn't interested in grass and let it grow any old how, so long as someone occasionally cut it. The pitted lawn was full of moles. The little boys liked to creep up and jump on the molehills, as if they stood a chance of crushing the mole skulls just beneath. But Mr Van Hoog would wave them off and come hurrying over with his trowel to scoop up the mole-heap spoil, which made excellent potting compost, so Barbara told me.

There was a field that ran down the far side of the back garden, a bitten-down field, more brown than green. A donkey lived in it, and a sunk-backed pony like a settee with the springs gone. They belonged to a Mr Jenkins, a squat little man just as unkempt and stout and bandy as his animals. He kept them for his grandchildren to ride and every so often would come with a couple of halters and lead the two creatures away.

'Why don't you ask if you can ride them?' I said to Barbara.

'Wouldn't want to,' she replied, carelessly. 'They're vicious. They bite.' And to prove it she shot out a hand over the fence towards the pony's neck. It pressed its ears back and showed us long, yellow, wicked-looking teeth. But sometimes I spotted the others feeding them. I saw the little boys rip up handfuls of lush garden grass and hold them, palms flat, under the animals' noses. Without painful results. And I remembered reading somewhere – was it in *A Pony for Patricia*? – that you should never go to pat a horse behind its line of sight; they couldn't see what was going on and it made them anxious. So what was Barbara trying to prove?

The Hennessys' garden was a paradise of disorder. You could look out on to the field and the trees, and the big hedge blocked all view of the road and the rest of the houses. Not a post-and-link fence or a garden gnome or a bungalow in sight. Which was exactly how they liked it.

* * *

Sometimes I walk with Hanny in the gardens here. It's usually sunny, but the wind's still cold. She wears a burgundy velvet dress with bell-shaped sleeves to hide her knobbly wrists, and a hooded coat made out of tapestry material. The tip of the hood has a long silky tassel, in dirty gold, just like something you might find in a church. She looks like a vampire, but still she makes me feel my clothes are wrong, and dull.

I have an Aran sweater, and a pair of jeans worn milky-white at the creases. I wear boots, or a pair of dirty tennis shoes. I thought I had just got them to the perfect pitch of dirtiness, but now I'm not so sure. I only wear the sweater when I go outside. Inside they always have the heating on and it's so hot and stuffy. Makes you feel quite ill. It's April now and I wonder if they are ever going to turn the heating off. You need to get out into the gardens to be able to breathe properly.

I don't wear any make-up. I never have. It has always looked stupid on me, making my face seem like a mask, like a painted-up doll. And, anyway, I don't like all those handy-sized pots and tubes, the way they're displayed in shops like penny sweets, pick 'n' mix. Too handy-sized. Take one – what's gone? – very hard to spot the missing item. Just like Kim's game. I was very good at Kim's game when I was a Brownie. Always could spot what had gone missing.

Some days Hanny wears thick black gook on her long black lashes. I don't know why she bothers, it just makes her look as if she's blinked into blackcurrant jam. But there are people who can hardly step out of bed without their make-up. They feel naked without it. They feel humiliated if people catch them with just their own faces on.

I showed the magazine quiz to Hanny yesterday. We had a good laugh about it.

Question ten: 'When choosing a birthday present for your best friend, would you (a) Shop for hours then end up buying something you'd really like yourself? (b) Grab some chocs or flowers at the last minute? (c) Buy her something practical you know she needs? or (d) Give her a special home-made gift?'

'Chocs,' said Hanny. 'Bloody hell. *Chocs!*'

All the answers presuppose that the reader is someone with loads of time and money, and overflowing with vague but loving thoughts. A kind of empty goodwill.

Hanny suggested, 'Maybe the quiz is called "Are you a Dippy Hippie or a Hard-faced Bitch?"'

Where are the real-life alternatives?

(a) You and your friend never exchange gifts.
(b) You pretend, convincingly, that you didn't know it was her birthday.
(c) You steal something.
(d) You don't have a best friend.

That first time when Hanny asked me my name, I paused and then said, 'Coral.' That was a new one, wasn't it?

16

A Family Likeness

When I was about ten I started to grow really fast. I began to shoot up, as they always put it. Like some plant getting thin and leggy for want of light and outgrowing its space. My mother was tall. I said, 'I must take after Mum,' when one of the aunts commented on my height. And then, because I saw Gloria give me a quick, dazed look – a hurt sort of look, or so I thought – I added, 'But I've got Dad's eyes.' It was true, I had wide-set eyes like Dad and Gloria and Stella, the chilly blue of roughened water.

So I knew I was lying when I told Barbara, 'I'm an orphan. I'm adopted. I'm not *really* their child.' I did it because I didn't want to seem *suburban*.

'Are you? Are you really?' said Barbara. 'I've never met anyone who's adopted before.' And for the first time in ages she looked at me with a gleam of real interest in her eye. 'Why?'

'Why what?'

'Why were you adopted?'

'*I* don't know!' I said indignantly. I hadn't got this far

in my thinking. I was only just beginning to appreciate what a dangerous field I had strayed into. Of course, on the one hand, I kind of thought I *was* adopted, wished I was, believed that somehow I deserved something better than the family I had. But, on the other hand, my rational self knew it was inevitable that I hadn't been, that the genetic make-up I saw all around me at breakfast, and particularly at tea-time on those Sunday visits, was, of course, my destiny and my doom.

'Who are your real parents, then?' Barbara asked.

'*I* don't know. How *should* I know? I was adopted at birth,' I said firmly. And I had a vision of the moment, some poor labouring woman lying back on a bed and a newborn baby, me, neatly trussed in snow-white sheets, being passed into the eager hands of my waiting parents. I hadn't a clue back then what really happened in childbirth. All I knew about was Little Lord Jesus and his swaddling bands. Funnily enough, the woman on the bed looked a bit like I used to imagine a Carolyn sort of mother would look, with her long fair hair all loose and her pretty face scrubbed of make-up.

I couldn't see any likeness to Tillie in Mr and Mrs Van Hoog. I found them both repellent, and alarming. Maybe she had their light-coloured eyes, but what else was there? She was bird-boned and her face had a sculpted look. They were both short and fat. I hate short people. I hate *fat* people.

We didn't have grandparents in my family – Brian and I had none, Mandy had none – so I had no idea what to expect of them. I didn't know how to behave around them, so I dodged into the shadows and hung back.

Mr Van Hoog seemed to have taken on the role of an

irascible park-keeper and treated the children like a pack of delinquents who haunted and teased him at his work. 'Get out! Get out of it!' he would cry, in his funny accent, and he'd growl and shake the tines of his fork at them, or pretend to sweep them out of the way with his broom. But they just rose to his challenge, loving it, waiting till he was looking their way and then jumping on the newly raked earth of his flower beds. When his back was turned they would steal his tools and hide them under bushes, or empty the watering can he had just filled. And then run away, laughing. With Isolde it was different. She was never naughty. So he called Isolde 'my princess', and ushered her round with an elaborate courtly air.

Outdoors, he was usually busy in the garden. Sometimes he would take a break and sit on his side of the veranda and smoke a pipe. But sometimes I followed Barbara indoors to look for her grandmother, into those quiet rooms where the sunlight had to lever itself at a steep angle over the hedge. And then we might come across him, sitting absolutely still and silent in a chair, his hands on the arms, his eyes open. Barbara didn't hesitate to perch on the arm of his chair and peck him on the cheek. I couldn't believe she would do this. It was as repellent as kissing a corpse in a coffin. He might very well *be* dead. He looked dead to me, or comatose at the very least, sitting there, unmoving, not dozing or reading or smoking his pipe. I don't know why he sat there like that. When I asked, Barbara would say, 'Oh, it's OK, he's just thinking.' Which really didn't explain it.

I was glad I didn't have a grandfather.

Barbara's grandmother liked to do embarrassing things. Once Tillie was sitting on the steps with Mattie between her knees, singing in her high and rather untuneful voice: 'All the ducks are swimming in the water, Fa-la la-la li-lo, fa-la la-la li-lo . . .' And when she stopped Mrs Van Hoog clapped her hands together, just like someone in the audience at a concert, as if Tillie had done something special. But all she was doing was singing a nursery rhyme, rather badly at that.

Mrs Van Hoog always had to be patting and pulling at the children, praising and complimenting them, squeezing them for kisses. She was the one, not Tillie, who smoothed down Barbara's hair, tucked in her blouse, or cried, 'Give me that skirt – it needs an iron,' or 'Just let me catch up that hem,' to which Barbara always replied by darting away. Oma responded to defiance by chuckling with laughter, like a mad old witch who couldn't tell good from bad. She loved to feed her grandchildren sweets and peel apples for them, carve slices like petals and post them into their mouths. And they'd just gape like baby birds and let it happen.

Barbara and the little boys willingly put up with all this, but with the older ones she had to be more circumspect. Tom just sloped away out of reach, slithering from her grasp, and she dared not offend Isolde's imperial dignity by poking and pressing her. She treated Isolde like a gracious, timid animal, a rare species of deer, who might be enticed into the open if only we were all still enough, quiet enough, beguiling enough. She offered food by holding the plate high, temptingly: 'Izzy, come try these? I made them for *you.*' And then, of course, all the starching and ironing and fine sewing appealed to Isolde's sense of propriety, and she was willing to allow Oma the privilege of looking after her clothes. She would stand waiting impatiently, with no air of gratitude, while Oma sank the point of her iron into the folds of a gathered sleeve. I had even seen Isolde sit while Oma slid one polished shoe after the other on to her feet, like the assistant in the children's department at Clark's. To the two of them, grandfather and grandmother, Isolde was a combination of the Sun King and a fairy princess. It was useful to me to see that even the Hennessy children weren't all equal; how one child could be treated completely differently from the others, not because she was special, but for the simple reason that she thought she was special. Maybe this was Mandy's secret weapon.

I don't know what Brian's was. Yes, I do. He was a *boy*.

It seems to me that this is one of the major things you learn in childhood: that not all families are like your family. You start out thinking that the way it happens round your tea table is the template for the universe. What else could there be? Gradually, by exposure, you get to learn some very strange things: that some people have parsley sauce with their fish, not everyone heats the milk for the coffee, and the father of the family may belch in public and even then fail to be censured by an embarrassed wife. The father taps his sternum, the wife carries on knitting, the coffee sits lukewarm in the cups. How extremely weird. And then you begin to wonder – is belching and cold coffee and parsley sauce the normal thing? What *is* the normal thing? Knitting and silence? Bickering and manners? Maybe it's a lifetime's work to sort it all out.

All I know is, at the time, I was frightened of Barbara's grandparents. Not because what they did was necessarily frightening at all, but just because it was unknown, strange. I was afraid that Mr Van Hoog would growl at

130

me, or even worse, that Mrs Van Hoog would wrap me in a hot embrace and force a segment of orange between my lips. They revolted me – their bodies, their clothes, their habits. Even the way Barbara's grandmother turned an apple under her knife with dizzying speed was foreign to me. We did not peel apples by that method in *my* circle.

I needn't have worried. They never did do anything unwarranted to me. It was as if they couldn't even see me. I was under a spell, enchanted. I could wander about, unhindered, like a little ghost.

Lorna asks, 'What did they tell you about the adoption? I mean, your mother and father.'

'My *adopted* mother and father?' I'm a stickler, but polite with it. I'm always polite to Lorna. My mother would be proud of me. I think the politeness is driving Lorna up the wall. One can only hope.

'Your adopted mother and father, yes.'

I think about this. 'Not much,' I say. She pauses to make a little note.

This is the worst thing, this making of little notes! Sometimes you say something that sounds as if it should be quite important, vital even, and she just sits there, hands unoccupied, and lets you go on. But say something stupid, or pointless, and there it goes, pen to paper, squiggle, squiggle, squiggle. What the hell is she writing? What the hell does she *know*?

That's why you should never say anything. Make it up. Tell lies. Hanny agrees with me.

'We're the only two sane people in this place, and I don't exclude the staff,' she said. 'We have to protect ourselves.'

'That's all right, I'm an incorrigible liar,' I told her.

'Incorrigible. I like that word.'

'I've always been a liar. No, that's not true.' I tried to explain, but Hanny threw her head back and laughed silently, her throat quivering.

'If you're like this in group sessions, you'd drive *me* mad,' she said, when she could speak again.

'What I mean is that I started off small, just making excuses. Or being evasive.'

'Everyone does that,' said Hanny.

'But later on you need bigger excuses – proper lies – because you're up to bigger things. You've got more to cover up.'

Hanny gave me her moody sideways glance, and hugged her knees. We were sitting on our usual bench, and she stuck out her chin and propped it on her bony kneecaps and began to look stubborn. 'What's all this?' she asked, staring ahead of her. 'You're not working up to the big confession, are you? Because I can tell you straight off, I'm not interested in anything like that.'

'No, I'm not.' I hoped I sounded indignant, but my voice came out all tight. I coughed to free it. 'I'm just giving you the benefit of my technique. *If* you want to hear it.'

It was the first time I'd stood up to Hanny. I might run Lorna ragged and have fun in the process, but then she was the implacable opposition, not my friend.

A beat of silence, a long, long beat. Then: 'OK, go on.'

'What I find with lying,' I said, and leaned my head back against the wall: warming up now, relaxing. If there was one thing Hanny and I both enjoyed, it was theorizing. '*Successful* lying, that is – it's keep it small. Keep it modest. Being a big, flash liar is like walking on a tightrope – too easy to slip off somewhere along the way. What I tend to find is that you don't have to give them much. Just the bare minimum will do. Don't pile it on unnecessarily, you'll only end up forgetting some of the things you've said. It's amazing what you *don't* have to say to get away with it.'

'Maybe they were never really listening in the first place?'

'Maybe.'

'Didn't care what you were covering up, so they didn't care how you did it?'

'Maybe.' I could feel my voice tightening up again. 'But not in here. Here, they're *fascinated*.'

'I prefer a dirty great lie, myself. It's more fun.' Hanny unclasped her knees and began picking at a mark on one of her crushed velvet trouser legs. 'When faced with the bitter truth, use bluff, bullshit, injured innocence. But that's just me. Everyone's got their own methods. And nobody's owning up. Not really. Whatever they say in Group.'

What I think is that everybody in this whole place is spinning some kind of fabulous tale, and Lorna and her colleagues are lapping it up, noting it down.

In the little room where we meet, Lorna and I, there is one picture. One small square picture plonked right in the middle of the wall. Its colours are so faint and wishy-washy they might almost not be there. There are overlapping circles, blobs of pale blue and green and pink, as if someone had dipped a pen in coloured inks and let them drip on to wet – very wet – paper. Perhaps it's designed to calm us down. But if, like me, you're used to more robust forms of art, it just makes your blood boil.

Like the Van Hoogs' side, the Hennessys' side of the house was full of pictures. Pictures of people, rather than flowers and fruit bowls and fields of corn. There was Tillie naked and Tillie dressed, and people I didn't recognize, doing ordinary things – bending over a kitchen table, sitting and reading, cutting wood, even people painting other paintings. Up the stairway there were portraits of the children. Someone I thought was Sebastian, a round-headed boy with a sweet protuberant lip, crouching and playing in the sand: this was Eugene, so Barbara told me. He had the family likeness. There were two little girls on a swing-seat: herself and Isolde when younger. Then a strange one of Tom with a bluish face, making him look rather pinched and cruel, and another of Isolde sitting with her feet tucked up on the sofa in the front room, turning the page of a big picture book. It was odd to see paintings of people I knew, especially if they didn't have their clothes on, but somehow even odder to see them of objects and rooms I recognized. The woman standing at a table was using Tillie's blue striped mixing bowl, and a fat black-haired man sat on the veranda of this very house. The paintings of the children were conventional enough, I suppose, but Patrick had laid the paint on in thick unyielding layers, had made the colours uncompromising, the blurriness of their features like them and yet not like. Isolde and Barbara on the swing were almost creepy, Barbara's eyes just dots and dabs of near-black, unaligned. Her expression was of boredom, and rebellion. But then how could that slab of grey-brown-pink, those curranty dots for eyes, be said to have an expression?

And then there were the women.

It wasn't only Tillie who was nude, but a large blonde woman only partly draped with a red shawl confronted visitors to the dining room, and along the passage a thin dark-haired girl sat upright on a hard kitchen chair, looking resentful and cold. Nipples and pubic hair, just like two eyes and a mouth, right in the middle of the picture, staring back at you. Barbara noticed me scurry past this one every time I had to follow her to the kitchen. 'For God's sake, what do you want on the walls?' she said. 'Puppies and kittens with bows round their necks!?' I felt myself blush.

She told me it was the habit of artists to paint human flesh. They had done it for centuries. It was high art.

'But why does it always have to be female flesh?' I asked.

'It isn't,' she said. 'Think of Michelangelo.' Which I couldn't, at that stage.

Tillie told me, another time, that there was nothing wrong with painting people naked. It was a challenge to the artist, she said, and it also got something deep and true about the sitter down on to canvas. The deep and true thing it seemed to me to get on to canvas was the terrible pendant nature of their breasts. I couldn't imagine how the painter could stare at some intimate part of the sitter, then stare at the canvas and carefully paint it, then stare back at the part again in order to get it just right, without thinking thoughts other than colour and shape and line. And the sitter sitting there, aware of the painter's eyes on their intimate places, and having to not twitch a muscle all the while.

So I learned to take my cues from the Hennessys. Nobody in the house turned a hair, walking past naked women with their breakfast bowls and their dirty washing, naked women their father had spent hours and hours staring at and turning into art.

17

The Club

'We'll form a club,' Barbara told me. 'It'll just be us in it. We won't let anybody else join.'

Which was flattering, but – also – disappointing. What was the difference, then, between our being best friends and being in a club? I would have liked Isolde to be allowed in, or even the little boys. Oh no. 'We'll be exclusive,' said Barbara. 'I'm leader. You're second-in-command.' But with no other troops to order about, my rank felt a bit worthless.

We constructed a camp out of sticks and blankets and old apple boxes, down among the fruit trees at the end of the garden. Barbara wanted to build a tree-house for our club headquarters, but the trees proved too stunted and shaky for that. So we had to make do with a prolapsing bivouac with a grass floor, which filled up with sheltering spiders and earwigs overnight. We crammed ourselves inside and Barbara turned on her torch.

'Close the door. Let's make it dark in here.'

I pulled the flap of blanket as far across the opening as

I could. Our backs bulged out of the sides of the camp.

'OK, we need some rules, and a badge, and a secret sign.'

I nodded eagerly.

'And we have to do a blood brotherhood thing, and take a vow.'

'Blood brotherhood?'

'Yes. I'll show you. Tom and Tom Rose and another boy used to have a club, in the summer house. They took a blood brotherhood vow. But then they spent all their time being horrible to the other boy. Three's not a good number for a club.'

She pulled a rusting penknife from her pocket and made me hold out my hand. She scraped the blade across the base of my thumb, several times, unsuccessfully. It left a white line, fading quickly as the blood rushed back into the unbroken flesh. 'You're meant to draw blood,' she said, 'and then shake hands, mingling both your bloods.'

'Oh.'

'We'll just do the vow. I'll get a better knife another time.'

I noticed she didn't try it on herself.

'We have to swap some secret that no one else knows, and then vow not to breathe a word. Ever. That proves our trust.'

I wondered what secrets Tom's club had divulged, and how the third boy had felt about trust.

'That must be Rule Number One,' said Barbara. 'Never to break that vow.'

We spent a happy half-hour drawing up a list of rules, and inscribing them on an oblong of hardboard scrounged from the summer house. 'We'll meet three times a week, at the club headquarters, here. Rule Two – you must give the sign before entering. Or if you meet another member of the club, anywhere. That's Rule Three.'

We decided on a badge, which was two apple leaves joined to a twig. This was my idea and I was proud of it: it was germane to our camp under the apple tree, also easily available, and inconspicuous. We didn't want anyone else to spot that we were wearing our secret society badges.

We couldn't agree on a sign. Barbara showed me her idea.

'But that's just like the Brownie salute,' I said.

'I don't go to Brownies.'

'Well, it is.'

'What's your bright idea, then?' she challenged me, folding her arms and sitting so far back that one side of the camp fell down. I made a feeble attempt at some other sign. Barbara looked unimpressed. 'God, now I'll have to mend *all this*!' she said, and turned her back on me.

It was occurring to me that clubs never did work out, whether you had two members or three.

'There's no point in having a sign, since it's just us,' Barbara said, once she had hitched the blanket up to a tree branch again. 'We'll have a noise, though, which you have to make before coming into the camp. To prove it's us.'

The noise was an owl-hoot, made through clamped thumbs into cupped hands. Barbara was better at it than me.

'That'll stop Seb and Mattie coming in,' she said.

But it didn't. Once they got wind of secret activities down in the orchard, they launched an offensive on our camp. They raided it when we were absent, flinging the rules and our scrap of carpet out. The next day they jumped on it when we were inside. There was a fight, with flailing legs inside grey blanket, and Mattie had to be wrestled with to get him to part with the biggest stick, which he was whacking and smacking into the mass of heaving bodies. I think I enjoyed this bit the most. I was taller than all of them, and surprised at my own strength. My lack of experience in fighting did not prove to be such a drawback.

When we had beaten them off and rebuilt the tent, Barbara took a brooch from the pocket of her shorts. It was shaped like a leaf. She unfastened the pin and stuck out her palm. She scraped it back and forth until a tiny intermittent line of red sprang from her skin.

'Now you.'

I bit my lip. The brooch pin felt hot, scratching, and finally stinging. I had borne it. I had shed blood.

'OK, shake.'

We clasped hands.

'What's your secret?'

I had been thinking about this. Indeed, I had been dwelling on it, worrying about it, turning possibilities over in my mind since the day before when Barbara first mentioned it. The big one was: I wish I *was* adopted, but I'm not – I lied. And I'd look her in the eyes and find the sympathetic gaze of a real friend, a true friend, who understood. Only I wouldn't say this. It was the secret of a very exclusive club, one member only: me. So, stumped for an answer, I said, 'I never tell my mum and dad where I am when I'm here. It's my big secret. I don't want them to know.'

'Why not?'

Because they wouldn't approve of me mixing with you, with your family. That was another thing I couldn't say. Barbara wouldn't believe it – such effrontery – even though it worked the other way. Barbara was always right, and always in the right. She could conceive of no other possibility.

'Because I want to keep it secret,' I said, half true. 'Because I want to keep you to myself.'

'Ooof!'

Barbara dissolved into a grey lump, and the semi-darkness inside the tent became blinding blue day as the blankets were dragged off me. Two feet in hard brown sandals came up in my face as Barbara, imprisoned, rolled over and over with Sebastian clinging round her blanketed head. We'd been the target of another guerrilla attack.

I never got to hear Barbara's deadly secret, if she had one. I never got to hear her swear 'Trust', and shake a bloody hand over my secret. We didn't bother to rebuild the camp that day, and by the next she had lost interest in a club which demanded meetings three times a week and adherence to a list of at least twenty tedious rules. I never got to be a real blood brother.

The funny thing about friendship, I learned, is that it contained an element of *hatred*. What you loved most in your friend was what you admired and wanted to have. I loved Barbara's self-confidence, the way she never thought before she spoke but just blithely spewed out her opinions on every subject under the sun, on things she knew about and things she must have been quite ignorant of. I liked this ceaseless stream of information and judgement. I didn't even mind her high-handed bossy ways. She never asked herself, 'What will people *say*?', which was refreshing after the caution and censoriousness of our household. I felt she was teaching me how to live.

I loved her great bouncy carelessness, but when it bounced off me I was desperately hurt. Her bumptious confidence could make me shrink. She always made out that it was Patrick and Tillie who had no time for suburbanites, for small-minded people, for tedious conformity. But it was Barbara who dwelt on the subject – bungalow kids, lace curtains, miniature windmills in front gardens – picking and pulling at it like a splinter, but just driving it further home. It was always she who raised the subject, as if she wasn't content for me to stay in disguise. She had to remind me of my origins, tease me with my danger. She was my very best friend, yet there were times when she made my heart feel as heavy as a rock.

So how did I explain all those hours, all those precious hours spent through the looking glass?

'I'm playing out!' *Playing out*. It would do, to begin with. Playing out was where my mother wanted us to be, not under her feet. Just as she wanted us off at school unless we were almost dying of something; otherwise we would have to be under her metaphorical feet, lying beneath the bedclothes, requiring to be plied with Disprin and barley water and to have our burning fore-heads felt at regular intervals.

And later, once my career swung secondary school-wards, I claimed homework as my excuse. My parents didn't appear to notice the disparity between my keenness to attack homework projects in other girls' houses, and my reluctance and resentment – which descended like fog, heavy and clinging – about undertaking any at home.

I remember that when Brian was little and just learning to tell the time he was given a book to help him. It had come from a church jumble sale, and I loved to look at it, even though I could already tell the time. It was about a mother and her two children and how they spent each hour of the day. Every new page had a clock-face to mark the passing hours. The children themselves were dull, two ciphers. Both had bunlike faces, and blank eyes like ha'pennies, brown and flat. But the mother – the mother was quite another thing. Elegant, lovingly drawn, her hair up in a French pleat, button earrings, a shirt-waister dress. Her lips, in two curves of the pencil, were like a lipstick print, her figure as hourglass-smooth as a Playtex girdle. And high heels. High heels all day long, except at two o'clock, when she kicked off her shoes and lay on the equally elegant sofa, reading and writing letters. At two o'clock the boy and girl obediently took a nap, though the boy was shown playing on his bedroom floor. Perhaps *he* was allowed to get away with it, so long as he stayed in his room. Then at three they sprang up, donned coats, and took a walk in the park, fed the ducks. The mother had flung on a duster coat and spiked a small hat on top of her French pleat. Though the wind blew a bow-tailed kite in the background, Mother's hat stayed firmly put. And at six Father came through the garden gate, baggy pinstripe suit and briefcase, waving a rolled-up newspaper in greeting. His wife stood waiting in the doorway behind their two offspring, a hand on the shoulder of each, smiling her welcome.

I loved it, I loved the order and routine, the heavenly predictability of it, the way the mother revolved around them all, except for that precious hour at two. But I loved her best for her carefree, carefully honed look. Her fifties *Vogue* model look. I can see her now, a Cecil Beaton version of a mother, if only her heels were even higher and if she leaned back a bit more from the hips. The sort who in reality banished the children to Nanny, so that she could lunch with her girlfriends at noon, peer stylishly through binoculars at the two o'clock runners at Ascot, and at six take cocktails with broad-shouldered men called Freddy and Boy. Midnight would find her dancing in a slinky backless frock, glancing unseeingly at us over her smooth white shoulder as she whirls past.

The book didn't actually go up to midnight. It ended at seven o'clock, with the children tucked up in their little beds. As all good children should be.

I don't know what happened to it once Brian learned to tell the time. I loved that little book. I used to pore over it for hours. Perhaps that was where I got the germ of Carolyn from, and the sort of mother she'd have.

And *my* mother? My mother did not want her hours to revolve around us. She had no idea of the work tiny children involved. Or perhaps she had just an inkling. Maybe that's why she plumped for house-trained pups, aged four and five. If we were outside, safely burning off our youthful energies, so much the better for the wear and tear on her upholstery, her carpets, her nerves. If only

Mum had worn high heels and a duster coat and taken us to the park, if only a be-suited Dad had swung his brief-case cheerfully through the gate at six, perhaps we would all have been happy then. Perhaps none of this would have needed to happen.

18

The Gift of Language

They never ask the right questions in here. They never look at the *broader picture*. How can you hope to find out about a person by asking trite questions and drawing the obvious conclusions?

When archaeologists dig up a skeleton, there's a certain amount they can find out: the sex of the person, an approximate age at death, maybe what they died of, some injuries or diseases they suffered in life. If they're lucky, and really industrious, they may be able to determine their status, how they were dressed and what kind of burial they had, what their diet was. And what does this tell us? Not a whole lot. Look at a skeleton and there is no means of knowing what that person felt when those empty eye sockets were still able to see, when inside that skull there was a brain to think with. It seems to me that it's just foolishness to pretend that you can know anything about them.

People have done that to me. They looked at the skeletal shape of my life and they've drawn their own conclusions. They sketched in a few facts and left out so much it took my breath away. They should have taken the broader view.

Even someone as tenuous as Uncle Bob can have an effect on you. But they're incapable of following the thread that brings Uncle Bob to me, to the Hennessys, and wraps us all in a loop. Do they ask about Uncle Bob? Uncle *who*? See what I mean?

We never went to visit my mother's brother, Uncle Bob. He always came to us, a maximum of once a year, if that. I have a memory of him in shirtsleeves in the back garden one summer. Just like a snapshot, and over-exposed at that, his white shirt and cheekbones and forearms blinding. But all the other years he came at Christmas.

He hadn't got a wife, and if he had a girlfriend he took great care to keep her hidden from us. He came singular, bachelor Uncle Bob, placid and cheerful. If the family had ever entertained hopes of Uncle Bob taking Stella off their hands, these had been ground into dust long before Brian and I came on the scene. There was no tension between Bob and Stella, no mutual anything when they were in the same room. Bob was always his usual pale and beaming self, Stella's mind on someone else entirely.

He stayed for just the two days, always arriving on Christmas Eve evening and departing on Boxing Day straight after breakfast. Cunning Uncle Bob. Christmas for us was a time of frantic church-going. I don't know how a household that was so driven by the Christmas spirit could embody so little seasonal cheer. We spent half the holiday in church thanking God and welcoming the arrival of the Little Baby Jesus, and the rest of it thanking relatives and welcoming the arrival of the end of the whole business. But long ago Bob must have turned his bland, round face up to our mother and said, 'You don't mind, do you, Edie, if I don't come with you?' And that was it. He never had to go. He stayed at home, with the newspapers and his pipe and a roaring fire, with instructions about the oven setting, wearing new carpet slippers he had (most likely) bought for himself, and free to tuck, unhindered, into the box of Turkish delight he had brought for us. If I had a Christmas wish, perhaps it was to be Uncle Bob. Just for the day. Or two days, at the most.

My mother should have enjoyed the Christmas morning service. After all, it was her choice to be there, not ours. But she was always tortured by thoughts of the dinner to come, worrying what was happening to the turkey. Was it turning as dry as a bone, or exploding in flames? I couldn't see how this could happen, short of the turkey climbing out of the oven, rubbing its bony little wings together in glee and turning up the dial itself, then jumping back in. Bob was at home, Bob who fended for himself on the other three hundred and sixty-three days of the year, surely Bob could babysit an oven-ready turkey without it immolating itself or him or the whole bungalow? But I was aware of Mum clutching her carol sheet very tightly and singing in that high cracked voice which showed the strain. Why is it that you can always rely on the voice of your own parent to ring out over all the others, a beat in front or a beat behind?

Her attitude to the domestic – as opposed to the sacred – Christmas was 'Well, at least *that's* over,' at every stage. The shopping, the wrapping, the sending of cards. The buying of ingredients and slopping them all together to make a cake, weeks and weeks beforehand. Covering the cake with the hard white paste of royal icing, days and days beforehand. She would whip up the surface into a snowstorm with the blade of a knife dipped in hot water, and settle the little wooden robin on top. The last act was to place the silver plastic letters spelling out A MERRY CHRISTMAS firmly in the centre. Then she'd stand back for half a second to admire her handiwork grimly, and say, dusting her hands together, 'At least *that's* done.' When we rushed to open our stockings in the morning: 'Well, now *that's* over, we can get ready for church.' The dinner, the exchange of family presents afterwards. She leaped on the discarded wrapping paper, snatching it up before it could begin to make a mess. My father some-times got to the point of saying, 'Sit still, Edie. You make a rod for your own back.' But 'If I don't pick it up now, it'll only get rammed down between the cushions,' she insisted, smoothing out the best bits. The best bits were always Uncle Bob's, because he bought new wrapping paper every year, unlike us, who saved it up from Christmas to Christmas, peeling off last season's sticky labels and snipping away the jagged edges. We thanked Bob for our presents, and he thanked us. 'Well!' my mother said, satisfied at last. 'Now *that's* over, how about a cup of tea?'

There was a routine to Christmas entertaining, as there was to everything else. Stella and Gloria, Eddy (if not on the high seas), Mandy and Bettina would join us for tea on Christmas evening, and we would join them for tea on Boxing Day, when everyone was too full to eat much anyway. This meant that neither household had to buy and cook an *enormous* turkey, only a *large* one.

Bettina was always left out of the obligations, being a woman on her own, and had a standing invitation to Christmas dinner at Gloria's. Tea, on either day, was mince pies and bread and butter and pickles and cold ham. And Christmas crackers, at generous Gloria's, and old silver threepenny bits pressed into what was left of the cold pud. My mother frowned on such frivolities. Perhaps it was because they were pagan. She could barely bring herself to have a tree – 'Needles all over the carpet!' – and was one of the first to buy a modern artificial Christmas tree, with leaves of shredded crispy paper and branches of palsied wire. What I hated most were its red plastic feet. We had to place our presents around its *red plastic feet*, which were like two clothes hangers joined at the hip. Why not, I complained, supply it in a plastic tub, with clean plastic earth, and a jolly red plasticized ribbon tied round it? 'Stop moaning,' I was told. 'Christmas is a time of goodwill.' We wired our Christmas fairy to the tree's three-foot-high top, and arranged the bells and baubles solemnly. 'It's for *the children*,' our mother intoned to the relatives. 'I wouldn't bother having one at all if it was *only us*.'

I didn't know then what secrets lay behind this modest claim.

The Hennessys went to church at Christmas, or most of them did. They went to midnight mass, a giggling, excited pack of them, Patrick's breath reeking of good cheer, leaving Tillie at home to stuff stockings and turkeys and keep the reindeers' hooves from breaking the roof lights of Patrick's attic studio.

None of this was known to me first-hand. I was next door, dining with simple Christian folk.

* * *

'It's all very well for Bob . . .' This phrase would always surface some time in the days after Christmas, usually from my father. He never finished it off, or explained how it arose, but there was a distinct feeling that it *was* all very well for Bob. He came to us as a guest in our home, and not for him the washing-up, the fetching of coal, or the making of pots and pots of tea. He judged finely how infrequently to say, 'Let me do that for you,' to which my mother, with a shocked expression, would reply, 'No, you sit down, Bob. You're a *guest.*'

My father wasn't so sure. I saw him gaze round sometimes, restless, as if he thought that Bob might just be able to lift that tea towel, if put to the test, or carry the dishes as far as the kitchen hatch. I could see him thinking, even before Boxing Day morning had arrived, *It's all very well for Bob.* Bob with his purpose-built flat with every mod con purposely built in; no garden for Bob to worry about, up there on the top floor. No wife or children to get on his nerves, or drain his pockets, or press him with trivial questions – 'How long is an ell, Dad?' or 'When are you going to creosote that shed?' There Bob sat, with the newspaper open on his lap and his long legs comfortably stretched out, toes warming by the fire, and nothing we children did or our mother said or our father implied by twitches of his head or the rearranging of small coins in his pockets ever impinged on Bob's sanguine composure. I used to keep an eye on his big-slippered reflection in the convex mirror hanging on the chimney breast, and he barely stirred.

And where did Bob sleep? Why, on the settee. No worry that Bob might wreck the upholstery or ram something uncalled-for between the cushions. For two nights Bob slept with a full complement of blankets and eiderdowns and pillows (redistributed from *our* beds, since we had no occasion to keep spares), with the added warmth of the sinking coals in the glassy fish-tank of the Parkray. So it was certainly all very well for Bob.

At some point in his career with the roof-tile and piping company, he was allocated a company car, which he grandly parked in our drive overnight. He and my father would go and admire it every year, talking of fuel consumption and road holding and cubic capacity. In the years when the old model had been replaced by a new one, they spent almost as long contemplating it in the freezing air as my mother did, in the humid kitchen, stuffing the turkey. And whatever Bob said, in encouraging terms like 'You really ought to think about getting one like that yourself,' or 'You can't beat it for acceleration,' or even (in consolation) 'Of course, it's not really a *family* car,' I knew what Dad was thinking. It's all very well for Bob.

The good thing about Uncle Bob was that he would often bring us presents we might actually want. His idea of boys and girls was gleaned from toyshop windows, which was not a bad place to start, from our point of view. The other things we got tended to be useful, things we would have needed anyway. Certainly mine were: a pen and pencil set, new socks and handkerchiefs, a hairbrush, a purse with my initial on it; never anything exciting. Brian was given more toy-like presents – Airfix kits, packs of balsa wood and glue, penknives with numerous useful attachments – though there was always an element of virtuous work in them. Even so, I was jealous.

The best present that Uncle Bob gave Brian was the International Spy Kit. It had a code book and a set of false moustaches; a handy booklet with instructions, like how to make invisible ink, and helpful tips, such as how to follow someone without them getting suspicious. It didn't tell you how to kill a man with a single blow or where you might obtain a false passport. Then there was a magnifying glass, a fountain pen that turned out to house a secret blade, and a set of (plastic) skeleton keys. The secret blade was as blunt as a butter knife, but Brian took it down to the shed to try and work up an edge.

The most useful item was the magnifying glass. Brian tried it out on ants' nests and spiders' webs and the back of his friend Pete's hand. He had more luck with little heaps of dry grass. If he was lucky and the sun stayed out, if he waited long enough and got the angle right, the spot of light intensified. A tiny curl of smoke, and the grass stems bent and crumpled into flame. Then he'd look up at me with a happy gleam in his eye.

The skeleton keys were no good at all.

Looking back, I think we could have picked up clues to Bob's secret love life from the presents he gave us. The year we had wonderful things from Hamley's Toyshop in Regent Street (price tags still attached) must have been the year he had a girlfriend he was trying to impress, a metropolitan sort of woman. He was showing her his generous side, his ability to be extravagant when the occasion demanded it, his kindness to children, his good family-man credentials. The year we had identical puzzle books was the year of the out-of-hand office party, the bad hangover, the passing regrets, the dash to buy something – anything – in a petrol station on the way.

Although we opened our presents under his gaze, after Christmas we always had to write thank-you letters to Uncle Bob. Our mother made us. It was because, she said, he lived *away*, implying that we spent the weeks after Christmas continually thanking our nearby relatives every time we saw them. Which of course we didn't. By mutual consent we drew a hasty veil over the embarrassing subject.

One year Bob gave me a dictionary and a thesaurus, a matching boxed pair. None of us even knew what a thesaurus was. I thought it sounded like some kind of prehistoric monster.

'Now that's a useful present,' my mother said, with her damning praise. She didn't know. She didn't know how useful I found it, how truly grateful I was. I didn't mind writing the thank-you letter for this present. I strewed it with *words*, like a spy sending a message to his masters back home, so that Bob would know how unusually welcome his present was. 'I will *endeavour* to *utilize* your gift, dear Uncle Bob,' I wrote, and 'I hope you had an *eventful* journey back to Basingstoke. We all trust you enjoyed the *festal* occasion . . .'

I read them obsessively, alone in my room, like dirty books. *Pellucid*, now there was a word, and *tormentil*, and *Eocene*. Words to charm the birds down out of the trees. English-speaking birds, that is. Lovely, wordy words, words to knock Barbara's vocabulary into a cocked hat. I savoured the words, and then swallowed them, letting them slip down my throat like melting chunks of coloured ice. I savoured them like Murray Mints, like Fruit Spangles, sucking out all their sweetness, letting their nourishment flow round my bloodstream and enliven all my cells. To me, those books were the equivalent of Mandy's shrine of sweets, everything in their pages to be worshipped and adored.

The following year Bob gave me a belt of gold chainlinks, in a style no longer fashionable. Or *modish*, or *contemporary*, or *topical*, if you like.

19

Group

I've started going to Group. I'm not sure if this is progress.

Group is always run by someone different. I hazard a guess that it's the most unpopular job of all. I think there must be a rota system, and I imagine them up in the staff room saying, 'It *can't* be my turn to run Group. I did it last week!' Or maybe they just pick straws.

I assume it is a weekly thing. *I* go weekly. Maybe there are groups taking place all the time, every day, only I'm not in them.

The first time I went it was run by Mike, a very long thin man with a faint fluffy beard and a jumper his mother made him. The sleeves reached his knuckles. He made us all sit round in a circle and think of one word, one word to sum up how we were feeling. Of course, it was very tempting to come out with a rude word. In fact, it was very hard to think of a word that wasn't rude for how we were feeling, being put on the spot by an idiot whose mother wasn't even capable of using a tape measure. I looked round at everyone in Group and decided that an outside observer would not be able to tell that Mike was any different from the rest of us. I was only one seat away from him. They started by going in the other direction, and I just prayed they wouldn't get as far as me before we had to finish. You didn't have to explain your word if you didn't want to, you just had to say it. Of course, they all wanted to explain. Trust the loonies.

The second time I went it was run by Moira, a tiny ant-like woman with red hair and a Scottish accent. Moira's approach was quite different. Whereas Mike sat forward in his armchair and knotted his tense white hands around one shinbone, and urged us with pleading eyes to come out with something, *anything*, Moira sat up arrow-straight, her short legs dangling like Goldilocks perched on Father Bear's chair, her little feet *en pointe* in order to make contact with the carpet. She wore black ballet shoes, which rendered the effect that much better. She commanded us with her fierce darting eyes to say something. And she didn't want just any old thing. She wanted something full of meaning. You felt likely to be picked upon. It was just like the old schooldays of spelling rounds and tables tests. 'Seven sevens – you!' And you would have to produce the answer to seven sevens, like some miracle, from out of your empty head.

Fortunately, she never picked me.

These are the people in Group. It is like something out of Chaucer, or Hieronymus Bosch. There's the Fishwife, the Old Crone, the Young Crone (they could be mother and daughter, perhaps they are), Beanpole, Wet Lettuce, Marsupial and me.

The Old Crone has a hooked nose and a chin that's

curving up to reach it, and I can see the Young Crone will go this way, too, in time. Beanpole is young, perhaps as young as me, but that's all we have in common. She unfolds herself like one of those expanding clothes airers when we stand up to leave. But she's always there before me so I don't have the chance to see her sit down. She's longer and stringier than Mike, even. His mother's home-knit jumper might fit her very nicely. Perhaps she's one of these non-eaters, like Hanny. The Fishwife has a voice like a corncrake and is fond of hearing it. She has a hectoring tone. Mostly it's the group leader she's hectoring, but sometimes it's herself, or the Authorities, or God. Wet Lettuce is just that – pathetic, weepy, her mimsy little-girl voice only just carrying across the vast six or eight feet of the circle to the rest of us. Marsupial is my favourite. She's not fat all over, just rather plump, but her belly is huge and saggy and she lets it swing down between her parted thighs as she sits, resting it oh-so-gently on the lap of her easy chair. My conclusion is it's the latest in a series of phantom pregnancies, a terrible recurring fantasy, and she has the stretch marks to prove it.

What a happy bunch we are.

I wish Lorna would have to come and run Group. I wish I could see the Fishwife going on and on at Lorna, not pausing for breath, not even pausing for thought. I wish she would have to face the Old Crone, whose infrequent but always enthralling gobbets of obscenity make Mike swallow, and blink his eyes open very wide. I wish she would have to deal, all at once, with Wet Lettuce crumpling into tears and Beanpole twisting her legs round and round each other agonizingly until some vein is likely to pop, and Marsupial sighing and giving off that vivid, swampy smell which she does whenever she's about to speak. Then we'd see what Lorna's really made of.

But that doesn't seem to be her job. I wish it wasn't *my* job, to have to sit there with them, to associate with them, be associated with them. They're clearly not normal people, and some of them are definitely unhinged.

I always try to keep my mouth shut. I don't want to say anything untoward.

Yesterday Lorna brought someone else to our little private session. He sat in the corner, next to the waste-paper basket, and said nothing. He was like a dormouse, so quiet and self-effacing that you really could ignore him.

Except that I didn't. I stared at him. We're so starved of events here – there's nothing much to do, nothing to look at but bad art, nothing to read but what we glean from other people's leavings – that it was really quite thrilling to see a new face. At least, that's how I felt. His hair was such a fine colour that you could hardly see it, but it was thick and upright, prickling out all over his head like an American astronaut's, and his eyes were as sad as a donkey's. He wore tiny steel-framed glasses, perched on the bump of his narrow nose. His face was unlined, shockingly smooth, just like a balloon. I've no idea how old he might be. He's one of those people where you just can't tell.

'Do you mind if I sit in?' he asked, right at the end, as Lorna was letting me go. I shrugged: too late. *Too late!* I didn't bother saying it.

He came again today. This time he told me his name is Dr Travis. Perhaps he's just learning the trade. His voice is soft. He sits quietly in the corner, with one leg crossed over the other. Or maybe it's a double act. Lorna's the tough interrogator, and maybe Dr Travis is to be the gentle one, the one who puts the cigarette to your cracked lips, only to have the other one knock it away again with a stinging blow to your jaw. Once Lorna's softened me up, maybe Dr Travis will let slip some remark, just in passing, gentle and low. And that's when I'll spill the beans. Out of gratitude at his kindness. So they hope.

Sometimes he writes in a little notebook with a pencil. His pencil is miniature, with a gold top. I can see it has a point carved with a knife, not a point sharpened with a pencil sharpener. I can't understand people who sharpen their pencils with a penknife. It doesn't give a decent end. That was something Tillie taught me, when I was at the kitchen table with the little boys, drawing: never to put up with anything less than a *sharp point*. Tom heard her and sniggered. It was all information, but was it *good* information?

There *are* more groups than mine. Hanny just told me that in her group Rose had talked about giving birth to a baby and killing it on a rubbish dump. Moira was leading the group and sat forward on her chair, electrified, pressing her little tiptoes into the carpet. Hanny said this must be something that Moira hadn't heard from Rose before, something that wasn't *in the file*. Hanny said she would have thought Rose was making it up – we're always making stuff up – but for Moira's reaction. 'I reckon people are here for more reasons than they give out,' Hanny said. 'I reckon everyone's here for something really extreme.'

Rose usually sits next to me in Activity. I've never heard her speak a word. Only those little noises in the back of her throat. Squeaking, mouse-like noises. I'd like to hear *her* story.

20

Nuns

When we were eleven we had to take the test for grammar school. Naturally, I failed. So did most of my class. We weren't expected to pass, and we didn't expect to. They didn't train us for it at my school. They let us rely on luck, and native talent, and most of us didn't have either of those. We were the whatever-per-cent, the large but humble majority, who were seen as somehow not *up to it*. I don't understand how a thumping majority can possibly be thicker than average; even with my standard of maths, that doesn't add up. But we opened the envelope and went where we were told.

Isolde was already at the grammar and Barbara automatically assumed that she would go there too. She told me so. Tom was at the boys' equivalent. They had to catch a train to get there. Barbara liked the idea of getting a train every day. There was a Paynes Poppets machine on the station platform that sometimes spewed out your sixpence as well as the packet of sweets. It was Paynes Poppets and train travel that attracted her to the grammar, as much as any standard of education she might receive there.

But Barbara didn't get through to grammar school. I could quite see if she'd spent her whole time making leaf-prints and dodgy pastry that they wouldn't be interested in taking her, and I was glad. Now she would have to come to the secondary modern with me and find out what life was really like. That it doesn't always – or even often – deal you the hand you wished for.

And if she came to the secondary mod with me, I would have a ready-made friend. We could spend every day together and break-times would be a cinch.

'Oh no,' she said. 'I'm going to St Mary's. It's a convent school. We're taught by nuns.'

'Are you a Catholic?' I asked.

'I can be,' she said, shrugging airily.

My mother had a horror of Roman Catholicism. The thought of nuns teaching biddable children made her shudder visibly with repulsion. But then I always felt that she went too far with the things she found repellent, showing off about how sensitive she was: bacon fat, frogspawn, nuns, women in tight trousers, they all made her sputter and gag as if poison was being forced down her throat. Histrionics. I mean, I don't like spiders, but if I see one in the distance I don't make a point of going over and stamping on it. Live and let live, that's me.

But nuns and *Barbara*?

'I bet they make you wear uniform. *And* turn up on time.'

'We're going to buy the uniform tomorrow,' she said. She sounded almost smug.

Her uniform, when we saw it, was very ornate. Tom

and Isolde, whose school outfits were reasonably plain, looked askance.

'Why has your hat got a French revolutionary's rosette on it?' Tom asked, drily.

'Just don't ask me ever to walk down the road with you,' Isolde said, folding her arms and turning away, putting her seal on the matter.

I thought she looked ridiculous. Well, I wanted her to look ridiculous. This was the Barbara who had sneered at my ordinary brown check school dress and said that the Wren wouldn't *want* its pupils all looking the same. As if they had some wonderful essential difference that must at all costs be preserved. And now she was preserving that difference by getting togged up like a Parisian Communard. But I didn't dare say anything. You didn't criticize Barbara. Or, at least, *I* didn't criticize Barbara.

On Sundays here they have a church service. You don't have to attend, but I think a lot of people go for something to do. The singing is terrible, but I just sit back on my hard wooden chair and let the white light wash over me. The windows of the chapel aren't stained glass, they're *frosted* glass. Not quite the same. Very nonconformist. Very public lav. I don't bow my head in prayer or sing the hymns or anything, I just sit. It's terribly relaxing. I never thought of church as relaxing before.

Perhaps I'll find God again. Or He'll find me.

On Sundays at home we were always very busy. In the morning we went to the main service, Mum and Brian and I, and Dad if it was a particular date in the calendar, like Easter or Christmas or Whit Sunday or Harvest

Festival; and in the afternoon Brian and I were expected to go back again, to Sunday school. Most of the children who went didn't have to do both. Sunday school was for little kids who couldn't be trusted to keep quiet during the sermon. We could be trusted. I had a handbag, a special handbag just for church, white with a gold metal clasp. I had little white cotton gloves. I felt very visible, walking down the road. We had to clean our shoes on Saturday evening, in order to be ready for church the next day. Brian had to wear a jacket, a fuzzy greeny-brown jacket just like a man's. For year after year we received mind-improving books on prize-giving day, because our attendance was exemplary.

Then adolescence hit.

I began to feel resentful, about the little handbag, the prissy gloves, all the fuss about getting ready as if God could see us, as if God could spot the dirty fingernail, the unbrushed collar, as if God was petty enough to get enraged about such things. I began to chafe at the endless, endless hours sitting there, being exemplary children, perfect church-goers.

It was Barbara's shifty attitude to religion that first got under my skin, like a worm, writhing away and making me itch and twitch. A hideous disease-bearing African worm, the kind we heard about when missionaries came to talk to us about their far-flung duties. With colour slides.

If Barbara could be, at one and the same time, a little heathen who spent her Sundays running about barefoot in the garden, playing swingball and It and tennis when God-fearing folk were in church, and yet be counted as religious enough to be taught by nuns, what was the meaning of it all? Some people seemed to be able to have it both ways, when it suited them. I just didn't understand. I began to wonder how *I* could have it both ways, how *I* could wriggle out of my obligations without paying a price.

'Patrick's a Catholic,' Barbara told me, 'and Catholics have to swear when they get married that they will raise their children to be good Catholics as well.'

'What about Tillie?' I asked. 'What's she?'

'Oh, Tillie's a Protestant. Dutch people are.'

'I mean, what if she doesn't want you to be brought up a good Catholic?' I had in mind my mother, shuddering at nuns. What if my father had been a Catholic? How would she have managed?

Barbara shrugged.

'And what about all the others, Tom and Eugene and everyone? Are they good Catholics? If they are, it doesn't show.'

Barbara thought about this, rolling her tongue over her exposed teeth like a horse. 'They are, but underneath. I'm the visible representative.'

'What, like – you're Jesus and they're the Holy Ghost?'

I had her there. Barbara, having spent all her Sundays playing poker and tennis, had no theology whatsoever.

So I went off to my new school, and Barbara went off to hers, braided and beribboned and decorated like a soldier in a particularly heroic army.

She made a friend there. She hadn't had a particular friend at the Wren, she'd said they were all too stupid or deranged to warrant her attention. I saw her walking back with this girl. They climbed down off the bus at the same place, and I saw them walking along with that slow walk which means you have more to say to each other than will fit into the space before you have to go your separate ways. I felt a stab of jealousy, quite unlike anything I'd felt before. It wasn't the dull ache that came when the girls at junior school cold-shouldered me. The two of them stood on the corner talking for a few minutes, then pulled away, and both began walking more quickly in different directions. I didn't know whether to catch her up or not. I trailed behind her like a spy, slowing my pace, ducking into the shadow of the hedge, holding my breath when she turned her head to glance both ways before crossing the road.

'Caro, what the hell are you doing? Get over here!'

Her voice was peremptory. She must have glimpsed me out of the corner of her eye. I stood up straight and walked towards her, my breath catching stickily somewhere in my ribs. When I got within reach she grabbed my arm, hard, and pulled me towards her.

'Come on, you idiot. Stop avoiding me. I want to know everything about your stupid day. Don't leave anything out.'

So I thought perhaps this new friend wasn't so important. I thought perhaps it would be all right.

'Secondary school now, eh?' my aunt Gloria said to me, on the first Sunday after term began. 'Very grown-up.'

I replied with just a painful grin, all stretched lips and no teeth.

'Bet they work you hard there?'

Well, no, actually. Not as you'd notice. Not yet awhile, anyway.

'No orange squash for Carol,' Gloria said to Stella,

who'd just come into the room and hadn't a clue what this badinage was about, or even that it was badinage. 'Too much the young lady these days. A nice cup of tea for Carol. Or would you rather have *coffee?'*

Stella mugged me a look. I mugged back. I think it was the first time we had ever exchanged any real form of communication.

'Didn't call it a secondary modern in my day,' said Gloria.

'Holloway Prison, more like,' Stella muttered.

'East End Lane School was its actual name,' Gloria told her, 'as well you know. You were three forms behind me.'

My mother sat quietly through all this. She wasn't an expert on education. I guess she had gone to some other school, some even more hopeless country school where everyone sat squashed into the same room and did their dismal best. She didn't mention where.

'And how're you getting on at school?' Gloria would ask, every so often. I felt she did this for form's sake. I guessed she wanted a multiple-choice answer: (a) very well, thanks, (b) fine, thanks, (c) not too bad, thanks very much for asking. I guessed she wasn't enquiring about the curriculum, or the school's approach to discipline, or hoping to delve into my exercise books.

And at home it was 'Have you started your homework yet?' and 'Have you *finished* your homework yet?', with regular inspections through the serving hatch between the kitchen and the dining table. I spread out my books. I sharpened my pencils. I must have had the sharpest pencils in the school. If there had been a prize for that I would have got it, year after year. I scratched my scalp with my sharply pointed pencils and wondered about the effects of graphite in the brain. And then the hatch doors would snap open and my mother's face would appear, breaking off from the washing-up. 'Carol!' The only way she knew how to enquire about school was to monitor the homework production line. But if I said I'd done it, and slapped my book firmly shut, she would nod and pull the hatch doors closed, and in a minute or two emerge, without her apron, and switch on the wireless and sit down to knit. And if I said I was off out to Mildred Clark's (Mildred Clark's!), to work on a joint history project, she would nod grimly, as if this was only proper, and add, 'Don't be late back.'

'We have to get it finished. It's due in tomorrow. Mildred's mother says she'll give me a lift home.'

I enjoyed the odd rococo lie. It was naughty, really. I relied on the arcane mysteries of the educational system to keep her in thrall. Maybe I wanted her to say, 'Hang on a minute, Carol.' I waved my lies aloft, like the red rag to the bull, but without success. The bull was disappointingly docile. It stood in the far corner of the field and turned its little, stupid eye away.

One good thing about secondary school: suddenly I was allowed to venture much further afield. My mother no longer bothered to throw a limit around the neighbourhood. Out of sight, I was out of mind. Once you could get on a bus unsupervised you could conquer the world, and there wasn't anything anyone could do to stop you.

Because the convent school was out of town, Barbara had to get a special bus to it. The rest of us used ordinary public transport. I would see the convent girls, in their sky-blue and navy and brassy gold braid, waiting in groups at special corners. There were no proper bus stops for them, just appointed places that they, and the bus drivers, knew about. It felt like a coded world, a world that excluded me.

'I can't play right now, I've got prep,' the new, serious Barbara said to me, when I called round. 'Don't you have prep? We have an hour each evening, minimum.' Well, I had *homework*, but it was rather patchy, and my teachers said they were going to let us take it easy at first. Break us in gently. Ten minutes to start with, maybe fifteen. Working up to as much as half an hour. They let us take it easy for a long time. I don't think they relished marking books at my school.

'I must change out of my tunic first,' she said, another time, standing at the top of their steps, while I straddled my bike on the path below. Her tie was still firmly knotted, her cuffs buttoned and clean. Could this be Barbara, who never even knew what she had on, who turned cartwheels in dresses, displaying her knickers, who stuck her hands right through the torn pockets of her shorts and waved them at me to make me laugh?

'We do Latin. Do you do Latin yet?' she asked, in a tone of voice that made me think she already knew the secondary mod drew the line at Latin.

I began to wonder if it was worth even trying to stay friends. But after a few weeks she got bored, and the old Barbara reasserted itself.

'Bloody nuns!' she said, running down the road to catch up with me, taking my upper arm in her hard, pinching fingers.

The nuns apparently had men's names, names they took on when they entered holy orders: Sister Ignatius,

Sister Benedict, Mother Francis-Xavier. 'Bad enough *looking* like blokes with no make-up and all bald under those veils, without calling yourself after blokes as well,' said Barbara.

And 'They're obsessed with sex. If we had absolutely no interest in boys they would put it into our minds, because they're always – but *always* – going on about how to protect yourself from boys, and what boys are after, and how we mustn't get led astray. They want us to be constantly alert as to the dangers of impure thoughts, but I bet we wouldn't have half so many if they didn't remind us about it so frequently.'

And 'Every week they make us bring in money for *the little black babies in Africa*. They write down everything you bring in a notebook, so it's not anonymous. It means you always have to bring something, and they know exactly who's brought the most, and they announce who it is.'

'But that's blackmail!' I said. I thought of my mother, who always gave me sixpence for the Sunday school collection. Never less, but never more.

'*I* don't think they send it to their missions abroad,' Barbara went on, lifting her lip. 'I think they keep it for themselves, and spend it on lipstick and high heels and booze!' And she went off into peals of laughter. But I was concerned.

'Do your mother and father realize what the school is like?' I asked.

Barbara just shrugged hugely and said, 'Oh, *them* . . .'

'You should tell them,' I advised. I thought that Tillie would write a letter, Patrick would charge up to the school, coat-tails flying, voice booming, surely? They

171

weren't like my parents, they wouldn't worry about interfering. To them, education wasn't something you took lying down. They would act first and then think about the consequences. I could imagine them – Tillie at a table in the sunshine, head bent, composing her letter on a big sheet of creamy cartridge paper, hitting just the right balance of politeness and persuasion; or Patrick, big and jolly, banging his fist on Mother Francis-Xavier's desk and saying, 'It's not good enough for my girl!', but with a nun-seducing twinkle in his eye. Diplomacy and dramatics: Barbara had both of these at her disposal.

But she didn't want my advice. She never wanted my advice. That wasn't the point. She wasn't even listening. 'I can see them all now, in the staffroom,' she went on, 'with their veils flicked back and their skirts drawn up, *red* mesh stockings and black patent stiletto heels, knocking back the whisky. 'Another wee drop, Sister Benedict?' 'Don't mind if I do, Sister Ignatius.' Glug glug. 'Sister Iggie, be a darling, give us a whiff of that latest perfume from Chanel!' And she leaned on my shoulder, weak with laughing. 'Oh God, just imagine it, I'm sentenced to stay there for another five years at least. I shall get expelled for insubordination. Just see if I don't.'

But she didn't.

Maybe if she had, maybe if it had been threatened, that's when Tillie or Patrick, or both of them, arm in arm, would have marched on the school, protesting her innocence. Standing up for their daughter. Like parents should.

What does Lorna want with me?

My head on a platter?

That's the way it feels, at times. That she has some deeply personal grievance against me, which she almost completely and cunningly hides. But not quite. It's as if she lets me see the tip of her annoyance, her anger, just enough to make me feel threatened. And then she hides it again. But why? I truly don't know what it is she's after. And her questions don't help. We cover a wide variety of topics, which she invites me to discuss. We go all round the houses, round and round, around one house in particular.

Sometimes I just want to jump up and shout: 'Say it! Say it! Just ask me directly and I'll tell you.' Just to get her off my back.

But will I?

21

Marriage

Bettina was getting married.

I couldn't think how it had happened. She hadn't put any effort into it, like Stella did. She had continued to come to our house with Mandy every Saturday afternoon, and to work in the hairdresser's all week. But suddenly she was marrying someone, a man called Roy Tiltyard. However had she found the time to meet him?

Our social pattern was disrupted. Mandy might be delivered on a Saturday, but was left abruptly, with a sharp kiss and a quick wave from her mother. Or she might not. Just as well. I didn't like her hanging around, scenting out my secrets. I didn't want to give her any extended opportunity to spill the beans. Though she never did tell. Not then, anyway. I don't know why. Mandy was super-devious. She was saving it up for the right moment, the one perfect moment for revelation, which she knew must come, if she bided her time.

Gloria took to visiting more often, sitting over the teacups with my mother. They said they were planning for the wedding, but it sounded like simple gossip to me.

'I suppose they'll be bridesmaids,' my mother said, nodding to where Mandy and I were putting together a five-hundred-piece jigsaw puzzle of 'The Hay Wain'. Please, God, no, I prayed; two years before and I'd have loved to be a bridesmaid. Not any longer.

Gloria pursed her mouth. 'Registry office,' she said, in a confidential tone.

'Oh yes. Of course . . .' My mother sounded dis-appointed. 'Does he have any family?' she asked, after another cup of tea was poured.

'She's not said much,' Gloria answered. 'But I know someone whose nose will be put out of joint,' she said, raising her eyebrows.

I could think of several people. My mother, for a start, believed that registry office marriages were as good as living in sin. It had to be church, under the eyes of God, for it to count. And then Stella: she was older than Bettina, she had put in so much spadework, with Dimitri, and Gerald, and Wally, had got them almost to the brink, but never quite over the edge into wedlock. It was humiliating, for a professional like her to be pipped at the post by a mere amateur like Bettina.

Wed*lock*. What a word. Like armlock. Or hemlock.

But Gloria was nodding in our direction. She tilted an eyebrow at us, and my mother turned ever so slightly and looked over her shoulder. At Mandy.

So it was Mandy's nose that would be put out of joint. Mandy's tiny white freckly nose. Her chocolate-seeking, secret-snuffling nose. She would no longer be the centre of attention.

'Will she stay on at Charisse?' My mother was the only

one who ever called the hairdresser's shop by that name. The rest of the family referred to it as 'Maureen's'.

'Who knows? She's an independent girl, I'll give her that.'

'Where will they live?'

'He's got a place out at Bossey Down,' said Gloria. 'Or is that his auntie?' she added vaguely.

Roy Tiltyard. We hadn't seen him yet. 'Haven't *laid eyes* on him,' as Gloria said, sucking in her cheeks. I gave a lot of thought to his name. A tiltyard, I fancied, was something to do with jousting. It was amazing that, in the centuries since jousts had been discontinued, the name hadn't been corrupted, worn away to something easier to pronounce. But maybe Roy's ancestors had been proud of the medieval connection, and kept reminding everyone to enunciate that second T.

'Will she be Mandy Tiltyard,' I asked Gloria, when we were round at their house in Beet Street one Sunday for tea, 'after the wedding?'

Gloria hadn't given this any thought – I could see it in her face. She stopped to think about it now. 'If he adopts her,' she said slowly, 'then she'll take his name. But she might stay as she is now.'

My mother came into the room, returning from the bathroom at the back of the house. Gloria coughed a bit and stirred her tea.

'What – Mandy Burton?' I asked, and suddenly realized that she shouldn't be called that. Bettina Burton, Mandy Burton. It didn't fit the facts, as I knew them. Or maybe I didn't know them.

But Gloria, lifting the lid and peering into the teapot, was more concerned at squeezing out a second cup of tea. 'Another cup, Edie?'

'I could do with one.'

'I'll just go and top up the pot.' She hurried out.

My mother turned to me. 'I hope you haven't been annoying your aunt Gloria,' she said. 'You children, you're always the same.'

I took the conundrum to Barbara. She seemed to have a natural grasp of such things. She said it was because she watched television. 'You can learn a lot from *The Wednesday Play*, you know.' We didn't have a television set, my mother wouldn't allow it. We listened to the wireless, which she kept tuned to the light music programme. Orchestras playing string arrangements of popular tunes. You didn't learn a lot from the wireless.

'If a person has the same surname as all the rest of her family, and her child does too, and she's a woman . . .' I could see Barbara getting impatient at this point, signalling acute boredom by rolling her eyes upwards so that the whites showed, so I hurried on: 'What does that mean? Is she married, or what?'

'Maybe.' Barbara shrugged one shoulder, lightly. 'If she married a man with the same name. A cousin or something. Cousins can marry.'

'What if she didn't? Could she keep her own name? And would the child automatically get her name, or its father's?'

'The father's.' She was firm about this.

'So if it has *her* name?'

'Illegitimate,' pronounced Barbara. 'Like Philip.'

'Who's Philip?'

'At *piano*,' she said, as if I was thick. 'Gwynne Wallis is Mrs Wallis's unmarried daughter, and Philip Wallis is her little boy. The *illegitimate* little boy. The little *bastard*.' She enunciated all these words clearly, so that even I could understand.

But I wasn't interested in the skeletons in Mrs Wallis's family cupboard, only in my own. Well, I thought, perhaps that explained the pitying looks, all the chocolate bars and baby dolls that flowed Mandy's way like iron filings towards a magnet.

'If the mother was married, the child would have its father's name.' Barbara held her hands out like two equally balanced weighing scales. 'If not, no wedding bells.' She dropped her hands to her sides.

'Crumbs,' I said. 'So Mandy's a little bastard.'

Sometimes I'd watch TV with Barbara. I wasn't terribly interested in television – 'What you don't have, you won't miss,' said my mother, and in this case it was true – but Barbara was, so if there was a programme that needed her attention while I was there, I went with her.

Patrick wouldn't have the television downstairs, said, 'Jesus God, it interferes with the brain cells. I'll not have the whole family sitting round the front room like morons, like you see through people's windows, mooning at the thing.' So it was in Tillie and Patrick's bedroom, whose brain cells were somehow all right, protected. You had to go in there and sit on the bed, resting up against the pillows they had slept on. Their room was small – though not compared to my parents' bedroom, or Gloria's and Eddy's which was even pokier – but small compared to other rooms in the Hennessy house. It was made smaller by the built-in cupboards, which Barbara said were there when they moved in and which her parents had always meant to get rid of, but never had.

Interior decoration was not really their strong suit. The cupboards, dirty white, with finger marks, ran across the party wall, clasping the bedhead in a series of intricate shelves and drawers and little side tables. There was even a wall lamp for each occupant of the bed, drooping over their heads like glass lilies-of-the-valley; they reminded me of the hair-dryers in Charisse.

On the wall by the door, above and below the light switch, were two paintings. A little one of Tillie, just head and shoulders. The painter had made her face too long and her expression bleak, and it looked as though she wore a halo. It wasn't very flattering. The other picture was larger, a multicoloured mess, random shapes in muddy reds and purples and browns. The initials, in thick black at the bottom right-hand corner, were A.L.L. An example of the Wren school of painting, I thought. But 'Our friend Arthur painted it,' Barbara told me one day, with a shrug. 'It's worth more than anything else in the house.' I didn't know what anything else in the house was worth, but it sounded impressive. If forced to choose between it and the print of the puppy and kitten on my bedroom wall, I'd be hard pressed to know what to say. *No thanks*, probably.

There were more cupboards on the other side of the room, with an alcove for the dressing table. This was where the TV stood, a small square set with a V-shaped aerial. It sat in front of Tillie's three-panelled mirror, so that we had the weird experience of seeing ourselves, from three different angles, watching. The watchers watched. Most peculiar. Barbara didn't seem to notice, but I spent as much time looking at our slumped bodies and engrossed expressions, the way our hair curled behind our ears, the way our shoulders rounded, as I did at the programmes I was there to see.

Anyway, being at the heart of the Hennessy stronghold was weird enough for me. I could barely follow the plot of Barbara's favourite hospital series or the urgent dramas of people in pubs, or laugh at comedians in bow ties, when two inches from the screen was something as intimate as Tillie's jewellery box, open and spilling where someone had been rifling through it. An eclectic mixture: pearls, plastic pop-it beads, tarnished silver bangles, tortoiseshell hair combs. And the brooch, just like a hawthorn leaf pressed out of copper, which Barbara had used that time, instead of a knife, to split our palms. To seal our blood brotherhood, our friendship. Perhaps it was Barbara who had been rummaging through. Tillie never wore jewellery, as far as I could see. There were glittering dustballs mixed up with the beads and glass, and the velvet shelves of the box were as bloomy as old grapes. I familiarized myself with everything else scattered over the dressing table: an enamel-backed hairbrush and a pink plastic hairbrush, a pot of face cream, a packet of Aspro, a pencil and a boiled sweet wrapper and some tweezers and the handle off one of the kitchen cupboards. I've always been hungry for detail; I've always thought there must be things to learn from picking over details. The saga of Tillie's bedroom was far more compelling to me than the saga of black-stockinged television nurses and their handsome, uncooperative doctors.

There was something I was keen to know – at night, who slept on which side? I didn't dare ask; they'd definitely notice the spooky degree of my interest if I said something like that out loud. The smell of paint and linseed oil and discarded clothes and something else permeated the room, permeated the bed so that I couldn't tell if where I sat was where Tillie rested her head, or Patrick his. It was desperately intimate. Here you could breathe in essence-of-Hennessy. Here it was almost too much.

Sometimes when we went in the little boys were already there, nestled down in the bed covers, watching a cartoon. Or Tillie would settle in with us, just as the smoky roofs of *Coronation Street* came up on the screen, and say, 'What a horrible place to have to live!' Sometimes Isolde consented to watch, though she insisted on perching on the dressing-table stool and never joined us on the bed.

And sometimes Tom came in, too, and portioned out his lengthy frame on the bedspread between us, just to annoy. 'Get your great feet out of the way!' shrieked Barbara, thumping him. 'I can't see the bloody screen.'

I wasn't so comfortable when Tom was there. His presence was distracting. He made the bed-springs leap up and down when he moved, his elbows stuck in me. I looked at his pale face sunk in sceptical torpor as he watched the screen. I watched him in the mirror, from three different angles. Once I caught his eye, in the big mirror panel, looking back at mine. Something inside me shivered. I didn't know if the feeling was horrible, or nice.

'Where did Bettina meet this Roy Tiltyard?' my mother asked.

'She did his auntie's hair,' said Gloria.

We were eating Battenberg cake at their dining table. Stella never seemed to be there these days.

'Stella's a bit *put out*,' Gloria told us, in an over-enunciated whisper, then went on: 'His auntie had been in hospital for a big op, and was convalescing at home, and she wanted someone to come out and do her hair, to cheer her up. That's how they met.'

I thought it wasn't a complete explanation. They hadn't moved Bettina and Roy Tiltyard into connecting squares, like on a chessboard. Was he the one who had actually hired Bettina for the hairdo, or did he just happen to be visiting the house when she called? And how was the interest kindled, and who made the first move? There were too many gaps in adult conversation; they left the vital bits out. You had to guess the connections, spin the spider webs between.

The wedding was to be in November. 'Depressing time of the year,' Gloria reported Stella as saying.

My mother made me a Black Watch tartan dress to wear, but we had to go into town to find black patent shoes to go with it. Smart coats were also a problem. We made do with brushing ours a lot, and Mum sent hers to the cleaner's. I remember going with her to fetch it. We had my new shoes in a carrier bag: they hadn't offered the shoebox this time. When they did we always said yes, because Brian liked to use them for making into garages and aircraft hangars. We stood in the chemical air of the dry cleaner's and the girl behind the counter rummaged for Mum's coat in a whole rail of coats on metal hangers, with yellow tickets safety-pinned to the lapels. We stood looking on – we could have told her it was the grey one, but somehow the etiquette of the place demanded that you didn't. It might seem like you were choosing a better one than your own, and laying false claim to it. Anyway, there was the ticket. No doubt the girl – not too quick on the uptake – would find the right one, given time.

I had no sense of premonition as I stood there, breathing in the dry-cleaning fumes. I didn't foresee my future, interchangeable with that of the girl behind the counter, the glum-looking, slow-off-the-mark girl. But then I never seem to have a clue what's in store for me.

Roy Tiltyard turned out to be a short man with absolutely no chin. 'Weedy little thing, isn't he?' was Stella's verdict, as she watched him from the sidelines. Her voice was tinged with knowledge, like a trainer sizing up rival horseflesh. But he was a man, and he was marrying Bettina, so all in all I think the family felt she'd got a good deal. By November Bettina was terribly plump, pinkly plump, and her hair full of electricity. She wore a whitish suit, ivory they called it, and a perky little hat with a net veil, and a spray of apricot carnations on her sizeable breast. In her high heels she was about four inches taller than the groom. I kept thinking about what I'd learned from all those novels, and how on their wedding night she would overlap and overflow his skimpy form. How she could, easily, quite overpower him. He looked pretty cheerful, despite this. I imagined her casting off her wedding hat, kicking off her high heels, and splitting the zip at the back of her skirt in her eagerness, while he lay on the bed in his wedding suit, his lower lip disappearing into his neck, smiling a nervous smile. I know I've read far too many unsuitable books, but it was difficult to get from *here* – stilted speeches and laughter in the back room of the Bull and Garland pub, my mother drinking bitter lemon with a lemon-puckered expression on her face because she didn't hold with public houses – to *there*, a riotous consummation in a hotel room up the coast, in only a few hours' time, while the rest of us were drinking our bedtime hot chocolate and examining the sore places on our feet where our new shoes had rubbed.

I found it the hardest thing to imagine, how people got on in private. How they really got on.

Mandy wore shocking pink. It clashed with her hair.

In the back room at the Bull and Garland pub, a place of quite unfamiliar smells and sensations, I watched my relatives and Roy Tiltyard's relatives. It wasn't often that an opportunity like this came my way. I made full use of my powers of observation. Ladies with fat bottoms (the Tiltyard side) capered in the middle of the room, doing some version of a country dance, arm in arm and round and round, to Lonnie Donegan on the jukebox. I wondered which one was Roy's auntie, so recently under the knife. They all looked in the rudest health. Their tight skirts, in electric blue and sugar pink, wrinkled spectacularly over their thighs. I thought I could hear the creak of their girdles above the music. Whereas my side of the family sat primly behind the small round tables, knees together, holding up their glasses as if about to make a toast. They looked as if enjoyment did not come naturally to them. Stella was subdued. The men (both sides) stood in huddles near the bar, or near to the door marked 'Toilets'. My father was letting his half of light ale go a long way. He wasn't, as my mother said, 'a drinker'. Nor was he likely to be, under her eagle eye.

I leaned my head towards Gloria and said, under cover of the music, 'What happened to Mandy's father?' Gloria was the one person you might ask, she had a taste for gossip, and whatever was in her glass was beginning to make her go loose-featured and giggly.

'Mandy's father? Oh, he was killed in a motorcycle accident, years ago.'

So he had actually existed. Bettina had not produced Mandy in isolation, like some self-pollinating flower, or a greenfly giving birth to replica female greenflies. 'Eleven years ago!' she said, and went off into a spasm of laughter, her shoulders shaking. I couldn't see what was funny about this. Mandy was eleven, almost.

'He always went too fast on that awful motorbike,' Gloria continued. 'Sometimes she rode pillion. Used to give her poor mother the willies.' So Bettina had a mother at one time, too. 'After he got killed, she used to refer to him as her fiancé. I can't blame her, it sounds better, doesn't it? Anyway, there she was, in the club. Never trust men on motorcycles.' And she burst into laughter again. I wondered if she meant a motorcycle club, which was no good if you didn't have a motorcycle to ride on any more.

They have a patients' lounge here which we are supposed to use for 'socializing'. Now there's a word. What image does it conjure up? Little groups in vibrant conversation, the clink of bone-china cups. Even – at a pinch – something fun and genteel, like a tea dance, or early evening cocktails. Greetings trilled across the room, a white hand waving and beckoning over the crowd. A gin-sling for me, please, darling! Another rum punch over here! Perhaps that's just the sort of thing that went on in this big, elegant room once upon a time, before the whole place was transformed.

The lounge is ringed with Scandinavian-modern chairs upholstered in bobbly tweed. To feel comfortable in one of these chairs you would need to be about seven foot tall, with no back problems and preferably no head, for the backrest reaches no higher than the shoulder blades. You would want abnormally long arms, but plump ones too, for the bare wooden armrests are hard on elbow and wrist bones. The chair cushions come in four colours: burnt orange, sludge green, brown and beige. Blue is still my favourite colour, I'm afraid, so no luck here. There are about twenty of these armchairs, plus some plastic stacker chairs placed around the walls. In the centre of the room is a circular coffee table which no one ever puts anything on. Not even coffee.

There are no seven-foot-tall inmates with bloated arms. Only the usual happy crowd. I'd rather stay in my room, but they don't like it. They like you to come in here and *socialize*. I look around for Hanny, but she isn't here. She's never here. Perhaps she's got some activity or session or something on at this time of day. Perhaps there's a non-eaters' group which she has to attend. I don't know. She's never said.

I choose an orange chair and slide into it. There's no choice but to slide, to slump, in these things. My mother would be horrified. And almost everyone fiddles with the upholstery, their fingers twitching along the arms searching for extra-large bobbles or loose threads to pull at. They're great ones for fiddling, twisting, turning, rubbing, scratching, scraping, here. I glance about and recognize Rose, and Marsupial, and the Young Crone. I recognize others, too, but they haven't got names. I can't be bothered to give them all names. Nobody ever introduces you, yet they'd really rather like it if we socialized.

And here comes Mike, wheeling in the television. It's a big old-fashioned set in a wooden case, perched on top of a trolley, wheeled in and then wheeled out again. There are only certain programmes we're allowed to watch, at certain times. Nature programmes, and some regional thing about country crafts and willow warblers and restored water mills. Nice safe stuff, so they think. But have they ever watched these wildlife programmes? Don't they realize the precise *nature* of these fluffy creatures in their attractive rural settings? It certainly is a jungle out there, with big beasts jumping on smaller ones, the swift dragging down the slow, the halt, the lame, even – and especially – the cute little baby ones. Another poor wildebeest bites the dust. There always has to be someone at the back of the herd, one whose unlucky day it is. A family of lions chew under the stripy haunch of a zebra. Its leg bounces gamely in the savannah wind, almost as if it were still alive and kicking. Perhaps it is.

Mike has left the room. Mike has popped out. Doesn't he know what's going on in here, what murder and mayhem? Nature red in tooth and claw, vividly imaginable even on black-and-white telly.

The woman in the chair next to me is rocking back and forth. Her strawy hair hangs over her face. I keep catching sight of her out of the corner of my eye. The TV switches its attention to small venomous things, things which dart and dive and shoot and spring twenty times their own length, catapulting out extravagant tongues, injecting and hauling and engulfing their victims in lethal webs, turning the internal organs of their prey to liquid before slowly ingesting them. Good grief. The woman next to me has begun to make a noise, a low, rhythmic, keening noise. Whether it's to do with what's happening on the screen or what's happening inside her head is impossible to know. No one else seems to notice. They go on picking at the bobbly tweed of their seat cushions, examining their hands, gazing blankly at the television. Marsupial lets out one of her huge impatient sighs.

Then it happens. My neighbour shrieks. You might almost think it is a macaw or a monkey, some background noise to the jungle warfare going on in front of our eyes, except for the volume. And how long it goes on for. She doesn't stop. She's grabbing the arms of her chair and swinging her body back and forth wildly, and screaming, *screaming*, at the top of her voice.

Mike pops back in.

Mike pops back in, looking like he's been shot, and dashes out again to summon help. Two assistants in white nylon – not the would-be friendly, civvies-clad likes of Moira or Trudy, this is the heavy mob – dive into position on either side of her chair, and the blonde woman is lifted bodily in the air. She shrieks again. The brief silence, the cessation between one scream and the next, is as ear-piercing as the noise itself. I slither round like an eel out of my chair and out of the way. I certainly don't want to be caught up in any of this. What on earth is she up to? Making an exhibition of herself! And us.

She flings herself sideways, out of their grasp, and as she hits the floor she starts banging her head, lifting it and banging it back down on the green carpet, as if her neck is a stalk and her head's a flower bobbing about in the breeze. But one of the assistants is kneeling astride her now and the other one gets her head, and between them they hold her still, and then something – *something* – happens. She goes limp. Mike hovers above them. They pick her up and carry her gently, like a sleeping baby, out of the room. Mike follows. Nobody else is looking. Everyone has turned their gaze aside, as if something unfortunate has taken place, and they are being polite enough not to notice. Some of them are looking at the television screen, where a coiffed blonde woman is smiling with all her many teeth and holding up a tube of Colgate toothpaste.

It was just as if she had been shot with the venomous dart of a jungle insect, shot and rendered insensible almost before she knew it. I creep back to my chair. The lounge is very still, preternaturally still, just like the jungle in the moments after a kill.

22

Sleeping Out

I'm almost fond of my room here. From up here on a fine day I can see endless blue, trackless wastes. My window looks over the back of the house and beyond the gardens to fields and woods. The view is prettier than any I've had before. I imagine it's the kind of view a Carolyn would have from her bedroom window. The fields are proper green, not bitten brown, and the woods are real woods – mixed deciduous, as they put it in geography lessons – with leafy trees in all different shapes and sizes. The hills are proper hills. In the evenings, out there is where the first star appears, before the sky has even lost its light. Sometimes, I lean on the window sill and – ignoring the room behind me which really doesn't fit the bill – I pretend I am Carolyn, just looking out, just gazing out on her garden and the countryside that surrounds her pretty house, and that in a minute or two I will go downstairs to supper with my lovely family.

I'm not bored here. Not really. I've always been used to waiting around for things to happen, things that don't usually bother to happen, anyway, in the end. I wonder if that's what they mean by *low expectations*. I've not had that much history, and mostly I've been the person drifting round the edges of the picture, looking on, not the one in the middle, doing whatever it is that the picture's about. And I've lost the first five years of my life, and there's a few months recently I've chosen to lose. Perhaps it is *all* entirely voluntary. I think that's what Lorna believes, and that's why she feels that if I wanted to I could rattle it out like dice from a shaker. My mother, the children's home, being adopted. The recent stuff, too. Rattle it out and see what comes up.

I can't imagine how Barbara would survive in here. With her, boredom is almost a disease, certainly a condition bordering on the chronic. She'd go stir-crazy by the end of the first day. They would have to use all those marvellous methods they try to keep in reserve, syringes and restraints, that kind of thing. What I witnessed in the patients' lounge. And you see it happening, sometimes, at the end of a corridor, or through an open bedroom door. We're always hustled away, hurried past, but I've got a good idea of what goes on. What goes on with poor deranged creatures like Rose, or the woman with blonde hair who wrings her hands. They'd have something up their sleeve for the likes of Barbara.

I would rather not go down to the patients' lounge any more. I would be quite happy to stay here and just watch the sky for hours; which, of course, is not approved of. But it's a bloody sight better than having to mix with loonies.

In a torpid spell of hot weather one July, Barbara and I hatched a plan. We were what – eleven? Twelve?

I worked it all out in advance. I said to my mother, 'I've been asked to stay over at a friend's house. To sleep the night. Suzannah Grey's.'

'Oh yes?' For once she sounded sceptical. 'Where does she live?'

Brian gave me a look, and I looked blandly back. 'Fairwith Avenue.' I named a road I knew would impress. I'd done my research.

'What number?'

'Fifteen. It has a white door.'

'A *white* door?'

'A white front door.'

Unfortunately she consulted with my father. This was a new development, conferring about my welfare. 'Dad will pick you up tomorrow morning. At nine o'clock. You don't want to *impose* on people.'

So after tea I took my overnight things in a duffel bag and set out, walking steadily as far as the roundabout, then taking the road out of town, past the café, doubling back through the rough ground beyond the houses and ending up in the pony's field that adjoined the Hennessys' back garden. Barbara was standing by the fence, watching Mattie feed the pony and the donkey with carrot tops.

'What took you so long?'

'Deceiving my elders.'

The plan was to sleep out on the veranda. Barbara said they'd often done it, when the weather was hot. She was always surprising me with things like that, things I was no part of, had no inkling about. I'd be feeling fine and dandy, in the swing of things, and then – wham! – by the way, here's something you didn't know, Carol, what fun we had when you weren't here. I could never make up my mind whether she kept such things from me deliberately, or whether she just forgot to mention them. God knows, there's plenty of information that people choose to keep to themselves. Just think of my family. Think of me.

On the Hennessys' veranda they had an old swing-chair with faded canvas cushions. I perched on it, my legs dangling, and watched while Barbara dragged a camp bed and a mattress across the boards. Down the garden I could see Tom unhooking the hammock. Tillie had bought it earlier that summer and hung it between the stoutest pair of apple trees. He carried it towards us over the lawn and tied it up to two of the veranda posts.

'Where's Tom Rose?' Barbara asked.

Tom shrugged. 'Gone home.'

'Good. We don't want him as well.'

'I'm having the hammock,' Tom said. 'Hands off. Touch it at your peril.'

I hadn't known that Tom was in the plan. I had thought it was just Barbara and me. Possibly Isolde, if she felt like it; maybe the little boys, too, if their mother said yes, and if they didn't drive Barbara mad with their whispering and noises. But in the end it turned out to be just Barbara and Tom and me.

Barbara went indoors for supplies, and came back with honey sandwiches, a KitKat and two hard green apples, which we added to the chewing gum and cupcakes stolen from the kitchen cupboard that I had brought. We sat on the boards of the veranda with our bare legs stretched out, feeling the daytime's heat coming up out of the wood, and talking in low voices.

The little boys and Tom and Patrick had gone far away down the lawn, playing some wild game that involved cricket bats and screaming and not too much else. I thought of my parents, beyond the hedge. They were probably indoors. My mother disliked the gnats that hung in clouds in the summer air. Perhaps they had the wireless on. Perhaps one of them leaned forward and pointedly turned up the volume, and gave the other a look that spoke volumes, too.

Then the boards creaked as Tillie walked down the steps and over the dimming grass, clapping her hands and calling for the boys to come in. But she must have given up trying, or got sucked into the game, for we heard her shrieks added to theirs.

'You can sleep on the swing-seat,' Barbara said, which I thought was very generous of her until I discovered just how hard the cushions were, sloping at an angle that made you roll towards the back. She set about making her camp bed into a comfortable nest. Tillie came back to the house, followed by the little boys. We could hear their feet going upstairs, doors opening and closing, pipes thumping, cisterns flushing, dishes and cutlery clashing in the kitchen as Tillie washed up. The garden was getting darker with a kind of floating dusk. The smell of cigarette smoke drifted round to us, and Tillie and her mother's voices talking quietly, in Dutch, I supposed, because I couldn't understand it. Barbara sat on her camp bed, pummelling her pillow. 'Something's biting me,' she complained.

I had so looked forward to this. I had looked forward to the long luxurious hours of being at their house, of being able to laugh and to talk – endlessly – what about

I didn't know, but I knew it would end up being about something important. Countless hours given up to conversation would have to lead to that. In the past, I'd always had to go back home, long before I wanted to. I had never stayed overnight with a friend before. I had never slept outside.

Then Tom came bounding up, shaking the boards of the veranda. The smell of sweat came off him. The smell of hot flesh, of rolled-on grass. 'Aha! The trusty hammock,' he said. He climbed in, fell out, swore, tied it up tighter. He stamped off, came back with a bottle of water, half of which he drank, then poured the remaining half noisily over his head. Splashes of it fell on us.

'What have you got, then?' He crouched down, inspecting our supplies, which Barbara had put into a biscuit tin and pushed under her camp bed. 'They're ours,' she said. 'Get off them!'

He picked up a cupcake.

'Get your own,' Barbara told him.

He opened his mouth and pushed half of it in, then seeing we were still watching, he slowly pushed the rest in with a delicate forefinger. His lips closed over the cake. When he opened them again on a smile made entirely of crumbs and icing, Barbara screamed.

I was afraid that this was how it would be. Tom showing off boys' tricks, bullying us just with the force of his presence, not allowing us to have those long hours of private conversation. But then Tillie came out. She walked round the side of the house carefully on bare feet, carrying a tray of little cakes. 'Oma made these, for the campers-out.' (Oma was not her Christian name but what Dutch children called their grandmas, I had found out. I

still avoided her. Too fat, too strange. Too wildly loving.)
Tillie set the tray down carefully on the boards, then
crouched down too, placing her pale square feet side by
side, then sat, swinging her legs down over the edge of
the veranda. She picked up a cake and ate it. Tom calmed
down at once, became just another one of us, reaching a
long gorilla's arm out of his hammock to pick up a cake.
And bite into it like a normal person, and chew and
swallow.

'Can you smell Grandpa's roses?' Tillie said, and we
could, because she'd suggested it. We tried to identify the
flowers we could smell on the warm evening air, and
the sounds of the birds settling down for the night. If I
had been transported to Brazil or India it could not have
seemed further away. I couldn't believe that my own
house was only next door, was just a matter of yards
away, beyond the bulk of the Hennessys' house and the
hedge. I closed my eyes and imagined myself in an
Arabian nights' palace, lying on plump cushions, eating
unfamiliar little cakes, breathing in the exotic scent of
roses. Tillie had gone away but came back again with a
glass and her tobacco tin. She set it down beside her and
started to roll one of her thin, uneven cigarettes. 'Get
under your covers now to keep warm,' she said to us. The
blanket I had smelled of the Hennessys' house. I breathed
it in as if I was drowning.

We could hear Isolde's voice high up indoors. I didn't
know who she was talking to, no one could be heard
answering back. Then Patrick appeared across the garden,
which was by now all one uniform grey.

'I'll be off out in a minute,' he said. 'I was going to say
was there anything I could fetch you, but you look well

provided for.' And he nodded at Tillie's drink, her cigarettes, her plate of cakes, her bare toes pulled up on the edge of the veranda. He put a hand on Barbara's side, through the blankets, and patted her. 'Sleep well, my beauty, and mind the bugs don't bite. But I'm sure they will.' He did the same to Tom, setting the hammock swinging. To me he said and did nothing, he looked tactfully across me as though I was nothing but air.

When he had gone Tillie stirred, swilling the ice round in her glass. She stretched her feet down from the veranda, and jumped lightly into the grass. 'Oh, well now,' she said. 'Hmm.'

'Mu-um?' said Barbara (who almost never called her that). But Tillie didn't reply. She just sighed. We watched her walk off into the dark.

Tom reached out a hand and lifted her glass, draining the last drops and the slivers of ice. Then he knocked her tobacco tin with the tips of his fingers, until it had slid into the shadows beneath Barbara's bed. We lay in the stillness, listening to the quiet. A sudden cough and snort nearby made Barbara cry, 'God, what's that!?' but Tom said, sounding sleepy, 'Only that horse over the fence,' and Barbara sighed, turning in her blankets, and said, 'Oh yes, the horse.'

I thought we were all going to go to sleep then, though by my watch – if I stretched my arm out and screwed it round into a shaft of light coming from inside the house, I could just about see – it was only half past ten. I was disappointed, I'd thought we would stay awake till well after midnight, would climb out to look at the stars. I became aware of how hard my bed was, how sloping, how prickly the blanket. My eyes strained open. My muscles were taut and my bones had begun to ache. I tried a yawn to see if I was at all sleepy – it felt unconvincing. Tom actually let out a snore. Then Barbara giggled. And sat up. Tom snored some more. Barbara leaned across and whacked him. The hammock vibrated, then Tom slowly, slowly, as if in a dream, slumped out of one end of it and slithered to the floor. He lay absolutely still. Barbara sat, unmoving. I leaned up on my elbow. Tom still had not moved. A last bit of his blanket unwound itself from the hammock and we heard the clunk as his skull dropped an inch or two on to the hard wood of the floorboards. 'Ow-how!' he said, sounding perfectly conscious, and we all let out a laugh. I was enchanted.

Tom unravelled himself from his tartan blanket and sat cross-legged on the veranda, leaning his head back against one of the wooden uprights. I could see the line of his throat against the darkness of the garden behind him. His Adam's apple stuck out. It was a boy's throat, quite different from girls'. 'She's not coming back,' he said. He reached out a lazy hand and drew Tillie's tobacco tin towards him. 'Ba?' he said.

'OK. Why not?' said Barbara.

He rolled her a cigarette. His fingers moved confidently, expertly. I stared in fascination.

'Your friend?' he said, meaning me. Not deigning to know my name, though I knew he knew it.

'OK.' I reached out one hand, casual too, and Tom crouched nearer to me in the darkness, holding up a match. I discovered it was an intimate thing, having a cigarette lit for you. Tom's unsettling nearness. That expert hand almost cradling mine.

'You're supposed to breathe in,' he said. Not very kindly.

It was like smoking a hot, flaming worm. I thought I must have seared my throat. There was no taste to it except heat, and then smoke. I did my utmost not to cough, and then dragged some air into my lungs, and leaned my head forward, hair over my face, while the tears popped into my eyes. I heard Tom's quiet, snickering little laugh.

Barbara climbed out of her bed and went indoors, coming back with the water bottle, which she passed around. She had filled it with lime cordial. My throat felt as if it had been ripped, and the cordial stung all the way down. She and Tom finished their cigarettes pensively, blowing out smoke into the cool darkness.

And then Tillie was walking over the grass again, materializing out of the night, barefoot, rubbing the backs of her arms. She didn't climb up on to the veranda but stood on the bare earth beneath it and reached through the railing for her empty glass and her tobacco tin, and saying, 'Don't stay awake too long, my doves,' walked towards the back of the house.

I thought I had found the ultimate happy family.

Some time later, half asleep, I heard Patrick come back, his footsteps heavy, and at least two others with him, making no attempt to keep quiet. The front door banged shut, lights flared all over the downstairs. Someone went into the kitchen, opening cupboard doors and calling out. They settled in the front room, although the other lights stayed on. I could hear the voices, Patrick's, another man's, a woman's with a throaty laugh, and now and then a half-sentence loud and clear: 'Lucky if she wants to . . .', 'Not if it was to save your life . . .', 'Thinks he's bloody Cézanne!', 'I care, and then I don't care . . .' I lay there, frowning in the darkness, frowning with the effort of making these patchwork phrases into something that meant something.

Later, much later, just as the birds in the woods started singing, I woke to hear Tillie's voice high up like a roosting bird herself, shushing Mattie who was wailing and protesting over something. 'Nah – nah – nah!' his voice went on, thin and peevish. 'Oh, Mattie, Mattie, Mattie, my little Mattie,' she said, almost singing. Whether he shut up or whether I fell asleep again first I couldn't tell.

Of course, I had to get up and out by eight o'clock, make my way over the dew-wet fields and right around to Fairwith Avenue, where I hung about behind the hedges until I saw my father's car come crawling along, and I jumped out at him from the driveway of number fifteen, waving enthusiastically, before he could do anything as silly as walk up to the white front door.

23

Mandy

Roy Tiltyard had moved in with Bettina, into the flat above Charisse. Bettina continued to cut and curl hair all day long, and Roy did some work in a light industrial place out along the coast road. No one knew what. It seemed to me that men's work when they were out of the home was literally unmentionable. What was it that they did all day? There are no names for it that mean anything. Unless they did something specific, like Wally, who drove a van. There again, it *seems* clear, but it isn't specific enough. Drove what kind of a van, filled with what, and for whom? An ice-cream van, a delivery van, a removals van? And Eddy, in the Merchant Navy, and Tom Rose's father, dead at sea – what was it they were doing? Did they haul sails and wrestle with the helm, sit at a table with radio dials in front of them and headphones over their ears, or pace the bridge and give instructions down a tube? You only got a hint of these things from films. What men might be up to in the oh-so-important world of work.

We all knew perfectly well what it was that women did. We could see them every day, indoors and out, scouring, scrubbing, plumping, patting, slopping and slicing. You had only to glance out of the nets to see Mrs Smith sweeping her front step and Mrs Jones hanging her Persil-white washing and Mrs Brown polishing her windows to a crystal sheen. You could see them from buses and trains doing much the same, or carrying string bags full of shopping or pushing babies in prams or waiting to collect their mixed infants at the school gate. Even those who worked (the other was not *work*, just housework) were clearly visible to the human eye: cutting hair, swabbing out the school lavs, sticking a needle in your arm and saying, 'This won't hurt,' or pressing the keys of cash registers in shops across the land. Even me, eventually, leaning on my counter-top at the dry cleaner's in the long stretches between customers. What I did was open for all to see, there was no mystery involved. Anyone could have done it. A trained dog could have done it. Though not the safety pins, I think.

Patrick, who was productive enough – I knew what he did and I even saw some of the results – worked at home when he wasn't teaching, and yet it seemed like play. He could saw wood and stretch canvas and make sketches surrounded by the riot and noise of his children and family and friends. When he could bear them no longer he could shut himself away in the attic, with all the windows open and music playing loudly, and still get his work done. But the very same circumstances had stopped Tillie doing the same work, had stopped her for years.

'She doesn't have time to do any painting,' Barbara explained to me.

'I don't get enough time. Time to paint. Not proper time,' Tillie said to me, later the same day. She leaned over the table towards me, pushing aside half-full cups and damp tea towels. 'You see, Carolina, I only have little wedges, little potato chips of time, sliced off the whole big proper thing. It's not enough.'

Which was bizarre in view of the fact that later I saw Tillie sitting on the back step in her usual position, chin on knees and arms around shins, doing nothing. Well, she was painting her toenails with Barbara's metallic blue nail varnish, and smoking a cigarette. She wasn't doing *absolutely* nothing. But in that household, in terms of inertia, it was as good as you were going to get.

I learned later that it was the kitchen Barbara was anxious for Tillie to paint. It was a dark and dirty pear-leaf green, had been all the time they lived there, according to Barbara, and she wanted it redecorated like the Van Hoogs' kitchen, fresh and yellow and glinting with light. She had even picked out a colour – 'Daffodil' – from a paint chart.

'I'll get round to doing it some day,' Tillie promised gaily, picking up a basket of washing to peg out on the line. 'But I like my house. I *love* my house. I'm perfectly content with it as it is.'

She paused in the back doorway, looking around. Her feet were bare and she wore terrible cut-off drainpipe jeans which made her look like Tom the Cabin Boy.

'You wouldn't want it all tidy and prissy and *clean*,' she told Barbara, and then ran off down the wooden steps. We heard her call back over her shoulder: 'In those sort of houses you can't do as you like, and you *always* do as you like.'

The Hennessys didn't have a scrap of wallpaper anywhere in their house, no cabbage roses, no twining ivy or limp bamboo. Their walls were painted, a plain backdrop to the pictures and the unmatched furniture. And I liked it, I found it restful. But I know what my mother would have said if she could have seen it: 'They should be ashamed of themselves. Chipped gloss paint, and finger marks everywhere. And I'd throw out that dreadful old junk they call furniture, if it was up to me. Not even antique. It's not as if they don't know any better. They know all right, they're just the sort that don't care.'

Bettina was a changed woman. She had always had a tendency towards plumpness, a generosity about the calves, a flapping of flesh on the upper arms. During her time as a fiancée she began to bulge, to melt and overflow, like warm ice cream squeezed between two wafers. Now that she was a married woman she inflated, a hot air balloon serenely wafting above the unimportant crowd. We all hoped, secretly, that Roy Tiltyard liked 'em big. He'd have to.

Mandy remained small and thin. When she was twelve, Gloria said, 'She'll start growing soon. She'll flesh out.' A horrible image, to my mind. She didn't. She stayed like a small wizened unhappy doll, while her mother blossomed and billowed. But she grew quieter. She lost her bully's confidence. Perhaps she'd got to the stage where little-girl tricks didn't work any more, but hadn't yet lighted upon any other techniques to replace them.

I had imagined that now Mandy was the child of two married parents there would be no reason for other people to cosset and spoil her. Surely she was no longer at a disadvantage? Everyone else had two parents, and had to put up with the situation, no excuses made. But the customers at Charisse still apparently saw her as a deserving case, a pathetic little mite, and when Bettina wasn't looking they buffed up already shining sixpences and shilling pieces and pushed them into her hand, muttering, 'Put that in your piggy bank, darlin'' or 'Get yourself some sweets,' as if her entire nourishment depended on them.

Which set me to thinking that maybe there was something they knew that I didn't know about Roy Tiltyard. Or about marriage.

I had my hair cut at Charisse now. I was able to observe these things. When I was little, Bettina had always cut my hair on one of her Saturday afternoon visits, making me perch on a kitchen chair with a box on it to raise me up to the right height. She brought her hairdressing scissors, and asked Mum for an old towel to drape over my shoulders. She damped my hair with water sprayed from a plastic squeezy bottle, mysteriously smelling of the hairdressing salon. And she and my mother would chat idly over my head, while I sat, as still as I could manage, trance-like, without even a mirror to gaze into. I could see why Mandy hadn't minded hanging round the salon. It was addictive stuff, even in the kind of enigma code they used because I was there.

'Poor old Gloria . . .' Bettina would start. 'That Eddy. Honestly.'

'Poor Gloria,' my mother would intone. And so it went on, a steady slow game of throw and catch.

'How she puts up with it.'

'She's too . . .'

'That Eddy.'
'. . . put upon.'
'I know.'
'All these years. You'd think—'
'I know.'
'*I* don't know.'
'*I* wouldn't.'
'Honestly.'
'Catch *me*.'

Like an iceberg, so much more unsaid than said.

'How's Stell?' Bettina would ask.
'She's all right.'
'Haven't seen her in a while.'
'She's well.'
'New man?'
'Nn-nn.'
'Could do with one. That Wally.' Or that Gerald, that Dimitri. 'Wouldn't touch him with a bargepole, myself.'

My mother would laugh. 'She needs to settle down.'
'Suppose she can't afford to be choosy . . .'
'Find a nice man.'
'. . . not at her age.'
'Mmm.'

Maybe they thought I couldn't hear, that being a child somehow sealed up my ears to adult conversation. I'm sure they believed it made my mind too slow to understand what they were on about. Which was usually their specialist subject: M-E-N.

I wanted to grow my hair long, and my mother wanted me to have it short. The compromise was somewhere between the two. Bettina cut my fringe halfway down my forehead and halfway round my head, like a Plantagenet king. The rest of my hair she cut in a straight curtain an inch below my earlobes, too short to put into a ponytail but still needing to be tucked behind my ears. Between cuts I might get it long enough to go into two stubby bunches which stuck out like shaving brushes. I think she did it deliberately.

But now I was older I went four times a year to Charisse. Bettina pronounced my hair *difficult*, holding up the end of a lock and letting it flop between her first two fingers, unimpressed. She cut it in a longer version of what I had had before. I was trying to grow out my fringe, but she always found the stray long bits and gathered them back in again, remorselessly chopping before I could say a word. I sat with my hands folded under the checked nylon bib that Ida Carr had wafted over me when I sat down, and watched silently as damp strands, longer than I could bear to part with, fell into my lap.

The salon smelled of hair dye and perming solution and the hairspray they kept in great gold silos. *Elnett. L'Oréal.* Exotic words, full of promise, promise of transformation. Photos of glamorous women with shining swirls of glamorous hair stood on the counter and hung in the window. They dangled the promise that such a look could be achieved here. They tempted you to point to one and say, 'I'll have my hair like that,' but that seemed to imply you thought you already had a wonderful Hollywood face to match. And it was obvious that the soft halos of curls in the pictures were a stratosphere above the parched lawyers' wigs that emerged from under the dryers, to be pecked at with the pointed end of a tailcomb, and sprayed and jointly admired, front and back, and paid for and covered quickly with a chiffon scarf for preservation from the weather outside. So you just put up and shut up, and never mentioned that the haughty Hollywood faces might be out of place.

I had always to go at a quiet time, when they could *fit me in*, so there were only ever one or two customers beneath the monstrous helmets of the dryers. They sat in their checked bibs, hands issuing out the sides to turn the pages of *Woman's Realm*, flicking through, hunting for the shocks and scandal of the problem page or the doctor's column. Or they did if they were anything like Barbara and me. Though Barbara was tougher with her advice than Evelyn Home or Peggy Says . . . 'Pathetic cow,' was Barbara's response to some poor reader's misfortune, 'she should just dump him.' Or, more radically: 'Cut his balls off!' It was not a remedy I'd ever heard suggested for Eddy.

The mirror in front of me reflected the bank of shell-pink dryers and just about everything else that went on in the salon. Ida Carr came round with the broom, taking away your hair before you could miss it. She wore navy velour slippers with stuck-on diamonds on the toes. Purple veins bulged over her insteps, snaked around her ankle bones and probably all the way up her calves, but these were hidden under a dingy black skirt and a pink overall, made of the same material as the salon's bibs. I wanted her to sit down and take the weight off her feet but she never did, always busy with the broom, or detaching curlers from boiled heads, or fetching the hand mirror so that customers could see the backs of their perms.

Mandy was usually there, in those fallow after-school hours, sitting on one of the chairs where people waited.

Sometimes there was another kid there too, a child or grandchild of one of the women under the dryers, and once there was a little dog, a Yorkshire terrier with its fringe in a tartan bow. Mandy never took any notice of them. She just sat there, knees drawn up and skirt pulled down over them, biting away at the skin beside her thumbnail. She didn't say anything, she didn't talk to me. Every so often Bettina might glance across, or not even bother to glance, and ask, 'Right, Mand?' as if to check that she was still breathing. Mandy would raise her eyebrows, or shrug her shoulders in response, a weary-of-the-world gesture, a seen-it-all and couldn't-care-less look.

And then Ida Carr would get even busier with the broom, and customers would snap the clasps on their handbags and purses. They waited until Bettina was concentrating on putting the coins into the right sections of the till, or had drifted on to the occupant of the next dryer, testing the next set of rollers and tucking cotton wool round overheated ears. Then a swift hand would take Mandy's hand from round her knees, and put a coin in her palm, and tuck her fingers up over it, tightly, so as not to lose it. Would pat her bony shoulder or her skinny knee, and a newly scented head would whisper sweet nothings in her ear. Would smile, and bustle out.

Mandy wasn't a little bastard any longer, and she obviously wasn't going to die of anything any time soon, so what was it that they were all worried about now?

24

Shopping: Two

When I was thirteen my pocket money went up quite a bit. This was because I was a teenager now. In the past it had risen by threepence, then sixpence, every year, which still didn't amount to much. Suddenly I was a whole two shillings better off. Brian wasn't pleased, even when it was explained to him that when he was thirteen the same rule would apply. He continued to moan every Friday night when the money was doled out, and every other time it occurred to him. Girls did not deserve to be preferred above boys, not for any reason – although he wasn't able to put it like that. And then he suddenly shut up about it. I have a horrible feeling that someone slipped him something – a lump sum – to keep him quiet. The old double standard, still alive and well.

Now that Bettina had stopped visiting every Saturday afternoon, Brian and I no longer had to stick around to entertain Mandy, do the family duty. Saturdays became a great stretch of flexible time, an oasis of freedom between the obligations of school days and Sundays. Barbara and

I took to going into town on a Saturday to wander round the shops. I actually felt the money burning a hole in my pocket, a lovely fiscal glow just where the coins sat. We usually walked all the way into town to save spending precious money on the bus fare; it took us about half an hour. Sometimes we went with Barbara's friend Gaynor, who got off the school bus with her, and sometimes we met up with another friend of theirs, a fair-haired girl called Jillian. My heart always sank when I heard that they were coming too, but I didn't have any choice in the matter.

When it was the four of us, I found that they preferred the shops that sold stationery and cosmetics. We'd wander round the counters, picking up erasers and pencil sharpeners and putting them down again, looking at the wrapping paper and the cards, trying out lipstick testers on the backs of our hands, spraying on sample scents. Barbara and Gaynor and Jillian weren't at all bothered by the penetrating looks of the salesladies in the department stores, but even so they chose to go to Woolworth's or the smaller shops, like Dorothy Perkins, where the staff were often Saturday girls, not much older than us.

One of us might buy a pair of tights, or a hairslide, or some decorated paper to cover a school textbook, but the rest would come home empty-handed, except for a few sweets. We always bought sweets. We became fiends for chocolate bars and caramel, for Polo mints, for gum. There was always something sweet or minty in our pockets, in our school bags. We had turned into Mandy.

In Barbara's bedroom, a dark little room on the ground floor, she had fixed up a tilting mirror and a desk lamp on top of the chest of drawers. We directed the lamp on to our faces and peered into the mirror. I drew my hair back, Barbara piled hers up. We made gargoyle faces, we simpered like film stars. In the end we drooped our mouths and came to the conclusion that we would always be ugly. Barbara kept a few lipsticks, Cover Girl and Yardley, in the top drawer of the chest. We tried them on – *Sugar Candy, Frosted Plum, Café-au-Lait*. One was a dark red. It left a stain even after I had rubbed my mouth with my hankie. 'God, why did you buy this one?' I asked.

'Oh, I didn't,' she said, absorbed in smearing pink blusher over her cheekbones.

'Is it one of Tillie's?' I said, thinking of that time she and Patrick had gone out all dressed up, the crimson frock and the deep red lipstick.

'Nah,' said Barbara, pulling a face. 'That's from one of our shopping expeditions.'

Which seemed like a contradiction to me. She was drawing a wobbly uptilted tail of eyeliner, the muscles of her forehead tense with concentration. She saw my expression in the mirror. 'It's nicked,' she said, and gave me a bored glance so that I didn't dare overreact. Then she licked the tip of her eyeliner brush and started on the other eye.

In Woolworth's, with Gaynor and Jillian up ahead, and Barbara clamping my upper arm, we strolled over to the stationery counter. Barbara stopped to examine the writing paper, so I stopped too. I had no choice. Barbara gazed critically at blue lined, at plain white, at airmail and onion-skin. None of them seemed up to the purpose she had in mind. The Saturday girl watched her.

'Do you have any plain cream writing paper?' Barbara enquired.

The girl bent to look beneath the counter. 'I don't think . . .' Her voice was muffled.

Barbara pinched me fiercely. My hand drifted across the counter top, hung there motionless like someone levitating, in the control of the spirits. The girl straightened up again. Barbara pinched me even harder.

'Isn't this it?' I asked, my voice surprising me with its innocence.

'No, that's lined,' the girl said, lifting up the pad my hand was wavering over.

'Oh well, thanks anyway,' said Barbara, and shuffled me away. 'Small,' she hissed. 'Something really *small*.'

In Boots the Chemist, we dithered by miniature tubes of sty ointment, throat pastilles, tiny packets of plasters. We sniffed the cakes of soap. We brushed our fingertips over the jars of lip balm. My legs had turned to jelly.

It was cold outside and the wind off the sea whipped up the side streets and flayed our skin. We halted on the street corner, shivering.

Gaynor, who had tooth braces and a long face that reminded me of a horse, rounded on me. 'You just can't do it, can you?'

Jillian, tiny and blonde and angelic, the sort of person no adult would ever seek to pin the blame on, said, 'You look so bloody guilty you'll get us all in trouble. And we won't have even done anything!'

Another weekend came round, and I called on Barbara. 'I'm going out,' she said. I didn't have the nerve to ask her if I could come too. I just didn't have the nerve.

I went into training. I stiffened my resolve. I practised my skills.

I went round and showed her, pulling out my tiny haul from a deep coat pocket.

One tester lipstick (only a stub left inside), one pencil eraser, one set of hair grips still on its card, one corn plaster, one bottle of clear nail varnish. I didn't say anything.

She studied them. She hugged me. 'I didn't want to leave you out,' she said. 'Honestly.'

I looked at her. I didn't know. With her green eyeshadow and her pearly pink lipstick on, you couldn't tell who she was any more. And I'd never known what she was really thinking.

As summer came around, it seemed to me that more and more we left the other two out. Barbara seemed content to stay at home, with just me for company. We played endless games of tennis over their sagging net. We swung in the hammock, and used the embryonic apples and pears that hung in the trees for target practice. Or we lay in the gloom of Barbara's bedroom and listened to crackly pirate radio stations and read magazines. The boredom and torpor seemed half the pleasure.

Barbara and I still went into town together, but not very often. Occasionally we lifted things, just to keep our hand in, but more often we didn't bother. It had been just a phase, a phase we'd largely grown out of. I thought that Gaynor and Jillian had fallen by the wayside. But then I discovered that Barbara was just as friendly with them as ever. As thick as thieves, I believe the expression is.

Jillian had perfected the bag trick. She was eager to show it off. We went clothes-shopping. We bought things and took them back for a refund, but saved every receipt, and wandered thoughtfully round the display rails, pretending to turn up our noses at what was on offer. We'd amassed a collection of carrier bags from every shop in town, fresh, new-looking ones, and put them to good use when the assistants weren't looking. My arms and legs felt weak again, as if the very bones and sinews had deserted me. Barbara appeared in a new green skinny-rib top, never paid for. Gaynor had got a chiffon scarf, and a necklace. But Jillian was the queen: she had a leather belt, a T-shirt, a short pleated skirt and a top like Barbara's, only in red.

'Doesn't the thought of getting caught at this ever worry you?' I asked once, foolishly, when we were walking along the seafront, eating chips, a carrier bag of stolen goods swinging jauntily from Jillian's arm. 'Surely the nuns tell you this kind of thing is wrong?'

Gaynor snorted. 'They tell us everything is wrong. *Breathing* is wrong.'

'Yeah, if you stick out your chest when you do it!' Barbara added, and they all went into gales of laughter.

'It's a sin, it's a sin,' Jillian said. She was obviously mimicking someone they all knew. Barbara leaned heavily on my shoulder, laughing right into my ear.

'It *is* a sin,' I said, and they stared at me and started laughing all over again.

But nobody did catch us. We were invincible. We carried out secret raids and escaped with our spoils. Or so I thought at the time.

I didn't want this kind of stuff. I really didn't want baby lipsticks, or round ponds of green or lilac powder with a mirror in the lid, reflecting one evil eye. I didn't want pencil sharpeners set in frogs' mouths or up pigs' bottoms, or pencils with tiny tassels, or rainbow-coloured erasers. The smell of those lemon-shaped soaps made me heave. I didn't want scarves and belts and tights – I knew if I ever wore them, they'd flash fluorescent signs that screamed 'Guilt! Guilt! Guilt!' to every passer-by. Especially those in the retail trade.

I'm sure that Barbara and Gaynor and Jillian didn't really want them either. I'm sure they could have afforded to buy them, if that's what they really desired. It was the adventure that was the thing, the risk, the thrill, the pure distilled wickedness they wanted. And the one-upmanship: whoever was the latest to steal something was *best*, whoever's haul was biggest was *boldest*.

This was how I fell out of love with Barbara. When we began our first forays into the world of petty crime I was desperate for her approval; by the time we'd finished I no longer cared. I had other fish to fry. It wasn't girls I was trying to impress now, it was boys. One boy. Barbara and I were still friends, but we weren't *best* friends. We might have been blood brothers, but we never took the vow.

'Let's see,' Lorna says, glancing at my file, which today is open on the table but too far away from me to be read-able. I don't even let my eyes stray in its direction. That would be much too obvious, and I like to keep Lorna on the hop. Instead I fix my gaze on Lorna, on her face, and when she looks back up, I gaze deeply and innocently into her eyes. No one finds it easy to be on the receiving end of that for very long, surely? Not even someone trained in the therapeutic arts?

She looks down again and says, 'Your mother wanted you to take piano lessons. She's musical herself. You say you played duets together.' She looks up. 'Did you enjoy your music lessons?'

'Yes.'

'Do you still play?'

Given the lack of a milk-white baby grand in the patients' lounge, what can I say? 'I'd like to,' comes my seraphic answer.

'But the lessons stopped. Can you recall when that was?'

'When I was about thirteen, fourteen.'

'Why was that?'

'They cost too much. We were teenagers. Teenagers are expensive. They eat a lot and have big feet.'

'I see.'

I realized the conversation we were having was possibly the smoothest and most pleasant we had ever had. Lorna looked down again. There was something different about her today. She was wearing new lipstick, *coral*-coloured. Perhaps she was doing it for me. My name on her lips.

'Did your mother put an end to the piano lessons when she found out you'd been shoplifting?' Lorna said, raising her head sharply, staring at me, shaking her pony fringe out of her eyes. 'As a punishment? Was that the reason?'

Hang on a minute – which mother are we talking about here? Perhaps she's trying to trip me up. And my mum didn't find out about the shoplifting for ages, not until there was a whole lot more to know as well.

I'm confused. I don't want to drop myself in it. I think I'll plead the fifth amendment.

25

Tom

It wasn't a crush that I had on Tom. I loved him long and slow, bad and deep.

Crushes are superficial, juvenile. You learn better, and grow out of them. If I had a crush on anyone, it was Isolde. I was daunted but impressed by her; wanted to look like her, to *be* her. She seemed so unbelievably adult, so composed, even when I first knew her. She had Patrick's hair, horse-brown and curly. She wore it long, often in a ponytail but sometimes gathered romantically up, like a girl on a Greek vase. Her pale, high-cheekboned face, with eyes that were just horizontal lines, narrowed and discriminating, was the pattern of beauty, to me. She persuaded me that she was truly special. But every time she glanced disdainfully round at her family, and sighed and said that the fairies must have swapped her at birth, I thought: how can you say that? How can you wish yourself out of a family like this?

That's how it was with Isolde. But not with Tom.

At first I hardly noticed him, he was just a *big boy*, lanky and harsh-voiced. Then, when I had sorted the Hennessys out from each other, and knew their names, he was the one I avoided. If there was one thing in the world I wasn't accustomed to it was *big boys*. I knew about *little* boys. And whiny little girls, and older girls, really – aunts and cousins and mothers all amounted to that, extensions of the female at all ages and stages. But big boys were strange and scary. Tom would swing round the corner of the hallway like a gorilla, one hand on the banisters, and lunge up the stairs, two or three at a time. Spurts of energy would propel him forward, or up, or down. Expulsions of laughter burst from his lungs. He and Tom Rose conversed with one another by shouting, like people coughing up blood – great gobbets and gouts of noise issued out of them, all of a sudden, stopping and starting again, racking their bodies as they ran and leaped about the house. I didn't know how Tillie could bear it.

Nobody else in the house seemed to notice the horror of this.

But then, I suppose, they'd been through Eugene.

Eugene I never saw. Eugene was a figment of Hennessy imagination, a monkey baby in a painting, old enough now to make his own way in the world. Barbara said he was learning to be an architect. He lived somewhere called Parsons Green (I imagined an olde English village) with some people called Dill and Arthur. Arthur had been Patrick's best man at the wedding. Dill was his second wife, his first wife, Eloise, having run off with a boy of nineteen. Two thoughts crossed my mind: one – wasn't Arthur worried about the possibility that his second wife might run off with another boy of nineteen (or thereabouts, I didn't quite know Eugene's age)? And two – that I had absolutely no idea who was best man to *my* father, if he had one. How was it right that I should know more about the Hennessys than my own family?

Barbara taught me a little rhyme. She would hop on and off the back steps, reciting it:

> *Monday's child is fair of face,*
> *Tuesday's child is full of grace,*
> *Wednesday's child is full of woe,*
> *Thursday's child has far to go,*
> *Friday's child is loving and giving,*
> *Saturday's child works hard for a living.*
> *But the child that is born on the Sabbath Day*
> *Is bonny and blithe, and good and gay.*

'What day were you born on?' she asked me. I looked blank. It had never occurred to me that I must have been born on a particular day of the week. '*I* was born on a Thursday,' she said happily. 'That means either I'll travel a lot, or have great achievements. Or both, probably. Izzy's Tuesday, Tom's Friday, Eugene and Mattie are both Mondays, and Sebastian is a Sunday's child.'

I thought about that. It seemed fair enough to me.

'What day was I born on?' I asked my mother, who gave me a blank look the equal of my own. 'What day of the week?' After a bit, she said, 'Wednesday.' Only later did I know that she must have been lying. Guessing.

Guessing, lying, making it up: what's the diff? We do it all the time.

So, Tom.

I can't really say what it was I loved about him. I can't go: let me count the ways. I always knew about his defects, and God knows he had enough. That's why it wasn't a crush or calf-love or any of those moony spoony patronizing names for adolescent heart-pangs. My love for him was always clear-eyed.

First he was an alien, a noisy gorilla, it was only his curly fair hair that I found fascinating and attractive. Then, just as Barbara and I were growing apart, I realized that he'd become the fixed centre of that turning household on which my eye was always focused. I could look at his sticking-out Adam's apple, at his big clumsy feet, or the way his T-shirt hung off his shoulder blades, and not delude myself that these things were beautiful, but know I loved them. I dwelt on them with affection. He always was bullying and egotistical and full of some enormous chip-on-the-shoulder rage to which I'm sure he wasn't entitled. But I didn't mind. I loved him. The fact that I could bear these things made me feel proud.

Then, at times, he *could* be loving, could be suddenly, strikingly gentle – with an insect, or one of his brothers, or me – in a way that made my heart stop. And he was always candid, and amusing, and inhabited his body, his long bony body, like an animal, perfectly at home with itself and with the physical world. He could happily lie down to watch television on double beds beside (almost) complete strangers. He could fall asleep at the table in the middle of a noisy kitchen. He could climb up the posts of the veranda and swing in feet-first through his bedroom window, and if you asked why, he might say, 'I didn't feel like taking the stairs.'

Of course all this was attractive to a girl of limited experience, limited physical experience (the physical means at my disposal being one ever-tidy bungalow, one bolted bathroom door, one family sure as eggs is eggs that God gave us our bodies in order for us to walk to church, and to cover them decently, and never use them to draw attention to ourselves). Of course Tom's physical presence was highly seductive. I succumbed. Of course I did. As sure as eggs is eggs.

Tom's friend Tom Rose was always about. Even more than me he inhabited the house like one of its rightful occupants. He ate meals with them, which I did not – or almost never – and he often stayed the night on Tom's bedroom floor. We always had to call him Tom Rose to differentiate; never Tom *Hennessy* and Tom Rose, just Tom and Tom Rose. He was tall, too, but wide-shouldered, with a nose about to become a beak; mean-eyed and unlovely, to my way of thinking. He was an appendage of Tom's, a shadow, a sniggering partner, a recipient of sideways looks, digs in the ribs. 'He lives with his mother, his dad died at sea,' Barbara had told me once. 'And he doesn't get on with his mum's new boyfriend.' (I wondered what she told anyone about me, in those sharp, potted histories she always had available, like the *Dictionary of National Biography*.) And why did this make Tom Rose ever welcome, and why did it make him not suburban? Almost the first I knew of liking Tom was knowing that I didn't like Tom Rose. In fact, I was horribly jealous of him.

We were in Tom's bedroom. We always seemed to be in his bedroom these days. As adolescents we needed the music, we needed the ambience of posters and joss sticks and old socks, and beds and floor cushions to lie on, rather than armchairs and other proper upright furniture. Isolde hated it, she glanced in at the doorway and then turned on her heel and walked away, her high heels tapping, just like someone already grown-up, busily pacing the corridors of their place of work. And Barbara was too impatient for quite so much indolence, got rapidly bored with languid sounds and smells, would jump up, chuck a balled sock or a paper dart at Tom, and depart. She didn't get on with Tom at all these days, and she had never liked Tom Rose. Which left just me and the two of them, perusing the latest music papers and album covers, and staring into space.

Tom leaned over and said to me, as if he'd just noticed my presence: '*Where* is it that you live?'

'Down the road.'

'Where exactly? Which house?'

'Next door,' I said, faintly.

'Next door? At *Mister Clipper's*?' And he made a gesture to go with it, an imitation of someone using hedge clippers, just like my father. 'Then you must be Caroline Clipper. Caroline Clipper!' And he laughed and laughed, rolling back on to the bed and hugging his ribs. He made more noise than he strictly needed to. 'She's Caroline Clipper!' he shouted to Tom Rose. Tom Rose was sitting on the floor cross-legged, idly rolling the poker dice. He laughed too, but only quietly.

'I'm not really *his*,' I said. 'I told you. I was *adopted*.'

'Oh yes,' said Tom, and his eyes locked with Tom Rose's for a second, and I knew they knew I was making it up.

'I wouldn't live there if it was up to me. But what can I do about it till I'm older?'

'Run away?' offered Tom Rose.

'As if I could!'

'Run away with *me*,' laughed Tom.

* * *

'Come here. Yes, *you*.'

When Tom kissed, it was with his jaw and teeth. This was a disappointment to me. I'd thought kissing must be like melting. That's what it looked like on TV. Instead it was a kind of grinding of hard surfaces. Something you'd really have to work at developing a liking for, like beer. The next thing, a split second after the gum-grinding began, was the shocking entry of his tongue into my mouth. It was very invasive, into somewhere as private as one's own mouth. Meeting lips was a meeting of equals; having Tom's tongue wiggling into my mouth was quite different. It was hot and lively, like some terrible pet that is put into your hands for a moment and gets instantly out of control, hurrying up your sleeves or down your neck, exploring, inquisitive. I must have reared my head away from him, because I felt his hand on the base of my skull, pressing me back down on to his tongue. God, if this is kissing, I thought, I had better go to Barbara's school and give myself up as a nun.

I have to say that, technically, Tom Rose had the advantage. I didn't like him at all, and kissed him under duress, but with him kissing was how I expected, a soft melting, a much more comfortable experience all round. He seemed to have lips where Tom had hard jaws, and he used them to cushion the place where we met, and his tongue only came out slowly and thoughtfully, a bit like a snail from its shell. His tongue sought my tongue, not my fillings. He seemed to solve the problem of the noses instinctively, as if there wasn't any problem there at all. If only he could have passed his technique on to Tom.

In Tom's bright, bare, dusty room, we sat on the floor,

pressing jaw to jaw. I was aware of other sounds else-where in the house: Patrick calling out joyously, 'Now isn't that always the way?', and a door slamming in the breeze from other open doors, and Mattie droning below in the front garden, and someone running lightly down the long staircase, tapping something hard and rattling on the banisters all the way down. I was conscious of the dustballs on the floor, and the smell of socks, and the droop of the red tartan blanket, frayed at the edge, as it hung off the side of the bed.

'Now me,' Tom would say, and a bit later, 'Now Tom.'

Did Tom Rose want this? Did Tom Rose have the same antipathy for me as I had for him? But then, as I had learned from the nuns, via Barbara, boys were only after *one thing*. They would use every opportunity that befell them to achieve that *one thing*, even with girls they had no other use for. Particularly with girls they had no other use for.

But perhaps in Tom's hands we were both powerless – experimental animals, laboratory mice – doing and being done unto as required, clinical and detached. For the purposes of the experiment, I was quite willing. At least, I was not entirely unwilling.

'I've got a boyfriend,' Hanny told me, 'on the outside. I don't much like him. My mother set him up for me.'

'Your *mother*?'

'My mother the matchmaker.'

'What, she wants you to *marry* him?'

'No. She just wants me not to be a social pariah.'

I glanced at Hanny. She was giving me her sideways

225

look. Her ironical look. I smiled. She was joking. Maybe none of what she'd said was true.

'His name's David. A *nice* boy. In my mother's words.'

There was a little silence, while we watched some faded brown and pink blossom bowl along the pathway in the wind just like the merry hoop of an Edwardian child in carefree days of yore. If ever there were any carefree days of yore. If Edwardian children were not just as sunk as us under the weight of their tweeds and their boots and parental expectations and parental neglect.

'Have you got a boyfriend?' Hanny said. 'I shouldn't ask. I hate to ask, really. That's the kind of thing my mother thinks passes for unaffected social chit-chat. That, and enquiring of newly married women if they're pregnant yet.'

'No,' I said, because it was true. A little truth. I had imparted to Hanny a little tiny truth.

26

Appendage

I got to be a sort of appendage at the Hennessys' house.

Adolescence is a funny time, when you're not one thing and you're not another; not a child any more, nor a grown-up. Neither fish nor fowl. A bit of both. It must have been the hormones, the great chemical inner sea washing about, throwing up equinoctial tides. It seemed as if there were long hours to fill, huge long pauses, when you were waiting to feel something, or do something, or be something, which you couldn't yet feel or do or be. Sometimes I just wanted to lie there and watch the light moving round on the wall, and let the almost pleasurable misery and boredom wash over me. And this was best done undisturbed. It felt as if I was always in the Hennessys' house, but that wasn't true. There were swathes of time at home, devoted to piano practice, homework, chores, to hiding in my room. There were whole days when I didn't visit the Hennessys, though never quite whole weeks.

Barbara was often out with other friends now, or

talking on the phone to them. (They got an extra telephone around this time. Mr and Mrs Van Hoog had always had one, but only the grown-ups were allowed to use it. Now there was a cream-coloured extension in the hall, and usually Barbara attached to it, sitting on the bottom stair.) If I missed anything it was the intensity our early friendship had, but I no longer minded if she wanted me or not. I felt I had no real need of her now.

I crept out of the corners where I used to hide with a book, I floated out from Barbara's wake into the open waters. And no one sent me on my way. No one suggested I shouldn't be there. It was lovely. I felt almost like one of the family then.

Sometimes I would sit on the veranda with Isolde, doing something useful like shelling peas or peeling potatoes. Chores didn't feel like chores when I did them here. She would ask me about school, or what I'd been reading, careful constructive questions, like a grown-up helping you join in a conversation. They were rather impersonal conversations, and restful because of it. Once I was sitting there, reading a book, while Isolde wrote a letter to some foreign penpal. Patrick paused beside us, a cheery beery smell about him. He stood on the grass and looked at us through the rails, wrapping one hand round the upright. There were curling brown hairs growing all over the back of his hand, and a bloody gouge on his thumb knuckle.

'Well, well, well, look at this, now. One's writing her memoirs, the other's reading 'em. I'd like to have the time you young ladies have at your disposal. Haven't I always said that, Izzy? That one day I'll devote time to study? Become a scholar. What do you say to that?'

I hardly dared look up. I think he was addressing me.

'A scholar and a gentleman. D'you think that's on the cards, eh, Izzy?'

'Doubt it,' said Isolde, and went on writing.

I liked to sit in the kitchen while Tillie cooked and Sebastian drew at the kitchen table. Sebastian was always drawing. He did highly coloured scenes of gore and destruction, of people dropping in flames from blazing aeroplanes, knights in armour with long sharp poles sticking right through them, chainmail warriors with axes splitting their heads. He liked to scatter careful vignettes of severed limbs, discarded bloodstained weaponry, vultures hovering, torn flags trailing in the puddles. Tillie would glance over his shoulder and say, 'That's very good. I like your horses,' or 'Good colouring in,' or 'Sharpen your pencil.' She never commented on the subject matter. Sebastian was a loving little boy who never, to my know-ledge, deliberately squashed insects or set small fires in dry weeds with a magnifying glass. He was often to be found cuddling with Tillie on the swing-seat, or cross-legged on her bed in front of the TV with his thumb firmly in his mouth. Patrick would tip him upside-down by his ankles and Sebastian just hung there, laughing, his arms lank and his corkscrew curls tickling the floor. 'You'll make a fine artist one day, boy,' Patrick said. 'They'll bring back narrative painting just for you.'

Mattie drew as well. Mattie drew brilliantly, replicas of what he saw, in thin, taut, scratchy lines. He drew the pony in the field, and the Hennessys' house, with the veranda and the two front doors.

* * *

229

I wish I had that drawing of Mattie's with me now. I wish I had it in here with me now. I'd like a picture of their house.

The Hennessys got a dog. When I first knew them they never had any pets at all, then one day Patrick came home with a dog, and suddenly they were fully fledged pet owners, canine experts.

Brian and I had kept pets before. I'm surprised our mother allowed them, but she set firm limits. Pets had to be small, inexpensive and short-lived. They couldn't come into the house – except the goldfish, which lived on the lounge window sill in a spherical bowl with a plastic castle to swim round. The others had to stay in the garden or the shed. None of them lasted long, not even as long as the pet shop suggested they should. Brian managed to smash the fishbowl, and just watched as the fish flapped wanly on the window sill, gasping its last. The mice ate their babies and then were found one morning stiff and cold. And the guinea pig escaped. That's what Brian said. He'd had it grazing on the lawn and it ran away under the hedge. He attempted to catch it with his hands, then hook it out with a stick. Neither worked. 'I tried,' he told me, 'but I couldn't get it. Good riddance! If it wants to live in there, it can. Just see how long it lasts.' I kept an eye out for it when I was in the next-door garden, but nothing materialized.

But now the Hennessys had a dog, and any pet experiences of mine were not to be compared.

Question: what would you rather have – a cuddly Labrador pup, or an elegant Siamese cat? I would imagine the most enjoyable bit about having a dog is having it as a puppy first. Puppies are playful. Puppies are always beautiful, no matter what the adult dog looks like later. They use their big feet and their big eyes to maximum effect. Long-haired ones are fluffy, and short-haired ones are velvety to the touch. They don't stink yet.

The dog Patrick brought home was full-grown, or as full-grown as it was ever going to get. I don't know where he got it from and they never said. It was another Hennessy mystery, a taken-as-read. Patrick called him Pickles, and there was no debate about that, either. Another nice part of pet-owning is deciding on the name. Brian and I had got into angry spats over this, and I'm sure the Hennessys would have spilt blood in the deciding. But they had to forgo this particular pleasure.

Pickles was a Jack Russell, though partly something else as well. He was mostly white, but with a round brown spot on his haunch just like a target, and his left front side was brown too, from shoulder to paw, as if he had his leg plunged in a pantomime thigh-boot. He was a tense little creature, hard to the touch, as taut as a cooked sausage about to burst out of its skin. He knew certain commands – 'Fetch!' and 'Sit!' – but found the spotlight of people's attention very stimulating and difficult. If they said 'Sit!' he would instantly touch bottom to ground, and just as instantly raise it up again, wiggling, waiting for the next instruction. He was desperate to know if you were pleased with his performance. Poor, insecure, over-eager Pickles. They would throw something, a ball, a stick, and shout 'Fetch!' and he'd run, get halfway there before he needed to look back over his shoulder, checking almost, was he on course? Was this what they'd meant? His back half would keep springing away and his front half, turning, would brake, and before he knew it his uncontrollable body had swung right round and he was still galloping, galloping, but in quite the wrong direction. He would finish up at their feet, sit down, neatly tucking in his hindquarters, and look up, smiling, keen to please. 'Where's the ball, Pickles?' they would say, and he'd look anxiously back over his shoulder, and smile up at them again. 'Where's the fucking ball, then?' Tom would say, shaking with laughter, and then skim an imaginary one, sending Pickles racing off again, body concertinaing.

Discovering how hopeless he was, the Hennessys made it a hobby of theirs – a point of demonstration – to humiliate Pickles. Patrick and the boys particularly liked to send him rushing off indoors, where his claws skated on the varnished boards and he bounced like a rocking horse, going nowhere. Isolde was his champion, crooning to him, 'Poor Pickly-wickly. Are they cruel to you?' and massaging his velvet ears. But even she couldn't resist the temptation to push his ears into silly shapes, giving him a ludicrous expression, and call out to the others, 'Oh, look, look! Quick, look at Pickles now! He's doing his hen impression.' Or his donkey, or his owl.

Poor old Pickles.

Poor Pickles, they never even bothered to take him for a walk. He went off hunting in the neighbouring fields and woods and came back with scratches, and with burrs stuck to his ears. I think the rabbits beat him up, the fieldmice bit his nose.

It was a dog's life, believe me.

Once Pickles came in with an injured paw. Sebastian and Mattie were very excited because he had tracked bloody paw marks right over the boards of the back veranda and into the kitchen.

'Oh, poor thing,' Tillie cried, picking him up. 'He must have caught his paw in something.' She wrapped him in a tea towel so that all his legs except the damaged one were trapped, and took him over to the sink. She wet the corner of another tea towel under the tap and wiped at the blood. Pickles struggled, growling in the back of his throat. He looked so foolish and helpless that she gave him a shake and said, 'Poor silly old thing!' He stared up at her reproachfully. I couldn't help thinking of the Duchess in *Alice in Wonderland* and the baby who turns into a pig. Except that Tillie was too nice to be the Duchess.

She cleaned his paw and wrapped it in a piece of bandage which immediately came off, and before the cut healed he walked around for a day or two with an ungainly tapping of his claws on the bare boards, three taps and a hop. And Patrick threatened to chop his leg off and fix on a wheel instead if he ever did it again, because he found the sound of it so infuriating.

Once Barbara no longer needed my daily, hourly presence, I could spend more and more time around Tom. Not strictly *with* him – you couldn't say *with* him, because he didn't exactly invite me – but then he didn't send me away or get up and go away himself. He sort of tolerated me, and sometimes much more than that. I was an appendage.

One of the things we did to amuse ourselves, Tom and Tom Rose and me, was play Monopoly. With them, Monopoly wasn't the quiet, plodding game that Brian and

I had passed time with at Aunt Gloria's, it was a full-blooded, fast and ruthless exercise of Machiavellian tactics. Sometimes even Barbara could be cajoled into joining us. My typical strategy of buying the cheapest streets never paid off here. If I was lucky I boomeranged from *Jail* to *Go To Jail* and back again, which, though frustrating, lost me no money.

Tom Rose was usually the Banker, doling out our funds as required. He squirrelled away his investments and then often turned out to be holding all the utilities and most of the stations. I never quite saw him buy them, and he always had piles of cash. I didn't trust him at all.

'Why can't someone else be Banker for a change?' I suggested once. 'I could do it.'

The boys exchanged glances and just carried on playing.

Tom never let us call it a draw. He forced us to play on until every player but one was broke and mortgaged to the hilt. I never won a single game. I lacked the necessary cruel streak, the lust for blood, the pleasure in seeing one's opponents writhe. Also, I was never allowed to be Banker.

'Let's go to the woods,' Tom said to me one day, as we sat on the veranda with nothing to do. Tom Rose was absent for once, so I had a chance to let him notice my special nature, my essential difference from every other girl.

'The *woods*?'

'Yes, the woods. Over the other side of the meadow.' The meadow was what they called the field that ran alongside their garden. 'The woods.'

Of course, I went. Thrilled, I went. He took my hand and pulled me after him, across the garden, through the barbed-wire fence and over the grass to the other side, where a wooden fence bordered a dense copse of low-growing, stunted trees. It didn't look inviting.

'I've never been in the woods,' I said. Too late.

'Never been in the woods? But they're only two fucking hundred fucking yards from your fucking house!' His voice got louder as he pronounced these words with great clarity. 'What do you do all day? What do you do with your life? Are you content just sitting next door in Mister Clipper's house, counting the flowers on the wallpaper? Waiting for the next cup of tea? *Like a nice cup of tea, dear?*' he mimicked, with a sneering expression on his face.

I looked at him, horrified. He must be able to see inside my head. Suck my brains out.

'Christ, some people!' he muttered, and stalked ahead, his hands in the pockets of his jeans.

The wood was very thorny. I could feel my clothes being caught, and torn, and then my skin. But I kept on going. What you had to do around Tom and Tom Rose was never let them know you disliked anything or were uncomfortable about anything in case they spotted it and persecuted you with it. You just had to smile and laugh along with them, and when you didn't understand something you had to laugh even more enthusiastically, to cover up your ignorance. They couldn't seem to bear ignorance. They couldn't seem to bear people feeling anything, except to find life amusing, or ridiculous, or stupid. You hadn't ever to *let on*.

Somewhere in the middle of the thorny, littered wood

there was a clearing, and an oak tree. It was broad and big, with low-growing branches dipping from its trunk. 'This must have been here years before all the rest. Look at the size of it,' he said, thumping its trunk. 'Go on, climb up.'

I hadn't ever learned to climb trees. It wasn't the sort of skill you picked up round our way, not with all those hawthorns. Even though it looked like a good climbing tree with stout horizontal branches, the first ones were still some way up, high above my head. The trunk was well-used, shiny with slithered footmarks. This was yet another thing Barbara had never mentioned, or shown me.

'Oh, God,' Tom said, in the kind of voice in which people say, 'I suppose *I'll* have to do it.' He swung his arms around a branch above his head, and then lunged his body into a pendulum effect. On the third swing his feet caught round the branch and he hauled himself up on to it. After that it was easy, footholds and handholds within reach all the way up.

I tried the same method, but couldn't get my legs high enough. Eventually I scrabbled them up on to the trunk and he hauled me, painfully, over the first branch. My ribs were scraped, right through my jumper. I climbed after him, holding my breath, not looking down.

We stood only about twenty feet up, I suppose, on alternate hitches, facing each other. But it felt very high to me. You could see out over the wood. You could see surprisingly far away. In my direction, over the bungalow roofs, towards the cluster of far-off taller buildings that was town, and in the distance a thin grey line not much darker than the sky: the sea. Tom faced the low green hills, the main road.

'I wish it was higher. I wish I could get right to the top,' Tom said. 'I've been higher, but you can't get *right* up there.'

'There are caterpillars in these leaves.' I was trying not to feel disgusted.

He grinned. 'Caterpillars, and spiders. All kinds of bugs.'

I wasn't going to let him put me off. I said, 'It's quiet up here.' It was. Miles away, you could hear someone whistling for a dog, but that was all.

'I know.'

We listened for a bit, hearing the quiet keenly. I think we'd scared all the birds away.

'Oh, I can hear Sebastian,' I said. He had started learning the trumpet. I could pick out its uncertain blasts, remote and barely musical. 'I can hear your house.'

Tom began kicking the trunk.

'Someone's always doing something in your house,' I said, happily. 'There's always someone there.'

I noticed that his sweet mouth was pressed into an angry line.

'I know,' he said. Kick, kick. 'That's the bloody problem. The bloody fucking problem.'

And that was the problem. I didn't seek to compare the two, our house and their house. I kept them completely separate in my mind, as if to place them side by side would be to damage or endanger them in some way. The Hennessys' house, household, way of life, was separate and complete; and so was ours. Just hold your breath, and don't look.

Only, of course, I longed to live there, to be them and not me, not we, especially not we. Because while we disliked and were dismayed by them, they despised and disparaged us. And who wants to be on the receiving end of that?

I said to Brian, casually, 'Have you ever been in the woods? Do you know the climbing tree?'

'Course I do. Everyone does. Me and Pete go there. We go right to the top.'

So that told me.

Once Tom showed me the oak tree, it became part of the territory I roamed in. Later that summer we found that someone had fixed up a swinging rope in its branches. Sebastian was furious. 'Someone else has been here! Someone else has been in *our* tree!'

There wasn't much space to swing, but it was the only big tree anywhere around. So maybe everyone did know it.

We took turns to climb up and swing on the rope. It was thick, and beneath the knot it frayed into a tassel like the feathers on a carthorse's hoof. You swung, twirling, leaf litter beneath your feet, the network of branches and leaves above letting flashes of sunlight down. The rope creaked suspiciously above you. Any minute it might break; your neck with it, or at least your legs and arms. But we couldn't keep off it. We hated giving it up for the next person's turn.

When it wore thin and frayed to breaking point, another rope appeared, and then another, hanging beside the rags of all the old ropes. I never found out who put them there but I bet Brian knew.

27

Seeing Is Believing

Hanny doesn't eat with other people. She has to eat alone in her room, and her meals are supervised. She's got a way round it, though. It's so boring, supervising her, she said, that they don't always watch, not all the time. She showed me how, inside her big bell-shaped sleeves, she has picked the deep hem undone and put a little plastic bag into it. Into the bag go bits of food, whenever they're not looking. 'I'm just like a conjurer,' she said, 'I'm so quick.'

'Maybe you could make your living doing that, when you get out of here.'

'What, sticking food up my sleeves?' she said, but I knew she knew what I meant.

When she folded her sleeves back to show me the plastic bags inside, I could see her wrists. They were as thin and white as I expected. And they had scars on them. One was white, diagonal, from the bottom of her thumb across to the bumps of her wrist-bone. The scar on the other arm was raised, red, with pink flesh around it, as if it were newer. It made me think of Barbara and our club, the blunt knife and the brooch pin and the blood brotherhood. I don't think Hanny had wanted to mingle her blood with anyone else's. And I don't think she'd just used a pin.

But I believe she must have meant for me to see her scars.

We were in Woolworth's once when I glimpsed Patrick. I'd never actually seen him out anywhere before, only driving away in his van. He was up at the far end, where they used to have the tea bar. He stood by the counter with a cup of coffee and chatted animatedly to the girl who was serving. I was with Barbara and Gaynor, but they were right across the other side of the shop. We weren't stealing anything, we didn't steal from Woolworth's any more: it was small-fry. We were just shopping, out for a wander, out for a look. I tried to drift past but Patrick saw me, caught my eye. He put out a hand, almost touching me. 'Well, hello there, Caro! What're you about?' I didn't quite know what he meant: what are you doing, or what are you drinking? His white cup was still in his hand. He might have been offering me a cup of coffee. I said vaguely, looking away, 'Oh . . . I'm just out shopping, with Barbara. She's over there.' I pointed vaguely. My face felt red.

'Well, well,' he said. 'Then off you go, quick. I'd better not keep you if the lovely Barbara wants your company.' And he turned back to the girl behind the counter, affability itself.

I hurried over to Barbara and Gaynor, and bundled them out of the shop. 'Your dad's here,' I said.

'Well, so what?' asked Barbara. Yes, so what? I didn't know.

But it was the first time a Hennessy, apart from Barbara, had *seen* me out in public. Had noticed me, had spoken to me.

At the secondary mod there was something called Social Service. This wasn't what it is coming to mean. It wasn't anything to do with unmarried mothers, or people who batter their children, or families that are not really functioning. Anyway, families did seem to function – as long as they knew what they were supposed to be like, they managed to keep up appearances. As long as they cared. And everyone knew what you were supposed to be like. Or everyone I knew, at least.

Social Service was helping people less fortunate than ourselves. It was character-building. It was raising money for charity by organizing a sponsored walk, or it was visiting deaf old ladies in the nearby home for the elderly. Or it was knitting squares. Each different year in the school did a different kind of Social Service, and in the first year the task was knitting. Knitting squares for afghans, the teacher said. I just hoped they wanted them.

'I've got to knit a six-inch square,' I told my mother when I got home.

'Well, go on, then,' she said. It might seem obvious, with all the knitting and sewing that she did, that she would have passed her skills on to me. But I had avoided learning. It's easy when you're young, always ducking out to play, needing to practise those bicycle turns, just having to get in some more roller-skate miles. But with secondary school came female skills. She took my clumsy hands in hers and forced them into the shapes for knit one, purl one. A lumpy bit of knitting, as disgusting as tripe in the butcher's tray, emerged from my needles. It was baby-blue, a colour she happened to have spare. The edges were steps and stairs, four inches wide at one side, seven on the other.

'Can't you do it for me?' I pleaded.

'Most certainly not.' Social Service was Social Service. The merit was in doing it yourself. You couldn't pay other people to do it for you. Or even *not* pay them to do it for you. I took my scrappy square in to school. I discovered that afghans were blankets, sewn together from even-sized squares of knitting. Mine failed the entrance test. I was put on stitching the squares together. Even this I was bad at. I hadn't inherited my mother's deft fingers.

Another kind of Social Service was taking library books round the wards of the long-stay hospital. This was for the more mature pupils. Somehow I had become mature, despite my incompetence over knitted squares. We were driven there during the lunch break by Miss Jessop, the RE teacher: me and Suzannah Grey and Mildred Clark. I think we were chosen because we happened to be wearing the most respectable skirts. Long-stay patients were not to be inflamed. We were given boxes of books and a hospital trolley with an eccentric offside front wheel. I don't know how this was supposed to build our characters, though it certainly gave us practice for a grand future as tea ladies, should we decide to follow that career path.

I expect what the patients wanted were Wild West novels and syrupy romances and good old-fashioned murders, and there was a sprinkling of those, well thumbed. But on the whole our barrowload of literary goodies was mind-improving, and it was with these we had to tempt the bedridden, and the frail-but-mobile types who congregated in the day room. A history of ecclesiastical decoration. Fruit-preserving for beginners. Beethoven and his world. A guide to the Swiss Alps. It was uphill work.

And then one lunchtime, on top of the pile I was sorting was a book about twentieth-century art. I sat down on a vacant chair and leafed through it. Let's face it, none of the patients was going to snatch it from my hands. They clamoured for Zane Grey and Georgette Heyer, not modern art. Thick paint, obscure shapes, stupid splattery canvases. I reached the chapter on portraiture, rather a thin one. On one of the pages, only taking up half the space (the top half was a scribbly head and shoulders of a miserable-looking old man), was a painting, 'Tillie: In an Interlude'.

It was definitely Tillie. Not by Patrick. I can't remember who it was by. But I noticed the date. Over twenty years ago. She sat, half sideways to the viewer, with light streaming down on her from a high window. Her dress was sky-blue, and lit white on the far side by the sunshine; her fair hair hung heavy like some thick crop stood ready for harvesting; her expression was far away, untroubled, thoughtful. Physically she looked just the same as now, except that she was very pregnant.

So Tillie was real. Tillie was famous. Tillie had really sat for artists out in the world, artists who got their pictures put in books. Hennessys existed outside of their house, outside my fevered imagination. I could hardly believe it.

My school took me off Social Service before the term

was up. They said I had stolen a book. I honestly thought that no one would miss it, but it was a bit too big to hide.

Hanny and I still have that quiz. I keep it as a bookmark, folded up in the back of my one book. The best bit about the quiz is that we don't know what the hell it's about and we don't have the answers. The first time we got to question twelve and completed it, Hanny said, 'OK. Let's see how we've done. What we scored. Are we the Hostess with the Mostest or the Pathetic Party Bore?' And then she screamed. It made me think of Barbara, that short, sharp, artificial scream of rage she let out when she got to the bottom of the column. ' "Turn to page 29 to see how you rate . . ." We don't *have* page twenty-nine. And rate as what? As *what*!?'

But once she got over her frustration it was better. It was better not to have the results. We could make them up. It kept the quiz interesting for much longer than a whole quiz would have been. We became obsessed by it.

Hanny leaned back and lifted up her knees, hugging them. She raised her eyes to the sky. 'You scored mostly As: You are a home-loving type with a deeply dull soul. You will give your future husband socks for Christmas and deny him your body.'

'Mostly Bs,' I said. 'You're a free spirit, a wild soul. A pain in the arse. Your friends loathe you and your family pretend you're not theirs. Throw away your hand-woven clothes and comb your hair. *Please*. As a favour to mankind.'

'This magazine begs you.'

'This anonymous magazine begs you—'

We saw Moira advancing down the path. Her tiny

shoes made miraculously fast progress over the paving slabs. She was coming towards us. We were laughing too much. Enjoying ourselves. We stopped at once and turned drab faces towards her. We didn't want to give anything away.

28

Discomfort

Today I came around the corner at the appointed hour for my little chat, just *before* the appointed hour, and saw Lorna standing there in the hallway with Dr Travis. She was saying something, something that sounded like '. . . getting nowhere fast, absolutely nowhere'. He leaned towards her a little, wearing that sweet, attentive but ever-so-slightly distant expression of his. He always looks like that, as if he is listening in order to be polite but really is not terribly interested. I like that about him. I prefer it. Lorna is avid, but he is just a well-brought-up boy, doing his job.

Then they saw me. And shut up.

I began to catch sight of Mandy in the high street.

Instead of spending her Saturdays in Charisse, now she went into town and hung around with other kids who were at a loose end. Rough kids, the sort I never spoke to and even avoided glancing at. I'd see her sitting on the ledge at the foot of the war memorial, swinging her thin bare legs. It wasn't meant to be a seat, just an innocent ledge, part of the memorial's design. Perhaps it was included so that mourners could rest flowers on it, or wreaths on Poppy Day. Only now it had become a seat for disaffected youth, lounging and kicking their heels against the meat-coloured marble sides. There was a horse trough too, from the days when horses made up a considerable part of the passing traffic, and the council had tried to plant it up with petunias. Only disaffected youth rested its bottom there and squashed the petunias flat. Perhaps in the days of horse-drawn traffic and war dead there was no time for disaffected youth. Perhaps little children grew straight from button boots and pinafores into work clothes and were too busy and too hungry and too tired to look around and complain. Far too preoccupied with scraping a living to go off the rails.

Then I saw Tom in town with a girl.

It was Mandy who drew this to my attention. Mandy was up at the secondary modern now, too. Sometimes we happened to pass in the corridors and would nod mutely, but that was the limit of our acknowledgement. She was usually with a gaggle of girls, those noisy and self-possessed types who never took any notice of the pecking order of age. I could see that she was emerging from her shell again. Whatever had gone horribly wrong for her had righted itself, or maybe she'd adjusted to it. I don't know. She was a closed book to me. Those opaque grey eyes looked at you but never let you know what she was thinking. I don't know what that says about the windows of the soul – maybe that Mandy had no soul?

Her face wore exactly the same look as it had when she

247

was a child, and I could see just how she would be as an adult. She didn't change as other people changed, their bones expanding and altering the proportions of their faces, prettiness arriving or departing. She stayed the same, with that mean-eyed, hunted, shocked white face, that undernourished face of hers, permanently starving for something she couldn't have.

I was standing at the bus stop one afternoon, feeling blank, just waiting, when Mandy appeared at my side. 'That boy that lives next door to you,' she said. I made sure my face stayed impassive. Mandy knew everyone, God knows how. Perhaps her years of eavesdropping on all the gossip in Charisse had equipped her with this knowledge. Her brain was a gazetteer, she had the town's complete set of mugshots and fingerprints embedded there. Just a quick flick and someone, anyone, could be located. There should have been a great future ahead for a girl with such talents. She went on, 'I seen him on the prom. In a shelter. Wiv a girl. Black hair, mascara. You know her? Paula, her name is. Paula Wright.'

Mandy watched me with her head on one side, her cheek bulging with gum. I gave her a theatrical frown, then an irritated grin. 'What? What are you talking about? What's that got to do with me?'

Mandy shrugged. 'Just thought you'd want to know.' And she slid away as easily as she'd arrived.

So then I knew where to look.

Seeing Tom with a girl actually wasn't as bad as imagining seeing Tom with a girl.

There was something about him – he was indisputably attractive, not only to me. Despite his light eyes and his pale lashes, his careless lack of chivalry. Perhaps *because*

248

of his lack of chivalry. So there was indeed a black-haired girl with a fair amount of mascara. But her hair was short, like a cap, and she wasn't at all pretty. She was even a bit fat. I caught a glimpse of them, not that same afternoon (although I looked, I wasted a good hour or more hunting him down) but a few days later. She was walking quickly along the seafront, and Tom was hurrying after her with that uneven loping stride he had at the time, as if he hadn't yet got used to his height and the terrible size of his feet. I had imagined them entwined on a seat, gazing fondly into each other's eyes, or worse. I watched the girl stop. Tom touched her shoulder with an outstretched hand. They exchanged a few words. The girl shrugged his hand away, and then they parted, walking off in different directions. Neither of them looked back.

This was OK. I could cope with this.

Later, though, I glimpsed the unmistakable back of his head in one of the shelters on the promenade. He had his arm around a girl with blonde hair. I saw them put their faces together. I saw them kiss. I saw their mouths open wide and their cheeks hollow in the kind of kiss where you eat the other person up. Not loving kisses, not melting kisses. Hard, pushing ones, where you tell the other person what you think of them, what you would like to do to them, given half a chance.

I see they have taken out the blocks of butter-yellow tulips and the blue forget-me-nots. The gardeners are at work now filling in the earth rectangles with other colours. One is full of busy Lizzies. I think they will be shocking scarlet when they all come out, to judge by the one or two that have opened flowers so far. They seem to have a craze for bright red in their colour schemes here, the colour of brand-new, just-leaked blood. Controversial, I'd say. Another bed is filled with silver-leaved plants, a fluffy silver velvet of the sort Hanny might well have in her wardrobe. I don't think these will ever come into flower; they're planted out for their foliage alone.

I asked one, of the gardeners what they were called, but he wouldn't tell me. He wouldn't even look at me, but kept his head down and dug away frantically with his trowel.

I've always thought the gardeners here aren't right in the head.

I went looking for Hanny. She was on our usual bench. She said, 'I've got a visitor. David's coming to see me this afternoon.'

I was astonished. It hadn't occurred to me that people visited, like in an ordinary hospital. Or a prison. Here I am, convinced that I've got a fertile imagination, and yet I never thought of this. Turns out I can't imagine further than the end of my nose.

'I think he's coming to tell me it's over between us.'

'Why would he do that?'

Hanny threw her arms out in a wide shrug. Today she was wearing an ice-blue mohair sweater, with long sleeves that she tucked over her knuckles to keep warm. Even in the summer sunshine she felt cold. 'Why not?'

I was still wrestling with the idea of a visitor, someone from Out There coming to see someone In Here. I suppose it could be said that sometimes *I* don't listen properly, either. But I tried to pay attention to her.

'I mean, what have we got going for us?' she went on. 'Me banged up like this for months. Him out in the real world. He probably wants a nice, proper girlfriend. One who likes him, for a start.' She laughed her husky humourless laugh, the one she saved for when she was staring straight ahead at nothing.

'He might not. He might just be coming to see you. See how you are.'

'Doubt it. No, he's come to finish with me. I can feel it in my bones. And I've got very sensitive bones, believe me.' She shivered and folded the spare volume of the sweater round her ribs.

I asked her, 'Will you be upset if he does?'

She turned to look at me. 'Why would I be upset?' Her stare was as bold and baleful as Mandy's. 'I told you, David was my mother's idea all along. Not mine. David's just a passport to make me look OK. In the *real world.*'

'Right. I get it.' I didn't know if I believed her. She sounded pretty upset to me.

'And we're not in the real world, are we, here? And we're not OK.'

Suddenly she laughed her brisk cheerful laugh, the one I thought was genuine.

'Don't tell me you thought we *were* OK!?'

She laughed so hard she threatened to fall off the seat.

When I saw her next day, I asked Hanny, 'What did he say?'

She looked at me blankly. 'What did who say?'

'David.'

'Oh.' She turned away, pulling her sleeves down over her hands, kicking at a fallen flower on the path. 'He didn't say anything. He never turned up.'

'What, not at all? No message, nothing?'

'Nn-nn.' She kicked with her other foot. The toe of her cowboy boot was scuffed.

'What happened, do you think?'

She shook her head. 'He chickened out.'

Hanny didn't seem at all bothered. I don't know what to make of that. Maybe he never existed at all. Maybe she just made him up.

29

Party

It's my birthday today. My nineteenth birthday. Gemini. The Twins. I can just picture the sign for Gemini, from one of Barbara's magazines: two identical figures sitting, knees up, back to back. Looking out in opposite directions. Not speaking to each other.

My birthday passes as spectacularly as every other birthday. Nobody sends me a card.

In Activity I made a birthday cake out of my clay and rolled a birthday candle and stuck it on the top.

'What's that?' Hanny said to me, and I said, 'A penguin,' and she said, 'It's not very good.'

Patrick and Tillie were having a party. A big party to celebrate their wedding anniversary, and her fortieth birthday, the dates of which were close together.

We didn't celebrate birthdays much in our house. Maybe it was the adoption thing, I concluded later. Maybe our dates of birth, birth to some unknown woman, somewhere in the world, were not important, were ludicrous to celebrate in that family. At the time I only thought that birthdays were low-key, having little experience of anyone else's. A card or two, a single present, wrapped, beside the breakfast plate, mumbled good wishes in the morning and then get on with the rest of the day as if it were any other. No cakes, no candles, no parties, no balloons.

So Tillie was forty. I was surprised. She didn't look it. She looked girlish, and like the Tillie of twenty in the paintings of her. Though now I thought about it, the skin around her eyes was dry and papery, a faint dove-grey. There were fine lines etched all over the backs of her hands as if, when she drew them from the washing-up water and dried them, the elastic sheen of youth was gone. She moved like a girl, and squinted and stuffed the hair behind her ears like a girl, but maybe she wasn't quite so youthful after all. How could I compare?

Stella was thirty-nine. I knew because Mandy had told me. Mandy was good for this kind of information. Bettina was thirty-one and Stella thirty-nine. My father was six years older, making him forty-five, and Gloria was somewhere in between. And who knows how old my mother was? This was a secret she felt it only dignified to keep, like keeping the size of her bust from prurient shop assistants. If Stella was thirty-nine and Tillie forty, which one looked the younger? It was hard to tell if Stella looked older or just like a member of a completely different species. Her powdered cheeks were rough peach-skin, her pierced earlobes creased down the middle, her bosom had a deep declivity Tillie could never hope to achieve. Yet Tillie had six children and Stella none. Perhaps it was true what Gloria sometimes claimed (though not on her own behalf, of course): children are supposed to keep you young.

'They're having a party? I'm staying over that night with a friend,' Barbara announced.

'How do you know it's that night?' asked Isolde.

'Because I'm just about to get myself invited,' Barbara called back, tearing down the stairs towards the telephone.

'If they're having a party, I'm staying here,' Isolde said darkly. 'To keep an eye on things.'

'Good,' said Tom. 'A party. Good.'

I knew, in the part of my soul that was Caroline Clipper, that a party was bad news. My mum and dad would peer out of the windows at cars coming down the street, and express their dismay at the number. They would tune their ears to any hint of noise, and worry and fret all evening, speculating on the exact nature of the event next door. There would be drinking, there would be revelry. It was summer and people would be bound to drift outside, windows would be thrown open. I didn't know anything about parties.

'What are you going to *wear*?' Tillie asked me, all excited.

'Am I invited?' I asked.

'Of *course* you're invited.'

In the event we hid upstairs.

Isolde, in a purple satin shift dress with a V-neck and a neatly darted waist, made it her job to wander round offering big plates of food. Tillie and her mother had made canapés, tiny mouthfuls of things, strange and mouth-watering and delicious. I was afraid to count how many foodstuffs I could not identify. Isolde drifted about, elegant and at ease. I could hear her voice: sing-song, chit-chat. It reminded me of the time I'd overheard Barbara talking with our piano teacher. Where did they learn this social competence? (Actually, I knew. It came in the package, it came with the deal: in the genes and as part of the upbringing. Nature *and* nurture. Wouldn't you bloody know it?) Mattie and Sebastian circulated, spoilt and feted – or studiously avoided, according to inclin-ation – by the guests, until they fell asleep in corners and were carried out of the way.

The nerve centre of the party was the kitchen, where most of the guests seemed to gather. It was from here, in the big double oven, that the baking trays of delicacies emerged. More, and different kinds, appeared from the old head-high fridge. Mrs Van Hoog swam back and forth through the crowd, taking a slow crawl to the sink for clean glasses, pushing with an onerous breaststroke back to the oven with yet another empty platter. The crowds parted only with greatest reluctance, hauling in the small of their backs, tucking their elbows away to give her an inch or two, glancing over their shoulders at her as if she was the hired help. Maybe they believed she was. She had on her sky-blue pinafore, and the hair pinned into her bun was escaping in sweaty curls. She kept her mouth firmly shut. Her expression was inscrutable. If she had been the hired help I would have guessed her politics were fiercely left-wing and she despised these lightweight revellers but did the work anyway and spent her wages on dynamite for others to blow them up. But she was Tillie's mother, the famously soft and spoiling Oma, endlessly prising open the children's mouths to tuck sweet cakes inside. She would do anything for Tillie. She would feed the five thousand, and wash the food down with drink until it swilled out of their gills again.

And there was enough drink for the five thousand. I had never seen so much all in one place, not even in an off-licence (and the only time I went in one of those was to buy a bag of crisps). It stood on all the surfaces, together with glasses tall and short, delicate or free-with-petrol tough. There were bottles of wine, and bottles of spirits in more shapes than I knew bottles came in, and brown beer bottles, and fat beer cans, and Patrick already had a barrel wedged outside on the veranda where people could just come and turn the beer on like a tap. And Tillie, or her mother, had made a drink called a wine cup, in a huge glass bowl swimming with slices of orange and apple and waterlogged brown banana, and even with petals from garden flowers. I was surprised anyone wanted to drink it, but it was going down fast, and every so often Patrick would seize the nearest bottle and pour generous quantities in.

So this was how you held a party.

I took myself to the kitchen, imagining I could be like Isolde and justify my presence by helping out. But Tillie found me nothing to do, kept whirling past me as if I was invisible. I picked up a plate and she whisked it out of my hands, and then turned, got grabbed and kissed on the cheek by someone, fell into animated conversation, and quite forgot about the plate. I was squeezed between the edge of the kitchen table and the bodies of yelling strangers who kept backing into me and stepping on my feet without even noticing. I knew no one, could talk to

257

no one, had nothing to eat and no glass in my hand. I was a party failure.

Tom's chin came over my shoulder and rested there, painfully. 'Come on,' he said, 'this is no place for the likes of us.' His arms came round my ribs and he joined his hands together at the front. He stood up straight again, removing his chin, but kept his hands where they were. 'Too many arty farts. Too many *Oooh hallooo, how nice to see yooo*-s.' It made me laugh: this was just what Tillie's grabber had said. Tom backed me out through the door, along the hall, and then posted me ahead of him up the stairs. I was sad to lose his hold on me. His lanky arms around my ribs were more intimate than any of those kisses had been.

Tom and Tom Rose and I sat upstairs on the floor of Tom's room. We could feel the music vibrating through the floorboards under our thighs, thrumming up our backbones, buzzing in our skulls. The dog, which had been confined to Tom's room to keep him out of the way, sat tensely beside us. Even he looked headachy and confused.

Tom had brought up a plate of food and a big can of bitter. Tom Rose made two holes in it with the can opener that was a fixture of Tom's bedside table, and attempted to drink straight from the can. 'Oh, *waste*!' Tom shouted, as it slid down his chin, neck and shirt. He found three glasses, misty, and probably used many times without benefit of a wash, in the detritus on top of his chest of drawers. He poured, also missing. The huge can was hard to manoeuvre. 'Oh, *waste*!' Tom Rose said, in his deeper voice, enjoying himself. 'No matter,' said Tom. 'Lots more where that came from.'

'Certainly is,' Tom Rose said, sitting back against the side of the bed, belching, deeply satisfied.

We heard the cackling laughter of people below on the front veranda, the shouted greetings when another car drew up. 'Nowhere to bloody park!' I heard a man call. 'Haven't you roped off a neighbouring field, Hennessy?' His voice assumed a honking, barking edge. 'I say, haven't you roped off one of your fields? The old hundred-acre would do.' I thought of my mother and father, twitching at the net curtains, horrified. I was horrified too.

The beer was warm and tasted of electroplated spoons. I drank it down like water. The more of it you had, the less you tended to react with a shudder.

Tom had turned his own record player on, was competing with some deeply thrumming music, jangling electric guitars and a synthesizer that seemed to be playing some other song entirely. The words sounded like 'Wait, wait, wait, why do-on't you-ou wait?' I didn't share his taste in music, I didn't seem to have any taste in music of my own yet, so I just tipped back my head and mouthed along as if I knew the words: 'Wait, wait, wait . . .'

'Why-hy do-on't you-ou *wait*!?' Tom and Tom Rose wailed, screwing up their faces, leaning their heads towards one another.

When that side of the record had finished Tom Rose turned it over and Tom scrambled up and loped off downstairs for more drink. While he was gone Tom Rose made no attempt to talk to me or even look at me. He could have been alone in the room. His foot thumped up and down on the floor in time to the music. Tom was some time. He came back with four bottles of beer and a clear glass bottle half full of gin.

I tried the gin, an inch in the bottom of my beer glass. That really made me shudder and gag. It looked so innocuous, watery, sliding around like glycerine. Tom took my glass and went to the window, tipping it over the veranda roof below. 'It's raining gin,' he called down. 'Just look up and stick your tongues out!'

I didn't bother to drink any more. I went to the bathroom and swilled my mouth with tap water and a dab of toothpaste. I had to queue behind three other people before I could get in.

When I came back, Tom Rose was looking at his watch. 'I have to go soon,' he said. I had to go too, but I always felt an idiot for saying so. In fact I should have gone long before, but that was too foolish to admit to.

Where did my parents think I was? At my friend's, up the road. I was hazy as to exactly which friend, which house. I let them fall into believing it was the new girl, the plump girl with the long single plait down her back, who had moved into the bungalow nearest the round-about. She went to my school – at least, we saw her in the uniform – and she was about my height. I didn't even know her name, though I had christened her Rosemary and kept it in store, just in case they should ask. I gave the impression we did our homework together, that is, I went off with books under my arm, without actually putting the notion into words. You couldn't even say that I had actually lied this time . . . my friend, down the road . . . well, here I was. It just wasn't that inert-looking girl with the pink-framed spectacles. It was Tom, lanky and lecherous. And Tom Rose, the inner parts of whose mouth I knew well, though he wouldn't even speak to me.

'But it's just getting good,' said Tom. 'Look, look, something special.' And he got out a tobacco tin, just like his mother's, with a scratched, intricate pattern of leaves on top, and opened it. Inside, amongst shreds of tobacco, was a long twisted white paper cigarette, very inexpert-looking. It reminded me more of a Tampax than one of Tillie's little roll-ups, which were match-sized and match-thin.

'Now, this . . .' Tom said, stretching out comfortably on the floor, 'is *our* party.'

We passed it from mouth to mouth. It was no good my saying I didn't smoke. Hadn't smoked at all, really, not since the hot worm in my throat on the veranda years before. At school girls smoked Number Six with a Polo mint in their mouths, the cheap version of menthol cigarettes. I usually accepted the Polo mint and didn't bother with the rest.

'Be a good girl,' Tom said, confidentially, winking like some old uncle. 'Don't be a drag.'

'Well, *do* be a drag,' said Tom Rose, laughing lazily, issuing a white layer of smoke out of his mouth, like some mountain mist, heavy and rolling, 'do *take* a drag.'

The beer, the gin, the toothpaste, the unfamiliar food, were curling around in my stomach like some restless animal trying to settle itself. The smoke flowed in and around, the smell of it was inside the channels of my head and around me, outside. I gritted my teeth, determined to hold on to my integrity, my stomach contents. I got up slowly, a bit unsteady. 'I've really got to go. I'm dead late.'

'Mr Clipper will wonder where you are. *Mrs* Clipper will be distraught,' Tom said, and they both laughed.

Laughed inordinately, lying flat on the floor with only their heads tipped up at a painful angle, rested against the bed. I could see Tom's bony ribs heaving up and down under his rucked-up T-shirt. I stepped over Tom Rose's legs and went out.

The stairs were a problem, see-sawing away into the distance, terribly long and steep. I held on to the banister rail with one hand and the wall with the other, and levered myself down, like a person on crutches. I had to push past a woman in a silver dress who was sitting on the stairs, jabbering into the telephone, and a man and a woman who were embracing. As I squeezed past I had to put both my arms around the man's back to steady them and myself.

'Oh, what's this?' said the man. 'Come on, sweetheart, the more the . . .'

I felt stupid and red-faced, and then it was over, I was through, and the front door was ahead of me, open. The deep blue, scented night. As I crossed the veranda the music downstairs stopped, and I could hear Tom and Tom Rose's voices from above, yelping out over the evening air, laughing, and howling like demented dogs.

No one was interested in how late I was. I think this time they'd forgotten all about me. I found Mum and Dad and Brian standing on the back lawn, in the full flood of light from the French windows, looking up at the strange glow thrown by flames above the hedge. Grey smoke blossoming up into the navy-blue sky, and burning sparks that shot madly up, darting and spiralling like houseflies, and turned into charred flakes which floated down, graceful and calm. Perhaps I should have noticed the smoky smell in the air when I came out of the

Hennessys' house. Perhaps I should have realized that the excited voices weren't just party voices. I was more concerned about walking straight and looking normal. About not puking into the roses. But no one even glanced at me.

'I wondered where you all were,' I said, trying to imply that I had been indoors for some time. 'What's going on?'

'More than a bonfire,' my father said, shortly. He sounded cross but the look on his face was triumphant.

'Maybe it's their summer house,' I said. 'Their garden shed. I mean, everyone has a shed. Don't they?'

'I suppose we'll have the fire brigade up here next,' my mother said. 'Though how they'll get through all those . . .'

We stood motionless, our heads tilted upwards. No more sparks flew up. The billow of smoke dwindled.

'Just keeping an eye on *our* shed,' my father said, looking back at me for the first time. He wore a weary cynic's expression now, as if he had to put up with neighbourhood riots every Saturday night. 'Making sure one of those sparks doesn't catch the roof alight. You go in. We can all go in now.'

We moved off slowly, Brian leading the way, his hands in his pockets, kicking a snail shell up the lawn.

That night the Hennessys' old summer house burned to the ground. It was assumed that a spark from the coals where Patrick was roasting half a pig had set it off.

Actually, it was Brian.

30

Home and Abroad

The day after the party we had Aunt Gloria to tea. My mother, with great bags under her eyes and a drawn expression which could have been removed if she had wished to, complained about the noise the previous night. 'No respect. No respect for other people at all,' she kept repeating.

But Gloria, most unsatisfactorily, only responded with 'The Crown and Anchor on the corner gets noisy some nights. Fridays and Saturdays, in particular. And the customers, going home! You can hear them all the way up the street.' Which wasn't what my mother wanted to hear at all.

While Gloria entertained the folks, I slipped next door for half an hour. The Hennessys were still tidying up. The smell of smoke and stale beer hung round the house. Tillie, in her jeans and a crumpled shirt, looking more bedraggled than usual, was stacking empty bottles in a cardboard box outside the front door. 'They're out the back,' she said to me. 'And Patrick's snoozing on the sofa.

He's feeling a bit fragile, so I'd appreciate it if you'd be quiet.'

I should have taken that phrase and presented it in a jewelled box to my mother. It would have proved beyond doubt her belief in the hypocrisy of the rest of the world. She could have lifted the lid every so often, as with a little musical box, and listened to the phrase, and gloated.

In the back garden I saw that the summer house was nothing more than a heap of damp black charcoal. Mattie and Sebastian had taken bits of it and were drawing rude cartoons on the paving stones. Isolde was sweeping cigarette ends and other debris from the back veranda. She gave me a 'What did you expect?' kind of shrug as I passed. Pickles was sniffing curiously at the path of her broom.

I found Tom sitting under an apple tree, eating cold leftovers. I sat down a quarter turn around from him, so that I could rest my back against the tree trunk, too. He passed me his beer bottle, and I took a swig. Here was my looking-glass life, the other side of the hedge, where people treated me casually, where I knew a boy, and drank beer. It was so weird that I turned into this other person when I crossed the boundary between there and here. Or was it that *they* turned me into another person, and my family, when I went home, turned me back?

'How did it happen?'

'Patrick and his medieval barbecue.'

Tom flicked his hand towards a coal pit where the end posts to support the spit-roast arrangement still stood. 'No one was paying it too much attention, and I think a bit must have flown up and caught the timbers of the shed.'

'Was anything lost?'

'Some tools and wood. No Leonardos, if that's what you mean. Eugene put it out.'

'*Eugene?*'

'Yeah, Eugene got the fire extinguisher Tillie keeps under the stairs. She keeps it in case the house goes up in flames, and all her precious pictures with it.'

I scrambled round to face Tom. 'I didn't know *Eugene* was here!'

Eugene had been somewhere in that thrumming crowd and I hadn't even suspected it.

'Yeah.' Tom sounded totally unconcerned. 'He wouldn't miss a party. Came up with his new girlfriend, Tamara.' He fell silent, looking down at the greasy plate in his lap, and there was something about the way he'd said her name that made me think he was silent in order to contemplate the image of Tamara.

'Is he still here?'

'Nah. Left this morning. Couldn't wait to get back to the Smoke. Doesn't like yokel life.'

'Do *we*?'

'Not much, but what can we do?' He sighed, and tipped the beer bottle right up, catching the last drops in his open mouth. I looked at the uncouth outline of his throat.

'I can't believe Eugene was here,' I said.

I never really believed in Eugene. I'd needed proof, and there was none. I thought of the monkey-baby in the painting. Now he was grown up, with delectable girlfriends. He was older than the others, a legendary sibling. Eugene had put the fire out in the summer house. Eugene was there and I had missed him. Eugene was the Invisible Man.

* * *

Barbara came back from her overnight stay with dyed hair. She and the friend (a girl I didn't know) had coloured it over the bathroom sink. It was dark red, a burnished red, eye-catching, but it didn't go with her complexion. The following evening we sat on her bed and worked our way through a stack of magazines she'd brought from the friend's house: *Honey*, *Nineteen*, even *Vogue*. She flipped pages, looking critically at skinny, soft-focus girls with huge eyes and blank expressions.

'How come Eugene is much older than the rest of you?' I asked. 'What was Tillie doing? She could have painted then, when she only had him.'

'Oh, she had two other babies after him,' Barbara said, offhandedly, not looking up from her article. 'But they died. They both had something wrong with them and they died just after they were born. Or they died before they were born. In the womb. I can't remember exactly.' She flipped another page.

I was shocked. Poor Tillie. And to keep on trying, so many times.

'It was lucky the rest of you were all right, then,' I said. She looked up. 'Are we?'

What if Tillie, to make up for those poor lost babies, had decided to adopt? Had decided to adopt a replacement to fill the aching void in her heart? What if they had chosen *me* from the children's home? I could have grown up with Tillie as my mother. I wonder how much would have been the same, and how much that has happened would never have happened, in those circumstances?

Well, it's no good thinking about *what if*.

As my aunt Gloria would say, 'It doesn't bear thinking about.'

Hanny Gombrich doesn't drink milk or eat any dairy foods. She told me she is allergic to them. I asked her how she knew.

'It gives me a rash. Anything dairy.'

'So what do you do?'

'They're supposed to be careful with my diet here, but they're not *that* careful. I think if they can't be bothered they just slop it all in. And I get a reaction.'

'Even to chocolate?'

'Of course to chocolate!'

'It's not just something you don't want to eat, then?'

'No!' She sounded most offended. 'Look, I'll prove it. Even if I don't know something's dairy, it still has an effect.'

She pushed back one sleeve to demonstrate.

'This is an old bit of eczema,' she said. 'The redness has faded but you can still *feel* where it was. It's from something milky in a sauce last week.'

She grabbed my hand and pressed it on to the skin of her forearm. It was true, it felt rough and dry, like you imagine a lizard's skin would feel. I took my hand away quickly, but she left her sleeve rolled back. Exposed like that, her inner arm was a basket-weave of delicate scars, more than I had seen before, more than she had showed me. She must have tried a lot of times.

I didn't know what to say, so I didn't say anything.

Today, under her tapestry coat, she was wearing black crushed-velvet trousers and genuine American cowboy boots. Bought when she was genuinely in America. Hanny has been all over the world.

268

I, by contrast, have never been anywhere. Our family didn't go away for holidays like other families did. If asked by some well-meaning neighbour, my parents would say, 'We're staying at home this year,' as if all the other years we had spent the fortnight in a caravan at Morecambe Bay or a cliff-top hotel in Cornwall. 'We're having *days out*.' Oh, days out.

Days out were purgatory. My mother would make us a picnic lunch, and pack it in transparent boxes that reeked of plastic and made the food taste of plastic. We had sandwiches and orange squash, and thermos flasks of tea, and bananas which putrefied inside their skins before the journey was halfway over. We took a blanket to sit on, and plastic macs in case it rained. And a camera to take a photograph of us having fun. To cap it all, Brian would sit in the front of the car. Mum sat next to Dad on the way there, and then on the way home – 'Fancy a change? All change!' my father would say – down Brian would plump into the space and comfort of the front seat, as if it was his God-given right. 'That's it. Ladies in the back. Just like driving the Queen.'

I think they liked it, men together, steering and navigating, in control of the car. I never sat in the front. Mum and I squashed into the back seat, in opposite corners, the picnic paraphernalia between us, our feet crammed into the narrow leg-space, not talking. It was always noisy in the back. We could hear Brian's and Dad's voices but we couldn't necessarily hear what they said. I stared out of the side window, or round Dad's head, but mostly *at* his head, the misty brown prickles of his short-back-and-sides, the waxy pink of his bald spot, the curious rolls of fat (and yet he wasn't *fat*) where his neck

269

met his collar. I wanted to see the open road, the rolling landscape, but all I got was the whirling grass verge and a view of the back of his head.

We went to places like some forlorn field indistinguishable from any other field, or a small hilltop – hilltops being few and far between in our part of the country and therefore thrilling. We liked a nice view. Sometimes we looked round an old church, or went to a stately home which had an open day. Very occasionally we went to the sea, but my parents, like a lot of people who have grown up in coastal towns, despised resorts and the trippers they attracted, and if we went anywhere near the water it was to bleak reaches of tide and shingle, acres of blade-like grass and piercing winds.

But the Hennessys, oh, the Hennessys did it differently. Of course they did. Once I went round in all my innocence, on the first day of the school holidays, anticipating endless time together, only to find that Barbara had already left. Flown the coop, hadn't told me a thing. This was early on, this was one of the first surprises, the sudden blows she delivered to me.

'Oh, she's gone away,' Sebastian said, hanging upside down by his arms from the veranda rail. His mouth hung open and his curly hair streamed towards the earth. 'She's gone to London with Isolde.'

This simple statement disorientated me as much as his face, the wrong way up. If he'd told me she'd been transported to Botany Bay I wouldn't have been more shocked. How did people just go? There must have been planning, packing, some thought beforehand. Some intimation of sudden departure. In our house even days out were planned for in detail, like a general drawing up his campaign strategy, taking all intelligence into account. Preparations were visible. But no, Barbara and Isolde had just taken off, like will-o'-the-wisps, like thieves in the night. Stolen away from me.

Or it might be to Devon, to Malvern, to Scotland, to Rome. I found that one or another Hennessy was always zooming off, at a moment's notice, to stay with someone's godmother or Patrick's half-brother or Tillie's old friend from art school. Tillie's extended family might all have died due to the Nazi occupation but Patrick's relations well made up for it. Hennessys, as I might have known, had a wealth of relations sprinkled across the globe, only too anxious to invite and entertain them, and a superfluity of friends just waiting to make them at home.

They went by train and car and sometimes even plane, in pairs and alone, on exotic adventures with fluid schedules and ever-shifting itineraries. Once when Barbara went to Paris to stay with someone I'd never heard mentioned before, called Joan (not a French name, I thought, in spite of Joan of Arc), I was told, 'She'll be back on Monday.' But when Monday came I learned she'd been despatched to Annecy to visit someone else. Annecy, I was told, had a beautiful lake and a very good climate. All very well, I thought, but why was Barbara in need of them?

Even Mr and Mrs Van Hoog went away every year for two weeks in the Lake District. They liked the mountains and the water. They always sent a postcard back, of Dove Cottage or Windermere or maybe just an unnamed misty island floating on a lake. I imagined them in their insect-like car, driving carefully down winding lanes, and stopping at recognized beauty spots to admire the view and then study the next leg on the map.

The exception was Tillie. Tillie never zoomed off anywhere. She didn't seem to need to visit London, or Dublin, or Paris. She barely even went to the shops down the road. Tillie stayed at home, as if she was the very necessary household god, the little deity of the hearth, the *genius loci*, without whom none of it could survive intact, or even exist.

31

Drifting

For a couple of years I was a Girl Guide. I only went because my mother made me – and because I'd been a Brownie, and that's what Brownies did next.

Our Guide group met on Thursday evenings in the community hall. Just as at school, we learned things that seemed to have no application in outside life, like tying complicated knots, and identifying predatory birds by their silhouettes in flight, and how to interpret signs and leave signs for other Guides. In the Brownies we had concentrated on semaphore. I was quite keen on semaphore, I liked stretching out my arms like the hands on a clockface and waving the flags at the end of them. But Guides did not stoop to semaphore. For some reason they did not envisage themselves standing on hilltops and signalling across open valleys. They saw themselves like La Longue Carabine, running trails through dense woodland, and made little signs from sticks and stones, leaving them in the middle of the pathway (where, of course, they could be kicked out of the way by animals or non-Guides), arrows for left and right, a circle with a stone in the middle for 'We have gone home'. It always seemed a bit of a cheek to me to get people out into a dark confusing wood and then signal 'We have gone home'.

I was in Kingfisher patrol. There were six girls, four of whom went to the grammar school and one who, like me, attended the secondary mod. She was a year older and at school we had never exchanged even a glance, let alone spoken.

Our patrol leader was a girl called Helen Ethersidge. She was fast and funny, and in another life I would have looked up to her. She had nearly black hair and a broad-boned face with thick pale skin, and I thought she was attractive. Not pretty, but attractive.

The very first week Helen showed us how to cook sausages over a bonfire, on the scrap of rough land behind the community hall. She helped us choose green sticks from the hedge for toasting forks so that they wouldn't go up in flames before the sausages were cooked through. When we took them out of the fire, the meat was black on the outside and raw in the middle. But they tasted much better than a lot I've had.

In another life I would have admired Helen Ethersidge and tried to be like her. It would have been better if I had. But it was too late by then. I had taken the Hennessys as my pattern, and look where that's got me.

While I was sent to Guides Brian went to Scouts, but he actually enjoyed it. They did much more energetic things than we did, and held open days when their families and friends could come and try out Scout activities for themselves. Scout activities involved rope ladders and walkways, jungle drums and inflatable dinghies. On open days the dinghies were not actually in water: they sat on the floor of the Scout hut and younger children climbed in and out, and sat down in them and waved paddles about. A large Scout in shorts, with hard-looking calves and scarred knees, stood beside the dinghies to ensure no damage was done. In a way it looked fun, the sort of fun Helen Ethersidge and I might have enjoyed. But I could hear Barbara's disparaging voice in my ear, and even worse, Tom's. *Is that what you do? You sing songs round the camp fire? You learn to tie knots? What for? So that when your knickers fall down in public you'll always know how to do a half-hitch with the elastic and save yourself further blushes?* Oh God, I couldn't be doing with that.

Leaving the Guides was surprisingly easy. I just stayed in my bedroom one Thursday evening, pretending to do some homework. My ironed uniform on its clothes hanger was ready and waiting. I ignored it. Brian was sent to remind me of the time. I said, 'I'm not going,' and, like a good boy, he reported this back to the kitchen. There was a further relay of messages: why was I not going? 'I've got too much homework.' 'Can't you do that another night?' 'No. I'm stopping altogether.' This brought Mum to my door, untying her cooking apron as if for a fight. She folded it and wrapped it round her arms, which she then crossed over her chest.

'What's all this, Carol?' she asked. 'Stopping Guides?'

'I've got too much homework these days,' I said. I held a maths textbook open on my knee for authenticity.

'What about your uniform?' she asked. The expensive uniform, which she had not been able to run up herself on the machine at home.

'We can sell it. There's always someone joining who will want it.'

And with that she exhaled loudly and turned away, unrolling her apron again. Another sort of person might have shrugged, but she didn't. Too lax, too sloppy, shrugging.

I couldn't believe it had been so easy. Well, at least *that* was out of the way. I would have done it ages before if I'd known. I quite expected her to put up an argument against my leaving, but she didn't seem at all interested, once she realized that some of the money she had spent could be recouped.

Piano, well, that was easy, too. I was telling Lorna the truth when I said it got too expensive. Almost five years of piano lessons, what an investment. As adolescence rolled inexorably on, my practising slackened off. 'If you're not going to practise, Carol, I'm not going on paying,' my mother said. We didn't shake hands on the bargain, but we kept to it. I think she was relieved, not just about the money but at the sudden lovely silence round the house. We were not a musical family. We had overreached ourselves. I think my five years of grindingly slow progress proved that.

Giving up church was harder. Too much at stake. This hit at the core of what my mother wanted us to be. There were so many rites and routines associated with it, the Saturday night shoe-cleaning and coat-brushing, coins for the collection put aside in a special jar. We would set out for church after breakfast every Sunday, my mother and Brian and me, leaving Dad oiling and sharpening the edging shears in preparation for his morning's work. These were the times I dreaded meeting a Hennessy – any

Hennessy, even Sebastian or Mattie – as we walked down the road, a pair and one trotting behind on the narrow pavement, all neat in our Sunday clothes. I prayed to the dear Lord for rain, because then Dad would have to get the car out and drive us to church, even though he would not go in himself unless it was a special occasion. Perhaps because of my lax and wicked ways, my prayers were answered no more often than the prevailing meteorological situation would allow.

I said I didn't want to go any more. Dropped my bombshell. 'I've grown out of Sunday school. They're all younger than me.'

'You can be a shining example to the young ones, then.'

'And the teenagers' group. It's so . . .' What? Condescending, embarrassing, lacking in cogently argued theory? I fell back on 'boring'.

My mother just looked at me.

'And I don't enjoy the morning service.'

Her expression showed me that she thought enjoyment had nothing to do with it.

'I'm plagued with *doubts*,' I tried.

She looked at me as if she had them too, all the time. There was a stand-off. Eventually she said, 'I'm not letting you make up your mind until you're sixteen. Then we'll see if you've still got doubts.'

'Fifteen.'

'No.'

'Fifteen and a half.'

She looked grim, but conceded with a brief nod of her head.

I never made it that far. She must have known that there was no leverage she could bring to bear that would make me go with them every Sunday. So eventually she let me drift. It was a funny feeling, beginning to realize that she didn't care. She'd concentrate her efforts elsewhere, on someone more rewarding. She had washed her hands of me. That was the impression I got, as I moved about the kitchen in my pyjamas on Sunday mornings. Even Dad in his old gardening clothes was more useful than me. He handed out more milk from the fridge. He tutted about the weather, and my mother tutted back. She and Brian sat up very straight at the kitchen table, neat and pressed and brushed, eating extremely politely like people dining at a hotel, so as not to get any crumbs or jam on their church clothes. Then they went out, without speaking to me, walking along the pavement briskly: a pair.

We still had our chores to do. Brian was allowed to take care of the lawn mower, to clean the blades, oil the wheels, scrape the grass-box out. He was strong enough now to keep the mower straight, press on the roller to achieve those neat green lines, that self-stripe in the fabric of the lawn. He'd inherited that responsibility. I don't know why lawns have to be stripy, what's so aesthetically pleasing about tame grass. It's only the way the grass blades lie, reflecting the sun, this way, that way. A trick of the light.

I knelt on the crazy paving outside the French windows, weeding. I pulled up a plug of bittercress, freeing a ridge of sand, a scatter of enraged red ants. The garden was past its best: sunflowers, flopping from their canes, ragged as old scarecrows, an edging of light blue ageratum like a trim of dirty nylon fur. The sun was dipping, our shadows long. From next door's garden nothing but silence.

Brian had stopped mowing, was kicking at the edge of the lawn by the hedge. On and on he went, tapping the toe of his shoe, waiting like someone who expected to be asked their opinion. I stood up and took my bucket of weeds down the path to the incinerator.

'The lawn's very dry,' he said, when I didn't say anything. 'It's crumbling away.'

'Oh yes?'

'We should put the hose on it.'

'Yes.'

'It's this hedge.'

Sucks the life.

'Put the hose on it, then.'

'Can't. There's a hosepipe ban. Not enough rain this summer.'

'Don't put the hose on it, then.'

'Other people do,' he said darkly, scowling. 'Next door do. I've heard them. I've seen 'em.'

Oh yes? Had he seen me, too?

'Other people are always breaking the rules.' He glanced upwards, at the dusty, dark immensity of the hedge.

'Then so can you. Once in a while. It won't hurt.'

He thought about it. Slow ticking over of time. Then he shrugged. 'No. Not me.'

'It'll be autumn soon,' I said. 'It'll start raining and never stop.'

But he was still standing there, hands in pockets, staring up at the hedge, as if the drought, the ban, the petty restrictions, and all the breaking of rules, every injustice in the world, were down to the Hennessys, every little bit.

Then we became economic units: Brian got a paper round, and I served, Saturday mornings, behind the counter in Mrs Drew's. The wool shop. Now it was incumbent on *me* to understand the secrets of two-ply and four-ply, to pluck, unerringly, a pair of size seven knitting needles from the close-packed display. It was up to me to slip the puffy packs of Kotex discreetly into thick white paper bags. Or – an innovation, this – the neat blue boxes of Tampax.

My mother, despite her love of the new-fangled, was suspicious of Tampax, in particular for 'unmarried girls'. They were not at all suitable. In her mind, unmarried girls – despite the incontrovertible evidence before her eyes from Bettina, from whatever she might know about the origins of Brian and me – *unmarried girls* were synonymous with untried girls. Untempted. Unspoilt. And Tampax were just so undeniably penetrative.

So I bought my own Tampax. I had ample opportunity, after all. And a staff discount.

Saturday morning in a wool shop was quite a Carolyn sort of thing to do. Not exactly hard labour; genteel and undemanding. I had high hopes of it that first Saturday. Perhaps I'd found my niche, the thing I could be good at. But by the end of the morning all I'd sold were three yards of ribbon, a thimble and a packet of darning needles.

Mrs Drew was upstairs resting her swollen ankles on a petit-point footstool. She suffered from 'veins' and 'blood pressure'. Her doctor had warned her to take it easy. Every time the bell on the shop door rang, she called down to find out the latest. At mid-morning I took her up a cup of instant coffee and a chocolate biscuit. Her apricot toy poodle was sitting on her lap, and kissing her with his horrible grizzled grey mouth. He got the biscuit. I'd had three cups of coffee already myself, perched on a stool in the little back room, trying unsuccessfully to tune her radio to anything interesting. At half past twelve I turned the shop sign over, pulled down the blind, and carried the day's takings upstairs to Mrs Drew. Nine shillings and sixpence. I think a Carolyn would have done better. With her winning smile and her delightful ways, she'd have purred the customers into extravagance. She'd have drawn them in off the streets like a magnet, and not let them leave till quantities of hard cash had changed hands.

The wool shop was struggling, on its last legs. People didn't knit so much any more, or make their own clothes. They liked to buy from the big shops in town, or send for things mail-order, cheap and cheerful garments with no hard work in them at all. They didn't like *home-made*. I don't know exactly how long the shop lasted after my nine months' stint as a Saturday girl, but, walking past one day, I noticed that Mrs Drew had pulled down the blind for ever. Had packed up the last few balls of wool and cards of lace and taken them home, to knit and sew through her twilight years. Or maybe not. Maybe she never partook of those homely female pursuits. Perhaps she got out the gin and the mah-jong set, even the little wooden sticks for making bets with, and invited all her old-lady friends round, and got them roaring drunk, and robbed them blind.

Perhaps. One can only hope so.

* * *

'Your brother,' Lorna says. 'Brian – hmm?'

So she has got round to him at last.

'When you were younger you were very close, your mother reported. Your *adoptive* mother.'

Then she does a thing with her eyebrows, a freaky thing she's started doing recently, raising them and looking at me, and then lowering one eyebrow on its own. Remarkable muscular control. I've tried it myself, without success, I have to say. There's a small mirror bolted to the wall in my room, and the first time she tried it on me I went straight upstairs and practised it in there. I looked like a gurning champion at a country fair, but I still couldn't do what Lorna does. It's very distracting. Maybe that's what she intends.

I try to keep my mind off Lorna's facial gymnastics and on what she is saying.

'You used to play together all the time, in the garden and the neighbourhood, with the local children.'

Yes, because there wasn't any choice.

'And you had friends in common.'

Does she mean those twins we forced to be our chariot horses? The little boy with the trike? *Mandy?* I really feel like saying something here. Almost.

Lorna grows expansive. 'From about the age of eight or nine, though, boys and girls tend to separate into groups of the same sex. Their friendships polarize. Girls loathe boys, boys loathe girls. Or they say they do. Does any of this sound familiar?'

'Polarize,' I say. 'I like that word.'

Lorna twitches faintly.

'You and Brian were no longer quite so close. You were busy turning into a rebel, while Brian was much more conventional. That must have been very galling for you.'

I feel a bit queasy.

'But later on, when your new friends palled, you got together again.'

That's the trouble with files, with reports, with the *official version* – you can see how they got the story they end up with, but you can also see where they've gone so very, very wrong. How they've ended up with fiction. Little Red Riding Hood picked up her basket and went off visiting, good intentions all round. What happened in the murky light under the trees is another matter: the wolf, the grandma, the woodcutter . . . How do we know for sure who was grinning, and whose blood was spilt? And just who was wielding that axe?

Lorna says, 'You and Brian, you're all each other has, when it comes down to it.'

She gives me a long look, not unsympathetic.

I want to say: no, you've got it wrong. He had Mum and Dad. They were always on his side. Or more on his side than mine. And he knew it, and he worked on it. Sticking his hand inside them like glove puppets, and wagging their heads, and watching me while he did it. And grinning all the time.

I want to *say something*. To Lorna. It's not fair. She has brought me to this pass.

I cross my legs and re-cross them. I fold my hands together, and look at my knuckles to make sure they're not too white. Very quietly, I clear my throat.

'Ever since the beginning, you and Brian have stuck together. You've had no choice, have you?'

I really don't like the way this is going, and I really, really don't like the way I'm handling it. If only Dr Travis were here, to pass me a glass of water or smooth his cool medical hand over my forehead. To light a cigarette and hold it to my cracked and bleeding lips.

But Dr Travis is away this week. At a conference. Hanny told me that, Hanny who always seems to know far more than I do. Maybe she indulges in pleasant conversation with him, maybe she chats away and asks anodyne questions and he tells her things. Ever since I sat in the narrow hallway at Mrs Wallis's and heard Barbara conversing with her like an old friend, I've always been amazed at people who can do that. I can't chat. I can only sword-fight. I am always *en garde*.

But right now I'm disarmed.

Lorna smiles at me, thinking she's won this round.

'Brian. How would you describe him?'

Actually, my hands are quite a normal colour and my fingers are relaxed. I flex them in front of me and say, 'We were never close at all. Circumstance threw us together.'

Lorna bends her head to make a note, smiling as she writes.

'I think, Cora, that we are beginning to get somewhere. At long last.'

Mike was taking us in Group today. We played the one-word game, as usual. Find a formula: stick to it. I think that must be the slogan printed on Mike's coffee mug up in the staffroom.

Strange to say, everyone was quite brief, almost restrained, in their ramblings and shamblings this morning. Marsupial's word was 'bedroom' – not strictly an adjective – but Mike's eyes bulged appreciatively. 'Go on,' he said, clutching both knees and leaning back and lifting his big shoes right off the floor.

I thought maybe we were plunging into a variant of the game – if you were a room in your house, which one would it be? – but it turned out to be just some lengthy garbled disquisition about not wanting to share a room with her sisters.

'So what would you say you were – frustrated?' he asked, and then left a meaningful pause. 'And is that what you're feeling like today?' He must have been having tuition. He's never been so direct before.

'Oh no,' Marsupial said, most reasonably. 'I was just *saying*.'

Perhaps Marsupial, despite her sighs and the smell of hot brown soup that escapes whenever she lifts her arms, despite the complete insanity of her precious, bloated, empty abdomen, was winding Mike up. Was taking the piss.

Then Mike turned to me. I was startled. What was the word for the day?

'Despair.'

I didn't mean to say it. It just popped out.

32

My Education

I cannot say we have ever got on well together, education and me. Eleven years, from five to sixteen, and neither side got much out of the transaction.

I could read and write and spell and do my numbers well enough, but not *well enough*, if you see what I mean. Not well enough to count for anything.

In the eleven-plus, we had an intelligence test. This meant endless questions where you had to fill in the blank word or add the missing shape. Most of the time I felt that the only answer I could give was 'Well, it depends . . .' There was no box to tick for 'Well, it depends . . .' There was no space provided to write down my equivocal reasons. I guess I didn't have the intelligence to pass this test.

At the secondary modern I was not regarded as anything other than part of the herd. Everyone who was no one went there, girls to the buildings on one side of the road, boys to the buildings on the other. Unlike my junior school, they were not that vigilant about our presence in class. Perhaps it was a matter of some relief when the worst pupils failed to show up. We put in a few years on the treadmill and then were regurgitated at the other end. If you wanted to do anything fancy, like O levels, or, heaven preserve us, A levels, you had to go elsewhere. You had to join the sixth form of the grammar. Hardly anybody ever did.

Nobody at the secondary modern picked me out and uncovered my special qualities. My work was equally covered in crosses and ticks, in B-minuses and C-pluses. We did geography, history, religious instruction, English, maths, a bit of science and a lot of *domestic* science. We did healthy games three times a week. Our teachers were those not good enough for better schools. They appeared to be divided into two camps: those who were interested in their engagement rings and those who were interested in preserving their virginity. The young ones with a bit of energy and a gleam in their eye came and went very swiftly. The old monsters in tweed suits and severe haircuts stayed for ever. I learned to sew a French seam, and that one should always pin and then tack and then sew, never just pin and sew; I learned to beat egg whites until the bowl could be turned upside down without losing any of its contents, to mould a Swedish meatball, to make pastry – shortcrust, puff and sweet. We drew up menus for a week and studied the finer points of bringing up a baby: fresh air, regular naps, everything sterilized. All this, together with subject and predicate, photosynthesis, the major exports of India, the lineage of all those Tudors and Stuarts, with a dusting of long division and algebra, was enough to fit us for our futures. Our futures as wives and mothers and Woolworth's salesgirls. Factory fodder. Maybe even Gough Electricals fodder.

I have never since sewn a French (or double) seam, or made, or even eaten, a single Swedish meatball. I know of no one who has. My mother, who made plenty of her own clothes and ours, didn't hesitate to sew straight from the pins; she couldn't be bothered to fuss with tacking and then to fuss with taking the tacking out. No one has ever come up to me and asked me the value of c if $(a + 2) \times (b - 3) = 2c$ when $a = 4$ and $b = 5$. I must say, I sometimes wonder to myself was he James the First of Scotland and the Sixth of England, or James the Sixth of Scotland and the First of England? But nothing depends on my being able to answer this except my own irritation. I know that a horse chestnut leaf has five, or alternatively seven, leaflets, and a buttercup five petals, but any curious person could get hold of the real thing and count, if they had a mind to do so. And I have never, ever, had to fill in the missing shape.

I got my education elsewhere.

Yet Lorna has said to me that I have (a) a wide vocabulary, and (b) a sharp mind, and what she hints at is: where did I get them from? Well, you can't inherit a wide vocabulary from a parent or parents you left behind at the age of one. So I must have used my sharp mind to pick it up somewhere. Neither nature nor nurture quite explains me. Maybe that's why Dr Travis sits there and writes so avidly with his little gold-topped pencil. I am an interesting study, a case in point.

I ignored my education. It was just a tasteless meal placed before me, something I had to eat before I could get down. Everyone involved was too witless to see my finer points. Why should I help them out? So I looked and listened and picked up and absorbed. You can get a lot just by absorbing. Maybe that's what I would have learned in science if our science lessons had gone a little further.

What I looked at and listened to was *life*. When I could get hold of any. And I read books, too, of course. Plenty of books. Thousands of books.

The value of c is 6, by the way. Not that anyone's asking.

My mother has a photograph, one of those whole-school photographs, taken when I was in the first year at the secondary mod. Had a photograph – perhaps I should say *had*. I doubt they've kept it, treasured it. I doubt they've kept anything. Swept the place clean. My books, my pyjama case, the puppy and kitten print from my bedroom wall. I wonder what happened to them? All erased, as if I had never been?

It takes a long time to pick me out in the photograph, out of the hundreds of monochrome faces. We were arranged in rows, seated on the grass, seated on low benches, then standing on the grass, then standing behind on forms and benches. It took ages to arrange us all. 'Hands still. Smile please. Say *cheese*,' the photographer instructed, a professional entertainer's chirrup to his voice. 'Knees *together*, girls,' hissed the deputy head. My face, belonging to someone tall for their age, is somewhere in the middle, somewhere towards the left. Once you have found me, my shaving-brush bunches, my heavy fringe, give away Bettina's touch; but the girl beside me has bunches too, longer, a bit darker.

The girl beside me is semi-blinking, glancing down as the shutter slides, which gives her the look of a dim carthorse. Others are smiling. There – now that you've got your eye in – further along is Mildred, and there is Natasha, half hidden behind a teacher's head. But look away, and it's hard to find us again. You have to search the rows of faces, find a marker: that teacher with the candy-floss hair, then go left for Natasha, back and left again, and – somewhere – there is me.

No one would pick me out from that crowd as special.

My school was not hot on careers advice. Miss Jessop, who had spent the entire thirty-five years of her adult life teaching religious education in girls' schools, was responsible for advising us on possible careers, between a full timetable of RE lessons and sorting out the Social Service rota. We had to go to see her in groups; there was no time for individual guidance. We were chopped up into alphabetical segments and sent along to find out how we might fruitfully spend the rest of our lives. Careers advice took place – there was no other space for it – in the medical room. The white enamel wall cabinet with the large red cross on it, the tingling smell of witch hazel, the big clean sink, lent a serious air to proceedings. So one day early in the summer term Mary Batty and Kay Bell and Christine Boyd and I found ourselves sitting on hard chairs in front of Miss Jessop, who looked uncomfortable and said, 'Well, girls, what did you have in mind?'

It was the you-tell-me variety of careers advice.

'Where does your experience lie?' Miss Jessop asked, and I said, 'The retail trade. Haberdashery. Knitwear.' I wasn't going to mention the sanitary products. Mary Batty helped in her dad's paper shop, and Kay Bell had sold ice creams on the prom, and Christine Boyd had done nothing at all (her mother was an invalid). We turned faces full of expectancy towards Miss Jessop, who fumbled with her yellow pearls. She had a manila folder in front of her on the table. A thin manila folder. 'Well, girls . . .' she began.

Perhaps Christine was hoping in her wildest dreams to be a nurse, and Kay fancied travelling to India in a hippie van, and Mary thought her dad should expand the shop – with her assistance – into prams and babywear. And I was definitely waiting to be plucked, inevitably, from the crowd, to be whisked away to London to take up my life as a single girl and to have fun. We didn't say any of this. To say it would have been to embarrass Miss Jessop further, to embarrass ourselves.

'Well, girls,' said Miss Jessop, toying with the folder but not opening it. 'You have some useful experiences behind you. I would advise you to start looking in the Situations Vacant column, to put your names down with firms who . . .'

I stopped listening. I watched the fluttering shapes of leaf shadows dancing over the table in front of Miss Jessop, and over Miss Jessop herself, transparent, carelessly dancing shadows, where the sun shone down through the lime tree that grew outside the window of the medical room. I drifted in and out of the sound of her voice. Words like 'loyalty' and 'punctuality', phrases such as 'good attendance record', 'many local businesses', and '. . . may not need any exams', leaped above the surface of my consciousness like flying fish,

291

only to disappear without trace, without meaning, again. I stared at the first-aid cabinet and wondered how much it must weigh, and what would happen if it suddenly fell off the wall and on to Miss Jessop's head. Somewhere in the branches of the lime tree, a blackbird started singing. And I felt, for the very first time, that I would not mind staying *here* for ever, in the safe smell of wood varnish and witch hazel, drifting in and out of listening, with the summery leaf shadows always playing over me.

'Remember, girls,' Miss Jessop said, sharply, as outside the medical-room door the afternoon lesson bell shrilled. 'When approaching a prospective employer, always dress neatly and respectably, always behave like young ladies. Always mention any useful experience.'

Kay Bell became a go-go dancer eventually, so I heard. Prancing about in the beer spills on a bar, dressed in tight black shorts and a red satin blouse, knotted just under the bosom. I wonder if she bore Miss Jessop's advice in mind as she approached her sausage-fingered future employer?

I shouldn't be so wicked. I got *my* job by following Miss Jessop's advice, although it was a route I could have worked out for myself. I bought the local paper and looked in the Sits Vac column. I was all ready to mention my useful experience in the world of haberdashery to the area manager, who agreed that I should 'pop in for an interview teatime-ish' the following Tuesday. He was on the telephone in the tiny back room when I arrived and he remained on the telephone throughout our short conversation.

'Look, Shirley – I know all about Ipswich,' he said, and flagged me into the room with one big arm. His suit jacket was light beige with a very faint check. One of the cuff buttons was loose and there was a mark on the sleeve. I was already practising applying my observation skills to the world of dry cleaning. 'Shirley,' he said, 'I'm not talking small-fry here.'

He nodded to me, and pushed some paper and a pen towards me. A telephone message pad, a bright yellow Bic.

'I know, I *know*,' he told Shirley, in the tones of a man who wished he didn't. 'I know all about that. Believe me.' He cupped one hand over the receiver and mouthed at me: 'Just fill in your details, love. The salient points.'

You tell me, I thought.

'Look, Shirl, there's nothing that *you* can tell *me*. I know. I saw the offending item with my own eyes. Name, address, national insurance number,' he added, in a throttled whisper, nodding at me. I stood to write. There was no room to sit down, and he was in the only chair. A wrinkling cup of coffee waited on the Formica desktop before him. 'No, no, Spiller's had it, Shirley. Take it from me, the man in the know. How old are you?' he asked me, frowning. 'Sixteen *when*? Write it down. Date of birth. Dee-oh-bee,' he added, as if in explanation, stabbing at the message pad with a forefinger. He picked up the coffee, elbow out, and sipped a mouthful, ignoring the skin that came with it. 'Spiller is *yesterday's man*, Shirley, my darling. Ipswich or no Ipswich. Take it from me.' He laughed, a loud, brigandish ha-ha, like a crackle of lightning over the wireless. There was phlegm in his lungs. The dry-cleaning fluid, maybe. 'Ever worked behind a counter before?' he asked me, and I nodded, beginning to speak, when he suddenly crowed, 'Shirl! If

I've told you once, I've told you a hundred times, Spiller's a dead man. No objection to working Saturdays?' he added, in a low voice. 'No? Well, a pleasure to do business.' He swapped the receiver over as Shirley's voice ranted out of it, and extended his right hand to me. 'When can you start?' In two weeks, I said. After my exams, after my birthday, when school would chuck me out with a grateful sigh.

Which was how I passed the rigorous selection process for the job.

'Bed-wetter, cat-getter, fire-setter,' I suggested to Hanny the other day.

'*What?*'

'Haven't you ever heard that phrase?' I asked. But she hadn't. For someone so well-travelled and worldly-wise, she's led a sheltered life. 'It's what they say about children who later on turn out to be bad. How you can tell.'

I gave her a long look, but she was just staring at the flower beds, at the red busy Lizzies which are now all in bloom. Screaming bright-red busy Lizzies. Under the glare of a grey summer sky they are migraine-inducing.

'It's a triumvirate of things, of clues that should set alarm bells ringing in people's heads. You know, people who know about these things.'

'What things?' Hanny asked. 'A *triumvirate* is the name for the three people who ruled Rome. Augustus, and Octavian, and Thingy. Or was Augustus the same as Octavian anyway?'

'I was only using the word to mean what I wanted it to mean,' I said. I felt we'd strayed off the point. And there was much more I'd wanted to say.

Hanny sat back, lifting her fragile white face to the non-existent sun, and closed her eyes. She wasn't listening to me; she often didn't really listen. In some ways she reminded me of Barbara. Getting someone to notice you is one of the hardest things, even when they're your friend: getting them to *really* notice you.

Later that afternoon, when it was too late, I thought: *triad*. Triad was the word I wanted. How could I have made such a foolish slip?

I remember the day Sebastian came running in, his face all twisted and dirty with tears. He grabbed Tillie from the kitchen and ran with her. We all followed, terrified by the bloodless look of her face, drained of all emotion until she could find out what it was she really had to worry about. Mattie wasn't with him, it was Mattie she was frightened for. We ran in a ragged line across the field and through the scrub till we came to the big oak tree. Mattie was there, sitting on the ground, scratching in the dirt with a stick. Tillie fell on him with little cries.

But it wasn't Mattie. Sebastian touched Tillie on the shoulder and she looked up.

In the tree, suspended from one of the old swinging ropes, twisting in slow circles, was a white shape, a long sausage. I stared: all I could see was a tent packed tightly into its carrying sack, just like Brian's Scout troop took when they went off to camp.

Tillie jumped to her feet. 'Oh, poor Pickles!'

She ran over to him, slowed his body, stilled the gentle swinging of the rope. She lifted his dead weight until the rope looped and she could ease his head out.

'Poor, stupid, *stupid* Pickles.'

For some reason she sent Barbara running back home for a sheet, and only when he could be decently covered did she carry him home, with the rest of us trailing behind, mutes in the funeral procession.

We buried him in the garden, at the far end, under the sickly apple trees. Tom sweated to dig the hole in the hard-baked earth, whacking it open with a pickaxe first. Then we laid Pickles inside, still wrapped in the sheet, and put in his newest bone, and scattered the tops of cornflowers into the grave, like sparkling blue dog biscuits. Barbara said some prayer for the departure of the soul, and Tillie and Sebastian kept wiping their eyes. Patrick had been away in London for a day or two and was expected back that evening, but they didn't wait for him. I got the feeling that it was all a bit hurried. Barbara said it was only because it was so hot.

I got the feeling that it was all a bit hurried because Tillie did not want anyone asking what had happened to Pickles. He got himself stuck in a tree, he got himself caught in a rope. She said, twice, that his paw was caught in the noose along with his neck, that he must have struggled to free himself but it was too late. She was so emphatic that she thought it was an accident. I'm sure she was sure that it wasn't. She wanted to get the horrible evidence out of the way as soon as possible and forget all about it.

I hadn't seen his paw in the rope. I had seen him hanging, like a long sad sausage.

How did I know that it was Brian who burned down the Hennessys' summer house? Well, I didn't at first. I was quite convinced by the barbecue-and-spark theory.

No need to look further. No need to be suspicious at all.

Then, one evening a couple of days after the con-
flagration, Barbara grabbed my arm, saying, 'There's
something I've got to watch on telly. Come *on.'*

We went upstairs to the back bedroom. Tillie was in
the bathroom, supervising the younger boys with their
teeth-cleaning and pyjamas, and Tom's door was firmly
shut, loud music pulsating beyond it. Patrick had gone to
the pub.

We settled down on the bedspread with a bag of
Maltesers. Barbara was the sort of person who couldn't
watch television without giving a running commentary.
'D'you recognize him? Not *him. That* one. See? He was in
that cop show on ITV. Played the sergeant. Oh, look at
her hair, good God! What *does* she look like?' She kept
shifting on the bed, propping herself up and then lying
down again. Maltesers were rolling everywhere. I got up
to retrieve a couple from the floor, and popped them in
my mouth. At home I could have done that without
getting a mouthful of fluff as well. Not that I would ever
have picked sweets off the carpet at home. Our kitchen
floor might have been so clean you could eat your dinner
off it, but that was not an idea we entertained. Germs,
and, anyway, *manners.*

It was a drizzly evening, which brought the dusk down
early. I glanced out of the window. There was someone
down there in the half-light, standing near to what was
left of the summer house, hands in pockets, surveying the
burnt remains. Not Tom, too chunky. I looked harder.
Someone wearing Scout uniform. It was Wednesday,
Scouts night. I ducked down so that I couldn't be seen
and peered over the window sill.

'Caro! What the hell are you doing?' Barbara asked tetchily.

'Spying.'

'Spying on what?'

'Foxes,' I lied.

'Whatever for?' She didn't really want an answer. She was rustling round on the bed, feeling under her back for a stray Malteser.

Out in the rain, the dusk, a chunky Scout was kicking at the long-dead embers with his toe, stirring the remains, admiring his handiwork. He glanced up, not at me crouching by the lit upper window, but at the hedge. In the half-dark I could have sworn that he grinned. And I knew, with a cold curdling feeling in my stomach, that Brian had a parallel life too, that Brian didn't always keep to his own side of the hedge. That Brian knew things and never mentioned them, for reasons of his own.

I sat back down on the edge of the bed. Barbara stretched out her palm with a single Malteser balanced on it. 'Want the last one?'

'No thanks.'

She clapped it to her own mouth, chewed and swallowed. 'Good.'

33

Sticky Decisions

If I had to choose my favourite painter, who would I come up with? Velázquez, or Rembrandt? Or someone else entirely? What if all the others had to go, and I could save just one from destruction, who would I choose? Hans Holbein, or Dürer, or maybe Leonardo. Though that's being a bit too obvious.

Barbara was always saying that kind of thing: what would you do if . . . ? Or: if you had to choose between . . . ? With her, it was to stave off the boredom. I'm not sure that she really wanted to know anyone else's answer.

So, Rembrandt, or Velázquez.

If I had to choose my ten favourite paintings, that would be easier. Nobody after 1870, I shouldn't think. Lots of portraits, a domestic interior, a frozen winter landscape, a still life. Or *nature morte*, as they also call it. Dead nature.

Of course, I have only seen them in books. And some of them only from postcards. Isolde was always good at sending postcards. You might expect it of her.

. . . or maybe Vermeer.

Once I asked Tillie that question, stupidly, as I sat at her kitchen table and she pummelled bread dough. 'Who's your favourite painter?' I asked, like silly girls at school sitting vacantly on desktops at break-time in rainy weather, asking, 'Who's your favourite pop star? Which one's your favourite out of the Monkees?'

'Who's your favourite painter? Rembrandt?' I thought I knew the answer, of course.

'Oh no,' she said, wiping stray hair away from her forehead with the back of her arm. 'Vermeer, I should think.' And she turned aside, said in a low voice, half joking, 'I know just how his wife felt.'

Then she heaved her bowl of dough over to the counter top beside the stove, and continued, educationally, talking across her shoulder. 'She had eight children, and when he died young, she had to sell his paintings to pay off all the debts.'

I don't know what I said in reply. It wasn't the kind of discussion I was expecting.

Tom took me to bed when I was fifteen and two months, which was not really, as he explained it, breaking the law. I can't recall his reasoning now. At the time it was convincing.

Tom's sexual technique was much the same as his kissing technique, and he was very bony. His hipbones grated on mine, just as his teeth had grated on mine. I wish I had enjoyed it more. I suppose in time I did.

How it came about was this.

Apparently Tom Rose had told Tom that I was madly in love with him, Tom Rose. He was very shrewd, and not at all likeable. When Tom thought that I fancied Tom Rose, it was all too much for him, and he had to do his bitterest best to muck it up for us.

What were they up to, those two? What the hell was going on?

If he had had any sense at all – Tom Hennessy, *my* Tom – if he had any use of his five senses, he would have known that I loved *him*. I thought he must know already. I'd thought he'd known for ages, and that was why he bossed me around and bullied me, because he knew I'd put up with it just to be near him. That I'd do anything he asked. Anything at all.

Tom Rose was a Machiavelli. What did *he* want out of it? I still can't work that out. Perhaps he wanted to believe what he said – that I fancied him – and hoped that by putting it into words it would become reality. Or perhaps he just wanted Tom to believe it, knowing how Tom would react. Stirring things up, just to see the effect. On reflection, I think probably the latter. The former is too much like how a girl might act, how a girl might wish things to be.

Maybe he wanted the reciprocal arrangement that obtained before, and knew he couldn't get it by himself. Maybe he was only after *one thing*.

I can still hear the words: 'Now Tom . . . Now me.' I can hear that silky tone of voice, see the sun filtering dust in strips across the room. I can hear the sound I made as I slid across the bare floorboards to cross the space between the two of them.

So Tom set about wheedling and cajoling me, a most unusual experience, and really not bad. It certainly made a change. He set about seducing me. His long limbs were filling out, he had a man's hands and a man's jaw now, and his settled deep voice was thrilling. When I lay against his chest I could hear it vibrating inside his ribcage.

He even consented to go out in public with me. Very occasionally we would be seen in town together. 'Oh, *him*,' said the girls at my school, looking at me with new eyes. They all knew, or knew of, Tom. He was a sixth-former at the grammar school. It was good for my reputation to be seen with someone as sought-after as that. That's what Natasha Maynard said, and I believed her.

So when Tom said, 'This is it. Come on, you will have to come to bed with me now,' what could I do?

It was evening and we were up in his room. I could hear Tillie down below in the garden, playing some wild game that was making Mattie scream. I could hear Patrick's opera music roaring out from somewhere up above. I could hear the heavy footsteps of someone – it could only be Sebastian – stumping up the stairs, patently *in a mood*. And I knew from old experience that they would leave us all alone, would not venture in. It would never cross their minds that here a girl and boy of certain ages, of certain dangerous ages, were alone together in an upstairs room, with access to strong drink and suggestive music lyrics and a bed that was wider than two foot six. I knew that in many a house in our town, the circumstances would call for a parental pounding on the door at least every five minutes, and in my own house a hedge away, the circumstance would never have arisen at all.

So no one was going to come to my aid.

'I could get pregnant,' I said to Tom.

'Nah, you won't.' He sounded very sure. 'Virgins never do.'

'Oh, Tom, don't be so stupid!' I said, but he just waved a little packet at me cheekily and added, 'Not with one of these.'

I'd seen the old dead-jellyfish things washed up on the seafront. And once in the black mud of a lovers' lane that Barbara had shown me. To me they seemed the antithesis of love, but they were its living proof. Proof that people did such things. Proof that people were wild to do such things, again and again, even in the most uncomfortable and undesirable of places. And there were girls in my school who were taking the Pill. They went to their doctors complaining of irregular periods, and were prescribed the Pill. There were side effects: perfect twenty-eight-day menstrual cycles and, by the by, no babies. There were girls in my *class*, it was rumoured, who were already on it. One girl, indeed, had grown enormous breasts where previously she had hardly any, so we had to give credence to the rumour. The oestrogen, apparently. It chilled me to think of people my own age having that knowledge, that very particular knowledge, of someone else's body parts. And someone else of theirs.

'We can't,' I said.

'Why not?' he asked, and when I didn't answer, he just shrugged lightly and put the packet down.

I heard Tillie in the hall, calling, and then Sebastian pounding back down the stairs, joyful again.

And I did love Tom, love him very badly, and if I didn't cede to his requests, God knows, there were girls in shelters on the prom who very likely would.

So I lay down like the Rokeby Venus on his tartan blanket and gave him what I hoped was a most inviting smile.

Of course, he fucked those girls he met on the prom. He'd fucked them before and he'd do so again, and never mind the fact that he had me there for the asking. Me, who loved every last molecule of him, nice and nasty.

But he slept with me, as well, because I was so convenient, only next door and in his house so much of the time.

And because it was one in the eye for old Tom Rose.

34

Onward and Upward

And then Isolde was gone. She'd gone to London to work as a personal assistant. Maybe it wasn't what her grammar school teachers had in mind for her – *a capable girl, clever, definitely university material* – but she upped and left at the end of her lower sixth year and moved to London. She had found herself a job through a contact of their friend, Dill Lopez-Lawrence, and somewhere to live before she went. She didn't tell anyone at home of her plans until they were settled. They wouldn't have stopped her, not the Hennessys, but she wanted to do it all by herself, or so she said. Though to me it looked like she had help every step of the way.

She sent me a postcard. She sent it to my house. The picture was a portrait of Lady Jane Grey from the Tate Gallery. On the other side it said:

Dear Caro,
V. happy here in London. Flat-sharing with Tamara. Just round the corner from us is Gordon Square where V. Woolf

used to live. I'm enjoying work at a big insurance company –
from my office window you can just about see the Thames.
   Love, Isolde

My mother couldn't read her dash of a signature and guessed Isabel. 'Who's this Isabel, then?' she asked, holding out the card to me.

'Just a girl from school.'

'Big insurance company. She's doing well for herself.'

This is precisely why I had to guard my life. Everything was deemed to be open for inspection. There was no room for secrets, for true privacy, in our household. Only the self-conscious privacy of the long dressing gown, the bolted bathroom door. If I hadn't kept a double life, I wouldn't have survived.

I was gratified that Isolde had remembered me. Perhaps she had sent postcards to everyone, luxuriating in her new independence, boasting of her freedom. But I didn't think so, somehow; I knew that she'd singled me out. I recalled that Tamara was the name of Eugene's girlfriend or ex-girlfriend maybe by now. I hadn't a clue who V. Woolf was, though, unless she meant General Woolf who fought in Canada, and whose Christian name I don't think I ever knew.

Of course, I know now. I've read *Mrs Dalloway*. But at the time I'd never heard of Virginia Woolf, and if Isolde possessed her books she must have spirited them away with her into the Van Hoogs' half of the house. You see, my knowledge depended on what the Hennessys were interested in, what they had accumulated over the years. And if the Hennessys hadn't got it, *I* didn't get it.

* * *

Sebastian got through to the grammar school, and Mattie was no longer at the Wren. He had gone to a special school – 'an *extra*-special school' as Tillie put it – where his flapping hands and ever-present wellington boots would not just be ignored in the tumult of careless welcome that was the Wren's educational approach. He'd gone to an extra-special school, where they were training him out of his boots, if not his other passions.

And Sebastian had grown ugly. I was so disappointed. His face appeared to be pulled and stretched apart by bones that didn't fit. The proportions had gone all wrong, leaving his best features – his eyes, his narrow disdainful nose, his well-drawn mouth – insignificant and upstaged by his new ploughshare jaw, his jutting eyebrow bones, the slabs of his cheeks.

'It's OK,' Barbara said when I remarked on it. 'It will turn out OK. Sebastian looks just like Eugene did when he was little – not that I knew Eugene when he was little, of course – and now Eugene's dead good-looking. But when he was younger – when I *did* know him – he looked terrible. It's just puberty,' she said, shrugging. 'Everyone has to go through it.'

About everyday things, Barbara was so knowledgeable. Yet she never so much as opened a book or gave any weight to her schooling, as far as I could see. Where did she get it from?

She tapped her forehead. 'Intuition. And TV.'

Tom Rose went away, too, to do an engineering degree at some university in Wales. I couldn't remember the name of the place, I didn't much care to. Tom was staying on at school to do re-sits. His A-level grades had not been very good, he had disappointed his teachers. It was hard to tell if Patrick and Tillie were disappointed in him, their attitude to all their children was so breezy, and besides, they knew of alternative strategies. They always had something up their sleeve.

At the same time that Tom slackly passed his A levels and I took my woeful CSEs, Barbara, at the convent school, was sitting O levels. Eight of them. She only passed four, and needed five at least to stay on in the sixth form. Oh, *Barbara* couldn't go to work in a dry-cleaner's shop. Or Woolworth's, or Gough Electricals, or selling ice cream in a booth on the seafront. But the Hennessys had something up their sleeve for her: a crammer.

I had never heard of crammers before. 'It's all right,' Barbara said, wafting the flimsy piece of paper with her results on at me, 'I'm going to a crammer.' I felt I'd had this conversation with her before, years ago, by the roundabout at the end of our road, after the Wren had let her down over the eleven-plus. For Barbara, as for all the Hennessys, there were always other opportunities.

If I sound mean, I was feeling mean. I was feeling the pinch, the pinch of different circumstances.

The crammer was in the next town, and Barbara rode off each morning with Patrick in his old white Austin van, though she usually returned by train in the early or mid-afternoon, long before he reappeared. She began to dress differently, to murmur lines of songs I'd never heard. Her wrists clinked with Indian bangles and her fingers were heavy with greyish silver rings. She wore the sort of make-up she'd always been rude about on the model girls in magazines. It was put on with a skill that showed great practice, and a steady hand. She was mixing with a new crowd now, a crowd, she implied, much more exciting than before. Both girls and boys studied there, even people up to the age of twenty, and the teachers were known as tutors and were called by their first names, and some by nicknames. I tired of hearing about Trevor and Linda and Mark and Dizzy even quicker than I had tired of hearing about Sister Benedict and Mother Francis-Xavier. *My* education was doled out in bland all-purpose places, where we were herded in and out like silly sheep, indistinguishable to anyone except our own mothers, forgetting all we learned and instantly forgettable ourselves, quickly replaced by the next generations. I could never get excited about it. Whereas Barbara's seemed destined to take place in highly specialized institutions, inward-turning and self-preoccupied.

Not unlike this one.

I'm sure that Hanny wants me to ask about her wrists. I'm sure that's why she keeps accidentally-on-purpose letting me see them.

On the other hand, I really don't want to ask her. There is some information which I don't care to know. And you can't un-know something once you've been told.

My thoughts about it are these, for what it's worth. Hanny is a sad person, she has a deep well of sadness inside her, like those sweets with a hard-boiled outside and a melted sugary centre. Sometimes the inside oozes outside. I don't suppose there's anything you can do about it. Some people are just like that.

How profound. I must share my thoughts with Group some time. Really drive them into supernova.

35

Information

What did my mother want of us? She wanted children, but they had to be neat and tidy and no trouble, outside the house or in. She didn't want us to have a life, except for a pared-down child's life, of school and well-behaved play. She saw that her duties as a mother were to feed us, house us, keep us clothed and clean, see that we went to school and church. See that we did our chores and knew our place.

Actually, she probably thought she was turning out model citizens. Doing a duty to self and state. Well, hadn't she taken in two little orphans of the storm? Two unwanted children, of irresponsible parents, and turned them into perfectly respectable members of the community? Give that woman a medal. Give that woman a round of applause.

Poor thing.

This is how she told me about the adoption: on my sixteenth birthday, in the middle of exams and a week

311

before I was due to leave school and go and work in the fumes of the dry cleaner's. After the presents on my plate at breakfast, but before the English exam that morning, she said, 'There's something I want to talk to you about. Later.'

'Why not now?'

'Later. When there's more time. When Brian's not around.'

Oh, I thought, I know what this is about. Sweet sixteen, never been kissed – better know what's just around the corner. I went off to school confident enough. With Tom as my tutor and all those books, I thought there was nothing she could tell me that I didn't already know. I laughed when I thought about how she might phrase it.

Back home in the dry silence of the early afternoon (exam over, free time – the weirdness of being out of school when others were bent over desks) she made a pot of tea in the stainless steel teapot and brought it into the lounge. Oh God, this was going to be serious! I had to keep my smile from giving me away.

'I'm having a talk with you today, which I don't want repeated to Brian.'

I nodded, grave and grown-up.

'It's high time you knew where you came from.'

Little shudders of laughter were running through my shoulders but I managed to keep them still.

'I've talked to your dad, and he agrees with me.' She paused, fiddling with the cups, rearranging them before pouring out the tea. You could hear it flowing into the cup, the house was so still. 'You're sixteen. You're old enough to know now.'

I know I'm old enough to know, I thought. I *know*.

Visions of Tom's creased bedsheets swam before my eyes, and him in them, and I was only glad that she couldn't read my mind.

'You aren't ours.'

The words were in Russian, in Latin, in Martian.

'Not by birth, I mean.'

The interpreter in my ear was beginning to filter through, but the time-lag was troublesome to comprehension.

'I mean, we adopted you, when you were little. We adopted Brian, too. You aren't ours, either of you.' She sat back, with her hands neatly together in her lap. Neither of us drank our tea.

The joke was over. I sat with my mouth open. The clock from my mother's mother's house (no relation) ticked away. Somewhere outside a car accelerated.

So. Not sex. Not how babies get here. Just how we got here.

'You *are* brother and sister, though. I mean, really brother and sister.'

No questions, m'lud.

Where did they think I was, all that time, when I was next door? They so obligingly swallowed my lies. Where did they really think I was?

Or did they just not care?

I can see that being adopted must make a difference. If you have a baby, give birth to a baby that you have created between you, you must find ways to accommodate its failings and frailties. It is *of you*, after all. If it grows up with an unappealing character, an unattractive face, you still have to love it, to find a way of loving it. But if you *adopt* a child and it turns out not as you expected, what do you do? Especially if you adopt it at four, at five, when certain nasty habits may already be entrenched. Especially if you haven't much of an idea about children, what they are like, how they develop, how naturally unpleasant they can be, in the first place.

So I think – I tend to think – that when I got to thirteen or fourteen or fifteen and I wasn't all they hoped for, maybe they just discounted me. Maybe they focused their minds on Brian, or on something else entirely, the crossword, or the garden. And let me drift away.

Lorna has always asked the questions, Lorna has always wanted to *know*, and I have always evaded her. It is quite easy to evade her.

Dr Travis, dear Dr Balloon-Head, is more difficult. I think he is a bit like Tom Rose being Banker in Monopoly, watching our moves and silently tending his piles of banknotes. And then, without noticing exactly how it has happened, you realizehe has tipped the balance of the game, that he holds the power.

That he has the information.

'Pharmaceuticals.'

We were walking round the garden paths, Hanny and I, trying to think of the most beautiful words we knew. It had rained all morning and we were desperate to get outside, so now here we were, she in her Pre-Raphaelite Brotherhood coat and me in my Aran jumper, hugging ourselves to keep warm. Layers of grey clouds and white clouds kept blowing over, and through them the sun could be seen as a clear disc, a yellow plate. We could look at it without our eyes hurting.

'No, not pharma*ceuticals*,' she said. 'Pharmacopoeia. Now there's a beautiful word.'

'Tangible.'

'Alchemy.'

'Vestibule.'

'Vestibule!' She started laughing. 'I always thought that meant a kind of underwear.'

'My brother hated the word *flavour*,' I said. 'Well, it turned out he hated it. One day he just squeaked when someone said it, and shouted, "I can't stand that word. It makes my teeth ache!" '

Actually, it showed he had depths I'd never suspected. I never thought anything affected him, especially anything irrational, like the sound of a particular word, and I never imagined that he had the power to describe how anything made him feel. I thought he was the most basic of human beings, functioning like a dog or a plant, moved only by currents such as hunger, tiredness, cold, the sap rising and falling according to the time of day, the time of year.

'I didn't know you had a brother,' Hanny said.

There was a silence. I had to ask, then, what she left me room to ask.

'Do you have any brothers or sisters?'

'No, I'm an only child.'

'My brother was adopted, too,' I explained. 'We *are* actually brother and sister. I mean, we were brother and sister before we were adopted. We were adopted as a pair.'

But she wasn't listening, as she often isn't. She said,

squeezing her arms to her emaciated chest, 'So, if I wither away to nothing, they'll have no one left.'

I looked at the sun scurrying furtively through the clouds. I didn't say anything. She never leaves me anything worth saying.

36

Sitting

It was two days after my sixteenth birthday that Patrick asked me to sit for him. He might have been waiting till I was of that age before he asked. But how could he have known?

And how could he have known how angry I was? That I was just in the mood, what with my newly acquired information, just in the right mood to shed my old skin. Shed it roughly, shrug it off and kick it aside.

I'd seen him drawing someone before. Two friends of theirs had dropped in on the way to some grand garden party, and he'd drawn the girl. She was in a dashing pink and black dress, with a cartwheel hat of crimson straw. He stood her in front of the old summer house and sketched her like lightning, in oil pastels, to get the colours in. We were playing French cricket, running up and down, but stopping to look over his shoulder every now and then. His model laughed a lot, holding on to her hat, which was taking off in the breeze. Her friend, a gangling, fair-haired, balding man, sat in a deckchair and drank from a bottle of beer. Sometimes he got up and handed the bottle to the girl. When he moved, the thin strips of his hair blew upright in the wind.

I saw the painting only briefly, when Patrick was man-handling it into his van one morning. He'd put it on a tall canvas; she was laughing, one hand up to her hat. A beer bottle stood on the doorstep of the summer house behind her. 'Selling this one,' he said, grunting as he hefted it on to the floor of the van, and then spread a white cloth over it. 'Doting lover. Still, he's getting a bargain. What'll it be worth when I'm famous, eh, Caro? When I'm dead and real famous, eh?'

So I said yes. Yes, I would sit for him.

I had never been in the attic before. We were not allowed. The only place in the house that was forbidden to us. Patrick's castle must remain unbreached, the draw-bridge pulled up, the portcullis firmly shut, when he willed it. Barbara had only described it to me.

I knew he had painted the bare brickwork white, and I imagined that – and the windows in the gable at either end, since it was knocked through into one long room – would give him the light he needed. But when I got up there, I found there were two huge windows set into the sloping roof, following its angle. The light felt as if it was pouring straight down from heaven.

'My north light,' Patrick said, while I stood there, eyes and chin raised, letting the pure white light of the overcast day flood down on to me. 'My good north light.'

If you stood on a chair – which I tried – you could see out, over the meadow next door, over the woods, over the top of the oak tree Tom and I climbed, inland to the low hills, like little hummocks. But most of all you could see the sky. Endless grey. Trackless wastes.

He told me to get down, sit down, sit on the chair (an old kitchen chair, very hard) just anyhow, however I sat naturally, and he began to draw me. It was the oddest thing, Patrick Hennessy, king of bonhomie, retreating into something else, something like a glass column, inside which he was strict and cold. I could see then – begin to see – how sitters might not mind his stare, might find it just clinical, just for practical purposes, of getting *this* angle right and *this* weight of flesh correct. I was all of a piece. My face was not prettier than my right foot, my eyes were not more important than my collarbone, the folds of my jeans where my knees bent had to be rendered with as much delicacy as the space between my nose and my upper lip. His eyes went, washed, scraped, over the surface of me; not seeking to look at *me*, or put me at my ease and make me laugh, which he sometimes did downstairs.

'Don't look so miserable, now,' he said. Breaking the spell. A whole half-hour had passed. I caught his eye. His eye was twinkling as it did downstairs. I preferred it when it didn't. I much preferred it when he kept things clinical. He started talking about his other pictures I might have seen about the house. The seat of the chair was very bony. My right foot was beginning to cramp. 'Now, the one of Arthur, Arthur Lopez-Lawrence, that's a grand one. Arthur was my best man, you know, when I got married to young Mathilde.' He didn't pronounce it harshly like *Matilda*, but made a breath of the H and ended the E like a sigh. I never thought of Tillie like that. *Young Mathilde*. Her name pronounced as a caress. I thought for the first time how much he must really, really love her.

The drawing was very interesting. To my mind there are three ways you want to look at a drawing of yourself. First is to see how another person might see you; then to see if it is, as a drawing, any *good*; then, last and most pressing, the vain bit of you just wants to know how you look, if you are pretty, or plain, or even – hold your breath – beautiful. A proper painter will not, I think, make anyone beautiful. A proper painter will be too interested in the fall of the light, the tone of the skin. A natural awkwardness of posture is just as desirable to them as a gorgeous fluidity, maybe even more so. John Singer Sargent was painting for money, flattering his sitters, their husbands and his own reputation. Rembrandt, I do believe, was not.

Patrick Hennessy had drawn me as a girl perched on a hard chair. There was another girl on just such an uncomfortable chair, in the kitchen corridor, only she was naked. I looked as thin and awkward as her. Not pretty, at all. Not a Carolyn sort of girl, no, never. Interesting, perhaps. I looked angry and resentful, as if I had just gone over and kicked the painter in the teeth and was wondering what would happen next. My wide-set eyes, I could see from his soft fluent line, were not the wide-set eyes of my father and his sisters. What I had always believed were inherited were only my own.

So maybe he had got me right. Maybe he had seen inside, to the deep true nature of things. Maybe he *did* have a painter's eye.

He didn't turn that one into a painting. It remained a sketch. I wish he had given it to me, but I don't know what he did with it.

The next one he painted. He came into Tom's room one day, when I was on my own, sitting on the window sill with a book, and he said, 'Come on, you. You're not busy. I need someone,' and he carried me off. So much for the value of reading. He put me on the old ratty green sofa that he had up in the attic, a piece of nineteen-twenties furniture with very palpable springs in the seat. He'd spread a red shawl diagonally across it – the same red shawl, I feared, that featured so briefly on the fat blonde nude downstairs – and he stuck me on that, with my back against the armrest and my feet up on the seat. 'Here, you can have your bloody book back,' he said, chucking it at me. 'Maybe that'll make you relax. At the moment you look like Mrs Scrubbit out of *The Woodentops*.' Which made me laugh, and so of course he'd achieved his aim.

'I might say that the Muse is upon me,' he went on, glancing to and from me to the canvas. 'But it's not so romantic as all that. I have to paint like other people have to eat. I get a pain in my belly if I don't.'

I thought this was romantic tosh as well.

He painted me, on the red and green, in my washed-out blue jeans and my white T-shirt. He made my hair a sort of reddish gold and my face very white. I was look-ing over the top of the book at him. In colour I hardly recognized myself. If I looked like anyone, it was my cousin Mandy.

I think he was better at drawing than painting. He put the paint on too thick, to my mind. And I can't stand that. But his drawing line was soft as a feather and instantly knowing.

I don't know what happened to this one either. My

sitting for him was never mentioned, it was not a topic around the household. What he did up there in the attic was sacred, and sacrosanct. Until it appeared on the walls. Or slid away, under cover, in the back of the white van.

In the little room off the hallway, Lorna leans nearer. 'Tell me about the house,' she says, at last. 'The house next door.'

I look at her. I am bored with this. Already bored.

'Let's talk about the fire. Tell me who was there.'

She's whispering. I don't respect her technique. It's as if she's expecting me to whisper back. Give up my secrets in whispers.

Of course I tell her nothing. It's private.

37

Gossip

After I learned that I had been adopted, I started going round to Gloria's.

Our social patterns had fallen apart. No Saturday afternoons, no Sunday teas – well, hardly, any more. Bettina had other fish to fry, and so did Mandy, these days. My little nuclear family – which wasn't really *my* family – seemed to retract into itself, with gardening or dozing over the papers replacing the pattern of regular visits. I was working at the dry cleaner's from Monday to Saturday, and Brian was often out, about his own business, though what that was I hadn't a clue.

The first time I dropped in, just before midday on a Saturday (I'd got tired of mooching round the shops to fill my lunch hour) I found Gloria in apron and slippers, a yellow duster in her hand. For the first time ever we sat in the kitchen, drinking weak instant coffee and eating Rich Tea biscuits straight from the packet. It felt different from those well-behaved family teas. More relaxed, as if I'd entered Gloria's world, the real world of the house in

Beet Street, hitherto unknown. Turning sixteen, like turning eleven, had taken me up a notch in Gloria's estimation.

'It wasn't my idea to leave it so long before telling you that you were adopted,' she said. 'But then Ted never listens to me.'

Although my father was their big brother, I got the impression that Gloria and Stella thought him weak, under my mother's thumb. They couldn't turn to him for advice or help, except over matters like plumbing or a leak in the roof. But then, I felt that they thought all men a bit weak, a bit lacking, when it came to the important things: matters of the heart, or family relationships. Stella wanted a man, like a badge, to say that she could get one, not because he would be of any actual use to her once he was got.

'My idea was to tell you gradually,' Gloria went on, 'get you used to the notion. Not hold back till some special occasion and then blurt it all out in one go.'

Though I couldn't see how you could pass on such information gradually, it did seem the kinder method. But I didn't venture to comment.

'I think adopted children should be told about it from the start,' she said, firmly. 'I think they should have their questions answered.'

But what if they're not in the habit of asking questions? What did you do in the war, Daddy? and Tell me about your birth pangs, Mama, were not topics that would go down well in our household. We never knew why they were so reticent, we just knew that they were.

'And then not telling Brian at the same time. I *mean*,' she went on, 'what a secret for you to have to keep! What a responsibility! Good thing you're a reliable sort of girl. Trustworthy.' I hadn't considered it like that until she mentioned it. 'I think he'll take it hard,' Gloria continued, 'when he does find out.'

It had never occurred to me that Brian would take it hard. It never occurred to me that anything much went on in Brian's head, intellectually or emotionally. He was the most transparent of boys, the most opaque. I took the last Rich Tea biscuit and thought about him. I suppose all brothers and sisters grow apart as they get older, get into the extreme polarity of teenagerhood. For us, it began with my defection to the Hennessys. I withdrew, when I could, from our joint world of garden and pavement and bikes and Mandy. And even before that, I'm sure we were just going through the motions. We did things together simply because we were both there. Not because we were alike, joined at the hip, at the brain. But because we were both lonely, I suppose.

What was he like? There wasn't much to tell. Like me, he went to the secondary modern, the boys' version. His school tie was always tightly knotted, black with narrow stripes of bottle green and purple. He wore the black school blazer which went shiny at elbow and pocket, and was supposed to wear a cap. I'm sure he would have worn a cap, except that the bigger boys always pinched them off the heads of small inoffensive pupils trying their hardest to follow school rules. He had grown taller, but not tall. He was still tank-shaped, stump-shaped. His round brown wire-rimmed glasses had been changed for ones with square black frames that were meant to look more grown-up. His hair was still cut brutally short when other boys' hair was growing long and shaggy. Boys were sent home from school for having hair over their shirt collars. The next year it was for having hair *two inches* over their shirt collars. Youth was rebelling, but Brian didn't join in. It was as if he couldn't be bothered with being a teenager. I suppose he had friends, but I hadn't seen any. Perhaps, like me, he kept them out of sight.

'I suppose it's your mother's decision to leave telling him till *he's* sixteen, too,' Gloria went on. 'He's a sensitive boy, Brian. Lord knows how he'll take it, *when* she tells him.'

Sensitive! I was tired of this. I wanted someone to worry about how *I* was taking it. Gloria's character analysis was not worth a light.

'Thank goodness you're a sensible girl,' she said, rooting through the cupboard for something more to eat. 'Always have been.'

She came out with a packet of Jacob's Cream Crackers. She couldn't see my face as she spoke. I'd had no choice but to be sensible, I thought. Not with my upbringing. My rebellions were really only slight, and never out in the open. True, I had given up Guides, piano, I had ducked out of the constant church-going. I had given up, in the last two years of school, doing homework and sometimes even going in at all. My attitude to school had become much the same as Barbara's to the Wren – you didn't learn anything much while you were there and nobody seemed to notice if you weren't. And I told the odd lie. But underneath it all I *was* a sensible girl. Look at all the shameful things I could have done – got pregnant in the fourth year like that girl who kept coming back and hanging round the school gates with a little shawl-wrapped bundle, as if she'd done something to admire.

Or I could have turned out like Suki Wooster, who ran away with a thirty-year-old man, failed to respond to the pleas of her anguished parents, and had to be publicly dragged home from Weston-super-Mare a fortnight later. Or the one with the dyed black hair in the year above who got badly into drugs and could be seen in the high street sometimes, ghost-faced and draggled, hanging round with thin young men who were clearly up to no good. Beside them I was as pure as the driven snow. Nobody *saw* what I got up to. There were no awful consequences to my actions. I was the perfect daughter.

But Gloria was kind. She settled back down at the table with the cream crackers and the butter dish. She gave me information.

Such as 'They didn't want a baby. Not a newborn baby. They were pleased when they heard you were four and five. Edie's never been one for babies. Doesn't know what to do with them. You should have seen her when Bettina tried to put Mandy into her arms, just a little scrap in a pink bonnet. No fear! Not your mother.'

And 'He ran away from home, once, Ted, when he was twelve or so. I remember there was an awful kerfuffle. He got himself hidden away on one of the fishing boats that used to work off the beach here in those days, and no one knew he was there till they were out at sea. He came back after a night and a day. He got a belting but we had plenty of mackerel for tea.' I couldn't imagine my father doing anything so exciting. I certainly couldn't imagine him telling it as an adventure, or even a moral tale. I wish he had told us. Maybe he was ashamed of his reckless youth.

Gloria's mouth ran away with her, after just a cup of

tea. She loved gossip. Perhaps it was because I was such a good audience. I didn't have my mother's prim puckered mouth if things got too plain-spoken, I didn't have her raised eyebrows and warning lowered lids – *because the children might overhear*. There were no children now, and no Edie present to put a spoke in things with her churchy ways and her snobbier-than-thou.

And so 'When Ted got married, he was twenty-six, and poor Edie was thirty. Your uncle Bob gave Edie away because her father was dead by then. I remember her mother, in this awful peacock-blue costume and a matching hat with a little veil. She wept all the way through, and when we were standing there for the photographs she kept saying, "I never thought I'd see the day." Which I didn't think was very flattering to Edie.'

It was of huge importance to Gloria that 'poor Edie' was as much as thirty before she got hitched. And *older* than her husband-to-be, as if that was somehow questionable behaviour. Gloria was sweet one-and-twenty when she married Eddy, much good that it did her. But it gave her an edge. She had been a successful young woman, competing and winning in the great female stakes.

'They met at a church outing. Your father was only there to help drive the bus. *We've* never been a church-going family, not much of one, anyway. Ted was helping Albert Hamer, who'd hired a bus with a dicey engine and didn't know the first thing about mechanics. They were on a trip to Ely Cathedral. Got talking to Edie on the way there, never looked back. *I* don't know. What people see in each other!' She laughed and shook her head and swung at a wasp with her tea towel. 'I think she'd given up hope. Well, *thirty*, in those days . . .'

I could see that it might have been humiliating for my mother to find she'd married into such a family. Gloria, Bettina, Stella, they measured each other and themselves by their ability to catch and keep a man. (It didn't really matter too much what kind of man, so long as he was formally enlisted.) I could see that she'd need all her weapons to survive, her religion, her standards, her tiny social edge. And then turning out not to be able to have children. At least, I assumed this was the reason why they adopted us. Gloria didn't volunteer any reasons, and I wasn't about to ask. Gloria had her own taboos, her own big silences.

'You don't mind me talking like this, do you, Carol?' she asked. 'I'd never say such things in front of your mother. But you're growing up now. You can't keep things from children for ever, can you? Doesn't do anybody any good.'

After that, I often used to drop round in my lunch hour, take my sandwiches, and we'd sit at the kitchen table, or if it was hot, on two kitchen chairs out in the back yard. 'You need to blow those fumes out of your lungs,' Gloria said at first. 'Dry cleaning, it's not natural. A good soak, that's what things need to get them clean.' That was until I let drop that I was allowed to do my dry cleaning for free. 'Oh,' she said, thoughtfully, 'I've got a coat upstairs that could do with smartening up.'

I didn't go when I knew Eddy was there. When Eddy came home life took on a new meaning for Gloria. There was a hurried, head-down look about her. She was always snatching off her apron and offering to make him a sandwich, a fry-up, a nice pot of tea. She didn't like Eddy to catch her doing any chores but the house had to be spotless for him. She was like a worried creature that thought at any moment it might be eaten. Eddy was affability itself. A small man, rat-faced, eyes fascinatingly close together, he swaggered around the place with his hands in his trouser pockets, whistling. The first time I went to the house in Beet Street and found him there – a surprise visit – he was outside the kitchen window, doing something to the frame that consisted of swiping it with a hammer and nothing much else. Bits of old putty flew out and landed on the paving stones at his feet.

'Hello, Carol,' he called, cheerfully. Remembered who I was, then. But that was presumably a talent he'd had to develop, given his way of life.

'I can't stop. I've brought these,' I said, and left a bag of jam doughnuts on the table. Gloria picked them up, vague and frowning, but I could see she was relieved as I backed out of the door.

I bumped into Natasha Maynard in the high street one afternoon. She was pushing a pram. Beside her walked an embarrassed-looking youth called Raymond Tozer. He was about Tom's age. They were married.

'Not seen you in ages,' she greeted me. 'Or anyone much from our class. Did you hear? Suzannah – Suzannah Grey? – well, she's gone off to work in her granny's hotel in Scarborough. Or Bridlington.' She rocked her pram back and forth in a professional manner, with one hand on the handle. The pram was huge, light blue, with shiny chrome fittings like an American car. From inside its depths the baby whimpered. Raymond Tozer gazed distractedly across the street. 'Or somewhere,' said Natasha, wrinkling up her nose, trying to remember. 'And Kay Bell's working in some sleazy pub. A few of the others are at that factory out Bossey Down way. But Mildred – guess what?'

'What?'

I could see that Raymond was getting restless. He had fifty years of conversations like this to look forward to, on chilly pavements and across garden fences, if he stayed the course. I could see the realization of it dawning on his still spotty features.

'She's a pop star in London!'

'*No!*'

Natasha pulled a face. 'No, actually, she's in hospital.'

Now I pulled a face. 'No!'

'Fell off her bike and broke her neck.'

'*God* . . . Is she paralysed?'

Named Mildred, and then paralysed from the neck down. That really would illustrate life's ironies.

'No. Not paralysed. The doctors say she'll likely make a full recovery. She's been very lucky.' She pumped the pram back and forth as the baby's squalling increased.

'How do you know all this?'

'My mum works as an auxiliary up at the hospital. Sees her every day.'

It always pays to have contacts, I thought.

'And what are you up to these days?'

'Me? I'm at Sketchley's.'

'Sketchley's? I might pop in and see you, then,' she said, grandly. 'When I'm out. With the baby.'

And I might be very glad. A visit from Natasha Tozer, *née* Maynard, seventeen-year-old married person and mother, even that would be welcome. There were precious few customers between the busy hours, which were first thing in the morning, lunchtime and at the end of the afternoon. People tended to see to their dry cleaning en route for other things. I had to take my lunches unsociably early or late. I kept a book under the counter. 'Don't let the customers see you reading,' the area manager warned me. Why not? Would it shatter the illusion that I was as dim as the job demanded?

Raymond was wandering off. Natasha lingered. I think she really wanted me to admire the baby. It wasn't something I had any practice at. I peeped under the light blue hood. 'He's very sweet,' I said.

'It's a she. Kerry-Louise.'

'How old is she?'

'Two and a half months.'

I looked back up at Natasha. Raymond was nowhere in sight. I was beginning to say something else, but Natasha said, 'Don't ask.'

Stella had a new man.

His name was Warren. He was a step up from Dimitri, from Wally. Even from Gerald, whose airs and graces, we decided in retrospect, had been assumed.

Warren had a house outside town and a piece of land on which people paid him to keep their horses. He had a wife, but she was in a mental institution, had been for years. He was quite open about this. 'Good God! Is his surname Rochester?' I asked, but of course no one was listening. Stella would not let on how she had met him. It was not like Stella to hide away a Man, but she was quite protective of this one. She didn't waft him into the house straight away just to prove that he existed. He was too precious to her for that.

And she changed. Subtly, she changed. I don't know whether he wrought the change in her, if he actually made the suggestions, or if she just responded to what she felt he would prefer. If I had to find a word for what she became, it was more *ladylike*. First her clothes began to change. She had always been one of those people you think of as underdressed for the weather. Her blouses were too fine and see-through, her shoes always strappy and peep-toed. She never wore a coat unless it was actually snowing, which it rarely does in our part of the world. A headscarf, a cardigan flung over her shoulders, an umbrella, were her weapons against what the climate threw at us.

Now she began with a pair of proper court shoes, filled in all the way round, still slender-heeled and feminine but not of the tart variety. Then she appeared in a twinset, not unlike the one my mother had; but quite unlike my mother's as it flowed over Stella's curves, and the cardigan – over her shoulders still, and buttoned with just one button at the throat – quivered with the movements of her body. She held herself and moved in a quite different way from my mother, as someone, I began to see, who was aware of herself and aware of men, of the effect she was having on them. By comparison, my mother was a clockwork female doll, one of those house-robots that we were always being promised by the newspapers would, in the near future, be available to take on all the squalid chores. But honestly, why bother investing millions of pounds in inventing them, when the world was full of people like my mother and Aunt Gloria, doing the job for free? Next Stella bought a dress, knee-length and fitted, but nothing like tight. It was a soft light brown, the colour of milk chocolate. Not a colour Stella had been aware of in the dyer's repertoire before. She looked – casually elegant. And rather svelte. Maybe she was getting slimmer. Losing weight, a fool for love. What a turn-up for the books.

I thought that Warren, on the whole, was a Good Thing. Stella had grown up, and calmed down. And he treated her better than the others had done, was easy with her, didn't actually appear to mind being seen with her and meeting the rest of her family. But Gloria wasn't so sure.

'He's already got a wife,' she said. And he was a bit well off and a bit middle class for Gloria's peace of mind. 'I don't like him. He's too polite. A bit suspicious, to my way of thinking' was how she put it. 'What could he want with Stella?' That is, if he couldn't marry her – what did he *really* want?

I could have told her, given my new worldly wisdom in all things pertaining to adult relationships, but we were not that close. Though we traded gossip and opinions, and spent happy hours flicking through the local newspaper or Gloria's weekly magazines, praising or shredding the reputations and looks of anyone who appeared within, we never touched on what I really thought. Warren was after exactly what Wally and Gerald and Dimitri had been after, and presumably got; they didn't marry her either, despite the fact that they were, supposedly, free to do so. What I really thought about Warren was what I could observe: that he brought out Stella's good points, and enjoyed them – her adaptability, her soft-hearted female nature, her ability to overlook or forgive almost all faults. And her sexual generosity.

I suppose this was the bit that was unspoken between Aunt Gloria and me. Was unspoken and unmentionable.

Perhaps Warren's wife is in here. I wonder which one she is? Perhaps she's Rose!

38

Discussing My Troubles

You see, what could I say?

I had spent all my life – at least, from ever since I could remember until my sixteenth birthday – wishing, hoping, pretending, that I was adopted. Telling other people that I was adopted. Explaining away anything I didn't like by the fact that I was adopted.

Until the day I found out that I was.

I could hardly go round to Barbara and say, 'Guess what? I really *am* adopted. I was just pretending before.' I'd been her friend under false pretences, and here was evidence of my big lie. And we weren't close, not any more.

I didn't feel I could complain to Tillie. To her my adoption was just a rumour heard from Barbara, an ordinary rumour. Supposing she replied, 'So what's the problem?' with a shrug, and went on rolling out the pastry?

And what on earth would I say to Tom, who I suspect never believed me in the first place?

It was all too humiliating. And I didn't want to feel humiliated, not in front of the Hennessys.

I wasn't allowed to discuss it with Brian. That was embargoed until *he* was sixteen. Not that I was in the habit of discussing much with him. I stuck faithfully to my mother's instructions. If he'd been a different kind of boy I would easily have defied her. If he'd been a different kind of brother I would have been glad to tell him, and find out what he made of the whole sorry tale. So that we could share our shock and sadness and excitement and curiosity. Or if he'd been another kind of brother altogether, a bluff and bullying sort, I might have enjoyed spilling the beans to him, and drawing out his feelings like those medieval torturers you see in etchings, slowly drawing out the entrails of their victims by winding them around a stake. But he wasn't like that.

It was almost as if we were not brother and sister at all. We had nothing in common. I was red-gold and blue, he was dark and hazel. Perhaps she had made it up, that part of the story. Who knows what she might not have said? She had lied for years and years, lied by omission mostly, but lies all the same. 'What day of the week was I born on, Mum?' A look, a thought, a blink – 'Wednesday.' That would have been a lie, too.

So there was no one.

I did try to talk to Gloria. Or draw her out, at least. I thought she might be amenable. I hoped she'd have some little gems of memory stored away, trinkets she'd just love to pull out and show me. It was like Barbara and me trawling through Tillie's dusty jewel box. I was eager to see anything she had. Good or bad, pretty or tawdry. It had to be better than nothing.

337

But 'Oh, I don't recall. I just remember going round to tea one time, after you'd arrived. Edie never said anything about the hows and whys of it. You know her. One day you weren't there, and then you were.'

'Just like that?'

'Oh, and Ted had done up the attic.' She frowned, and dipped her biscuit in her tea. 'Though that was years before.'

'But you said she never wanted a *baby*. She must have talked about it sometimes.'

Gloria shook her head. Perhaps the hows and whys of it were painful to her. Gloria and Eddy were childless. I didn't know if this was by intention, or just bad luck. Or maybe she wanted them, and he didn't. You never know. Married since she was one-and-twenty and nothing to show for it; not even Eddy, half the time. But these were the unspoken details, the secret life of married couples. I thought it so unfair that Gloria and my mother should speculate quite openly about Stella because she lacked the entitlement to privacy of the married state. Not that all married states were private. I thought of Tillie, who had had six children, eight if you included the poor lost babies, and then the op to put a stop to more. If I had landed in another family, then I would have known all. All, and maybe more than I wanted to hear, sometimes.

I used to lie about being adopted as an excuse. A way of saying, 'It's not my fault.' It's not my fault I live here, look like this, have this mother, this father, this deeply unnoticeable way of life.

I used it like that pendulum swing of belief – total belief, no belief – that people have about sudden changes in fortune. Gloria was convinced that one day she would win a million on the football pools, and followed with great interest the activities of those who had a big win, always commenting, 'Oh, I'd never do that, or buy that, or go there,' or 'Oh yes, that's what I'd do'. Even my father, who didn't do the pools (all forms of gambling were eschewed in our house) talked about the grand day when his ship would come in. We'll have a new car when my ship comes in. We'd build a glass porch, or have a pond with a working fountain. Or a trip to the Isle of Man. It was a way of saying what they'd do if they had the money, but also if only they had the courage and audacity and style to go with it. It was a way of saying what they'd do if they had turned out different people from the ones they were.

And yet they used it as a dampener too. Mention anything expensive or unlikely and Dad would say, 'When my ship comes in,' which meant, in other words, no. And Gloria, if you suggested something heavenly and desirable, said, 'Oh yes, when I win the pools,' in just the same voice as she said, 'And pigs might fly.'

So I swung between knowing, really knowing at the bottom of my soul, that I was not from them, and knowing, really knowing, at the top of my canny brain, that this was all a fantasy. That I was really just as dull and ordinary as all around me were.

Well, all except my chosen people.

Hanny is keen to discuss my adoption. I wish she wasn't. It's one of the few topics that make her focus on me rather than on herself. This morning she said, quite out of the blue, as no one had ever said it to me at the time, 'I wonder why your real mother gave you up to be adopted?'

Mum told me where I came from, in as few words as possible, and then she dropped the subject, closing and pursing her lips. Signalling that nothing more was to be asked or said. And we were not a family that asked or told anyway, not a family who rolled out the words, the tales, in an endless stream of placing and framing and decorating. We were a family who behaved as if words cost money.

Gloria told me, but what she told me were little glinting bits of gossip, items of interest to her, minute relics picked out of *her* past. She hadn't the mind or the education to take the wider view. Nothing existed but in relation to her, and her family, and her neighbours, and her town where she had been born and grown up and lived her whole life. Everything was filtered through the sieve of Gloria. And the mesh of Gloria's sieve was very narrow indeed.

Hanny turned out to have a fertile imagination. She sat there with her pointy fragile knees bent up inside her skirt, and her bony wrists clasped round her knees, and her raspberry lips considering and framing questions that were all lively curiosity, and never noticing my shut face, or my tight voice.

'I wonder if she was married? I wonder if her husband died in an accident or something, and she got ill and couldn't cope with you any more?'

'She must have been married,' I said. 'She had two of us.'

'Oh, yes. I forgot about your brother.'

My brother.

'If she wasn't married, she was a very bad girl!' Hanny laughed, throwing her head back and showing the ridges

340

of her windpipe. 'Oh, a *very* bad girl. Welcome to the house of bad girls, every one of us a different kind. They've never known what to do with us bad girls.'

Then 'She could have had kids by loads of different men! The authorities just took 'em away as they popped out.'

I didn't think this was even worth answering.

'Or I wonder if she just died? Of TB or something, or a bus ran her over, or maybe she died in *childbirth*. So then you were orphans and you had to go into a home.' Hanny sounded as if she were recounting a story, a thrilling story that had happened to someone else. In a book, or a film. She sounded enthralled.

'She might not have wanted to lose you at all. She might have *had* to give you up. For your sakes. For the best. There are lots of reasons why women have to have their babies adopted.'

'Or she might have been glad to get shot of us,' I said. 'And I wasn't a newborn baby.'

'She might have been very young. I mean *really* young. They might have forced her to give you up.'

'Who?'

'Her *parents*,' said Hanny, with some spite. 'Or she might have had loads of other children, and you two were just the last straw. Her womb might have been hanging out, like those women before the National Health Service who could never afford to go to the doctor and didn't know what contraception was.'

'That's just repulsive,' I said.

'Maybe she beat you. Neglected you. Maybe they took you away.'

I hadn't thought of this. I hadn't thought of much, to

tell the truth. I'd just thought of me, tricked and stupid, adopted and *really* adopted. I didn't like to dwell on the idea of being ill-treated. Perhaps because it sounded more convincing than the rest. Or perhaps because it rang a bell.

I wonder if I remember and have chosen not to? After all, it must be quite possible to choose *not* to remember certain things.

One thing I do remember – approaching my fluffy pyjama case with my hands stretched out in wonder. It couldn't have been a present, it wasn't wrapped. Nor was it flattened and matted with use, but soft and white as a Persian kitten. Thinking about it now makes my heart beat faster. I'm sure this was when I was five, on that first day: it was waiting for me on my narrow little bed in my brand new bedroom.

If I can remember this, why can't I remember the children's home from just the day before, or earlier that very same morning?

I was told I had a visitor. I was stunned. Who? Aunt Stella, now Mrs Warren Pike. A shock at first, but then I thought: well, who else would come? Stella was the only one with any guts.

Trudy came to fetch me, escorting me along a corridor I'd not been down before, a narrow switchback corridor I never even knew existed. Trudy's massive bulk nearly touched both sides. I followed her, mesmerized by the jolting of her buttocks in their tie-dye drawstring trousers. It gave me something to think about, other than the impending visit. She showed me into a small room, furnished with two easy chairs and a coffee table. There was a window covered by a white blind. The door to the room had a big panel of glass in it, the sort of glass they favour round here, with a layer of chicken-wire inside. Further down the corridor there were several more doors. Rooms where people had visitors. Rooms I never had an inkling of. Maybe I'm not that clever, after all.

And there, in the middle of that first room, stood Aunt Stella. Poised, stylish and positively svelte. I think she must have shed a few more pounds since we'd last met. She wore a plain grey linen dress. 'Grey' and 'linen' were not words I would ever have thought to associate with Stella. Her cardigan, in the palest shade of pink, was draped over her shoulders. I realized that a cardigan over the shoulders was still Stella's signature, though it was more likely to be cashmere, now, than nylon. Her hair was smoothed into a French pleat and she wore plain pearl studs in her ears. She reminded me of the mother in Brian's tell-the-time book: the one I thought a Carolyn sort of mother would look like.

Maybe I could pass Stella off as *my* mother. We could track down Lorna and do a double act for her. It might be worth the risk, just for the confusion I'd spread.

Trudy said, 'I'll be right outside.' And closed the door. I looked round and her big moon face was there, in the safety glass. I gave her a wishy-washy smile.

Good old Stella. She held out her hand and I thought for a moment she wanted me to shake it, but she was just showing off her engagement and wedding rings: a complicated modern design, gobbets of gold and three bright diamonds.

'We did it very quietly,' she explained. 'Well, his wife had only passed away three months before.'

I remembered – the wife in the mental hospital. I stopped myself from asking if she'd died on one of his visits. No, Warren was a kind man, a gentleman. Look at what he'd done for Stella, made an honest woman of her, a rather elegant woman, too.

'We slipped into the registry office one Friday lunchtime. Just Warren's mate Nige and his wife as witnesses. I'd have asked Gloria but Eddy was home. And we wanted it private as possible.'

'Did you have a honeymoon?'

Stella giggled. 'Yes – *Paris*.'

So Stella had been abroad, the first of the Burtons to venture so far.

'You must have got a passport?' I said, thrilled.

'Yeah. Handy, too. We're off to Spain for ten days in September.'

I thought of how far she had come, and how tricky the journey. The useless men who crowded her past, and her family at her back all the time like dogs barking behind a wire fence.

I said, 'Lucky you,' and the words fell into a little pool of silence between us. There wasn't even a clock to tick away the moments.

Stella looked longingly at the ashtray on the coffee table in front of her.

'You can smoke if you want to,' I offered. I was the hostess, after all.

'No, I won't,' Stella said, and then a moment later grabbed a pack of Rothmans Kingsize out of her handbag and swiftly lit one. She blew the smoke out sideways, upwards, and held her hand at a ladylike angle. I saw her glance at the door, and looked over my shoulder.

'That's Trudy,' I said. 'She's all right.'

'One of the staff, is she? I thought they'd wear uniform.'

'Some of them do.'

A long pause. I wondered if we could send Trudy to fetch coffee and biscuits. But it wasn't really the sort of place that provided room service.

Question: your favourite aunt comes to visit. Do you (a) lay on a slap-up tea at home? (b) take her out for a meal? or (c) ask her what the hell she's doing here?

Stella gazed at me. I felt her eyes roaming up and down, maybe in just the same way that I had scrutinized her. I wondered what she made of me.

'Thank you for coming,' I said.

'You have to be family. They won't let you come unless you're family.'

'Oh, I didn't know that.'

But then it was becoming clear that I didn't know anything.

'How are you?'

'OK.' I thought of what Hanny had said. *Don't tell me you thought we were OK!?*

Stella ground her cigarette out, and looked as if she wanted to reach for another one right away. She twisted round to the window, but you couldn't see anything out of it. I wondered if there were bars hidden behind the blind, in case anyone was tempted to make good their escape. But then there weren't bars on the garden, there were just flower beds and hedges, and the eagle eyes of the staff. I looked round for Trudy again, and caught a glimpse of her broad tie-dyed back. I wondered how long these visits were supposed to last.

'No one else has been to see me,' I said, making my voice sound breezy.

'No. I know.' Stella's eyes were cast down now. 'You're not cross, are you?'

'I didn't expect them to.'

My mother had visited me, once, in the place I was in before this, a day or two after I'd been taken there. She wore her mackintosh buttoned up, and a hat, as if for church. She had her standards, despite everything. She whispered, through tight lips, 'How could you do this to us?' I was pleased that she never came again.

Stella asked, 'D'you mind if I have another smoke?'

I shook my head. She clicked her lighter nervously several times before managing to make a flame. I had never really got the habit of cigarettes but that first curl of smoke smelled beautiful to me.

'I could come again,' Stella said. 'If you wanted me to.' Her eyes were cloudy blue and doubting. 'I drove over. It's quite a nice drive. The different countryside, and so on.'

'Yes. I'd like that.'

She exhaled a long plume towards the ceiling. She was still clutching the lighter, and for something to do she held it out to show me. 'Warren bought me this.'

'It's nice.'

Stella remembered something then, and quickly took her hand away.

'Warren's good to you.'

'He's great.' She was picking up her handbag now, girding her cardigan more firmly round her frame. The last thing she did before standing up was to lean forward and decisively stub out her cigarette.

'Have a nice time in Spain,' I told her.

'Oh, I'll see you again before then.' She was halfway to the door, and through the glass panel Trudy stood to attention.

'It's nice to see you, Carol.' Now that she was on her way, the words seemed to flow more easily. 'You eating all right? Getting enough fresh air? Is there anything I can bring you, next time?'

'A book,' I said.

'A *book*?'

Trudy had the door wide open now, a look of bovine patience on her face.

'What kind of a book?'

'Oh, any book,' I said. 'A thick one. A nice thick one.'

39

Flesh

'Why don't you want to eat?' I asked Hanny today, in Activity.

We were making snowmen with our clay. They're the easiest things to make, one big round blob topped by one small round blob. Then you can cut the details of eyes and mouths and buttons with your fingernails, if you have any.

Hanny bites her fingernails right down. They're shallow and boat-shaped and set deep in the stubby tips of her fingers. I hadn't really noticed this before. You would have expected her to have long, delicate hands and slender almond-shaped nails. Even if you bit almond-shaped nails they would still look all right. Hanny has the hands of a person who has been forced to go grubbing through rocks and earth for the whole of their life.

I had lowered my voice to ask her, but clearly not low enough for Hanny.

'For God's sake, Coral!' she growled at me. 'Not *now*.'

I shivered when she said my name.

*   *   *

It was hardly any time before Patrick asked me to sit for him in the nude.

I sort of knew from the very first that it would happen, that it would have to happen, but I told myself that really he wanted me there in my jeans, on kitchen chairs and shawl-bedecked sofas, that my wide-set eyes and golden-red hair and bony knees in faded blue denim were quite enough. And he was always painting people clothed, clothed and busy, clothed and just sitting there, musing or reading. I hadn't posed on the veranda yet, or at the kitchen table. I hadn't had my go with the blue striped bowl. There were plenty of alternatives to work through before we had to come to *that*.

But just like with Tom, it was very hard to say no.

Hadn't his wife and his daughter educated me all about it? What were my arguments against it, given the weight of artistic tradition and the evidence right here in the house that nobody minded at all?

'It's a bit cold,' I said. It was October, and chilly up there.

'Would you like to go down by the fire, then, the nice bright fire in the sitting room?'

No, of course I wouldn't. Thank you very much.

I sat on the sofa, which he had covered in blue this time. I leaned my jaw on my hand, and my elbow along the green plush arm. I crossed my ankles and kept my knees together. I stayed as still as I could, which was utterly still. It was very much like waiting to go in and see the headmistress. Except that my nipples were standing out like doorstops with the cold.

I didn't particularly want to see what this one looked like. I knew how he saw me by now, I was acquainted with my degree of attractiveness, or otherwise.

And he always slapped the paint on too thick.

Maybe if Rembrandt had asked to do me stepping out of the bath, or Velázquez, a half-torso, I would have let my shawl drop and looked tenderly over my shoulder at him. They would have let the light melt over me, like cloth-of-gold, like finest lawn, clothing me before the eyes of others. Shielding me with centuries-old dust-in-light. I would have shone, and been glad to do so.

But Patrick is like someone making shapes with clay. He plasters scraps together, leaves his thumbprint sometimes, makes flesh as choppy as a windy day in a maritime study.

I wonder what Tillie would have painted like?

I mentioned to Barbara that he'd painted me in the nude. I just wanted her to know that I could do it. She was astonished.

'Good God! You wouldn't get me agreeing to that,' she said. 'Not that he'd ask me anyway. I'm his daughter. It'd be like incest.'

So thank you for that, Barbara. Yes, thank you for that.

Another time he painted me naked, standing up. At least this time the weather was warmer. It was just after Easter and the temperatures had shot up, sending everyone out into the sun with their white arms and legs on show in unaccustomed summer clothing. I had to stand up under one of his roof lights, with the spring sunshine pouring in over me, leaning against an old-fashioned upright cabinet he'd recently acquired. He never bothered to paint his nudes caught in the act of washing or dressing, as if to give an excuse for the acres of bare flesh, but had them standing, sitting or lying, staring back at the artist, empty-handed and aimless.

There was something wrong with my pose. He came over to rearrange me, moving my left arm, then my right, interfering with the angle of my feet, then coming back to touch my jaw, my neck, my chin. His hands felt rather warm, very dry, and, just like a doctor's, were completely unembarrassed. Just as he drew his hand away from my chin he brushed my cheek with the side of his thumb. Accidentally, or otherwise.

Brushed my skin like he pronounced *Mathilde*, the slightest sighing caress.

At the end of the session, I decided to be brave and bold. I had got my clothes back on by then. 'Do you ever sleep with your models?' I asked, briskly, as I bent to do up a tennis shoe.

He was cleaning brushes. 'Absolutely,' he said, 'I swear by it,' not bothering to look up. He spoke just as if he was saying, 'I swear by linseed oil, or paraffin, or real beeswax,' or whatever the tools of his trade were. 'Except, of course, the men.' And then he looked up, and gave me a Hennessy kind of grin.

I hurried away down the attic stairs. I thought of what Barbara had said: 'It'd be like incest.' I thought of the fat blonde nude, and the thin dark one. I thought of his late-night comings and goings and the voices round the house that I could not identify. And I thought of Tillie.

Which makes me think of another time, several years before. It was autumn, quite cold, but we were sitting out on the veranda in a patch of sun, turning up our faces like

351

basking seals, or elderly trippers in the seafront shelters. There was Barbara and me, and Tillie in the swing-seat covered by a blanket, and Mattie asleep with his head in her lap. We were doing some word game, I-Spy, or B for Botticelli. (I had enough education to cope with the latter by then. I knew who Botticelli was and could offer M for Michelangelo all of my own accord.)

In a pause while we gazed around searching for objects beginning with M, I heard the descending squeals of laughter from up above, peals and squeals of what could only be described as a *musical* laugh, something I'd only come across before in literature, and only second-rate literature at that.

'Mackintosh,' I guessed.

'Where?' demanded Barbara.

'It's what the pony wears in very bad weather.'

'But he's not wearing it now, is he?'

'Minestrone,' said Tillie.

'Oh, come *on*.'

'Meteorite. Mandolin,' said Tillie. 'Marguerite of Anjou.'

There was nothing out there beginning with M. The laughter fell in peals and rolls, arpeggios of laughter, on and on.

'Who *is* that?' I was forced to ask, though usually with the Hennessys I retained an air of casual detachment, as though nothing in the world could or would surprise me.

'Freddie.'

'There's nothing beginning with M,' said Tillie. 'We give in.'

'Don't be so *boring*,' said Barbara. 'Look *harder*.'

'*Freddie*?'

'Yes. Are you really looking?'

'How can it be Freddie?' I asked. The musical laugh was clearly female. It stilled for a moment, and then came gurgling again, this time on an ascending scale. As if naughty fingers were tinkling up her ivory backbone.

'Short for Frede*rica*,' said Tillie in a flat voice. 'Mistletoe.'

'There isn't any mistletoe.'

'I thought there might be but my eyes aren't good enough to see it,' said Tillie, in a conciliatory tone. 'Not as good as yours.'

'Who's Freddie?' I asked.

Barbara gestured with a flick of her head. 'The fatty in the red shawl.' Her head flicked towards the dining-room window. The big nude. The big fat red-shawled nude. Frederica. 'Come *on*. Keep guessing.'

'Metal. Metal as in barbed wire,' I said.

'No. Give up?'

'We give up,' said Tillie.

There was another sort of squeal, a quite different sort of squeal, from above. Tillie put Mattie's head aside from the blanket and jumped up.

'Give up,' I said.

We heard Tillie running down the back veranda steps.

'It's *marguerite*. They're still in flower, just about,' said Barbara, pointing to a grey clump with two straggly white flowers on show.

'Well, I didn't know that's what they're called,' I complained. Mattie sat up, scratching himself.

The squeals had disappeared now. All was silence from above.

'Tillie almost got it with Marguerite of Anjou.'

'You should have let her,' I said.

353

We could hear Tillie. She was chopping firewood down by the summer-house step. Chop chop, chop chop.

40

Co-operation

'They don't like me, you know,' Hanny told me. 'They think I'm a pain in the neck.'

'Who?'

'Travis, and Moira, and Mike. And the rest.'

'Not all of them, surely?'

'They've got me down as Un. Co. Operative. They'd be happy to see me dead.'

'Not *Mike*. He's so wet, he wouldn't wish harm on a fly.'

'Don't you believe it.'

As if the mention of his name had summoned him up, Mike appeared on the lawn to gather everyone in. The others assembled docilely. We were on our usual bench, hidden on three sides by hedges. Maybe he wouldn't see us.

'I'm not going,' Hanny said. 'I like it out here. And I hate it in there.'

She kicked off her shoes and put her bare feet up on the seat, hugging her knees. 'I think we should go on strike. Stay out here all night.'

I looked up at the sky. 'We'll get cold in the night, and wet if it rains.'

'You've got no spirit of rebellion, have you?'

'I wouldn't say that. I'm just being practical.' She was the one who was always shivering.

'We're OK in our little corner. We'll be just fine.' Hanny made both her hands into pistols and aimed them at the figures on the lawn. 'We'll be like Butch Cassidy and the Sundance Kid. They'll have to surround us with troops to get us out. I loved that film.'

'I never saw it.'

'You're joking.'

'I'm not.'

'Where is it you live – Timbuktu?'

'We used to have a cinema in the high street, but it closed down because of a leaky roof. When it opened up again, they'd turned it into a bingo hall.'

'No kidding?'

'I've seen *The Sound of Music*, and Cliff Richard in *Summer Holiday*.'

'Poor you.'

Mike was walking steadily down the path towards us, holding out his arms like someone driving cattle. 'Sorry, you two, but it really is time to go in.'

'We're not coming. You'll never take us alive.' This time Hanny raised a shotgun, and squinted down the sights.

'That's not funny,' Mike said.

But Hanny let him have both barrels anyway, right in the guts.

We aren't allowed to go into each other's rooms here, though I've often walked slowly past the open doorway of Hanny's. She's got the same blue-checked bedcover and curtains as me; some people have green. On the wall-shelf she has arranged a photo gallery. Her parents, grandparents, numerous cousins and uncles and aunts, the family cat, her grandmother's cairn terriers, all in silver frames. They watch her push the food around her plate and practise sleight-of-hand with her sleeves.

I've got no such thing. Our family were not much given to photography, and they weren't that keen on displaying the results. In Gloria's house the only ones I remember were a touching picture of her and Eddy on their wedding day, and two posed studio portraits of her long-dead mother and father hanging above the sideboard in the front room. Taken in their early twenties, when they were engaged but not yet married, they faced each other, looking lugubrious and far from young. Sometimes, if she was doing the dusting or putting away knives and forks in the cutlery drawer of the sideboard, Gloria would chat to them: 'All right, Mum? All right, Dad?'

'You can't ignore them,' she told me, quite seriously. 'It wouldn't be polite.'

At home the only photos on display were of Brian and me, aged seven and eight, in what must have been our peak year as satisfactory offspring, taken by the school photographer against a sky-blue backdrop. Both of us in neat uniforms, my hair not yet long enough for bunches, Brian's wet-combed across his chubby forehead. They stood for years on top of the piano, not looking down on me as I practised but gazing away across the room, as if desisting from comment. All the other family photos were kept in a single album, hard to fill, with snaps of us in front of stately homes or picnicking in windy fields on our days out. A few of Bettina's wedding, and an old one of Stella, Gloria and Eddy in deckchairs, with the big clock on the prom recognizable behind them. Maybe Wally, or another of Stella's unpromising beaux, took this snap, crouching down with the Kodak and instructing them all to say 'Cheese!' The rest of our annual school photos were tucked inside the back cover. There were no pictures of us as babies (of course) or of Mum and Dad in that blank time before we arrived.

The Hennessys went in for paintings, not photographs. But I had one record of Tom, taken in the automatic photo booth that Woolworth's installed after they ripped out the old tea bar. One day when we had nothing better to do, Tom and I crammed inside and posted our coins. We squashed our faces together and arranged our expressions in the mirror, waiting for the flashes to start. After the fun Tom could barely be bothered to wait for the results to drop through the slot. 'We'll look like gibbering idiots,' he said, leaning against the booth with his arms folded aggressively, putting off any other potential customers.

I waited, and I picked up the strip of four tiny photos. In one Tom was grinning like a death's-head. My eyes were huge with the flash, except for the last one where they were screwed up, laughing. I didn't keep that one, or the death's-head. I snipped them up, but carefully scissored between the remaining two, and gave one of them to Tom. I don't know what he did with it. In mine Tom just looked like a pale and ugly boy with a bad perm. But it was the nearest thing I had to a picture of my love.

Every summer Brian went to Scout camp. Stayed for a week in a damp tent with five other smelly-footed boys. One year I said to Mum, 'I'm sleeping in his room while he's away. It's OK. I checked with him and he said yes.'

Of course I hadn't checked with him. He wouldn't have approved. Very jealous of his territory, was Brian. As if he had something to hide.

So for a week I slept in the built-in bed up near the stars. The ceiling sloping over me felt strange. Even in the darkness I could feel it there. I was aware of myself up high, like on the deck of some old-fashioned ship, a vessel of exploration, the *Pinta* or the *Santa Maria*. Breasting into the waves with me dozing at the helm, out on the bowsprit, up in the crow's nest. It was away from every other room, every entanglement and obligation in the house. You could breathe. No wonder Brian liked it up here. He never had to sleep downstairs in the belly of the house, like a slave in a slave-ship. I left the windows open so that the smell of the night could drift around me, and I heard the night sounds come in. You couldn't hear that kind of thing from my room. The bird hoot, the fox yell, and sometimes the wonderful sound, like a powerful zip unzipping, of a motorbike engine tearing away up the main road.

Bikers hung out at the café by the roundabout. During the day it was family time, trippers welcome – bring the kiddies in, madam, plenty of room! But in the evening, motorbike boys assembled in the forecourt, swaggering round, gunning their engines, shouting out in rough voices. And Mandy had been seen there, on the forecourt, hanging out with greasy bikers. It was Suzannah Grey who told me, when we were in our last year at school.

'That Mandy Burton – she's your cousin?' she said, stopping abruptly in front of me in the corridor one day.

'Sort of cousin. Distant cousin.'

'What's she like?'

This was a fatal question to be asked at school; a cryptic question. You could never be sure if the person asking was a sworn enemy or a bosom friend of the person being asked about. The only thing you could be sure of was that they had some good and as yet hidden reason for asking. I took the politic way out and gave the smallest shrug.

'Does she go with greasers?'

'*I* don't know.'

'You know the transport café by the roundabout?'

I nodded.

'Saw her there, getting on the back of some dirty great motorbike. Bloke looked about forty. *How* old is she?'

That was the reason, then, the delight of scandal and gossip, the satisfaction of rubbishing someone's reputation in front of their kith and kin. Publicly, in a corridor seething with other girls. I wasn't quick enough to think of asking how Suzannah saw her, what Suzannah was doing in the vicinity. My best retorts are only ever in my head.

So Mandy had felt the call in her blood of her poor dead motorcycle-riding father. I could see her there, in my mind's eye, all too easily. Pinched white face under the brilliant lights, gum-chewing jaw hard at work, bump-and-grind hip jutting out, bantering with bikers. Great big bulky men in studded waistcoats and fingerless gloves, with ratty beards and stubbly jowls. Dirty hands and black-rimmed nails. She had found her niche, her true home. God knows what they made of her. Skinny mascot doll to dangle from their handlebars? Baby delinquent in need of a good fright, or a firm hand? Maybe they just took her home to her mum. They say there's honour among thieves.

Not that there was any among the ones I knew.

I didn't mean to waste time thinking about Mandy while I was up there in Brian's room. I meant only to sleep, afloat, try it out, while I could.

When he came back from camp he was angry with me. I didn't tell him anything, but I think Mum must have let something slip, mentioned it in passing – 'Oh, that was very kind of you, Brian, letting your sister borrow your room. Not that I can think why she'd want to.' And he was furious! But he showed his fury in sly, cold ways. He trod heavily round the house for days, not attempting to speak to me unless it was necessary. He'd pass the salt when asked, but leave it just outside my reach. He'd turn out the light if he left a room and I was still in it. He never said anything about it at all. He never accused me of taking his room, sleeping in his bed, trampling all over his territory. Maybe Mum didn't tell him, didn't need to. Maybe some animal sense of his picked up the wrong smell, the rumpled rug, the footprint discernible only to the most intense and spiritual of native trackers. After all, the sheets had been changed. And I'd aired the room quite thoroughly with those wide-flung windows.

The other thing that he did was take my latest book, one I was borrowing from the Hennessys, and burn it to a little heap of ashes in the wire incinerator down beside our garden shed. I didn't see him do it. But I couldn't find the book, not on my bookshelf, under the bed, or even in Tom's or Barbara's room where I might well have left it. I didn't like to ask anyone if they had seen it. But I'd gone out to unpeg the washing for Mum – see, I was still biddable, in small house-trained ways – and I spotted something in the incinerator. I looked more closely: a new pile of ashes and a triangle, an inch wide and two inches across, of dun cloth-covered board with a minute gold line just inside the rim. I knew exactly what it was. No one should burn books. No one should burn anything as blameless as Rosamond Lehmann's *Dusty Answer*. But Brian had.

And after that he was back to normal. Back to *usual*, I should say.

Sometimes I look about me at the people in here and wonder if they were ever normal. If they ever, at one time in their life, walked down a street or round a playground without anybody staring at them, whispering, pointing them out. Maybe they were ordinary people, once. Perhaps they had friends, real, normal friends, not just someone whose mother had insisted they be friendly, out of pity's sake. Not just some aunt or cousin, acting as a surrogate friend, because there wasn't – never would be – anyone else, not from choice. God, I wonder if any of them were married, once, on the outside? Were loved and cherished and desired, had someone whose face lit up when they walked into the room? Someone who *longed for them*. I wonder if any of them had children of their own?

I wonder if they remember?

Actually, it's hard to imagine it. It's even hard to

imagine Mike, or Trudy, or Lorna, for that matter, finding anyone weird enough to want them, fancy them, yearn for them from afar. Hanny and I are definitely the only two normal people in this place.

Oh, and there's Dr Travis. I can imagine him with a mum and a dad, I can see him in a pleasant family setting. I can see him having dinner with his girlfriend at a restaurant table, snow-white linen and gleaming china. I can imagine them raising their glasses to each other over the small vase of carnations that sits between them. I can see the pair of them quite clearly. The funny thing is, in my mind's eye, *she* looks a bit sort of Carolyn-like.

'You haven't *been* . . .' Lorna says, pausing on the word dramatically. I don't admire her technique. She's chosen the wrong sort of word to emphasize. Far better a noun, or a decent verb, something more specific. I wait for the rest. '. . . very *creative* in Group, Cora.'

Oh, my mistake. I thought it was Activity that we were supposed to be creative in. I thought it was there that we gave ourselves up to the sordid secret shapes in our minds and let them take substance through our finger-tips. Once at school I got given a C-minus for a composition, and the remark was added (in red ink): 'You must show more imagination!' Since the title set for the composition was 'A Day in the Life of a Penny', I think I would have been justified in replying the same. Why should we produce more than our superiors are capable of coaxing out of us? I wouldn't mind if my clay penguins or my snowmen were judged and found wanting. Lorna must know by now that manual dexterity is not one of my strongest points. Though, in mitigation, perhaps she's not been a party to most of the discussion around that subject.

Does this mean that they all report back to Lorna? I hate to think so, to think of Mike and Moira and Trudy observing my every word, my every significant silence, and telling tales. I try not to think about that side of it at all – what the point of all this stuff is.

'You do not – apparently – play a very full part in Group.' She pauses to stare at me from under her thick pony's fringe. 'You don't say much, you don't cooperate. And you don't say much to me, either.' She pauses again. This must be the technique for the day. Well, it's one I'm good at, too.

'Yet I would have thought you'd find it easy. To say something. Anything. Anything that comes into your head. You can be very articulate when you want to be, and I thought you were good at making things up. That's something you *are* good at, Cora.'

All this comes with huge pauses in between. During which I look at the dreary painting on the wall. Or I look at my hands, at my fingernails rimmed with clay. As if this time it is I who have clawed my way through earth and rocks.

'Do you bite your nails, Cora?' she says, following my gaze, changing tack. Being wickedly cunning, so she thinks. And Dr Travis jerks into life to write this down.

Do you bite your nails? Have you got a bike? How high can you jump? Can you do this? *Can* you?

'I have it on good authority . . .' (Oh yes? Whose?) '. . . that you like to make things up. Do you like to tell stories in your head?'

She leans back and folds her arms. Today she is wearing the blouse with the necktie made out of the same material. As she folds her arms the tie loops out like an enormous single bosom.

I don't make things up. I just see things – what they are, what they could be. If anything, I see too much, too clearly. That's what they don't like.

She tries again, a new direction. I am getting so tired of this. 'Do you have a temper, Cora? Would you say you had a quick temper? Do you sometimes react violently, before you've had time to think?'

'No, I haven't,' I reply, just to surprise her. Just to keep her on her toes. 'I'm easy-going,' I add, and to prove it I give her a happy little shrug. An easy-going kind of shrug. You're not annoying me with this line of questioning, you're not trying my quick-erupting temper, that little shrug says.

'You know, it would be much better,' says Lorna, rather sternly, as if she is a headmistress and I am the harum-scarum madcap of the fourth form, 'if you could try to be more active in Group. Don't hide your light under a bushel, Cora. Will you think about that? Will you give it some serious thought?'

I nod. Serious thought is something I'm always ready for. In fact, try and stop me.

Lorna gathers herself and I think we've finished, but there is something else: 'You've led us a merry dance, you know, and so far we've let you. Merry dances are always worth watching. But don't think I don't know what you're up to.'

And Dr Travis gives her a sharp look. A quick flick of a look before returning to his notebook, in which he is now writing nothing. But a look all the same. I saw it. Nothing passes me by.

So I try. I really try.

It's Trudy's turn to run Group. She doesn't look well. She pulled the short straw today, and she really doesn't look at all well. I wonder if it's her period? I wonder if it's her time of life? I've no idea how old she is – it's difficult to tell with very fat people – and she has a permanently cross expression, which may be there because she *is* permanently cross, tugging all that bulk around with her, or it may be just the weight of her flesh that pulls her facial muscles into a scowl. I hate fat people. And I hate short people, like Lorna, like Moira, a minute ferocious doll of a woman, and I hate thin people – no, that's not true – but I hate *gawky* people like Mike. They really aren't physically blessed, the people here. It's no beauty contest. I bet Moira went round with the straws, up there in the staffroom, and arranged it so that poor fat wheezing Trudy would get suckered. Because nobody else feels like doing it, for God's sake, and Trudy should pull her enormous weight.

We sit in the usual circle and Trudy decides that we'll play a new game. Picture postcard, it is called. Remember somewhere you've been, something interesting you've seen. Let the image pop into your mind just like a picture postcard. Tell us about it.

Fair enough.

I remember Tillie slamming down a lump of pastry on the table. Not on the marble pastry board (a marvel, this, white and cloudy grey and black, swirled through like a monochrome version of Raspberry Ripple ice cream). I don't remember why, just her tight lipless mouth, and her hand over the slamming pastry.

And the way all the plates jumped on the table top.

But the Old Crone has taken the stage and is yattering on about something, a man and a car and a policeman, and everyone else has to wait.

I remember Tillie saying, 'Oh, there you are, my little doves,' and 'Let me in,' and kneeling up on the bed, her own bed, while we tugged at the pillows and shuffled ourselves over. She switched on the white lamp above her head and Barbara said, 'Oh, *Muh-um*! It gets reflected in the screen. We can't see a thing now!' And Tillie turned it off.

It always disconcerted me to hear them call her Mum. To assert that connection, that umbilical claim.

It used to disconcert me at first when I heard them refer to her as Tillie and call her it to her face. As far as I knew, mothers didn't operate in the realm of Christian names – they forfeited those at the moment of giving birth. It seemed to trespass on the boundaries between adults and children, tipping everything sideways, to go flashing Tillie's Christian name about, using it as if they were equals. The grown-ups whose first names I was permitted to use were supposed to be strictly prefixed with 'Aunt' and 'Uncle'. Even Bettina was referred to as 'Dad's Cousin', and Mandy as 'Your Cousin'.

Oh, there I go again. Drifted away from the postcard, away from the game. Must try harder, pay proper attention. Wet Lettuce is lisping faintly about some incident fossilized in her past, and Trudy lies there, beached, in her orange-upholstered easy chair, eyelids half closed. Even if I came up with something creative, chances are she wouldn't recall it by the time she gets debriefed.

Here's an image that keeps popping into my mind, bright as a picture postcard: a sunny day; our street is jammed with fire engines, and I can see Barbara running, with a dress like an old-fashioned bride's yanked up above her knees, and her feet bare on the bumpy tarmac. She's running like mad towards her house.

41

Desperate

These are the kind of questions that Lorna asks me. She is getting hard, and desperate.

– Tell me more about when you and your brother used to play together as children. Who tended to choose the game? Was one of you naturally the leader?

– Did you keep secrets from each other, or did you like to tell everything?

– What about if there was a disagreement with the other children? Would Brian stand up for you? Or did you, as big sister, tend to protect him?

– Who would you say got on best with your mother, your adoptive mother?

– Would you say you were closer to any of your aunts? Was there anyone you thought you might have preferred as a mother?

It all sounded a bit too close to home.

And one day, when Dr Travis wasn't with us, she said, 'Do you have any feelings about your *real* mother? Do you ever think of her? Are you angry with her?'

Although what I normally did in response to her questions was refuse to reply, or talk at length about something else, this time I was surprised into saying, *'What!?'* because I really couldn't see what this had to do with anything.

Because, honestly, I never thought about my real mother. Even all those lunchtimes when I went round to Gloria's in search of a friendly face, a source of information, the one thing we never talked about was my real mother. She was of no interest to me. The idea of her did not cross my mind. I had enough on my plate as it was.

Lorna began to tell me about some changes in the law that were being considered, that would allow adopted children, once they were adult, to search for their real parents. If the new law went ahead, adopted children would have the right of access to their records so that they could trace, or have traced for them, their real mother. The term she used was *biological mother*, which sounded rather disgusting to me. A bit of my *adoptive mother* coming out in me, I thought, and felt a smirk flit across my face.

Lorna glanced sharply at me. You have to watch them all the time. *They* are watching *you*.

'Of course,' she said, 'this will only apply to those adopted children who want to find out about their origins. Who choose to seek the information. And it will have to be carried out very carefully, with a lot of counselling and so on beforehand.' She's very keen on the value of counselling. Well, it keeps her in paid employment. 'And the biological mothers, they won't have any rights to trace their children. It won't be a two-way thing.'

'Bit of a shock, I should think,' I said, pausing for a

lengthy yawn, 'to find the baby you cast off twenty years ago standing on your doorstep.'

'That's why the legislation has got to be well thought out,' Lorna said. 'These things could potentially be very traumatic.'

I wish Dr Travis could have been there. I would have valued his silent opinion.

'I'm really not interested in my *biological mother*,' I said, pronouncing the words in a way that showed her what I thought of them. What I thought of Lorna and her crowd, and their revolting jargon. 'I'm not interested in mothers at all.'

'Well, it's interesting that you should say that, Cora,' she replied, 'because that's what *I* think is at the root of all your trouble.'

I'm sure she would not have said that if Dr Travis had been there. I have a feeling that she's overstepped some invisible mark. Perhaps I've made her go too far. Perhaps I've driven her to it.

The time came when Brian was sixteen and my mother must have told him. Or perhaps she delegated the job to Dad, to keep this private matter in the appropriate purdah of the sexes. I don't know.

I don't know because no one ever mentioned it.

I said to Gloria, the week after his birthday, 'Have they told Brian yet? Do you know if he's been told?' And she said, 'Oh yes, he's been informed.' So they had mentioned it to *her*.

I went home and kept a watch on them all. Nothing had changed. Nothing had changed from before his birthday to after his birthday to the time when Gloria told me, 'Oh yes, he's been informed.' I looked at their bland impassive faces and found nothing. Except that they were so stiff and impassive and bland that anything at all might have been going on behind them. Absolutely anything at all.

I thought they were ridiculous, the whole pack of them.

It's funny how your parents go from being the centre and limits of your world to being almost irrelevant. When you are little they are everything. They control the world and inform everything that you do or is done to you. You know nothing beyond them, and everything you *do* know comes through and by way of them. Even things they know nothing about they have an opinion on and *their* opinion is *your* opinion. This must be true of all parents. They don't have to be megalomaniacs to achieve this – it just comes about through raising small children, who will unerringly tumble out of windows, wander under cars and fall into water if left to their own devices. They cannot even feed themselves, or reach a light switch or a door handle. They need fresh air, regular naps and everything sterilized.

And then you turn twelve or thirteen and these lordly beings, the sun and the moon, are eclipsed. Or just shouldered out of the way. Your world extends to places they have never gone, people they don't know and will never know. Their wisdom is shown up for the sham it is. They get their information out of newspapers, for God's sake. Might as well come off the backs of cereal packets. You get yours from the real world. You do things you know they've never done, and never will do. You become a denizen and then an expert in a world completely unfamiliar to them.

It's like the reflection in the convex mirror on our chimneypiece. *They* are the people crowded to the edges. They're still in the room but they are small and hopeless, and *you* loom big, bigger, biggest, the centre of the universe.

Lunchtime, at the dry cleaner's. Not strictly lunchtime, more like eleven fifteen, because that's when I'm allocated my lunch break. The other assistant, Lois, who has ankles the same width as her calves and has to wear special shoes which her feet melt over the sides of, is holding the fort. Her lunch break is from two to three. I sidle forth into the high street, not hungry yet. Whoever *is* hungry at eleven fifteen? These are the choices: a windy walk along the prom, a gentle stroll through hosiery and handbags in one of the department stores. Coffee in a thick cup in the Wimpy (they had closed the Woolworth's tea bar by this time). Window-shopping, wandering along pavements pocked with chewing gum, pink and grey and black, like all the stages in a nastily deteriorating skin condition. It was all right for a day, but not for every day.

I go into the big stationer's. There's a blast of warm air at the doors, and ahead of me a rack of ornate, pinky, primrose, silvery greetings cards proclaims, 'Don't forget Mother's Day!' Daffodils and bows and smirking kittens. Beyond are the shelves of notebooks, address books, account books, hanging packs of pens and pencils, ink cartridges, fluffy pencil cases in lurid colours. I stop and survey them. I don't want anything here, but it wastes a minute, two, three. I turn aside and read the 'funny' birthday cards, which aren't funny at all. They're obsessed with sex and ageing. I'm obsessed with youth and life. One of the sales assistants, who is kneeling, slipping sheets of wrapping paper over separate wire slats, glances sideways at me. Perhaps she thinks I've got dirty fingers. Perhaps she thinks I'm soiling the goods.

Gloria once bought a candlewick bedspread. 'Shop-soiled, it said,' she proclaimed proudly, unfolding it for us. 'Half price!' The rose-pink fringing was fluffy with dust, an insubstantial, fine-textured dust, a shop sort of dust, and a dusty-coloured panel lay diagonally across the spread. 'It'll come out in the wash,' Gloria said, the enthusiasm in her voice already draining away under the steady examination of my mother's eagle – you might say *professional* – eye.

'You wouldn't catch me buying anything that was *shop-soiled*,' my mother said. 'I like to have everything new.'

'Oh, I like to have everything new,' Gloria replied, catching the wind in her sails again, 'but *want* can't always *have*.'

'It *is* new,' I wanted to defend her. 'It's just shop-soiled new.' But I didn't say anything.

Want can't always have. I dabbled along the magazine shelves, came to the books, paused. I never wanted those jammy jars of coloured lip gloss, those bottles of nail varnish round and glowing like Christmas tree lights. But these, slippery orange Penguins, mind-provoking Pelicans with swimming-pool-blue backs. Lovely little hardbacks, just the size of a one-person box of chocs – what a treat! When selecting a gift for a friend, would you choose (a) the latest Edna O'Brien with soft-focus cover? (b) a fusty fawn Evelyn Waugh with jazzy jacket design? (c) an Agatha Christie drawing-room comedy? or (d) any old thing that would fit in your pocket without a fuss, or a giveaway bulge?

You may not be able to teach an old dog new tricks, but *old* tricks, now that's quite another thing. My sleight-of-hand amazes me, when the motivation's there. Look, girls! Look, Jillian! Watch me, Gaynor! My quicksilver fingers dipping and delving, my casual expression as, instead of turning tail and guiltily, flush-faced, hurrying off down the aisle, I slowly flick the pages of a dictionary of quotations, peruse the index, make a mild mental note of the price. And put it back. I am a customer, entitled to stand here with a wasp-jacketed copy of *Teach Yourself Greek* in my unpersuaded hand. I catch the eye of the assistant, who looks enquiring, but no, I am decided now: not Greek, not this year. I slide the book back into its proper place in the shelf, and walk slowly away. Barbara, you would be proud of me.

I am not proud of myself. At home, in my bedroom bookcase, I have a growing number of volumes, including a dictionary of quotations, pocket-size edition, of course. My mother thinks I buy them with what's left of my weekly pay after board and lodgings have been deducted. I could. I *could*. But I don't. A little voice at the back of my mind tells me I am entitled. Those responsible for my parlous education whisper to me that I am a deserving case. And anyway, I have read everything the Hennessys have to offer. And I have a lot of time on my hands.

I know what it was that Barbara and her friends were after, too. Not the stuff itself, not the *things*. But the lift, the buzz, the high. I feel it. All dreadful words. Uncle Bob's thesaurus would be ashamed of me. The excitement, then, the exhilaration, the fizzy intoxication of that moment when an object of desire slips into your hand, liberates itself, surrenders itself to the other side. The sheer bloody thrill of it.

It was hot in the gardens this afternoon, thundery and overcast. There was a brittle roar in the distance. More staff came hurrying outside. I could see Mike trying to herd people indoors, glancing up at the sky and making hopeless, beckoning movements with his arms.

I said to Hanny, 'There's going to be a law to let adopted children trace their mothers. Their *biological* mothers.'

'Oh yes?' Hanny wasn't paying much attention. She was too busy watching Moira getting nearer to us, rounding up the sheep. She fanned her face with a sprig of leaves she had torn off a bush. 'I do hope it storms,' she said. 'I love watching the lightning.'

'Lorna told me.'

'*Lorna?*'

I'd meant her to say, 'Told you what?' I wanted her to say, 'What was it Lorna told you?' and 'Why was that?' But she didn't. So I didn't prompt her, push her. She wasn't really interested in what I had to say, and I wasn't about to humiliate myself. I'm too proud for that. And you have to look after yourself in here.

I'd forgotten. Lorna doesn't mean anything to Hanny. Hanny doesn't see Lorna, has never had an interview with Lorna. All Hanny's individual time is with Dr Travis. Now that's what I call unfair.

'Look at them. What are they trying to do?' she said, letting out a laugh, indicating Mike and the confusion of people hurrying for the doors.

Hot, heavy spatters of rain fell on us, on our bare faces and our knees.

'Here it comes!' sighed Hanny.

Moira stood before us. We were the last. 'It's raining. You have to come in now,' she said.

'We like the rain,' said Hanny, smiling at her.

Moira was unmoved. Her tiny mouth – no bottom lip at all – was a single cynical straight line.

'Too bad. Besides, Hanny Gombrich, you're wanted, inside.'

Hanny rose, and Moira turned away to go back up the path, missing as she did so Hanny's little gesture, supplicating, lifting her hands and putting her injured wrists together, ready for the handcuffs.

Lorna asks me, 'What do you see in the future, Cora?'

Well, there's fun and love and life for starters, I could say.

She's got her sympathetic, syrupy voice on today, which always puts my back up. I don't need her sympathy, thank you very much. She's gazing at me with her head on one side, like a friendly robin on a Christmas card.

'Cora?'

I live from day to day. I don't make plans. Plans only lead to disappointment. I grub through earth and rocks just to keep my head, as they say, above water.

If I were a Carolyn sort of girl, even now, even here, I'd have things to look forward to. Because a Carolyn sort of girl would be cherished whatever she'd done, would be forgiven, because a Carolyn sort of mother would love her come-what-may. Would feel that bond, that protective bond, from the very first moment she saw her newborn baby's head, or, way back, when she was first aware of that kicking inside her swelling body.

But let's be frank, I'm not a Carolyn sort of girl, and where you'd find a Carolyn sort of mother is beyond even my powers of imagination.

'There is a future for you, Cora. You'd better start believing in it. It will be here sooner than you think.' What does she mean by that? 'I think that would really help, Cora, if you started believing in something.'

42

Scissors, Paper, Stone

We didn't have clay in Activity today. We had paper.

Trudy was taking Activity. I imagine it is a better job than taking Group, in that the staff don't have to get anybody to talk, even if they do have to sweep up all the mess afterwards. Trudy seems even more plump. She wears an outsize T-shirt and her baggy tie-dyed trousers clasp her thighs. Her circulation is less than good and her red toes stick out of her Jesus sandals like a row of radishes. Her cheeks turn bright pink and she breathes hard, just going round giving out the paper. I wait for her to fall on the floor unconscious due to some kind of aortic spasm. *Then* what would we do? Scramble to escape? Or sit there looking dumbly at each other? I'm afraid the latter's more likely.

We are each given a square of black sugar-paper, which is not really black but a sort of anthracite. It looks matte and dusty, like cheap coal. On top of this Trudy lets float down a square of crimson tissue paper and then another of deep lipstick-pink. I hear her wheezing breath coming round for a fourth time behind our chairs, handing out circles of raspberry-coloured tissue. I hear the rasp of her thighs in their tie-and-dye. When everyone has her ration, Trudy subsides into her own chair and pauses there a moment. Then she lifts her heavy shoulders with a sudden deep breath and shows us how to tear the red tissue paper into strips and fringes and how to stick it on to the black sugar-paper in layers. Of course, we have no scissors. In the middle of the table is a white two-pint kitchen basin filled with innocuous flour-and-water paste. Each of us has a plastic spatula, with rounded ends and a soft, flexible handle. We'd be hard-pressed to do any harm with one of these. Except maybe stick them down our throats.

I can't see the therapeutic point of pasting fringes on to sugar-paper but around me everyone is having a go. Marsupial frowns, sweats and sighs. Rose tears her tissue into fingernail-sized pieces and lets them flutter to the ground. At least with clay we are allowed to make what we want. And personally, I would not have chosen all these reds, not with Marsupial and her phantom pregnancy, Rose the putative infanticide, Hanny and her criss-crossed wrists, and Lord-knows-what other dubious female problems there are in our group. The crimson, the deep pink, the crushed raspberry, are all too indicative. Or maybe that's the point.

Either that, or it was all that was left in the store cupboard.

Hanny is late. Hanny is very late. We have all started tearing and sticking and she still hasn't arrived. The woman with the long earlobes is murmuring to herself, Marsupial and the fair-haired girl next to her begin to talk, some nonsense about the weather and how it gets you down. Outside the sun blares through big windows and a true-blue sky flies like a flag. Trudy lets flow cheerful comments and compliments all round the group, like a successful party hostess, making us feel embarrassed if we don't join in. I have no one to talk to. Hanny isn't coming. I notice, at last, that Trudy hasn't laid a place for her at this female dinner table with its black mats and red red plates. I pull the crimson, then the pink tissue paper into strips. I stick them on to the black background. But I take the little circle of raspberry and pleat it into a flower.

The quality of careers advice on offer at other schools must have been far superior to mine. Also the parental expectations, the family ability for map-reading round the highways and byways of life. In the second autumn after I left school, Tom went away. He had managed to improve his A-level grades and got a place at university in London. And Barbara had crammed her five Os, and embarked on a foundation year at the art school where Patrick taught. I was astonished. She'd shown no particular talent or desire for this area of operations before. And here was I, still behind the counter at the dry cleaner's.

If my parents were schooled in the University of Life, it must have been one of the smaller and quieter departments, some kind of distant extra-mural forcing house. A mushroom shed, maybe. Dim and quiet and undisturbed.

'Think yourself lucky you've got a job,' my mother kept telling me. 'And not just one that's seasonal, either. You could've been selling ice creams. Then what would you do come September?'

And Brian, Brian had started at Gough Electricals. He went off with Dad every morning in the car. My nightmare of a line full of dancing blue overalls was coming to pass. They both took a packed lunch, which my mother prepared, because they didn't like the canteen food. Didn't trust it. I don't suppose Brian even got the chance to try it. So he was launched in life. Weirdly enough, they were both very proud of him. He was keeping up the family tradition, you might say.

'Is that really what you want to do?' I asked him, when I found out where he was going to work.

I stared at him, into his hazel eyes, light and flecky like fried bread which the yolk of an egg has run into. He didn't look anything like me, never had. When Mum told me that I was adopted, was there a split second when I'd thought: so that explains everything!? I don't think she gave me time – she followed up so quickly with *But you are brother and sister*. She didn't even give me a second in which to think.

Brian still had his schoolboy haircut and those pinpoint freckles spattered over his nose, but his skin had coarsened with the oily explosion of adolescence. His expression was surly and blank.

'Do you always have to do everything people tell you?' I pressed him.

'*No*.'

'But that's what you're doing! Don't you ever want to shake people up? Give them a bit of a surprise?'

'Don't get so angry, Carol. You're always in a stew.'

'But don't you?'

'What for?'

'Just *because*. Just to show you can.'

'Well, I could if I wanted to,' he said, not looking at me.

We were standing outside on the lawn. He glanced up at the great wall of the hedge, and scowled, and then turned away from me. 'I'm going to get the shears,' he said.

'Brian!' I called after him. I almost shouted, and then thought better of it. We never shouted this side of the hedge. Somebody might hear us. But I wanted to grab him and shake him. I wanted to shake him till his head jangled about on its shattered neck and his eyeballs fell out, like some cartoon creature.

I caught sight of Barbara one day, coming down the steps of the bridge at the station. She must have just got off the train, back from a day at the art school. She wore a long silky dress like the one Gloria is wearing in her wedding photograph, heavy satin, gathered beneath the bust, a smooth skirt flowing to her feet. Gloria holds an armful of flowers and Eddy, firmly, in the crook of her elbow. Barbara held a big art portfolio tied with black tapes. Her dress was a yellowish ivory, like something hidden away in a cupboard for a long time and then brought out into the glaring daylight. The hem swooped and drooped. Over the top she had on a ragbag crocheted cardigan, much like the one she used to wear to the Wren – maybe the very same one, since the sleeves were stretched tight around her upper arms. Beneath the uncertain hem of the frock I could see scarlet clogs. Her hair, henna-red, hung to her waist, still without benefit of comb. She was wearing sunglasses. They made her eyes blank, hidden.

She walked right past me, scanning the traffic for a space to cross the road. She didn't say hello or nod, or even seem to glance in my direction. Perhaps she hadn't seen me? Or failed to recognize me?

I don't think for one moment that was true. I'd have recognized *her* anywhere.

When his re-sits were over and he was waiting to take up his place at university, Tom spent six months as, variously, an assistant house-painter, a waiter and, finally, a van driver for a soft drinks supplier. He rode around all day with his arm out of the van window, ending up with a tanned right arm and a pale left one. Well, it seemed exotic to me. I stroked the silvery hairs on his tanned arm as we sat together, drinking beer, in the sunshine on the prom. Tom upended his bottle above his open mouth, catching the last drips, and then balanced it carefully on the upright of the railings in front of us. 'Finito,' he said. He lay back, wiping his mouth with one hand. '*You* could get yourself another job,' he said to me. 'You don't have to stick where you are. You could be a waitress.'

But I had seen those waitresses at the restaurant where he worked. They were college girls, university girls on vacation, they had a swing to their walk and a gleam in their eye. Their names were Sarah, Suzannah, Julie, Elaine. That's why they were chosen. Their high heels clicked like flamenco dancers' and they earned a fortune in tips. 'More tips than me, especially when they twitch their bums,' Tom complained. And laughed in lascivious delight at the remembrance of them. I hated those girls. But whatever he said, Tom, in his snow-white shirt and black waistcoat, with his pale curly hair just perfect for the year, got more than enough tips.

'You could learn to swing your hips.' He patted my thigh and laughed. 'Get some hips first and then learn to swing them.'

'I couldn't,' I said. 'They wouldn't hire me. I'm clumsy, I'd drop things.'

It was an excuse. I didn't even like their eyes when I walked into the place. They looked you up and down, summed you up in a split second. Summed you up and flicked on to the next person to walk in. Dismissing you.

He didn't know. I had tried once, swallowed my pride, sashayed in, asking. Eager to mention my previous experience, of dealing with customers, of keeping a ready smile. Some hope.

He had never known the truth of it. It wasn't just there for the picking.

I was hoping that Patrick would ask me to sit for him again. I thought he might get me some work modelling at the art school, I'm sure he could have. He could have said to all his colleagues, to his students, 'I've found a wonderful life model. Very patient, very still. Born to it. You must meet her.' He could have said, 'She's the perfect inspiration, the perfect muse. You won't be able to resist her. Naked *or* dressed.'

I might even have proved brave enough to out-stare Barbara, if I'd had to model for her class.

But then I remembered that what he'd actually said was 'Come on, you're not busy.' *You'll do.*

And I thought that maybe, all down the centuries, that's what it was. Rembrandt's Saskia, Elizabeth Siddal,

Camille Doncieux (later Mrs Monet), Vermeer's golden-haired girl with the egg-shaped face. Perhaps what was the most compellingly lovely element about them all was their *convenience*. 'Come on, you're not busy' – blind to the babies, the baking, the master's socks to darn – 'you'll do.'

Isolde often came back to visit, as if she couldn't keep away. Didn't like it when she lived there, longed for it now she'd gone. Maybe she missed Barbara, and Mattie and Sebastian. Maybe she missed her mum and dad. She'd be suddenly there in the golden sunny evening, leaning over the veranda rail and pulling the roses towards her, examining them critically, as if she still lived in the house. Smart, jewel-like, a finished creation: her own work of art.

When she hugged me I caught the scent of her perfume, deep and strong. Not like the patchouli everyone my age reeked of. And she hugged me when we met, taking my upper arms in her hands and leaning close like someone highly practised in the social arts. I fear I was a bit wooden. She was nicer then, gracious to everyone in the house, not carping and disdainful as she had been. She played the perfect guest.

I always thanked her for her postcards. 'When you come to London,' she said, 'we'll go to the Tate – have you been there recently?' I mumbled something and she carried on. 'You'll love the Hayward, and the special exhibitions at the National Portrait Gallery.'

Yes, I'll love them. I will. And for a while it seemed a certain thing, a thing that would unavoidably happen – though I didn't quite know how – in the natural course of time and events. I would go to London, I would be a single girl, I would have fun. I would continue my education. In some way, some very special and totally deserved way, my real life would begin. I just had to wait for it to start.

In October Tom went to London. He was allocated a room in a student hall of residence. But if he'd rather, he could lodge at Eugene and Tamara's. (They lived together now, so Isolde said, in a crummy flat in Notting Hill.) Or with Arthur and Dill, if he cared for more homely comforts. He had a choice. I waited for my invitation, from him or from Isolde, to sample the heady sights of London, to taste the wicked fruits.

None came.

I'd been brought up to be fatally polite, not to be pushy, never to *impose*. I waited, and waited.

Tom arrived home, on Christmas Eve. I'd thought it would be sooner. Barbara told me that university terms were shorter than school terms, and the schools had broken up the week before. I'd been counting off the days: no Advent calendar for Christmas, only for Tom. He had a small beard, which didn't suit him. It made his pointed chin appear more pointed, and because it was pale it looked transparent and fake; a young lord out of amateur dramatics. It didn't matter, my heart still leaped to see him, the familiar way he moved, his long body and long legs. Despite the ridiculous beard, my heart still jumped. Tom Rose was home too, a strapping *man* now, in a striped rugby shirt.

I hadn't got a Christmas present for Tom. It was difficult to get him anything that was meaningful enough, without laying myself open to ridicule. I felt unequal to any choice. Besides, any present got from round here, anything small-town or suburban, would be beneath Tom's notice. In the end I settled for a bottle of whisky, bought as we sailed arm in arm past an off-licence, on our way into town. I stepped out of the shop and handed it to him, in its paper bag, pressed it into his chest, with a laugh, as if it meant less than nothing.

He hadn't got anything for me, of course. No little London knick-knack, nothing exotic from far afield. But then that's boys for you.

In the last year Tom had developed a taste for pubs and clubs. There weren't that many of them in town, but there were enough. Or we borrowed Patrick's van and drove into the neighbouring town, which offered more. We drank and smoked, and in the seedy darkest ends of dark pulsating rooms, Tom bought all kinds of pills and powders. There was always a fold of paper or a bit of silver foil in his pockets, just like small boys who constantly have twists of cellophane from boiled sweets or the gold wrappers of cream-line toffees about their persons.

But now he found the brightly lit pubs and the dirty sweaty clubs were not up to his new standards, or even as satisfyingly, seedily bad as he recalled. He sat with us at a wet, brass-topped table with his pint of beer and sneered over the top of his hand-rolled cigarette. When I asked him how was London, he just put out his lower lip and shook his head, as if he couldn't possibly say. I think even Tom Rose felt left out, surpassed, as if, of all of us, Tom had chosen the grown-up option, the world of London, and glamorous emaciation, and unspeakable depravity. He was certainly thin. When I lay next to him on his tartan blanket I could play the piano on his ribs. His sexual technique had changed. He'd learned a thing or two at university. I can't honestly say that it had got any more tender.

Suddenly it hits you. You realize how stupid you've been. You begin to understand that all those wonderful things you were counting on to happen – because they must happen, mustn't they? otherwise life would be unbearable – won't happen at all. You won't come across ten thousand pounds just lying in the road, and you won't get that beautiful snow-white horse. Nor will anyone spot your special talents – do you even have any? – and whisk you away to a future worth all that waiting. To fun. To life.

You begin to really grow up now. Childhood is over, finished. *Finito*. Sorry – no sneaking back to the safe confines of dreaming how it might be one day. One day has come. You look around and realize that this *is* life, horrible boring horizonless life, what you see before you. Tough luck. Hard cheese.

It just took so long for the thunderbolt to strike me. Maybe I simply didn't want to see.

Perhaps I shouldn't generalize. Maybe those amazing things do happen to some people.

So Isolde never asked me, maybe never intended to ask me, asked me only as an automatic part of her newly acquired social graces. Or perhaps I'm being unkind. Perhaps she thought that *every*body went down to London sometimes – surely they must? – and that when I was there I would surely drop in. Or that I would be there as part of Tom's entourage. Tom would invite me.

Tom, who leaned his chin over my shoulder or put his hand roughly through my hair as he was speaking to someone else, as if I was his pet or part of his furniture, Tom would surely ask me there.

Only Tom never did.

Lorna tells me Hanny Gombrich has gone. She tosses this remark away like someone throwing a winter scarf off on entering a warm room. She tells me – when I decline to ask – that Hanny has had to go away. The treatment here wasn't working, she says.

I say nothing. I even give her a little smile.

But when I'm walking down the corridor away from her, I feel sick. I hope that Lorna isn't standing in the doorway of her room, watching me. My hands tingle. My feet keep walking but I don't know how.

This is how it is with friendship. This is how it always ends. They go away, they always go, because something else looks a better option, and because they never loved you enough in the first place.

43

Library Books

My God, there is a library here!

You know who told me about it? Wet Lettuce. Of all people, Wet Lettuce enjoys a good read.

Which means she'll be disappointed.

I have only just found it, a small room, shut away, windowless, as if they were ashamed of it. There are two shelves of books, half empty, and a trolley standing in the middle of the floor, taking up most of the space. One of those trolleys they use in the public library when they are putting back all the returned books. It has upward-sloping shelves at the top so that the books can lie with their spines to the ceiling, easily seen. At the public library, people always hang around the returned-books trolley as the librarian fills it up, waiting to catch a glimpse; as if the books that other people have chosen are likely to be far superior to anything they might choose themselves, from off the ordinary shelves. Personally, I never use the public library, not unless I need to look something up. Or if I can't get books elsewhere.

This trolley is empty, except for a square biscuit tin and a blue biro, the transparent plastic sort where you can see the tube of ink inside. The people in here could do things with a biro like that. All kinds of things.

And I've been subsisting for all this time on *Little Women*. I've read it four times so far. Jo is the obvious favourite, the one you identify with. Personally I think Marmee is a stinker. You're supposed to like her but she's so kind and noble it positively reeks. Laurie, of course, is lovely. He's made for Jo, you'd think. Laurie is the boy next door.

So what kind of books might they have in here? Safe books, neutral books, soft pappy comforting books, like the kind of food that builds up poor undernourished bodies, damaged systems, digestive tracts that must not be put under the slightest stress or strain. *Complan* books.

Not something like *Jude the Obscure*. That might give people ideas.

When I say ideas, I mean what my mother meant by the word. She didn't mean things you might get from Plato or St Augustine, or even Marx and Engels. Philosophical, political. Her definition was more all-encompassing. She never liked ideas. Ideas were matches in the wrong hands, fireworks bought by under-age children from less-than-scrupulous shopkeepers. Dangerous, potentially damaging, troublesome. Ideas were not neutral. 'You'll be giving her ideas,' she might say, or 'They've got ideas above their station.' Heaven preserve us from *that*.

The whole point of books, it seems to me, is that they give people ideas. They furnished me with ideas for years, ideas I would never have picked up otherwise. Ideas philosophical, political, sexual, metaphysical, ideas general and ideas specific. They stretched the inside of my head like a very large foot pushing its way into a very tiny slipper. And whosoever the slipper fits . . . Well, you don't get to marry the prince, but it certainly is your pass-port to other worlds, beyond the kitchen hearth and the cinders.

No wonder my mother was suspicious of them.

So what do we have here? To lighten our darkness, to lighten our burdens in this vale of woe? Well, there were several romances, to judge from the vivid covers, but no doctor/nurse ones, not very healthy in this context. Various animal stories, a paperback autobiography of someone who moved from London to Cornwall and had a happy life, an abridged book-club version of the *Pickwick Papers*. Something uplifting about a nun. And a book of light verse, covered in soft blue blotting paper. I could feel the strawberry-flavoured nourishment smoothing its way through my body already. I wondered if this was the kind of dairy produce Hanny Gombrich was allergic to. I looked at my arms to see if I was coming out in blotches. They all have that feel of cheap books, too, books no one cared about sufficiently, when bring-ing them out, to print them on good paper, with reasonable margins around the blocks of text. The paper has that rough, pulpy feel, as if it is made of pressed breakfast cereal, and already it's turning yellow. The pages won't open well, they're stuck too tightly to the spines. These books don't actually want to be opened and read.

I have borrowed the volume of light verse. Someone has written the title on the paper cover in the turquoise

Quink we all favoured in the third year at secondary school. The verse is all very inoffensive. Still, it makes a change.

I borrowed it and I signed it out in the exercise book on the library trolley. Someone had already ruled the columns. I wrote the title of the book and my name and the date I borrowed it. Well, no, not *my* name. I put Hanny Gombrich. Only because she's the one person here whose first name and surname I know.

Ever the dissembler.

The other night I saw an ambulance pull up. When there is any urgent business to be seen to they don't bother with the hundred and twenty shallow steps that wend their leisurely way through flower beds to the big front door. There is a service road that comes in round the back of the buildings. I can see it from my room. An ambulance drew up and a couple of men in uniforms sprang out, and opened the back doors, and disappeared. After a bit someone was stretchered inside it. Doors shut, driver jumps up in the front. Five minutes and it was all done. The ambulance drove smoothly away. No flashing lights, no sirens.

And now Rose is absent from Activity.

First Hanny, and now Rose. It's getting lonely in here.

I wonder if Hanny went home? I refuse to ask. Or have they sent her to some far more specialized place, where they've strapped her to a bed and plugged her with tubes and pumped the very life force back into her? Where they purée roast beef and Yorkshire pudding and proper gravy and flood her system with nourishment? I can imagine the kind of stare she would give them, a basilisk stare, full of the bitter knowledge of humankind, that would turn them to stone inside their crisp white uniforms.

Actually, I can't imagine Hanny anywhere but in this place, on our usual seat, on the afternoons that were fine enough for them to let us out into the gardens. Hanny only exists here, and then.

Perhaps I made her up.

Question: you're redecorating your room. Would you choose (a) a strong modern colour scheme? (b) pastel shades and pretty florals? (c) plain walls and floor to show off your collection of valuable antiques? or (d) keep to the same as before but freshen it up – you don't want to spoil the homely atmosphere with its family photos and mementoes?

This is what I wished I had: Mattie's picture of their house, executed in thin lines with a hard pencil – 2H not 4B – a technician's, not an artist's pencil.

Patrick's sketches of me. His paintings – sitting, standing, in my jeans and naked, staring hard at him, bold as Manet's Olympia, as if to say, 'What the hell is it to you?'

My photo-booth picture of Tom, ugly as it is.

The dictionary and thesaurus that Uncle Bob gave me.

My fluffy pyjama case.

That's probably all.

Not much to ask, is it?

Lorna has surprised me, appearing in my room. She has never been in here since that first day. She stands by the window and picks up my copy of *Little Women* between her finger and thumb, like someone picking up an item of someone else's dirty underwear. A shred of evidence. I'm sure she isn't supposed to be here. She is supposed to see me in the room off the entrance hall, with the dinky picture. She is overstepping the mark again. Out of desperation, I like to think.

'You're very privileged to be here, you know, Cora.' If she had an ounce of sensitivity, even an eighth of an ounce, she wouldn't call me by that name.

'*Cora.*' I must have muttered it. I didn't mean to.

'What's in a name?' says Lorna in a sing-song voice. 'A rose by any other name would smell as sweet.'

I look at her blankly.

She's in a good mood today. '*Romeo and Juliet,*' she says, with a smile.

Oh. I never read that one.

She runs a fingertip along the window sill, almost flirtatiously. Not looking for dust.

'While you're here, you have the possibility of taking advantage of all that we can offer.'

She was talking about Group and Activity, I suppose. Making the most of Mike's long shins and Moira's pointy toes. Learning how to make snowmen and penguins out of clay. And finding out just how badly off other people could be, people like the Old Crone and the Young Crone and Rose.

'Benefiting from our expertise. While you're here.'

There seems to be some veiled threat in those last words. She continues to look out of the window at the sunny fields. Her voice is light, as light as a bit of thistledown bowling over the flower beds, wafting over the grass. Of course, what an innocent piece of thistledown is doing in the circumstances is letting the wind cast it where it will so that it can land and in no time at all send up a *thistle*.

Lorna remains at the window. There's more she wants to say.

'I know you don't think much of us here, Cora. I know you try very hard to despise us.' She pauses, maybe to let it sink in. 'I can understand that.' Her voice is reasonable, so very reasonable. Shockingly reasonable. 'It's not so strange. You need to think that we don't know what we're doing, that we can't succeed. That we're never going to get to the bottom of things. That you're cleverer than us.' Another pause, like a lead weight in the air. 'Don't you, Cora?' Nothing. 'Don't you?'

She takes a turn around the room, light on her feet, like someone just dropping in to see what the place is like. As if she's never bothered to visit these upper rooms before. Just curious. She gets back to where she started, facing me.

'And you are very clever, Cora. You are. I'm impressed.'

Oh no. Please, no. Please don't let Lorna be the only person to spot my special talents, pick me out from the anonymous crowd. Please don't let her be the one.

She looks down at her empty hands. 'Such a pity, Cora. Such a pity.'

After another long silent minute between us, she asks, 'Do you want to know what I think we've got here?' I am sure she is not allowed to do this.

'No. I don't. No, I don't, *thank* you,' I say. We are so well brought up. Always say please and thank you. Never put our elbows on the table because that would be bad manners; never put our shoes on the table – even for cleaning – because that would be bad luck. Always mind our Ps and Qs, not that I have ever known what they were supposed to stand for. Probably something in Latin, which was not on my curriculum. I am thinking all these things rather hard, and rather loud, in order not to hear what Lorna is saying, to shut her out. To shut her up.

It's July, and hot outside. Lorna is wearing her lemon lacy-knit top and – hooray – not the brown check skirt but a new one in fawn cotton. It's hot indoors too, and I'm sitting here in my jeans and my washed-out mauve T-shirt, which was once a blazing purple but is now the exact faded colour of a Parma Violet pastille. Fugitive, that's what they call these colours that can't last, won't last, run away.

It's hot, and through Lorna's peek-a-boo jumper I can make out a salmon-coloured undergarment with a panel of lace insertion which does not coincide with the lacy panels worked in lemon wool. Here is someone patently unprepared to deal with life, telling me I must deal with mine.

'I'm sure you do, really. I'm convinced of it. It will be such a relief to get it out into the open, won't it? Finally unravel all those made-up stories, get to the bottom of what's real and what's not. And then we can begin working on that.'

She gives me a look, a sincere kind of look, as if to say *We both know what I'm talking about, don't we?* Only I don't, I haven't a clue what she's going to say. But I'm sure she is overstepping some mark, and that this is a deliberate strategy, the latest move in her campaign against me. I wonder if I should report her to the authorities? Except that she *is* the authorities.

She sits down beside me on the bed, in that prissy way

of hers, knees and ankles together, hands clasped in her lap.

'So here's what I think happened, Cora. You tell me if I'm wrong . . .'

I will be forced to put my hands over my ears, which is probably safer in the circumstances than putting my hands over Lorna's mouth. Or round her throat. The last thing I want to hear is her professional opinion.

So I turn the sound off. I sit here and watch her, and her mouth moves. She is a frog, an alien, one of those puppets on TV whose rictus mouth moves in no synchronization whatsoever with what the human voice overlaid is saying. Lorna speaks and I listen, but I can't hear her and I can't see the shape of the words her lips are forming.

I sit here and I am a still life, a dead nature.

44

Desert Island

Stella came to visit me again. Mike was on duty this time. He showed me into the same featureless room as before. The window-blind was up. Outside I could see a small enclosed garden, a bench-seat and a climbing rose. It was a pity we couldn't sit out there. But summer rain was dripping off the leaves, making them vibrate. A yellow rose petal dropped on to the wet paving stones as I watched.

Stella and I sat with the coffee table between us. She had laid out her cigarettes and lighter next to the ashtray, all ready.

'How is everyone?' I asked. I hadn't dared to say anything last time. I'd been shocked to see Stella here at all, didn't want to frighten her away with importunate questions.

She leaned forward, broke the cigarettes out of their cellophane, and lit one quickly. 'You know Bettina's pregnant again?'

I didn't. How would I? Everyone had been doing things while I wasn't looking.

'Little Lisa's not a year old yet. She swears it was planned but I don't think so. That girl never planned a thing in her life.'

I tried to sound casual. 'And what's Mandy up to these days? Now she's a big sister?'

Stella exhaled smoke sideways and made a face. 'Don't ask.'

The silence stretched out. I could hear a blackbird outside, singing as sweetly as if it wasn't raining.

'How are Ted and Edie?' I couldn't bring myself to call them Mum and Dad. Stella looked stunned for a moment, then rallied.

'They've moved. Well, they couldn't stay in that house. They've bought a flat in Colchester.' So, no more garden; no more straight edges, or clicking of shears on summer nights. 'Your – she's gone back to bookkeeping, and he's got a job with the Parks Department.'

That should keep him happy, I thought. In a manner of speaking. It would take his mind off his problems. Miles of municipal edges to keep in shape. Perhaps they'd let him have a go with the ride-on mower, too. Colchester would soon be famous for its impeccably striped public lawns.

'And Brian?'

There was a tapping at the door. I looked round. I could see Mike through the glass panel, holding two plastic cups on a tray.

'Good,' said Stella in a heartfelt voice. 'I could do with a drink.'

Mike helped us transfer the cups, along with two plastic spoons and several sachets of sugar, to the table. 'No biscuits, I'm afraid,' he said, 'I wasn't quick enough.' He looked from me to Stella but I wouldn't meet his eye.

'What's he on about?' she asked, as soon as he was behind the door again. I shrugged. I wasn't about to describe the domestic arrangements to her. I wasn't going to give anything away, if I could help it.

Stella lifted her cup and took a sip. 'Is this tea or coffee?'

I shrugged again. 'You were going to tell me about Brian.'

She put the cup down and said, 'Brian – Brian's got a social worker. He has to go to some centre or other, couple of times a week.'

That will go down well. A Supervision Order and a social worker. No wonder they'd moved to Colchester.

Stella was glancing round again, appraising the decor. 'But it's not bad here, is it, Carol? They let you have a bit of privacy. Give you tea – or coffee! Not like prison visiting, is it? Not that I know first-hand, but you see it on TV, don't you? Will they let you out, you know, for little trips and that?'

'I don't know.'

Hanny would know. Hanny would know all the ins and outs of the rehabilitation programme. Except that it was too late for me to ask, and it didn't do her any good: knowing. You can have all the information – jolly good information, too – but if you don't use it, it's no help. If you don't know how to use it, or if you don't choose to.

I think I let out a great big sigh, because Stella leaned forward and squeezed my fingers with her large, warm hand. We weren't a family that touched a lot, and I found myself feeling unutterably grateful for that spontaneous human contact. No one ever touched me any more. My eyes were hot and watery.

'It's all right, Carol,' Stella said. 'All right?' Though she had no idea what she was talking about.

'I haven't told anyone I'm coming here,' she went on. 'It's none of their business what I do or don't do.' She threw her head back and gave a quick laugh. 'It never was. Not that they thought that way.'

'You always were the subject of gossip,' I told her.

'The *subject* of *gossip*.' She seemed to relish that phrase, and lit a fresh cigarette in a leisurely way, and sat there smiling for another moment or two.

'And now it's me, instead,' I said. That wiped the smile away.

'No, they don't talk about you. They don't mention you at all.'

'Not even Gloria?'

Stella shook her head. Today she was wearing white linen slacks, and she brushed a speck of cigarette ash off her spotless knee.

'Do you still work at the fish-and-chip shop?' I asked.

She grinned. 'No, course not. Haven't for months. I'm a *housewife* now, aren't I? I should think it'd be bloody boring if you hadn't slaved your guts out behind a counter for most of your life, but I *like* it. Bit of washing-up, bit of dusting. Lord and master's tea on the table in time for when he comes home. It's a piece of cake.'

'What, the lord and master's tea?'

Stella giggled. She tapped the back of my knuckles with

one peach-painted nail. 'You're doing all right, Carol. You'll be all right, you will.'

I should have wept and fallen on her neck, but we didn't do that kind of thing. Not in our family.

She gave me an earnest look. 'You've just got to get yourself sorted out, Carol. They'll get you sorted out, and then we'll see . . .'

This was all too much, too close to the bone. I gave the garden a fierce examination, and Stella busied herself by rummaging in her bag.

'I got you a book, like you asked,' she said. 'You said you wanted a thick one. I hope it's all right. You know I'm not a great book-lover.'

She pushed a big book over the table at me. It was almost as thick as it was wide.

'First I thought of bringing the Bible, but then I thought you'd probably read most of that, in that Sunday school she sent you to. So I got this instead.'

I could read the title upside down.

Stella shot me a hopeful smile. 'Like they say on *Desert Island Discs*: the Bible, and Shakespeare.'

My eyes felt hot again. If you had to choose a fairy godmother, Stella in this latest manifestation would certainly do.

Mike was rapping gently on the door. He poked his head inside and said, 'Time's almost up, ladies.' Like a cheerful barman.

'I'll come again, after Spain,' Stella said. 'Promise.'

I felt bruised. I'm not used to anyone being nice. As Mike escorted me back to the lounge I looked at my fingers where Stella had touched me and felt them burning, like a saint's stigmata.

* * *

Once I attempted a peace treaty with Brian. We were both over sixteen, we were both adopted – there had to be some common ground. Act like grown-ups, start again.

So, up the steep red-carpeted stairs. Brian was working at his desk, leaning over a notepad. Whatever he was writing or drawing, he covered it up with his arm as I stepped into the room. He expected me to say, 'Your tea's on the table,' or, 'Mum wants you.' The windows were open. I inhaled deeply, drew the summer evening air into my lungs: top notes of freshly mown lawns and night-scented stocks, cut with a dash of petrol from the main road. Stay-at-homes and getaways. Nostalgia for that week, that single week of nights spent up here, washed through me. I shut my eyes and rocked gently on the balls of my feet.

'What d'you want?' Brian asked grumpily, because I hadn't spoken.

I said, 'Do you remember, in junior school, that first time I ever bunked off and you helped me by taking a note to my teacher? A forged note?'

I recalled that feeling that I had back then, the joy of bending him to my will.

He gave me a mean look, as if to ask why I was bringing that up. His eyebrows had thickened to ridiculous levels, wayward hedges themselves now, above the rims of his glasses.

'You do, don't you?'

He took off his glasses and rubbed the lenses with a corner of his handkerchief.

'Ye-es.'

A monosyllable that conveyed 'Maybe I do,' and

405

'What's it worth?' and 'Where's all this leading to?' I know I've said he's not an expressive sort of boy, but sometimes he can pull the rabbit out of the hat. Or at least coax it to peep over the edge.

'You remember the International Spy Kit that Uncle Bob gave you?'

Now he couldn't help it: his mouth creaked into a semi-grin.

'The keys were crap,' he said.

'The plastic skeleton keys! I wonder what happened to them?'

But he turned his back to me and bent over the notepad again, crooking his arm around his pen. He clearly wasn't one for nostalgia.

'And that kid with the trike?' I tried. 'We put rocks in the back, remember?'

Nothing, not even a grunt, this time.

'See, we used to have fun together,' I insisted. 'Way back when. Think how much we both hated Mandy. Those plans we always made to steal her sweets.'

'Carol?' His voice was head-down, blurry.

'What?'

'I'm busy. Get out of my room.'

I took one step backwards. 'I'm just saying that we did.'

He looked up again, his eyes heavy-lidded with boredom. 'I know how to have fun,' he said. 'Just not *your* way.' And then his head went down again, over his secret work.

I was going to leave, I was halfway out the door, but I stopped. 'I know about your fun,' I said. 'I know about you.'

Nothing moved – not a finger, not a hair – but I was

sure he'd heard me. People go still like that when they're listening, when they're really listening.

Tom didn't come back at all that Easter. Tom Rose did. Tom Rose was a good boy, a loving son, and came home to see his mother. He dropped into the dry cleaner's one afternoon and asked if I would come for a drink. 'OK,' I said, with the brilliant sparkling enthusiasm of one who has nothing else to do.

In the pub that evening Tom Rose said, 'What d'you think of Tom's place, then?'

Tom Rose was big, broad, most convincing. His hands around the pint glass looked as if they could mend a car or chop down a tree. He sat with his legs apart in that male fashion, as if their testicles are just too amazingly enormous to be housed comfortably in the space of an ordinary chair. The seams of his trousers strained around his thigh muscles. It was just like being out with a real grown-up.

'Tom's place?'

'His flat? What did you think of it?'

What could I think? A place only visited in my imagination. At an address I hadn't been vouchsafed.

'When were you there?'

'In February. Just for the weekend.'

'Oh, yes.' I nodded, as if I'd known all about it. 'Not bad.'

'It's such a *tip*. A dump. I don't know why he didn't stay in hall, or lodge with his well-off friends. I would.'

'Well, so would I. But you know Tom.'

We paused, considering our knowledge of Tom. I moved my glass – martini and lemonade – in circles on the wet table top. I'd never really got a taste for alcoholic drinks and tended to choose something sweet and innocuous.

'You know, when we used to play Monopoly,' I was moved to ask, 'did you sometimes cheat? About buying the stations, I mean. And the electric light company.'

Tom Rose laughed, his old snickering laugh, though deeper now.

'Oh, always.'

'No wonder I couldn't win.'

'No wonder.'

I didn't like the way he laughed. It was always as if he knew something that other people didn't.

I slept with Tom Rose, all through those Easter holidays, when his mum was at work at the dairy products factory out near Bossey Down. His bedroom curtains were thin and the daylight came in. He had some characteristics that my Tom never had, making me feel, during those very minutes, those slow, short minutes when nothing much else existed, that this was what it was all about. The future, and fun, and love. In some ways I hated to do it, but it was all information, and some of it was good information.

I lay back on his pillow and Tom Rose stroked my hair. It was getting quite long; I hadn't let Bettina's scissors anywhere near it in the last two years, except to trim the split ends. Tom Rose's hand felt tender at first and then, because it kept going over and over the same place, irritating. I twitched out from under it.

'What are we doing, Caro?' he said. 'I mean, for fuck's sake, Tom and everything?'

So I told him. I thought he'd understand. I said it

lightly. 'We are the Hennessys' toys, and when they stop playing, we're left alone in the toybox.'

'Where d'you get that from?'

'I worked it out.' And I was reading *Tess of the D'Urbervilles*.

Tom Rose leaned up on one elbow and propped his head on his hand. There was a stripe of sunshine across his chest. 'You know, sometimes you're really quite clever, Caroline Clipper.' He rolled over and got up, pulling his jeans on quickly with his back turned. 'But it's all bollocks, what you said.'

He'd taken to wearing fluffy checked lumberjack shirts, and he picked one off the floor, sniffed it and tugged it on, still buttoned, over his round rugby player's head.

'You ought to do something with your life, Caro. Get another job, or save up some money and just get out of here.'

He kicked a balled sock across the carpet, and sat down grumpily to pull his loafers on over bare feet.

'What are you waiting for?'

I lay there, trying to formulate an answer. A clever one, or a heartbreaking one, I wasn't sure which to go for. And then he added, 'Get a move on, for God's sake. My mum'll be home any minute.'

Which showed me just how much Tom Rose wanted to know the inner secrets of my heart.

45

Love, Oh, Love

I went round to Gloria's one evening after work to deliver her newly cleaned winter coat. Pillar-box red, it was, with crinkly gilt buttons just like little ginger biscuits. It didn't suit her, made her look washed-out. 'What on earth's she gone and got herself now?' my mother murmured, the first time Gloria appeared in it. But I loved the blaring, loud colour of it, and Gloria for being so bold as to choose it.

I hooked the coat in its polythene shroud round the banister rail.

'Cup of tea?' Gloria asked me, and disappeared into the kitchen.

Stella was in the front room, tying a flimsy scarf round her neck preparatory to going out. The doorbell rang. 'It's open!' she sang out.

Warren stepped into the room.

'Where's my dream girl?'

He reminded me of late-period John Wayne, on a bigger scale than a normal human being, chest like a meat safe, and wearing high-belted, shapely, flowing trousers.

'Here I am, lover boy.'

Stella was munching her lipsticked lips in the mantel-piece mirror. She met my eye in the reflection and winked. 'Tell us, then, Carol,' she said, 'have you got a boyfriend yet?'

Warren put his hands in his trouser pockets and politely feigned deafness, gazing at the ceiling. He let his eyes range intimately over the light fitting. I said nothing.

'Well – have you?'

'Give the girl a break, Stella,' Warren suggested.

'She's seventeen. She ought to have a boyfriend by now. Go on, Carol, you can tell us.'

'It's a sensitive age.'

'No, she doesn't mind.'

'Stella!'

'You don't mind, do you, Carol?'

I smiled and shrugged, a minute smile with clamped lips, a minute shrug, like an itchy twitch.

'Carol?'

What could I say?

'Yes.'

Why not?

'Oooh! Is he nice?' She opened her mouth and touched the corners where upper and lower lips joined with the tip of her little finger, blotting up stray fuchsia-pink lines.

'No, he's horrible,' said Warren. 'That's why she's going out with him.'

'I'm only asking.'

'Yes, and maybe Carol doesn't want to tell you,' he said,

taking her by the upper arm, putting his lips to her ear, tucking his big nose into her shampoo-and-set. 'Maybe it's private, Stella.' And he whispered something else into her ear. Stella giggled. She nuzzled at his jacket. It was embarrassing to watch such behaviour between people of their age. They pulled apart.

Stella was determined. 'What's his name?'

'Take no notice of her, Carol. She's just being nosy.'

What should I say? Not the truth, that wasn't my style.

'Go on, Carol, tell us. Tell your auntie Stell.'

'Dave.'

'Oooh, *Dave*.'

'Stell-*a*!' said Warren, half laughing.

'Where did you meet him?'

'She's an interfering old bag, Carol. You don't have to tell her anything you don't want to. Just tell her to mind her own business.' He picked up Stella's handbag from the chair and pushed it at her.

'I'm only taking an interest in my niece, Warren. I'm only wanting to know how she's getting on.'

Taking an interest. These weren't the sort of questions my mother ever asked me. Though presumably she ought to have hoped for a boyfriend, a nice steady boy, and then marriage, a white church wedding, for me. The famous *settling down* she set so much store by. And children, one day. *Grand*children. Unless because I wasn't hers, not really hers – and lately proving it with a vengeance – she didn't care any more. My putative children wouldn't be her grandchildren. Not really hers at all. They could be anybody's.

'We're on our way, Carol. Don't you worry. Come on, Stell, old girl.'

'Less of the *old* girl, if you don't mind. I was your dream girl a minute ago.'

He patted her bottom and stepped over to the door.

'Just tell us where you met him,' said Stella.

'At a friend's house,' I said.

'Oh, not very romantic,' she said, face all tragedy, eyebrows awry.

'Where we met wasn't very romantic,' Warren told her.

'It'll always be romantic to *me*,' she replied, pummelling his back as she pushed him out of the door.

Sometimes I wonder if the Hennessys ever knew I was Tom's girlfriend. I wonder if they ever saw me in that light.

For so long I thought they were the most delightful, intelligent, lively beings, whole humans where the rest of us were half-humans, sprightly gods where we were heavy-limbed, blinkered mortals. I really believed that they offered me something, extended a hand, out of sheer generosity, because they had so much and because they saw I deserved it. I thought they were a household of pure, unconditional love. But, to tell the truth, they were very good at *not* seeing, not really feeling, at staying each within his or her own column of glass. And refusing to look out.

To tell the truth: something I find quite hard to do. Even to myself, at times. The truth's not very palatable – easier to look away, curl your lip, push it aside, like a plate of something you really don't fancy. Hanny might have been on the right track, after all.

That last year I spent less and less time at the Hennessys'. But I still used to visit Tillie when I could.

Sometimes I'd find one of the younger boys there, sometimes even Isolde on another of her trips home. But in a way I liked it more if it was just Tillie, all on her own.

I was in the kitchen on one of my afternoons off, making a pot of tea. I hadn't asked if I could, and I wasn't asked to do it. It was just something I felt like doing. There was nowhere else that I would behave so free and easy, not at any of my relatives'. At Gloria's or Bettina's I felt like a guest, and at home making the tea was a chore which I left to my mother unless I was actually made to do it. But in Tillie's kitchen there were no rules, it was come and go as you please.

I rinsed out the teapot with hot water, swilling it round and round in circles, and tipping it into the sink.

Tillie was standing by the ironing board. There was a pile of clean clothes, folded as she'd taken them down from the line but still crumpled, in the basket at her feet. Mrs Van Hoog had had a spell in hospital and while she was there Mr Van Hoog had withdrawn to his chair on the veranda, catatonic, apart from the drift of smoke from his pipe. Now Tillie was washing and ironing their clothes and cooking all their meals.

She gestured at the basket. 'I thought I'd have more time, now everyone's so grown. But it's never-ending. I was hoping to get back to painting again.' And then she shrugged. In the quiet we could hear birds singing.

'What is it you're doing?' she said to me, a frown in her voice.

I held out the teapot to show her.

'I mean, these days? What do you do with your time? Are you studying?'

'No. I left school ages ago. I've got a job.'

414

'Oh. Where?'

How could she not know? She was Tillie, who cared about me. She *must* know.

'In a shop.'

I didn't want to say the words – *dry cleaner's* sounded so dull, so humiliating.

'Which shop?'

She gave me a look, as if to say, 'Do I know it?'

'It doesn't matter,' I replied.

There was a long pause, in which I lifted the lid of the teapot and stirred the water round. I didn't want tea any more. My hand felt heavy and slack.

'They've all rather left you behind, haven't they?' she said, looking at me with such opaque blue eyes that I couldn't tell what she was thinking. I waited for her to ask, 'Are you lonely?' or 'What is it that *you* want?' I waited, teetering on the edge, waited for a real conversation. I thought we might bare our hearts to each other. But when she looked at me thoughtfully for a moment longer, her eyes were still opals, blue and obscure; and then she glanced down and went on with what she was doing. Which was ironing a shirt.

Tom came back in June, after his exams, and immediately resumed his old life as if he had not ignored me for six months. We met up two or three times a week. He'd catch me as I was leaving work, or drop in during the day, or send a message through Tom Rose. It was all quite casual, as if I was rather far down his list, but it was something solid, too. Something to grab hold of.

After an evening out Tom never escorted me to my door, seldom accompanied me home down our street.

He was always badgering Tom Rose to find some even later-opening place to go to, and I had to get up for work in the morning. So I'd walk home alone. It wasn't ideal, but I was used to the empty streets and the shadows, with just the occasional dog walker out and about, or a despondent figure loitering at a bus stop. I clutched my keys in my pocket and held to the vague plan that if anyone ever grabbed me I'd be ready to knuckle their eyeballs, quick as a flash. Oh, and knee them in the groin for good measure, too.

One night we were sitting at a table in a pub (we were always sitting at a table in a pub) and Tom leaned across and touched me, softly, on the cheek, fitting the long fingers of his hand across my neck and moving his thumb along my jawline from hinge to chin as if he were measuring me for something. He did it with one eye on Tom Rose's expression. I don't know, I have never known, what it was that lay between them. Rivalry, complicity.

I don't know that he ever touched me so tenderly before or after. I died of love that moment.

But it reminded me of Patrick's hand, his caressing thumb, that time. That first time.

We only did it once, Patrick and me. Just the once. Maybe it was his way of initiating his models, putting his stamp on them all. Welcome to the club: here's your badge, and here's your secret sign.

After he let his thumb rest on my jaw that time, and I asked the fateful question about sleeping with his models, I knew the game was up. Well, they were all irresistible to me, Hennessys, and they knew it. It was only a matter of how soon.

Up close, his dark eye gleamed, and the little fine lines, the hail-fellow-well-met crinkles of laughter around the corners of his eye, were coloured with a thousand glittering pigments. I thought perhaps he was impregnated with the materials of his craft. His *art*. I should say *art*. But he was crafty. His hands were dry and warm, negotiating with such clever, intimate knowledge all the planes and angles he had studied so well. We were in the attic. The day was hot and the breeze came and went like a lovely current, tangling over my skin, now warm, now cool, as Patrick moulded me to the shapes he wanted and I complied, as a good model should.

And then I knew. I knew that all those lolloping nudes, century after century, had done just the same. Marked with the artist's stamp: 'I had her. She was mine.' Perhaps that was half the allure for the audiences, not just the naked flesh but the knowledge that this woman was available, not only to look at, had been available to the artist and might, even if only in the world of imagination, be available again.

Or, in some cases, this man.

Oh, Lorna, do not let me catch you reading my thoughts. Or you will certainly mark me down as troubled, sexually troubled, confused, mixed up. When in fact I have worked it out as plain as day.

We were in the attic and I could hear, on the breeze that filtered through, the usual sounds of the Hennessys' house. Doors slamming, Sebastian's music – he had inherited Tom's old record player – someone running urgently down the stairs. Somewhere Tillie called a name, and somewhere else Mattie, chanting something, jumped repetitively on and off a wooden step.

It was always *in the house*, they did their wicked deeds even *in the house*. And afterwards, when I had pulled my clothes on again, I wondered if Tillie hadn't called out *my* name. 　　　◆

So when Tom took me gently by the jaw and looked at me with love, for Tom Rose to see, I melted again. I felt my soft insides dropping away. I was foolish. Maybe *he* was the Machiavelli. But I was reminded of Patrick's thumb, and how I had lain down with Patrick on the old green sofa, knowing how many times it must have been used, and I had heard Tillie singing in the kitchen below. And I smiled at Tom, such a smile as would break his heart if he knew what I was thinking about.

Well, it would if I had my way. But I think his heart was whole, it was impregnable – unlike mine – and I don't know if suspecting Patrick and me would have made the slightest dent. A bit of hurt pride, maybe, a bit of peevishness at the loss of a possession. Like when Sebastian accidentally stepped on one of his favourite records and broke it. But not horror, desolation, enraged jealousy.

I wondered what it would take to dent his tinny heart? Crack it open, really hurt him? I would have liked to know. Suddenly I wanted very much to find that one thing.

46

Monopoly

Today it is raining as if it will never stop. And it's St Swithin's Day. I heard Trudy telling one of the ones in uniform. The guards, Hanny used to call them. 'That's it, there goes the rest of the summer,' Trudy said. 'Just my blinking luck.' As if the foul weather were a personal insult to her, and that was all she had in the world to worry about.

No chance of getting outside today, but no one to go outside with.

The guards. I always think of Hanny in the past tense. I don't suppose our paths will cross again.

Last year on this day it was beautiful, clear skies and stunningly hot. A good omen. And it was my afternoon off. Tom borrowed the Van Hoogs' little car and drove us out to a field by a stream. Just a nondescript field with some trees and a stream, and black and white cows across the bend in the river. I brought the food, and Tom brought the dope and a transistor radio, and Tom Rose brought a bottle of wine which he stood in the stream to keep it cool. We felt like connoisseurs. We lay back in the grass and sunbathed and listened to the grasshoppers. Tom tried to find a music station with good reception on the radio but it was hopeless, and in the end we just tuned in to the grasshoppers, to their wheezy rhythms. The sky up above was forget-me-not blue, criss-crossed with puffy vapour trails, and tiny, winking aeroplanes spinning new trails just for us.

I thought that even though I had waited a whole year for a day like this, it was worth it. I was blissfully, wordlessly happy. My arms were above my head, resting in the dry spikes of the grass, and I could feel Tom's thumb and fingers loosely circling one of my wrists.

Tom said sleepily, 'What shall we do now? I know, let's play Monopoly.' Nobody stirred. 'First to throw a six starts. Amazing! I threw a six, very first go.'

Then Tom Rose murmured from behind closed eyes, 'So did I. Wouldn't you know it?'

I stared up into the blue. 'Me too,' I said.

'No, you didn't.'

'You couldn't have. Three sixes in a row, too much of a coincidence.'

'Yeah, *you* can't start. You'll just have to wait till your next turn.'

'Jump jump jump. Park Lane. I'll buy it,' said Tom.

'Waterloo Station, *I'll* buy it,' said Tom Rose.

'Waterloo's not on there,' I complained. 'Marylebone, King's Cross, Fenchurch Street and . . .' I couldn't remember.

'Waterloo. Sure is. Is that my change? Why, that's very handsome of you. Thank you, I will.'

'Jump jump jump. May*fair*. That's for me,' said Tom.

'What about me?' I said, forcing myself to laugh. 'When's it my turn?' I scrambled to my feet. They still lay on their backs, arms over their faces, shielding themselves from the sun.

'Community Chest. Just my luck,' said Tom. 'Wait – look at this! You have come first in a beauty contest.'

'In a beauty contest!' Tom Rose chorused. 'Win ten thousand pounds.'

'It's not ten thousand. It's never ten thousand,' I protested. I kicked Tom lightly in the side with the tip of my shoe. He was shaking with laughter, Tom Rose too.

'Come on, Caro, have your go.'

'Have your go or we'll have to go for you.'

'Oh, too late! Jump jump jump. Goddammit – Go to Jail.'

'Go to jail, Caroline Clipper,' said Tom, extending his arm and raising a harsh pointing finger at me.

And that's the way it was, that's the way it always was, Tom pulling the strings and Tom Rose cheating to keep up with him. It seemed like we were having fun, but I'm not sure that we were.

I walked into the Hennessys' kitchen, looking for Tom.

Tillie had to think for a minute. 'He's gone to a music thing in London. With Tom Rose. Back tomorrow, though.'

It was like a punch in the stomach. I lowered myself on to a chair, and did what I always did with Hennessy information, claimed prior knowledge. 'Oh, was that today?'

I existed on scraps.

But Tillie was still here, alone in the quiet kitchen,

weighing out butter and flour, and Tillie was enough.

'Would you do something for me?' she said.

She might not have been able to read minds but she ought to have been able to read faces. I blinked in case mine gave away too much. 'Of course I would. What?'

'Go and pick me some rhubarb. About this much.' She gestured a vague measurement with her hands.

It was disappointingly mundane, but, for Tillie, anything. 'Sure,' I said, and smiled.

The rhubarb patch was down at the end of the garden, by the fruit trees, where some years, if he was feeling like it, Mr Van Hoog cultivated sprouts and kale, and leathery lettuce, and radishes like crimson bullets. (Vegetables were not his forte, too dull and demanding.) And where the children, if they were feeling like it, though usually they were not, hoed and raked and weeded for him. Or – more likely – raided the currant bushes.

As I walked down the garden I could hear the grating, drumming sound, like stones in a grinder, of the lawn mower next door. My dad's lawn mower. These sounds were always lying there, just there, open to inspection if anyone cared to. Our lawn mower, our clacking shears. The Hennessy voices, their ringing self-confident cries. 'It was definitely *out*, Caro. That's thirty-love.' 'Unpeg that washing for me, Carolina, there's a honey.' 'Oh, come on, Caroline Clipper, can't you do better than *that*?'

On the concrete base of the old summer house Patrick was putting up a new shed. He'd planned to for ages, said he needed somewhere for the less glamorous end of his business, the tools and spare bits of wood. Like most things he planned, nothing had come of it. But today,

today I could see him standing there with a hammer in his hand, a panel of wood propped against the tree stump. The makings of a shed were all around him. And with him was a man, a young man, perhaps the most beautiful young man I had ever laid eyes on. They were surveying the pieces of wood laid out at their feet. I walked on down the path towards them.

'It's just a simple piece of construction,' I could hear Patrick saying. 'Any fool could do it,' and the other man laughed. His head tipped, his dark curly hair fell back. I saw the shape of his brown throat. I've always been a fool for throats.

'What are you laughing at?' Patrick growled, with fake displeasure. 'Laugh at an old man like me, would ya?' He rubbed his hands together as if he meant business and set his feet wide apart. 'We'll see about that, Eugene. We'll see about that.'

But Eugene, a tall Florentine angel, a *Portrait of a Young Man* by Raphael, by Titian, by Giovanni Battista Moroni, just went on laughing.

I walked past. I went on down the garden, ducking my head under the slumped branches of the apple trees. I found the neglected rhubarb thrusting its stalks snakily out of the couch grass. I pulled that phallic species of vegetable, fruit, whatever you want to call it, I pulled this much (a Tillie's-width, as indicated), just enough to make a fruit pie for all the Hennessys. And then, with the stalks tucked under my arm, I walked back.

Eugene was stooping now, steadying a length of wood, using the tree stump as a saw-horse, and Patrick was standing with arms folded, watching him. I stopped on the path, six feet away, wondering if I might be introduced. But neither of them said a word, or looked my way.

Despite it all, despite everything, everything they had ever done to me or said, I had become invisible again.

47

Going to the Bad

I was in the high street one day when Stella drew up beside me in a car.

'D'you want a lift?' she cried, and it would have been churlish to refuse, so I accepted to please her, willing to be driven somewhere, anywhere. The car was a Hillman with a wide bench seat in the front, luxuriously padded in fat corrugations. Stella patted the seat and I slid in. 'Now don't get mad at me, Carol. I haven't passed my test yet, but I needed to pop into town and Warren was away, so I just took the L-plates off.'

She pulled the door of the glove compartment down and there they were, two white plastic squares with luminous red Ls and little pieces of string through the holes top and bottom.

'Warren's present to me. Not brand new, of course, but it's in very good nick.' She drew smoothly away from the kerb with all the assurance of a legal driver. She was living with Warren by then, at his house out in the countryside. *Openly* living with him, as my mother insisted on putting it, every time she referred to Stella.

'He's been giving me lessons. He's very good, very patient. Not like they're supposed to be – husbands, boyfriends.' She glanced in the rear-view mirror, changed gear, took a left into the next street. 'It can be the end of a marriage, so they say. Teaching your wife to drive.'

She was all efficiency and composure. She wore a navy-blue dress with white buttons, and navy and white leather court shoes. Her earrings were little dots of white in her lobes. Warren was absolutely the best thing that had ever happened to her.

'Where're we going then? Or are you happy with just a little drive round? A little sightseeing tour?'

'Shouldn't you just do your errand and get back home as quickly as possible?' I asked nervously. Would I be an accessory if we were stopped?

Stella let her head drop back and a rich, loose laugh came out.

We turned against the traffic and came on to the seafront road. Stella drove regally along the front, looking out at the sea from time to time, or commenting on the passers-by. I knew it was all an act to impress me, and I *was* impressed.

'I don't know, some of these people, they can't know what they look like or they'd never dress like they do. Look at that one!' She was enjoying herself. Her star was rising, while Bettina's was eclipsed.

Bettina was having a baby. I wondered if it would have Mandy's mean-eyed features *and* Roy Tiltyard's lack of chin. Or did Mandy's looks come from her father, dead at twenty and cross about it ever since? Bettina was suffering, sick all the time, losing all her blossomy plumpness even as her abdomen expanded.

'The flesh is just falling off her,' as Gloria said. 'It's awful. It reminds me of her mother, poor soul.' Bettina's mother, it turned out, had died of some sort of rapidly progressing cancer. Gloria could not name it, of course. She made a face and mentioned some 'internal trouble' and then 'a terrible complaint'. Bettina's mother had swelled right up like a balloon, and then just wasted away. Apparently.

I still went to Gloria's at least one lunchtime every week, and heard about Warren on the one hand, gentlemanly and generous, and Roy Tiltyard on the other, still living in the flat over the hairdresser's, staring helplessly while Bettina retched over the basin, 'no help to man nor beast'. I trawled up the gossip for want of anything more interesting. I was very glad to hear that though fortunes could go down they could also go *up*.

We came to the end of the promenade, did a U-turn in the car park and set off again.

'There's your cousin,' Stella said, nodding and raising her eyebrows at the same time.

I glanced over and saw Mandy, the nearest in a crowd of teenagers hanging around by one of the shelters. She was still skinny, still rather small, with a well-used look about her, and a repertoire of exaggerated gestures and expressions like a female impersonator. She favoured imitation leather motorbike jackets, and miniskirts when everyone else had switched to long, and bare mottled legs in clumpy shoes. As we looked she took a step backwards, slapping a boy on the arm of his leather jacket, either laughing or shouting, with her mouth wide open.

It looked aggressive but it could have been a joke. No one else in the crowd took any notice. The boy's face, we saw as we passed, was transfixed in a snarl. Mandy swung away from him, twisting out of his grasp, beginning to walk off rapidly. The last we saw was her little white face screwed up and her wide mouth enunciating, even for those not trained in lip-reading, a clear instruction.

'She'll come to the bad, that one,' Stella said, not, I thought, without a touch of satisfaction.

But who did come to the bad? Not Mandy, or not more than might be predicted.

It was us. Brian and I, the model citizens, the Scout and Guide, the church-going children of modest, careful parents. We were deemed in need of 'care and control'. Maybe it was our genes coming out, our doubtful inheritance. God knows what kind of stock we came from – horse thieves, mountebanks, cut-throats. Really, someone should be responsible for checking up on this sort of thing. Maybe that's how our parents explain it away, as they sit quietly over their tea, with the radio tuned to a light music programme.

There were a number of reports written on us prior to the court case, to try and work out the state of our minds and the complications of our background. On paper Brian looked so much better than me. Of course he would. Perhaps that's what he'd been up to all those years, with his solemn church-going, his diligent Scouting, his excellent attendance record at school and work: making sure he appeared, to all intents and purposes, squeaky clean. He might have been an indifferent school pupil but he turned up without fail, and never cheeked his teachers or noticeably got in with the wrong crowd. In fact the only thing his teachers noticed about him was that he didn't seem to be a part of any crowd. And he'd clocked up enough responsible adults elsewhere to vouch for his character. They said he was a quiet boy, eager to please, even, one might say, easily led. Oh, and good with his hands.

I didn't go down so well. It was known – how was it known? – that my doctor prescribed the contraceptive pill for me; that I had smoked and consumed illegal substances; that I was identified as one of a group who stole from local shops. I was a compulsive liar. Added to which, I had been a poor achiever throughout my school life, and a sloppy and casual figure behind the counter at the dry cleaner's. I had dropped out of all improving activities and appeared to have no aim in life. How all occasions do inform against me. I was clearly out of my parents' control at an early point in my adolescence. Witnesses attested to my unreliable temper, my short fuse. A disturbed start in life was blamed, and defects of character, which the valiant efforts of my hard-pressed adoptive parents failed to correct. I was trouble. I had all the potential for bad that Brian appeared so lacking in. It was a puzzle to them.

No one seemed to think I might have been persuadable, susceptible. That I might have been easily led by more experienced and manipulative souls. That at numerous points in my life I might have done things, not because I wanted to, because I deliberately and unreservedly made the decision to, but because there wasn't any choice.

Also I wouldn't cooperate. I wouldn't answer their questions. I wouldn't talk. That really got to them. Even worse, sometimes when they were questioning me I wanted to laugh. Perhaps they saw the ghost of it flitting about my features, a twitch of a smile, too much glitter in my eye. No one likes to think that a house burned down with someone inside it can provoke a little flicker of laughter. No one wants to think that death, accidental or deliberately caused, would make anybody snigger. I can't wholly blame them for taking against me, in the circumstances.

But I was thinking of the weight of evidence they already had racked up against me and here's what made me want to smile: if only they had seen my portraits as well, my bold and naked flesh, the way I stared out of the canvas, furious and provoking. Then they would have formed an opinion, unshakeable and black, of my defective character. Then there would have been no room in their hearts for doubt.

Dr Travis spoke to me today. I oscillate between thinking he's Lorna's boss and Lorna's minion. I don't know. He could have been putting in a good word, a kind hint, while she was out of the room. Or he could have been giving me an ultimatum. The final word, from the top man.

Yes, on second thoughts, I think that's it. I don't think he's training to be anything, I think he *is* it.

What he said was 'Carol.' My heart warmed to him. It's pathetic to think I have sunk so low that I feel the use of my name is a kindness. My real name. My own name, the name that I am used to. Or one of them, at any rate.

'Carol, I want you to think hard about this.'

I began thinking hard straight away. It was like the

Intelligence Test, like my examinations. I thought hard, and my capacious mind, my razor-sharp mind, flew to bits.

'This is a place of treatment. You will not stay here indefinitely if they think the treatment is not helping you.'

I could tell his words were carefully chosen, but, for once, carefully chosen words didn't offend me. I don't like to think of people feeling that they have to plan how they are going to speak to me. I hate feeling that they are treating me like a piece of glass. A stick of dynamite.

'We would like to think that you are being helped. Making progress. But you must do some of the hard work, too. You must try to help yourself.'

I don't know why I thought his words were kind.

'Will you try to do that? Will you? Carol?'

I nodded.

Smoke in the air: the smell of ruin. My head buzzed. I couldn't think straight.

Mandy had come round, Mandy, who we hadn't seen in months, had dropped in for a visit, hot on the scent of disaster. The fire engines had only just gone.

Skinny as a twig in her drainpipe jeans and studded denim jacket, she sat in our lounge delicately drinking tea. 'Burned to the ground?' she asked, craning to see out of the window. The hedge was battered, but still intact.

'Not to the ground,' my mother said. 'But pretty bad. Bad enough.'

'Who raised the alarm?'

'The lady at number twelve. She saw the smoke when she was hanging out her wash.'

'Anyone hurt?'

Mum pulled a face.

'*Je*sus,' said Mandy, and I saw my mother flinch. 'They're best mates of yours, aren't they, Carol? You were always in and out.'

My mother was staring at me, but I was staring at Mandy.

'That boy – that Tom – you know, the one you fancied? Don't tell me he's got hurt?'

My mother was staring at the carpet now, looking as if she had swallowed a fly. Mandy sipped her tea, unperturbed. 'Where's Brian today, then?' she said. 'What's he get up to these days?'

'How's your mother, Mandy?' my mother asked. 'Is she blooming?'

'Bloomin' obsessed. She's papering the spare room with teddy bears. All over.'

'What, in her condition? Isn't Roy doing it?'

Mandy reached over to the sugar bowl and popped a lump of sugar into her mouth.

'Roy doesn't know his arse from his elbow. He'd be no help.'

I sat listening to this conversation, saying nothing. The buzzing in my head diminished and then rose again, like a swarm of bees getting closer. And it stayed there until the next morning, when at breakfast my mother opened the front door to two policemen. She looked back down the hallway at me: horrified, but not, I saw, surprised.

48

Fun

Every year in the first week of August the funfair came to town. It set up in a straggly park behind the high street, and local boys got into fights and local girls got up the duff and local everyone got fleeced, and then the fair moved on. My mother disapproved of it on various grounds: it was *common* and *dangerous* and *a waste of money*. I went once with Barbara and Jillian, and I agreed; even on a sunny afternoon you could feel the menace. Dubious-looking men – far worse than the bikers at the café – hung off the rides, calling out to us and cat-calling across the alleyways of mangled turf to each other. They took our money and shut us into rattling seats, peering up our skirts as we whirled away. They laughed when we clutched at our hems and clung to the rail and each other and screamed. And when we stumbled off and staggered away they still shouted after us, though their eyes and hands were busy with the next customers. We drank Coca-Cola and ate candyfloss to calm our stomachs, lurched between the stalls where tides of evil music clashed, and shook our heads at the hard-looking women who promised we'd win a giant teddy with a mere handful of hoops. I hugged my arms around myself, longing for Barbara and Jill to say they'd had enough. To my mind, all this *fun* was deeply depressing. I never went again.

Until last summer. Last summer Tom said, 'First week in August, isn't it? Is the old fair still in town? We've got to go.'

We were sitting in the garden of the Crown and Anchor, Gloria and Eddy's local pub. It was only a back-yard, but the sun slanted down into it nicely, and Tom Rose and I were tired after a day earning money. Tom had been on the beach. The slope of his nose was pink with sun, and his habitual pallor was beginning to shift into something healthier. He kicked my outstretched foot and said, 'Come on, we must. All the fun of the fair?'

'We're tired,' I said. I admit my tone might have been a bit whiny.

'What's all this *we* ?' Tom glanced from me to Tom Rose and back again, his eyes bright with wickedness.

'I mean we've been hard at work all day. Unlike you.' Tom had taken up his job as a waiter again, but he only worked the busy weekend shifts.

'All the more in need of a bit of recreation, then.'

'Anyway, the fair's not fun,' I said.

Tom gave me his scathing look. 'It's a *fun*fair, no?'

'Are we going or not?' Tom Rose asked. He picked up his pint glass and drained it obligingly.

'One more drink first?' I pleaded, which was not like me.

Tom and I said nothing until Tom Rose had come

434

outside again with fresh glasses. Then he turned on me and said, 'You're in a rut, Caro. A big fat stinking rut. Like this whole town.'

I looked at his reddening nose. 'And you've had too much sun. It's made you cross.' But everything made him cross these days.

He ignored me. 'Can't you see it? You've been in a rut your whole life.'

'I don't think that's exactly possible. I—'

'I'm trying to help you, can't you see? You could do something good.'

Now Tom Rose made his contribution: 'You could do something *spectacular*.'

'Yeah – spectacular.' Tom liked that word.

'Like what?'

Tom's wide bony shoulders made the most eloquent shrug. 'I dunno. Firebomb the dry cleaner's, for a start.'

'That'd go down well,' Tom Rose agreed.

'That'd give this town a hint.'

The sun had slipped behind the houses by the time we left, and the air was getting chilly: a stiff breeze straight off the North Sea. I was still in the respectable blouse and skirt I had to wear for work and beginning to shiver.

'I *hate* the fair,' I confessed to Tom Rose, as we lagged behind. Tom loped along in front, covering the ground eagerly and much faster than I would have liked.

Tom Rose shrugged. 'I don't care either way. But there's bugger all else to do.'

We could hear it first, and then smell it, before we could see it.

Tom turned round to us and inhaled dramatically. 'Ah, the unmistakable aroma of hot dogs and vomit.' He

435

threaded his arm tightly through mine, mainly, I think, to keep me walking. 'I told you you'd love it! I'll win you a panda.'

'I don't want a panda. I want to go home.'

He relinquished my arm. 'Fine. Fine. Off you go. Tom and me'll just puke our guts up on the Waltzer, and again on the Teacups, and you'll have to miss it. No, you go.'

Which, of course, did the trick. As he knew it would.

They went on the Waltzer, they went on the Teacups, they went on the Shake 'n' Slam. I don't know if that's what the last one was called, but that's what it did. I stood behind the barrier and watched the pair of them, hugging myself to keep warm. A group of girls I vaguely recognized wandered up and stood beside me. 'Look! There's Tom H. and Tom R.,' one of them shouted above the swirl of the music, and a quiver of interest rattled through them. They were all pretty girls, with long legs in tight jeans and hair like a shampoo ad. I thought that they went to the grammar school; their accents fitted, and they weren't quite as slutty as some of the other gangs of girls already roaming the fairground, looking for trouble and fun. I felt like an idiot with my conventional work clothes and my long face, which seemed as if it had just got a yard longer.

'Hey, Tom!' another of the girls shouted, as the ride swung dizzily round our way. All four waved. I hopped from side to side, my feet cold on the damp ground. The boys' faces swept past, ugly with the G-force. I couldn't tell if they were delirious with joy or pain or fear. The grammar school girls giggled and hid their faces in one another's hair.

Tom H. and Tom R. That was a new one on me. They'd

never been as equal as that on Hennessy territory. I knew that my Tom was an object of general desire, but Tom Rose?

I walked up and down, trying to warm my feet. The ride was slowing to a halt now, people stood up in the cars, ready to scramble out. The scrawny youth who manned the entrance gate turned and said, 'You next, is it, girls?' and the grammar school gang turned away, squealing. Tom and Tom Rose jumped down.

Tom grabbed my hand. 'You missed a treat there. We were going so fast we actually swallowed our puke back in. Now, what next? Bloody hell, Caro, you're freezing!'

Tom Rose caught up with me. 'You *are* freezing, Caro.'

He was wearing one of his lumberjack shirts over a black T-shirt, and he shrugged it off and wrapped it round my shoulders. It smelled faintly of sweat, and beer, but, underneath, his mother's washing powder. I pushed my arms into the sleeves.

'Thank you.'

He waved a dismissive hand.

The grammar school girls came up behind us. 'Hi, Tom,' they chorused. I turned to look at their clear sweet smiling faces, but they couldn't even see me. I was no competition, in my neat skirt and somebody else's plaid shirt. I hadn't spent an hour in front of the mirror in preparation for this evening out. Even if I had, it wouldn't have done me any good.

'I know, let's go and shoot something.' Tom glanced round at his new audience. 'How about it, lay-*dees*? How do you like the sound of that?'

At his insistence we passed up the first shooting gallery, which had ducks as targets, and carried on round the dingy canvas alleyways until we found another one with battered tin figures out of a Wild West saloon.

Tom counted through his coins. 'D'you want a go, Caro?'

'No.'

'Come on. Have some fun.'

'I'd be no good.'

'Damn you, woman, have some *fun!*'

'I told you I didn't like the fair. I'm only here because . . .' But it was obvious why I was there. I didn't have to put it into words. Anyway, Tom was busy lining up his rifle, concentrating on the first target.

I watched the targets come clacking round. The first one had a black hat and turned-down moustache. Both rifles missed. The next figure was a Mexican towing a mule.

'Get the donkey!' shouted Tom. He squinted and fired. 'Fucking sights are useless!'

But the mule went down to Tom Rose's shot. A cry of glee went up from the four girls, and Tom Rose turned round to take a bow, missing his opportunity as the following target creaked into view, a John Wayne type in a worn white hat. Nothing. The next was a bartender with apron and slicked-back hair.

'He looks like Mister Clipper,' Tom jeered, bending to his shotgun. 'Let's get Mister Clipper.'

The target clanged and fell backwards. I didn't see who'd hit it. Maybe they both had. Tom turned to me. 'Jesus, Caro, *so* sorry about your dad.' Behind me, the grammar school flock all giggled again. A fat bent creature trundled across the target area, waistcoated and staring. 'And there's her creepy brother!' Tom cried. 'Get the weirdo brother, too!'

438

I'd had enough. 'I'm going home,' I said, and began to pull Tom Rose's shirt off.

'Oh, come on, Caro, it was just a joke.' Tom abandoned his rifle and came over. 'Don't go. You know I can't resist a joke. I didn't mean it.' He put his arms tight around me and kissed my forehead. The grammar school girls were just a blur on the periphery.

Tom Rose downed that target, and then the next.

'*Shot*, sir!' Tom cried, in a crusty English voice, and clapped his hands high in the air as if he were at a cricket match. I wriggled out from underneath.

'Don't get in a mood, Caro. Anyway, we haven't been on the dodgems yet.'

I could smell a sweet burnt smell. 'I'm going to get some candy-floss,' I said. 'Want some?' But nobody did. I glanced at Tom Rose and saw that he had his arm draped around the shoulders of the blondest girl. Boys don't touch without intention: that hand on the elbow, on the small of the back, is never just there by accident. It's planning to lead to greater things.

The trampled grass was littered with lolly wrappers and chip forks. I queued behind a fat woman. The sky was quite dark now, beyond the fairground lights, and the wind had dropped. Maybe next year I wouldn't be here, I'd be doing something *spectacular* and would never have to come back.

When I got to the dodgem cars the session was under way. They sparked and banged and tangled, and their passengers' heads flew back like executionees. Tom Rose and the blonde girl were sharing one car, Tom Rose in charge of the wheel (of course) and busily charging a metallic blue car which my Tom drove. In it was another of the girls, hanging on to his shirt and screaming fit to burst. The session ended, cars coming to a sudden halt as the power went off. Their occupants stood up and climbed out. Both Toms stayed. The ride boy swung from pole to pole, and I saw them hand him up more money. The poles sparked and sizzled, the cars started up again. I watched them for a minute more, and then I walked away. The candyfloss stuck to my lips and disappeared on my tongue. I had only myself to blame. I didn't know how to have fun.

Stones against my window. I knelt up on the bed and lifted the curtain. Tom was standing in our driveway. I made a face at him and held up my fingers: two minutes. I climbed into jeans and a sweater. I wasn't going to a moonlit assignation with him in my suburban night attire. I picked up my keys but didn't dare to shut the front door properly – the latch always clunked and my parents' bedroom was only a whisper away. I tiptoed up the drive. Tom had vanished behind the hedge. At the gate he grabbed me and rolled me into the sharp-smelling leaves. His hands were cold, and his breath smelled of beer.

'Where'd you get to, Caro? You just disappeared!' He made magician's gestures with his fingers, and an explosion with his mouth.

'Shh!' I said, but he took my finger from my lips and fixed me with one of his vampire kisses. I pushed him away again. 'How did you know which was my room?'

'I always knew. I'd see you staring out of your window all the time.'

He knew. He'd always known. He knew everything about me; or thought he did.

'What do you want at this time of night?'

'I've got a plan!' he said, grinning. 'It's great. I had to tell you. I was going to tell you earlier, but then you skedaddled.'

'What plan?'

'For when I go to America.'

If he had hit me over the head with a blunt instrument I couldn't have seen more stars. Tom had a plan, and I was in it and so was America. Something *spectacular*.

'America?'

'I thought you knew.'

How? Tillie could have told me, or Barbara. Or Tom himself, as a matter of fact. But none of them thought to.

'No. I don't know anything. When is this?'

'Couple of weeks. I've got an exchange trip arranged with an American university. For a year.'

So Tom, that slackest of students, had somehow wangled himself an exchange. A year in America and I could go with him. I put my arms around his waist. His cheek was warm against mine; his voice echoed through my head. As if our thoughts were joined.

'And when I go,' he said, 'you can have my job.'

A jolt, a lightning blast. My head throbbed with it.

'Your *job*?'

'Yeah, it's only weekends – they won't want the bother of finding someone else. I'll tell them you'll cover for my shifts.' He stepped back and regarded me. 'Get yourself some high heels and a little tight skirt, you'll do fine.' He gathered up my hair with one hand and pulled it back behind my head. 'And mascara. A bit of make-up wouldn't hurt, you know.' Again he leaned towards me but this time he rubbed noses Eskimo-fashion. His nose was so sharp.

'You're off to America?'

'Great, isn't it? I might stay on if all goes well. I can see myself in America.'

He was grinning, drunk, so pleased with himself and the life he'd got sorted out. So stupid.

I stepped away from him.

'I don't want your lousy job. I don't need it. In my spare time – time which *you* don't know about – I'm a life model. I pose for artists. Loads of them. And I sleep with them, too. That's all part of the deal. Patrick started it. Your dad started me off. He was the first one.'

What banal little words. They sounded as dirty and suburban as I felt.

'Yeah, sure.'

He was still grinning, still pleased with himself.

'It's true.'

'No, it's not,' said Tom happily, his grin wide and crazy like a cartoon animal's. 'Because you're Miss Caroline Clipper, and you never do anything *your dad* wouldn't approve of.'

It wasn't true. If he had given it even a moment's thought he'd have known it wasn't true.

I hissed at him, 'I don't know who my dad is, so how the hell could I do anything he wouldn't approve of?'

Tom's grin was still in place. Nothing got through to him.

'I don't know who my dad is, I don't know who my mum is. I'm nobody from nowhere. You don't know anything about me and you never have!'

It was a shout, a scream. The noise of it shattered the still night air, rang off the rooftops and the windows and the empty milk bottles standing neatly on the step.

I tore back down my pathway and pushed open the front door. As I passed, the curtains in the bay window twitched, but no one came out of my parents' room and nothing moved inside the house.

49

Out of Friendship

I was getting up from lunch and saw that Moira was hanging about in the doorway, eyeing me. She came over, that trotting pony-walk she always does making me irritated before she even reached me.

'You're down for a visitor this afternoon,' she said. Consulting a scrap of paper in her hand, frowning over the scribble on it, she added, 'Two o'clock. Tom?'

I wonder what a heart attack feels like?

I went up to my room and stared in the mirror. At least I could comb my hair. Wide blue eyes stared back, looking as wild as a rat in a trap. I'd like to say I barely recognized myself, but sadly I did.

There was a time I would have died for Tom to come and see me. Not now. Perhaps I could say no, perhaps I could refuse a visitor who had come *all that way*. Despite the pleasant drive and the delightful scenery they might well be pretty fed up, after making so much effort. It might go against me, too, with Lorna and her colleagues. Not cooperating, yet again.

I put on my least faded T-shirt, and the more faded of my two pairs of jeans, and combed my hair. I held out my hands to see if they were shaking. They were. But maybe not enough to be visible to someone else.

Moira walked me down the corridor. We passed the first room, and the second and the third. She opened the door to the last room, which was bigger. There were two windows, and three chairs. On the middle one, with his knees apart and his hands clenched and his head bowed, sat Tom Rose. It was the first time I'd ever seen him wearing a tie.

Of course it wouldn't have been Tom Hennessy. I don't know why I ever entertained that thought.

Moira had shown me to the room, but it was another member of staff who waited outside, one of the uniformed ones, in a buttoned white tunic; tall and very broad, more than a match for Tom Rose. Should the necessity arise.

I sat down carefully. My knees were still shaking. Tom Rose looked older. His forehead was corrugated with permanent-looking lines. He didn't smile – at least he pressed his lips together and stretched them, but it could have been an expression of pain, or wind, or displeasure. I couldn't tell.

'Hi,' I said. It was a silly little word and it quivered in the air between us. *Hi.*

I could more or less understand why my aunt Stella had come to visit: a mixture of curiosity and guilt. I had no idea why Tom Rose was here. I hoped to God Moira wasn't busy behind the scenes arranging us some tea. I wanted this over as quickly as possible.

'I had to say I was your cousin,' Tom said, squeezing his knuckles even more tightly and looking sideways, not at me. 'They won't let you in otherwise.'

'Thanks. You shouldn't have.'

'On your mum's side.'

Poor Uncle Bob, I thought. But let it go.

'Didn't they check?'

'How? Show them my birth certificate? It wouldn't be the same name anyway.'

'No, I suppose not.'

'They wanted ID, though. I just showed them my student card.'

He sat there glowering at the floor. I didn't know what else to say.

When his voice came out again it was a croak. 'How're you doing?'

'OK. What about you?'

That was when he looked at me, looked up, hollow-eyed.

'I don't know, Caro. You tell me.'

I hate these visitors. I hate the way they have the right to come here and invade you. I'm glad Hanny's boyfriend never showed up. I'm sure that would have been the final straw for her. David, sitting here, wringing his hands and looking cow-eyed and apologetic. It's all right for them, they can walk out of here and get in their cars and go home, back to their lives and their little everyday worries. They can gaze out at the attractive scenery, and maybe stop for tea and scones on the way home – or, better still, a couple of stiff drinks – and thank their lucky stars they're not banged up in here with the loonies.

'You look different.'

'I thought I looked remarkably the same.'

'*Remarkably*. You always did come out with those big words.'

I didn't think that *remarkably* was a very remarkable word.

'So, what are you up to these days?' I asked, to head off any more questions from him.

'I've finished uni, got a job in London now.'

'Oh yes?'

'Pays peanuts but it's a foot on the ladder. I'm staying with Barbara. She shares a flat with two other girls.'

'Anyone I know?'

Tom Rose shook his head. 'Friends from college. Barbara and me – we – we're kind of – going out.'

Barbara and Tom Rose? Now there was a turn-up for the books. I thought she'd always hated him. Circumstances must have thrown them together. I hitched my feet up and sat cross-legged in the easy chair. It might even be possible to enjoy this visit.

Tom Rose stretched his arms out in front of him, cracked his knuckles, stretched his hands over his head and brought them down on to his face, rubbing the whole surface, keeping them there. I couldn't see what was going on behind them.

'It's been rough for her – she's had a rough year.'

It's rough in here. *I've* had a rough year.

'What about Tom? Did he come back?'

'Yeah, and then went away again.'

'Where is he now?'

'Um, Boston, I think. He chucked in his course, and he's working as an assistant to some sculptor. Someone

Patrick knew from way back when.' Of course. To London, to Boston. Typical Hennessy trajectories.

I was getting tired of this.

'Why have you come here? Is it to gawp?'

'No. I came because of Barbara. She's got a bad conscience.'

She's got a bad conscience?

'Because when the police said it wasn't accidental, she put two and two together.'

Don't tell me: five?

Barbara, whose advice to troubled women was always impatient and extreme – 'Kick him straight out!', 'Cut off his balls!' – recognized a gesture when she saw one. Or believed she did.

'And you came all this way just to tell me this?'

'I've come out of – out of friendship. Because she feels bad enough as it is, and – about you, she feels—'

'But why would she think that?'

He looked as if his belly was giving him a pain again. I hoped it was. I hoped his guts were mangling.

'She knows what your temper's like.'

I don't know what she means about my temper. I've told Lorna I don't have one. Isn't my word good enough?

'The big bust-ups you and she would have. That final falling out.'

I unhooked my legs – they were stiff with cramp – and stretched them to the floor. I could see now that my tennis shoes were ragged and filthy. So much for the glass slipper; now hand me that woodcutter's axe.

'She said you were mightily pissed off at Patrick, and she could quite guess why. He's the love'em and leave'em type.'

Or the don't love'em and don't even bother to leave'em type. Use and discard, then pretend they never existed. Erase them from the record.

'And you were always in the house. Even when everyone else had gone. She said Tillie said' – God, it sounded like playground tittle-tattle! – 'that even then you'd hang around, when there was no one else to talk to, that you'd plague Tillie. Taking up her time. They didn't know how to get rid of you. You were getting as bad as your brother.'

'And Tom? What did she say about me and Tom?'

He had the grace to look uncomfortable.

'Not much.'

I tried to drill into his eyes with mine, make him look at me again. He knew how it was with me and Tom, he knew all about those odd arrangements. He was part of them.

'And what did you say to her?'

'Not much, either.'

'Well, that was probably for the best. The truth's not very palatable.' He winced, but I think it was only at the big word.

'The truth is, it was always you more than him, Caro. And you wouldn't see it that way.'

Oh yes, I did. That was clear from the start. But I existed on scraps. That's the way it is with a pet, a pet that's not really cherished or loved but kept out of habit, under sufferance, out of guilt. Not that Tom ever felt any guilt. He was blissfully unburdened with that. They all were.

Tom Rose coughed and carried on, grumbling into his hands again. 'Personally, I think she was being a bit harsh. I mean, we both spent a lot of time there, didn't we? We both preferred it to what we'd got at home. And it didn't seem a problem. Not for a long time.'

I glanced back at the door. Maybe I could call the guard. Maybe I could request his assistance with this young man who was bothering me. He might enjoy rugby-tackling a visitor for a change.

Tom Rose said, more firmly now, 'But you've got to move on, Caro. You can't keep stuck in one place all the time.'

I thought he was referring to my prospects now, to the future, and life.

'Everybody grew up and moved on. And you stayed the same.'

I felt weak, washed up. But something rankled.

'What did you mean about Brian? My brother?'

Tom Rose rubbed his forehead again, and took a surreptitious squint at his watch. He was as exhausted by this as I was.

'Oh, that he was a creepy little sod. Everyone knew that. Lurking, spying, setting little traps and leaving signs he'd been there, just to make you feel – I dunno – not right. Not quite safe. That's how Barbara put it.'

Barbara, who stormed through the world scaring nuns and shopkeepers – feeling not quite safe?

'She found a mouse paw in her hairbrush once.'

'She *what*?'

'Found a mouse's paw in her hairbrush. Just a paw. Dead, obviously. Someone had put it there, for her to find, in her room.'

'She's just making that up!' Anyone could have put it there; she had a house full of brothers. And besides, Barbara didn't possess a hairbrush.

'And he was always setting fires. In the woods, in the fields. Just little fires. But he knew how to do it.'

'This is just Barbara's say-so.'

Tom Rose looked to be in pain again.

'I don't know, Caro. It's all just one big mess.'

So that was Barbara's version of me – now I knew. Best friend, blood brother. But we never took the vow.

'She didn't say it *was* you. And she was angry and upset. Devastated.' Now there's a big word. 'She just told them where to start looking.'

So it was Barbara. I never knew that. I thought those two policemen arriving at the door, and the flock of professional-thises and court-appointed-thats who followed on, were just part of the inevitable parade. Because opportunities aren't just there for the taking and nearly everything ends in trouble, anyway. Because I'm the sort who always looks guilty. Because somebody finally picked me out from the crowd.

Tom Rose sat back in his chair, collapsed now, hands loose on his substantial thighs.

'Was she right, or not?'

Tillie: In an Interlude

Raining again. Trudy was right. So I'm stuck here in the patients' lounge, feeling the opposite of patient. 'If wishes were horses, beggars would ride.' That was another of my aunt Gloria's phrases.

I close my eyes and wish it was a fine day, that I was *out there* somewhere, with the sun shining and a sweet breeze blowing. I wish I was Carolyn. I'd be bowling along through the pleasant countryside, not a care in the world. Driving my own car (open-topped, of course), and wearing a summer dress and big sunglasses and my hair tied back with a scarf to keep it out of my eyes. The car's a birthday present from my father. ('Second-hand, darling! We don't want to spoil her,' my mother warns him, but with an indulgent smile.) I'd be on my way to a party or a date, the whole weekend a glorious expanse before me. I press down the accelerator and feel the tug of the open road, the fields and hills around me beckoning.

Or, better still, I'm out in those green hills riding my milk-white horse, with just the thump of his hooves and the clink of the bit and the birdsong for company. And any moment now I'll gather up the reins and spur him on and we'll gallop off over the horizon, as far as we can go.

If wishes were horses.

I close my eyes and wish it with all my heart, and then I open my eyes again and I'm still here.

It's dangerous, anyway, wishing with all your heart. Sometimes what you wish for comes true, but in ways you hadn't meant. Or not entirely. If you wish really hard for something bad to happen, and it happens, then you must be responsible. Surely.

Today Lorna's bouncing with energy. She's full of fleeting smiles and twinkly glances, as if she's on to something. Me.

She studies the file, pursing her mouth like someone in front of a baker's window, trying to choose the most delicious cake. 'Your brother was always the practical one. Good with his hands. And you were the one with ideas.' A pause, one of her clichéd dramatic effects. 'And both of you were angry with your mother.'

No, that's not it. That's not it at all. If we were angry with anyone—

'To go back to my earlier point . . .' she says.

What does she mean? It's not a game we're playing here. It's fact versus fiction. Life or death. Brian's a man of action. I've always been the dreamer. That's how I'd put it.

There is nothing to keep me here. There might be locks on the doors and plenty of safety glass, but there are no bars on the windows, no security fences, no watchtowers and spotlights and screaming dogs. Only miles and miles of open countryside to stop us running away, just fields and woods and pleasant rolling hills.

There is nothing to keep me here but Lorna's firm looks and the gentle voice of Dr Travis urging me, 'Will you try harder, Carol? Will you try?'

And the thought of where I might go instead.

I know what Lorna would like me to say, in order to *make some progress*, and then, she hopes, *move on*. And presumably she has got my best interests at heart. Though I know what Hanny would say, too: don't you believe it! But Hanny doesn't know Lorna, her dealings were all with Dr Travis. Dr Travis got her out of here. Or maybe he let her down. I would like to get out of here, and not back to that place I was in before, that stank of institutions and sounded like an execution, that slamming and slamming of doors. *I'd* like to move on.

To be honest—

To be honest, I say, and in my mind I'm stopped by Hanny's hollow shout of laughter that picks up and punctuates every contradiction, every slip from form.

To be completely honest, though, I'm tired. Exhausted. I'm not fit to step out on to the tightrope. I can't remember half of what I've said.

They said I got Brian to help me. They said he believed the house to be empty. They said I had given him the information.

But Tillie never went away.

And I knew that.

This is what Lorna wants. She wants me to say what I did. She wants me to say that I climbed the wooden steps ahead of Brian, because I knew that the door was always unlocked, on the latch, waiting for a bold kick or just the gentlest pressure of fingertips. Or that I led him round the creaking boards of the veranda, trailing my hands along the flaking wooden window ledges, showing him by word or simply by gesture how tinder-dry, how ready the whole place was, set like a batch of kindling in a hearth, just lying there and waiting for a match. That I took him to the back door, and into the silent kitchen, where glasses stood upturned on the draining board, and a handful of ox-eye daisies fading in a jar. On the table a small loaf left to prove, in the blue striped bowl, under a damp tea-cloth. Only a small loaf. The Van Hoogs were away, Tom in America, Patrick and the boys camping in France. That I knew all that. No one else at home.

Into the passage, so unusually quiet that the sound of the quiet and of the dust circling slowly through the afternoon air was palpable, like a gauze scarf falling softly over our heads and settling on our shoulders. The black-haired girl in the passageway staring her baleful stare. How Brian might have paused, staring back at her cold flesh.

And so into the hall, where the blue curtain hung in dusty folds at the foot of the stairs. No sound from beyond it. Up the stairs, with the brown runner worn around the stair ends by so many feet, so many journeys up and down, so that you felt your feet going from beneath you at each step, without ever quite slipping. Up through slabs of sunlight, picking out the dusty, dirty stairs. On to the landing, the smell of dust, Hennessys, and above all wood, wood, throughout the house.

Throughout the house the dry paper of a thousand books, comics, magazines, dry begging fabrics, curtains, horsehair, tartan, shawls, the slippery manmade fabrics of the clothes in Tillie's wardrobe. Canvases, stacked, and flammable oils. Up, up, through the house.

Into the white attic. The long white attic, where the breeze always blows. Or not. On hot, still days like this one at the very end of summer, the attic was a furnace under the roof tiles, collecting all the heat that rose from below.

What would we have seen then, Brian and I, always supposing I had led him, deftly, with all my knowledge of the house? Would we have found Tillie, in an interlude, painting? Lost in thought, standing before a canvas, magnificently flooded with light, with aspects of light?

Or perhaps she stood there in front of a blank canvas, blank herself. It had been so long, she had lost her touch. Or lost touch with any ideas she had of how to convey an image, or what image to convey.

I prefer to think she stood in front of a half-finished picture, a painting of tenderest luminous light. She stepped back a moment, holding the brush, just to see how she was doing. She was doing as well as ever.

In the heavenly stillness of the empty house, as she painted, Tillie would remember how it was to be undisturbed, to fall back into concentration like falling headlong into still green water. Immersing herself, letting go, sinking to the bottom as the weed streamed past, not heeding the calls back to the surface. There was no one to call her back to the surface. Not today.

*   *   *

Did they think it was there that we dropped the first match? Did they think that was how she was when the house went up?

What shall I say? What do you want me to say?

THE END

Acknowledgements

I would like to thank Francesca Liversidge for making this possible, my delightful editor Sarah Turner for her insight, and the rest of the team at Transworld for their boundless enthusiasm and commitment. And lastly – but never least – I would like to thank Brett for his tireless support and belief in me.